JUSTIN NEWLAND was born in Essex, England, th
His love of literature began soon after, with swash
tales of adventure. Undeterred by the award of a
Imperial College, London, he worked in IT and

G000127190

His tastes in literature are eclectic, from litera
fiction, with a special mention for the existentialis
reading history, ancient and modern, then got lost in the labyrinths of mythology,
religion, and philosophy.

In 2006, he found his way back to the creative keyboard and conceived this
novel, *The Genes of Isis*.

His short stories in anthologies include 'The Fool of Abbot's Leigh' in Hidden
Bristol and 'Fisher of Men' in North by Southwest (both published by Tangent
Books). 'Vallum Hadriani' is published in *The Dark Half of the Year*, a collection
of ghost stories by North Bristol Writers.

He writes historical, fantasy and speculative fiction with a supernatural bent
and lives with his partner in plain sight of the Mendip Hills in Somerset.

THE GENES OF ISIS

JUSTIN NEWLAND

SilverWood

Published in 2017 by SilverWood Books

SilverWood Books Ltd
14 Small Street, Bristol, BS1 1DE, United Kingdom
www.silverwoodbooks.co.uk

ISBN 978-1-78132-608-4 (paperback)
ISBN 978-1-78132-609-1 (ebook)

British Library Cataloguing in Publication Data
A CIP catalogue record for this book is available from
the British Library

Page design and typesetting by SilverWood Books
Printed on responsibly sourced paper

Egypt knows you, but do you know the Egypt in you?

SAYING OF THE ANCIENTS

It came to pass that the Source gave authority to Semjaza to rule over the angels of the sun, the children of heaven, who were called the Helios. And He entrusted them to deliver the Surge, the next step in the evolution of the children of men.

On Mount Hermon did the Helios descend to Earth with their assistants, the Solarii, only to find the children of men tardy in their development and wholly unprepared for the great boon of the Surge. The angels tarried in the astral light and when they could tarry no longer, the Helios sought to deliver the Surge lest it pass its time of flowering. So the Helios passed through the veil and appeared in their astral guise, the winged hornet. They covered the children of men in a cloak of golden astral pollen and stung the daughters of men, revealing to them untimely knowledge.

And the women bore monstrous hybrids, fathered by fallen angels, mothered by fair maidens, yet cursed with the rude nature of the creatures of the forest. All men and women were blighted by the hybrid seed and could only give birth to hybrids. For want of a miracle, the children of men would grow old, wither, and die, all because of the Helios.

The Solarii smote the Helios, covered their faces with darkness, and bound them for eternity beneath the valleys of the Earth. In Dudael did the Solarii make an opening in the desert and cast the hybrids into it and separated them from the children of men by invisible shields tethered with the fineness of the astral.

EXTRACT FROM THE BOOK OF ENOCH

PROLOGUE

Sometimes when I sit alone and the night draws in like a curtain of fine black soot, my skin becomes ultra-sensitive. I can feel the slight vibrations of a shadow, or detect a passing wraith vainly seeking its way home. Each nerve fibre develops its own echo, so as the feeling travels from my fingertips, through the palm, along the forearm, then flashes through the scapula, it culminates in a resounding crescendo in the caverns of my soul.

Stillness ushers in this state, a strange quiescence that comes from afar. It is as if I were afloat in the midst of a great galaxy, where the sound of the millions of years hums in the inner chambers of my mind like a gentle but mysterious symphony.

When I touch its panorama, I see with my own eyes, but in a way subtly different to normal vision. I watch with other eyes. Other eyes – how is that possible? There is only me, isn't there? But there *is* something else – an entity – that sees *through* my eyes, that sees what I see. How can this be? That I can see? That the other can be? Yet I tell you it is so.

They are the Eyes of the Watchers.

When they attend me, I feel their primeval power and authority. Without prejudice or bias, they watch. From the gentle awakening of my body in my mother's womb when the fiery spirit entered therein, to the time when one day I will exhale my last sigh, they are vigilant.

When they are far away, I long for them to return and grace my existence. When they are near, the Watchers are both a passion and a comfort, for I know that they convey what they witness through me back up the great ray of creation. They tell me I am not alone and simply never will be.

Their duty and dedication is to write, as well as to watch. They are both silent witnesses and faithful recorders. Etched for eternity in the planet's living archive, they have recorded, though not in hieroglyphs, nor on papyrus or carved on stone, her secret, invisible vault – the astral light.

As I write this testament, they watch and record. One day, the Source will turn the celestial pages of what I've written and weigh it in the balance. Life is a continuous exercise of spiritual due diligence, and my actions here will determine my place in the next life.

My name is Akasha.
I am mother of you all.
You are the children of angels.
And this is our story.

PART 1

The Great Winds

CHAPTER 1

The Wheel of Change

Akasha stared despondently at the pale green dress hanging on her door. It was the traditional attire for anyone visiting the Emerald Cavern. Ah, who would ever want to sit in that awful chamber and come out infertile? Not her. Yet everyone in Samlios was obsessed with it. "We have to do what the Solarii tell us," they would say. Well, they might have to, but she didn't. No, there was something intrinsically wrong with the idea and she wished there was some way she could avoid stepping over its threshold.

Mind, if the winds howling outside the temple and the clamour of the night bell were anything to go by, there might yet be a chance. Clouds of crimson dust scraped against the window like a scaled serpent, jarring her nerves. The winds moaned through the temple's cloisters, muffling shouts and cries of alarm. A door banged open and then slammed shut. She moved across to the window and for a moment, the visibility cleared. In the centre of the cloisters was the silhouette of the old oak of Samlios. The winds had already stripped its early spring leaves, but at least it was intact.

A sense of foreboding quickly replaced the feeling of relief. Squinting through the billowing dust, she swallowed hard, her mouth dry. The winds gathered into a swirling vortex around the oak. A loud and ominous cracking plunged the city into silence. The winds had severed one of the oak's thick lower branches, which lay forlornly on the earth. They toyed with the rump of the branch, rolling it repeatedly. Then they tore into the main tree with such ferocity that even the trunk strained its mighty sinews. Like a vengeful deity, the winds scraped at the tree until, with a noise like a clap of thunder, the huge trunk cracked. Slowly, like some titan felled in battle, the great oak tilted and plummeted to the ground. Its upper branches smashed through the window of Akasha's cell. Covering her head with her hands, she ducked behind the window ledge.

The oak of Samlios was broken, snapped in two by the winds' vitriol. Reputed to have been planted by old Enoch himself, it was a symbol of the isle's strength and endurance. But why these winds? Had they offended the Source? Were the winds a pestilence, or a cleansing? Her mentor would know. She had to ask Shamira.

Akasha pushed against the door but the buffeting wind prevented her from opening it even a crack. Trapped, she yelled for help. Her cries echoed back to her and her hopes of rescue faded. As the wind abated, the door fell ajar. Then the breeze picked up again, snaking through the gap, ruffling curtains and sucking her green dress out of the window opening.

Well, that was it. She wasn't going anywhere near the inside of the Emerald Cavern now. Leaning headlong into the winds, she squeezed through the tiny opening. The door slammed behind her. A moment later, her nightcap sprinted down the corridor ahead of her.

She joined the throng of people fleeing the temple and emerged into a heaving maelstrom of salt and sand. The particles hit her with such speed that she felt like a thousand minuscule daggers were piercing her skin. Dust drove splinters into her eyes. Buffeted by the winds, she struggled into the bared teeth of the gale.

Outside the temple entrance, the winds had toppled the statues of the divinities from their plinths. They lay on the ground in undignified fragments, their long reigns brought to a sudden and premature end. The path to the Step Well was strewn with branches and debris, all coated in red dust. Off the lee of the isle, two waterspouts stretched from the angry seas right up to the heaving sky waters. Swarms of gulls and sea birds swooped and dived in the air stream, blown about like stray twigs.

Staggering down to the Step Well was an achievement in itself. The portico had collapsed. The night bell swayed back and forth, issuing a terrible din. Akasha ducked to avoid a branch that flew at her, as if thrown by some invisible hand.

Tros the Gatekeeper was staring down into the Step Well.

"The oak of Samlios! It's gone!" Akasha yelled.

Tros lowered the scarf over his mouth. "There's nothing we can do," he shouted back.

She thought he was probably right. "What are you doing down here?"

"The men are trying to pin some material over the pool." Tros pointed down to the pool at the base of the Step Well. He was ever the practical one. To survive the onslaught, they needed to protect the city's main source of fresh water.

"Let me help."

"No. Shelter in the cathedral with everyone else," he said.

After what seemed a lifetime of evading the deadly winds, Akasha finally glimpsed the murky outline of the cathedral on the peak of Spirit Hill. The winds had left a crimson deposit on the outer crystal surface of the cathedral. Next to it, the Emerald Cavern was the same. She murmured a prayer of thanks to the winds for sparing her visit to that dreadful place.

She crawled along the ground like a snake, and eventually slumped against the cathedral doors, her body aching. Her face stung from the swirling sand, and the salt spray parched her lips. Hiding from the claws of the storm, she glanced across at the marketplace. Splinters from the flagpole lay strewn over the ground. The market stalls were scattered, broken into tinder. What was the point of this devastation? The hybrids? Or the Solarii? Or both? Everything else in their lives was, so she guessed the wild winds might be too. Anyway, Shamira would know.

Hundreds squeezed inside the rotunda, not one of them moving. It was as if the tempest had sucked out their spirits and turned them to stone. No one spoke, and their eerie silence was in stark contrast to the raging storm outside. Glum-faced, the men stood around the perimeter, backs against the wall. The women sat huddled together in small groups in the centre of the rotunda, comforting each other and nursing the injured. The cathedral door creaked open and everyone looked up. The wind howled through the gap, roaming like a disrespectful spirit around the chamber. Tros and his band of windswept stragglers were hustled into the room by the force of the breeze, and the door slammed shut again behind them.

Akasha finally located Shamira, who was tending to an elderly woman named Irit.

"There," Shamira said, patting the old woman's hand. "You've had a shock, but you'll be fine. You've survived worse than this. Take a sip of water." Shamira turned, noticed Akasha for the first time, and greeted her warmly. "I'm glad you're here. I was worried about you. Are you all right?"

"Yes, I think so," Akasha said, catching her breath. "Except there's terrible news. The winds demolished the oak of Samlios, snapped it in two."

Shamira grimaced. "I feared as much, but at least we're safe here. We must be strong. Look, here comes the high priest."

Panion headed towards them with his characteristic loping stride. He offered greetings to those around him, but spoke directly to Shamira. "We've never been confined in the cathedral like this before – not by winds, not by the inclement seas, not by the sky waters, not by anything. These are winds of change. You're the augur – tell us, what's your reading of the runes?"

Akasha was Shamira's apprentice, and her mentor was always telling her about these mysterious runes. Invisible to the naked eye, they ran through the astral light in the same way currents and tides and vortices moved through water. When prophesying, Shamira's expression took on a pinched look, and when she spoke, it accentuated her lisp.

"Our human friends, in Cathay in the east and the Land of the Clouds in the west, as well as the Solarii in Egypt, will feel the sting of the great winds in their faces. In the physical realms, the tempest will break the rotten bough, allowing renewal and rebirth. Everything begins and ends in the astral light, the unseen causative realms. There the wheel of change takes another turn on its axis, as the future seeps into the now. What we witness are its grand, spectacular effects. Only that which belongs to the future will survive."

Akasha's mind whirled with questions. She wanted to belong to the future. How could she achieve that? Shamira could see into it, couldn't she? She must know.

Panion was persistent. "Was there anything in the runes about the Surge?"

Shamira pursed her lips. So typical for a pythoness.

"These winds herald the last days of this epoch," she said. "The Source is desperate to unveil the next one. Already the Source has issued the Surge, which lies dormant inside every one of us, its release restrained by the scourge of the hybrid seed. First, remove the stain. Then and only then will we be able to drink from the refreshing spring waters of the next epoch."

So the winds were ushering in something new, and that was the Surge. That was profoundly significant. Akasha loved hearing about it. If only the Surge would flower in her lifetime, she'd enjoy wondrous new faculties that had never before existed, and arts and skills no one had ever conceived of. She'd join a race of geniuses. The winds were propelling the wheel of change, driving out the past and bringing in the future, fast.

The end of an epoch. These were more than interesting times.

CHAPTER 2

Sovereigns of the Sun

Horque wiped a particle from his eye and squinted into the crimson cloud. His chambers were set back from the Jizah pyramid field but, despite the billowing dust, the glare from them was almost blinding. Dawn was breaking and he'd been awake all night dealing with the manifold repercussions of the winds.

The winds... By Horus, he was tired of them. When would they cease? There were never these horrendous problems in the astral. Sitting back in his chair and fingering the hawk motif on the armrests, he drifted off into that curious state between wakefulness and sleep. He gathered his astral form, the black hawk, at the nape of his neck and instructed it to fly off into the boundless freedom of the astral light. From there, he scouted the Solarii in the Lower Lands and the Upper, flew west to check on the humans in the Land Between the Two Rivers, and then in a flash the hawk was hovering over the Pyrenes Mountains and the Whispering Tower. The winds even bound the humans of Samlios in their Crystal Cathedral. They blew everywhere.

In the astral, Horque relived the huge sense of liberation enjoyed by his ancestors, the first Solarii arrivals on Earth. They had divided their astral consciousness, like twins separated at birth, leaving half on the sun – their *ba* – and crossing the great sky waters with the other half – their *ka* – on their way to Earth. The sun was more than a source of light and warmth; it was the home of his solar double. Horque's dream, and that of every Solarii, was to reunite *ka* and *ba* and bask amidst the supreme glow of the astral light of the sun.

The howling winds and a growling stomach pulled him from his reverie.

Tarsus, his human manservant, arrived at the door.

"What is it?" Horque murmured through a fog of tiredness.

"I've brought you some fruit," Tarsus replied.

Horque grunted. These Semites were a mixed blessing. While providing useful domestic service, they were also both awkward and cantankerous.

Horque plucked one of the grapes. It tasted sweet, though left a sour aftertaste, albeit a mental one. There was another knock on the door and in walked Marim.

"What news?" Horque asked.

His deputy lowered the scarf from his nose and mouth. "Protector," he said, "the winds are chafing. They destroy our crops. The billowing dust clouds contaminate our wells."

That wasn't good news. If the winds didn't stop soon, famine and thirst would stride amongst them like demonic twins. Uppermost in Horque's mind was the state of repair of the pyramids. Death by starvation was one thing, but to perish by lack of sun-fire ambience was quite another.

"Are the winds inhibiting the normal absorption?" Horque asked.

Marim took a deep breath. "The breath of the gods has gouged small indentations in the surface of all three pyramids. Thus far, they continue to absorb sun-fire ambience during the day and emit it at night, as normal."

"That is my reading too," Horque confirmed. He would have been able to sense any lessening in the nightly emissions. He was Solarii, after all, and sun-fire ambience was their astral lifeblood.

"Yes, Protector, the seals are intact."

"Good. It's vital they remain that way. The moment they wear down beyond the normal level, I want to know. Understood?"

Marim nodded and said something, but a huge gust of wind drowned out his reply.

"What are the dispositions of the hybrids?" Horque asked, raising his voice. For the Solarii, it always came back to the hybrids. "Are the Horus Wing craft continuing their flights into Dudael? Are our astral shields holding them in the desert lands? Keep the hybrids at bay – both from humans and from us. I don't want to hear of them mixing with humans. The hybrids are a scourge on the face of the gods. They've already contaminated the humans with the hybrid seed. If the hybrids carry more diseases and infect the humans, we'll never get the Surge released in those little people."

Marim wiped his palms against his skirt. "The breath of the gods is opaque," he said. "Clouds of particles and sand churn in the air. The Horus Wing flyers can't see far enough to scout in the lands of Dudael. The dust clouds caused two accidents yesterday."

"Accidents? No one told me. What happened?"

"One flyer crash-landed, and the other got entangled in the branches of a tree," Marim replied.

"Are they all right?"

"The pilots were injured, so I called for the healing priest. Khephren applied the curing power of the ankh to their wounds, and with the grace of Hathor, they are recovering."

"I was referring to the craft, not the men," Horque snapped. What was Marim thinking of? "We have barely a score of Horus Wing craft. They're finely wrought flying machines and are irreplaceable. On the other hand, the men *are* expendable."

"I-I understand," Marim stammered, bowing his head.

"Where are the craft now?" Horque was losing patience.

"In the Temple of Horus. According to Berux, they can be repaired."

"The word of Berux, I trust. Yours, I'm not so sure about anymore."

"I will improve," Marim replied.

"As my deputy, the men look up to you. Pull yourself together and remember the flyers' code: *Nothing but order, efficiency and dedication.* And no more mistakes. Mistakes are for humans, not Solarii."

"Yes, Protector," Marim said. "But there's one more thing. Despite the hostile conditions, a few flyers have ventured into Dudael. They searched the caves of the western valleys where the hybrids gather. They found ten of the beasts lying prostrate, partially covered by debris."

"Dead?"

"It appeared so. The flyers looked through the whites of their eyes into the astral light and saw no life emanation from the bodies."

"So they *are* dead. These winds of the pantheon *are* behind our backs. That is an aid to our sacred task." Horque rejoiced in the news. That made a change; usually the hills and dales contrived to hide the hybrids from the Solarii, but for once conditions were working in their favour. Ten fewer hybrids made their final task easier.

"Report to me the moment the craft are repaired. I want them all out scouring Dudael as soon as the winds abate. In the meantime, continue with a state of full vigilance. I do not want to find the men sitting around the chessboard with their chins cupped in their hands. Execute my orders in full. You're dismissed."

Marim left him alone in his chambers, the morning breaking around him and winds gusting strongly. Another day on Earth, another day as an incarnate. What ignominy! At least the winds had blown in some good tidings.

Horque swallowed hard. A wave of homesickness washed over him, like a nagging at the soul. It was a terrible itch, never satiated. The urge to end the gross humiliation was obsessive, as was the need for him and his people to return to their rightful places, sovereigns of the sun.

CHAPTER 3

The Dance of the Winds

Akasha lifted her scarf over her nose and notched another mark on the cathedral wall – one for each day since the winds began. She counted a round score.

She'd seen nearly nineteen summers and her youth was seeping out. Bound by the cruel chains of these winds to the altars of the cathedral, she bemoaned her fate. This was supposed to be the flowering of her youth, a period of intense natural discovery and learning through trial and error. Yet she'd paced out every step in every nook and cranny of the cathedral. Its sheer height and majesty couldn't disguise the bald truth that it was, to all intents and purposes, a prison, not only for her, but also for her people.

She'd occupied herself by nursing the sick. The people of Samlios were more accustomed to the night skies and the open panorama, and this enforced detention seemed to suck the life force from them. Akasha found she possessed calming energies, laying on her hands to one, bringing comfort to another. Only Irit failed to respond to her newfound healing powers.

Despite this new knowledge, Akasha was desperate for adventure. She'd run up and down the flights of stairs that led to the top of the rotunda dome and pester Shamira to let her go outside with the men. On the first day that the winds abated, she accompanied Uriah to the Step Well to bring back the much-needed water rations.

"She can help carry the amphorae," her father said. "We need to fill as many as we can."

This was the first time she'd emerged from the cathedral since the winds began, and Akasha couldn't believe the scale of the devastation. Cracks had appeared in the domed roof of the Emerald Chamber and one of its walls had caved in. The rest of the city was as broken as the oak of Samlios, its streets cluttered with debris, mauled by the winds. She was appalled to find all manner of creatures of the feather and of the fur, their small, fragile carcasses buffeted by the winds and left lifeless against the rude rock crystal of the cathedral.

"What have they done to deserve a fate like this? They're innocent creatures," she complained.

"This carnage is such a waste." Tros was sympathetic too. "I don't understand it either."

They reached the Step Well. Overnight rain had soaked the spiral path that coiled round the sides of the well, all the way to the pool at the base.

"Mind, the path's slippery. You'd best stay here while we fill up," Tros advised. After a while, the men returned with amphorae full of water. They left them leaning against the pillars of the portico, and set off down the spiral with more empty amphorae.

While she waited for their return, Akasha stared disconsolately across to her home in the arc of residences. It was there that she spotted a creature darting between the dwellings. She dismissed it at first as an animal scavenging for food. But no, there were two more and they had…human bodies. They were lycans: hybrids with the head of a wolf and the body of a human. Alert to her smell, the three simultaneously turned their heads in her direction. They stood up on their hind legs and… Wait…they were heading her way!

She gasped. What to do? All she knew of hybrids was hearsay. Most said they were dangerous, violent and unpredictable. Their appearance was grotesque. And in their nature, they contained two highly conflicting urges: the angelic and the human. Some, like Irit and the other mothers who'd given birth to them, offered them care and kindness. Akasha was surprised to see them here, because they mainly kept to the Needles in the interior of the isle. Sightings were rare, and even when hybrids did approach, they'd never venture into the city. Until now.

Her throat dry with fear, she squealed down to the men at the well base, but the winds drowned her cries. The lycans moved nearer. The leader had a golden mane. He bent his snout into the onrushing winds, ears slanted back. Akasha backed against a pillar. As tall and proud as an oak, the leader fixed her with an impassive, fearless stare. He had the snout, whiskers and pointed ears of wolf, but he was human in body from the neck down, except for his downy auburn fur. The other lycans edged closer. She froze.

"No, don't!" she cried, and turned away, fully expecting them to leap on her and tear her to pieces. Was this it? Was she to suffer a mauling? Her heart was beating, *drum-drum, drum-drum*. She smelt their animal odour, heard their steps nearby. She glanced back and saw to her shock and relief that they were walking away, clutching full amphorae in each hand. After what seemed like an age, the leader picked up two more amphorae and sloped off to join his kin.

19

She slumped to the ground, terrified, and exhausted. By the time Uriah and Tros returned, the lycans had gone. She reported what had happened to the men.

"Are you all right?" Uriah asked. "I'd never imagined they'd attack you."

"They didn't actually attack me," she protested. "But they stole our water."

"I'm going after them." Uriah sounded bullish. "We can catch them, teach them a thing or two."

"I don't think so," Tros said, the voice of reason. "They're familiar with every blade of grass in the Needles. We'd never find them, certainly not in these winds."

"All right, but they're not coming back into the city," Uriah insisted. "We've kept them in check for years, and now this? What will happen when the winds cease, that's what I want to know?" Uriah didn't wait for an answer, merely turned and stomped back to the cathedral.

Akasha and Tros stumbled after her father. Confused by the confrontation, she wanted answers to her questions.

"Who was the lycan with the golden mane?" she asked Tros.

"That sounds like Jarda."

"Irit's child, by Semjaza?"

"The same." He nodded as they reached the safety of the cathedral.

She'd encountered a real live lycan. If they were so violent, why *didn't* he attack her? It was so confusing.

Akasha didn't sleep that night. She lay awake, listening to the winds howling around the cathedral rotunda, singing to her...

Open the door,
Scrape the claw,
The Emerald Cavern
Is no more.

At dawn, she found Shamira.

"Now the Emerald Cavern has been destroyed, what will happen to the Covenant of the Firstborn?"

Shamira glanced at her. "The covenant," her mentor said, "is an agreement with the Solarii to help us humans out of the huge mess created by Semjaza and the Helios."

"But what do we need this covenant for anyway? Aren't the Solarii just trying to control our lives?" She was sure they were.

"The Solarii were originally sun-folk, immensely powerful angels who've passed through the veil and adopted human form. Somehow, using their phenomenal astral powers, they've established a circumstance where, when one of us dies, the first child we conceive after the death will be a normal human in appearance, free of any animal or hybrid features. That is the Covenant of the Firstborn and is a precious lifeline for the human race because it means *we can reproduce*. Eventually, we need to return to normal, when we can procreate whenever we please. Until then, the Covenant of the Firstborn allows the Solarii time to work out how to do that and without it, young lady, we're on the long, slow road to extinction."

My, it was a mess. But Akasha had some news of her own, some intimate news, to share with her mentor. "Since the great winds, I've become a maiden. I've started the cleansing flow. I'm able to give birth. I'm unique amongst Samlios women."

"Congratulations. But you'll have to keep your desires in check. You don't want to give birth to a hybrid, do you? Besides, all the men and women in Samlios have – unlike you – breathed the vapours of the Emerald Cavern, so they're all infertile."

"I know that," Akasha murmured. She was ready to bear children. But there were all these rules and obstacles. The world was too complicated.

Shamira saw it otherwise. "You're different to other girls," she said, her eyes bright like the fires of the sun. "You've the mark on you, the sign of the Basilisk That Slays. You can fulfil a special destiny that's important to the future. To do so, you'll need to walk a long, hard path. At the moment you seem more interested in bearing children."

Shamira was right. Akasha was young, and had put off making such a commitment. Was now the moment to do so? How could she know?

"I'm your mentor," Shamira reminded her. "You're an apprentice of a rare and unusual art in which you'll be trained to summon the astral entities of the basilisk. They are what they are: that is the nature of divine, astral forces. To deal with them safely, you must be who you say you are. Abuse their power for personal gain and they'll rend and demolish you. I'm telling you this for your own good. It's about time you made up your own mind about what you want."

Shamira folded her arms and stared at her.

"I...I feel like one of those birds out there, blown off course, lost."

"These winds aren't only in Samlios, they're all over Earth. Everyone's frustrated: us, the hybrids, even the Solarii. Our lives are in abeyance until the winds blow themselves out, and I counsel you to reflect on this as a matter of urgency."

"I'll do that," Akasha said, and she meant it.

For the next eight days, Akasha thought of nothing else. What did she really want – a child and a family, or a role in the future, such as the one Shamira was promising her? On that spring day, one moon after the beginning of the great winds, she lowered the scarf around her mouth to wipe her lips, to take the bitter taste of the winds from her mouth. Water, she needed water. Then she belatedly remembered that what little was left was reserved for the sick and needy. Irit was not the only one struggling to recover her health.

The fury of the winds had prevented anyone from venturing outside the Crystal Cathedral since their last visit to the well pool, ten days before. If the winds didn't release them soon, they'd block the cathedral door. Then if they did manage to extricate themselves, they might find the waters of the pool no longer drinkable. She began to smell her own fear.

None of the men knew how to unlock their prison gates. In the end, they advocated patience. But patience would not and did not stop the winds. Their three religious leaders were also in difficulty: disturbed by the tempest, their clairvoyant astral powers had failed them. The people of Samlios lay around the cathedral floor, staring at the vaulted ceilings, palisades and towering columns. Hands on chins, they pined as much for the open air as for a drink of water.

Outside, there was a crash. It sounded like a large piece of mortar thumping against the bone-dry earth. Everyone looked up.

"The cathedral's breaking up," Callisto cried. Some women began wailing, while others whimpered and mewed. Fear drew its talons across their faces. The men rushed around, bumping into each other, shouting at shadows. Some tried to push open the heavy wooden door, but it was a forlorn effort.

As if in a trance, Akasha stumbled into the centre of the rotunda. Everything seemed far away and a mist descended in front of her eyes. The other women moved out of her way. There she stood, eyes closed, swaying from side to side, surrounded by an increasingly profound stillness. She began to turn in the same space, as if orbiting some invisible sun. Widdershins she spun, drawing in the subtle energies from the astral light. The gentle tune of a lullaby passed her lips and she sung to herself, the same song the winds had sung to her.

She heard another crash of stone from outside, and then more screams. The women wailed. The men shoved desperately against the entrance door. The astral light pushed against her. Arms outstretched, she turned, spinning, humming. She spun on one foot, then the other, until she felt dizzy. She carried on the dance, whirling until the heady feeling passed, thrilled at her own fluency. Increasingly, she felt tenderly possessed by some entity from the astral light that directed every sinuous move. The majestic singing came from inside her soul. Her body felt serene, at one with the humming. She surrendered her soul to the instructing entity that guided her volatile and fluid movements.

She mimicked the howl and gust of the winds. She uttered a soft mewing sound, then a hissing and a moaning. Calling the winds, she spun faster and faster, summoning the elemental power of the tempest. Turning, twisting, she beckoned to herself the forces that drove the winds. Her white cloth dress whirled around her in a vortex of power.

She could see the winds in the astral. They were violet currents with clouds of indigo, heralds of change that seeped through invisible gaps in the walls. Turbulence circled her as she spun, and she commanded it to come to her, to occupy her, to possess her. She felt exhilarated, sublime: step by step, she *became* the eye of the hurricane. Quiet and still inside herself, while all around her was incredible, tremulous motion. The essence of the storm enshrouded her with dark wings.

She felt every sinew straining at the leash. The elemental powers were tearing her asunder. Her mouth opened wide and she yelled, long and high. A crystal in the rotunda smashed into thousand fragments, each one a lost dream of a lost people. From outside came a roar, as if the foundations of the earth shook.

Every nerve in her body was shredded. Her mind raced. She fought to keep pace with the brutal storm-entity as it ripped at her sinews, stretching them beyond breaking point. Her temples thumped like a beating drum. The winds' majestic power inflated her lungs and gave her great power.

As she danced and the winds danced with her, she saw startling images flash before her mind's eye. It was a dream vision of what would be, and of what was to come. The cobra, her astral insignia, reared up out of her soul. Floating above her physical body, she looked down on her dance and the winds, and on the dance of the winds. Above the cathedral she flew, high above Samlios, over the isle and into the very midst of the sky waters. Faster and faster, they streamed above the earth. Tides flowed in the air. Currents of water moved in and out of the ebb.

A vortex appeared in the midst of the waters. Through the watery gap, a light flickered in the distance, growing nearer and stronger. Akasha saw that the light was a white angel, who carried a silver trumpet in one hand and a blank scroll in the other. The seraph shone with intense luminescence, wings as translucent as a dragonfly's. Shafts of light emanating from the angel bathed the surrounding waters in diaphanous turquoises and greens.

In her dream vision, a group of humans mingled in peace with hybrids. Marooned on a rocky outcrop, they cried out to the seraph for deliverance. The angel blew on the silver trumpet, sending out a clear crystal note that reverberated throughout the starry domains of the firmament.

The rains began, a drizzle at first. Drops of water fell and grew into a stream. The waters in the sky knelt on the ground and soaked the caverns and deeper recesses. The ground sucked the waters from the sky. The waves washed through the empty hollows and the dry wells, filled the valleys until the tides breached the hillsides and the lower mountains, and reached above the tree line. The waters rose to the tips of the highest mountains, where the humans and hybrids huddled together in fear. The waters lapped at their feet and an ocean spread out before them where once there were the clouds and the void. A searing bolt of lightning smashed into the huddle of humans and hybrids. When the clouds of dust cleared, the smell of death was everywhere. Even the mountain peak was flat.

In her dream vision, everything was black.

Akasha crumpled to the ground.

When she awoke, Shamira was cradling her in her arms. Bleary-eyed, she looked around the rotunda at a scene of rich celebration. The people hugged each other; others plunged to the floor, and raised a prayer to the Source.

"What happened?" Akasha murmured.

"The winds have stopped," Shamira said, with a triumphant air.

A loud crack broke the sense of exultation. For a dreadful moment, Akasha feared the cathedral was breaking up. Some of the women screamed, until Callisto cried out, "Look!"

The men had opened the entrance doors and let the familiar green half-light of day stream into the cathedral. Fresh, still air filled Akasha's lungs. All around them was eerie silence, while inside her a high timbre rang in her ears. Her body ached from exhaustion, thirst and fear.

"Akasha's saved us all from certain death. We're delivered," Panion crowed. Everyone knelt to listen to his prayer. Elation and relief lifted the anxiety from their faces.

Propped up by Shamira on one side and Thera, her mother, on the other, Akasha hobbled out of the entrance. The trees looked like misshapen monsters, their branches lopped, their trunks twisted, and their crowns bowed over in obeisance to the great winds. The cathedral had sustained damage to some of the crystals on the roof and the Emerald Cavern had suffered further weathering. All the citizens emerged into the quiet morning air and drunk deep of its freshness. Some kissed the ground, and clutched clods of earth with reverential awe.

"Who is Akasha to have becalmed the winds?" Tros asked.

She wanted desperately to reply. The winds had shown her, the dance had instructed her. "I'm an apprentice Basilisk That Slays, and Shamira is my mentor," she said weakly.

Shamira smiled with her eyes, strong and warm. "What do you remember of the dance?" she asked.

"I remember spinning and turning." In an instant, she reconnected to the elemental power of the dance, lost her balance, and stumbled. Shamira supported her.

"The astral light filled me with a supreme power, one I've never felt before," Akasha explained, her voice quivering with emotion.

The Five Hills of Samlios looked like the dales of the underworld: bare trees snapped in two, some with just a stump, the rest of the tree stripped and torn asunder. The survivors were bent over, with branches flattened, frozen in the act of bowing to the very thing that tore them apart. Out beyond the harbour was the ocean, smooth and benign.

"The winds were inside me, tearing at every fibre of my being," she continued. "I was terrified. I thought the winds were going to tear me apart. Then, a voice whispered in my soul. 'Be quiet, be still.' So I was. And the winds obeyed my command: they went quiet too. It was sublime."

"These are divine entities," Shamira claimed.

"There's more," she said, struggling to get the words out. "I had a dream vision of what is to follow these winds."

"What did you see?"

"The fall of the sky waters. There is to be a flood."

As she spoke these words, a veil between Akasha and her destiny fell away and she could see her own future more clearly. The first stirrings of her great quest rose in her and she found the words to clothe their passion. She was to preserve the human race, resolve the tragedy of the hybrid seed, and free the Surge.

A woman let out a wail of such grief that everyone turned to see who it was. Callisto stood over Irit, who had slumped to the ground just outside the cathedral entrance.

"She's gone," Callisto cried. "The winds have taken her."

PART 2

The Hybrid Seed

CHAPTER 4

Hybrids' Assault

Horque awoke in his residence in the administrative district of the White Wall. He tucked his black hair inside his cloth headdress and put on a shirt, a linen skirt, and sandals. As the emerald green rays of the sun cast long early morning shadows, he stepped into the water court and sat watching the fountain spray a cascade of drops into the air.

Then the nausea struck him. Oh, the odour was obnoxious and, worst of all, pervasive. He lent over the pool and breathed in the fragrance of the sweet-smelling water lily. Slowly the loathsome smell receded, but the rank odours of decay were a poignant reminder that he and his Solarii didn't belong here. To be on Earth was an extremely odd experience for a Solarii. How did humans cope with it? They were endemic, so they didn't suffer the same trials and tribulations as the Solarii.

Facing the shadows, he shifted in his carved sycamore chair. The arches of his feet flattened onto the cool of the marble floor. Reciting the Morning Prayer reminded him of their great undertaking:

Raise yourself, Horque.
Make this the day the hybrid are banished from the face of the Earth and so
Rectify the faults of the Helios.
Fulfil thus the terms of our exile.
Heed the call to cross the Winding Waterway in the sky
And return home to my double on the sun.

The great winds had blown away the creeping paralysis of complacency that had infected Solarii society over the years, especially the Horus Wing flyers in his charge. To remedy that, he'd promoted Berux over Marim and ordered him to intensify their search for the hybrids. The sun had risen and set nine times since the winds had blown themselves out, yet to his annoyance the pyramid field still had debris strewn over it.

He headed to the outer yard, where he found Tarsus hunched over his Horus Wing craft, preparing it for flight. These flying machines responded exactly to the flyer's mental instructions and state of mind. They were things of beauty. Physically, the machine bore more than a passing resemblance to a twin-backed throne, adorned with an array of pipes and straps. The dull glint of the morning sun touched the lip of the horizon, highlighting the craft's smooth veined surfaces. As a good omen, he touched the engraving of his family's insignia on the crown of the seat: a black hawk, wings wide, talons bared, beak open, swooping down on its prey.

Spine erect and with his feet resting on the base platform, he settled into the seat. The red granite backrest was smooth, the armrests even and firm to the touch. Tarsus pulled the retaining straps tight across his barrel chest.

Horque mouthed the special utterance to cause a mental nexus to the craft.

O Horus, revered son of Isis,
Grant this petition
To fly like a hawk,
And ascend into the sky.

The craft shuddered and moaned softly, writhing like a lover beneath him. It was as if the granite block had become sensate and joined to his being. He instructed it to lift, and it dutifully hovered above the ground, spewing a cloud of dust from its downward exhaust. Ascending above his residence, Horque mentally guided it along the main aerial pathway and then downriver to the Jizah pyramid field.

Sunlight sparkled off the specks of foam below him. An empty barge tacked upriver, heading for the southern quarries towards Thebes. He passed over the bustling market and turned inland towards the incandescent gleam of the trio of pyramids: the King's, the Queen's and the oldest, the Pyramid of Records. Next to them was the enigmatic Sphinx, the source of the astral shield for the whole pyramid field. Protecting his eyes from the glare, he noticed a movement near the Records Pyramid.

He couldn't believe what he was seeing. It was Marduk, the legendary hybrid, a huge creature with the head of a black bull, legs like those of a great bear, and arms like tree trunks. He'd clambered halfway up the side of the Records Pyramid and slithered back down its smooth, polished surface, a slide only halted by dextrous and inventive use of his powerful serpentine tail. Horque stared in horror as the frenzied demon slowly clawed his way back up the side of the pyramid to the apex where he sat, furred thighs astride the capstone. Marduk raised his arms in triumphant salute to a knot of hybrids below him, who revelled in their leader's newfound position as king of the pyramid.

Horque was seething. Where's Berux? Why wasn't he fighting them off? He's responsible for securing the pyramid field. There's an impenetrable astral shield. It's supposed to confine the hybrids to Dudael. How then have they escaped from the holding area?

Marduk gripped the capstone with arms and legs. Twisting it left and right, he tried to wrench it from its moorings. Surely, he'd fail. The capstone was solid electrum-encrusted rock. A small puff of dust drifted from the capstone into the morning air. He'd shifted it! Marduk pulled and heaved, and cubit by cubit, it gave way until the apex sheared off from the main structure. The sheer weight of the dislodgement propelled him backwards, tracing a crescent arc in the air. He landed on his back halfway down the side of the pyramid, locked in a weird embrace with a huge lump of rock.

This was defilement. The pyramids were solar furnaces that collected the rays of sun-fire astral ambience during the day and released them at night. Looking through the whites of his eyes into the astral light, Horque had the odious vision of all those stored rays splurging through the gash at the top of the pyramid, like a plug dislodged from an active volcano.

Strangely, it gave him an idea. Fire and flame – that was the way to repulse them. He mentally transmitted his orders to Marim, stationed with the Horus Wing flyers at the Temple of Horus.

Come quick. Bring torches, ankhs and an ashlar. Force the hybrids away from the pyramid field. Then we'll dispose of them.

He gripped the armrests of his craft until his knuckles went white. What else could he do while he watched a bunch of renegade hybrids destroy the pride of the Solarii civilisation? The loss of astral sun-fire energy was catastrophic. He was so shocked he momentarily lost the nexus to the craft, which tipped over and dropped like a stone, only the retaining straps preventing a fatal fall. As he righted it, he saw Circone, a one-eyed bear of a hybrid, lift a boulder as if it were a child's plaything. Repeatedly, he smashed it into the limestone fascia of the Records Pyramid, fracturing the surface and rupturing the inner astral storage membrane. Behind him, a lycan and a pananthrop – a hideous creature with a man's torso and a panther's face – combined to batter large rocks into the same spot. A huge hole appeared as the pitted surface casing fell into the interior of the pyramid.

Horque shunted his craft above the spot, and noticed the shadowy outline of a tunnel angling into the pyramid's innards. The hybrids had inadvertently revealed a hidden entrance. Or did they know it was there? Surely not? He was even more astounded when a seething black torrent of insects gushed out of the tunnel. The swarm headed straight towards him. In a flash, he took evasive action. No sooner had they passed him, the gush of air rocking his craft, than they were gone, and the dark cloud had disappeared from sight. He swished a few of the bees off his body. No, they weren't bees, they were hornets. How did a swarm of hornets get *inside* the pyramid?

In the distance, a vapour trail traced the flight of Horus Wing craft, grey-white against the pale green sky. Each one wielded a bright wicker torch, the flyers' orange-yellow flames reflecting on the polished limestone surface. There was not a moment to lose; Marduk had regained the ruptured capstone and sat there waving his hands above his head, roaring indiscriminately.

Marim steered his craft at the bull-headed monster and at the last moment, swerved over his head, singeing the beast's ears and elevating his craft just beyond the reach of the bull-man's flailing fingers. The other flyers dived in and out of Circone and the other hybrids, jabbing their flaming torches into their eyes. Horque grinned with satisfaction. He was right – the hybrids were terrified of the naked flame.

Another danger was imminent. The huge amounts of astral sun-fire ambience released by the pyramid created a highly flammable atmosphere in and around the field, so much so that the flyers' torches left an extended trail of flame like a long yellow-orange pennant. The flyers had to take increasingly drastic action to avoid these lithe, fiery streams.

Marim manoeuvred his craft back and forth before Marduk's line of sight, eventually causing the bull-hybrid to tumble over and slide inelegantly down the angled pyramid surface. As soon as he hit the ground, Marduk bolted in the direction of the Sphinx, lurching along a deep gully that sloped into a disused quarry. Roaring with rage, Circone and the other hybrids followed close behind. They smashed bloodstained fists into the gully's steep ridges. Arriving in the pit of the quarry, they were surrounded by steep rock inclines.

So far, so good. Now to close the trap. Landing near the quarry lip, Horque unstrapped himself and got down. Marim and the flyers arrived nearby.

"Give me the ashlar," he demanded.

Marim gave him the shiny conical device. "What are you going to use it for?" he asked.

"I'll show you," Horque replied, inserting his fingers into the cone.

Once he'd made the nexus to the ashlar, a pale blue astral ray emerged from the apex of the cone, seared through the air and into the gully wall, where it opened out into the quarry. He manoeuvred the ray to cut deep incisions into the rock, tracing out a huge triangular block, like the ones he'd seen the stonemasons use to build the pyramids. With adept movements, he enticed the block out of its bedrock until it eventually toppled down the rock face and landed in the gully below. The agile pananthrop tried climbing over the smouldering block, but it had wedged so neatly into gully that the creature slipped on its sheer incline and fell back into a heap on the quarry floor.

He'd trapped them.

Realising their predicament, Circone bellowed his contempt. Marduk was incandescent with rage. Horque almost found it amusing, although he wasn't sure what humour was, even though Tarsus had tried to explain it to him. Obedience, he knew. Discipline, he knew. Service, he knew. Humour? Where did that belong in the grand scheme of things?

"They're pathetic," Marim said scornfully.

Horque had to agree. The hybrids bore an uncanny resemblance to the dread creatures of the underworld, which was where they were about to be sent. The men clutched their ankhs to use them as weapons – fingers around the loop and the pointed end directed at the hybrids.

"Fire at will," Horque ordered.

Each weapon spat a lethal bolt of concentrated flame that traced an arc of death into the quarry. A red tongue of fire seared into the hybrids. The smell of scorched flesh was horrendous. The explosions threw up clouds of smoke and dust that spewed out of the quarry and stung Horque's face. Coughing and spluttering, he turned away and lifted his scarf over his mouth. As the pall of smoke cleared, there was no trace of the hybrids. The ankhs had turned them into tiny droplets of water, skin and bone.

"Marduk and his vermin have been vaporised." Marim smirked.

Horque allowed a wry smile to flicker on his lips. Now he had to deal with the cause of this despicable act.

"Where are Irex and Javian?"

"Here, Protector," Irex said. He was tall, even for a Solarii, with a square, jutting chin.

"Berux has questions to answer. He must pay the penalty for...that." Horque gestured towards the smouldering Pyramid of Records. "Javian, I want you to find him. Look in his quarters. Look in the taverns. Look in the harems. If you have to, look in the underworld. Just bring me Berux."

"Yes, Protector." Javian saluted and left.

Next, Irex delivered the damage report.

"The King's and Queen's are relatively intact but the Pyramid of Records sustained serious damage..."

"...Which takes us back to the parlous situation we endured twenty years ago," Horque replied.

"When we only had two operational pyramids?" Irex asked.

"Yes." Sometimes he felt like he was dealing with dolts. Why couldn't they think for themselves? Following orders was important but when it stifled initiative, it often led to missed opportunities.

"And that was when, in the absence of sufficient sun-fire ambience, we suffered from the scourge of the wasting disease. Don't you think the same will happen now?" He lathered his words with sarcasm.

"Y-yes," Irex stammered, his face shadowed by the fear that affected all Solarii at the mention of that painfully slow killer.

"Don't worry, your *ka* will survive. But I want the Records Pyramid fully operational in three days' time."

"That...will be hard to achieve," Irex admitted.

"Any longer than that and the wasting disease will grip the people by the throat." Horque could not allow that. As Eye of Horus, Protector of the Pharaoh and His People, and Guardian of the Pyramid Field, he was responsible for the people's welfare, and any longer than three days would jeopardise his position. In these fractious times and with the flood coming, he was not going to allow that to happen.

"Have you forgotten," he went on, "that when the Solarii first cast a shadow on Earth and walked in the rays of the sun as incarnate beings, we only needed one solar furnace, the Records Pyramid, to store sufficient rays of sun-fire ambience to nourish our *ka*? Now we need three. What does that tell you?"

"That the pyramids' storage capacity is slowly reducing," Irex said.

"Exactly. And that's because the fundamental bindings in the astral light are fracturing and fragmenting. It is also affecting the sky waters. Didn't you hear that our high priest has predicted the coming of a flood?"

Irex nodded. "I did. If Cheiron says it's coming, it must be true."

"Three days. Get on with it."

Irex bowed and left.

"Yours orders, Excellency?" Marim asked.

"You are to secure our boundaries," Horque told him. "The hybrids must have breached the astral shield around Dudael. Something is awry with the Sphinx, the source of the shield. Put it to rights. There must be no repeat of this incursion. Is that understood?"

"Yes, Protector." Marim turned on his heel.

As Horque returned to his Horus Wing craft, he swept off a pair of dead hornets from the seat. That swarm of hornets niggled him. The last time he recalled hornets in an incident such as this was long ago when the rebel angel Semjaza, aided by the chimera Pazazu, Marduk and other hybrids, had tried to sabotage the construction of the Records Pyramid. They had failed, and Semjaza ended his life trapped inside the pyramid. The workmanlike hornet was the astral insignia of the Helios, but surely that was as far as the coincidence went?

34

CHAPTER 5

The Oak of Samlios

Akasha awoke in her cell in the temple. She peered out of the window opening across to the west. Everything looked the same: the arc of residences, the rounded peak of Out Hill, the rolling hills in the Needles. Even the sky waters above, huge surging torrents of water suspended in the air, maintained a semblance of normality. In the six days since the ending of the winds, nothing had changed, and yet everything had changed.

After the exhausting dance of the winds and the dream vision of the flood, she'd been cared for by the two women in her life: Thera, her mother, and Shamira the Pythoness. While Thera nurtured her back to health, Shamira nourished her with the latest tidings from the city and around the world. This morning she arrived with more.

"Your dream vision has captured everyone's imagination," she said, head as still as a snake's. "From Pearl Land to Cathay, from Land of the Clouds to the Pyrenes, everyone wants to know the answer to one question."

"What's that?" Akasha asked.

"There's a lot of water up there." Shamira glanced at the sky waters. "It would be nice to know when it's going to come down."

Akasha shrugged. "Even I don't know that."

"If you can say anything at all, it would help," Shamira said, "and would undoubtedly save lives."

For days, Akasha had reflected on this knotty question, but she hadn't managed to squeeze any more insight from her memories of the vision. She took a deep breath. "I saw nothing about the timings in my premonition. But I have certain beliefs about it."

"What kind of beliefs?" Shamira asked.

35

"First of all, I don't believe that whoever or whatever sent me that vision will bring the flood tomorrow, leaving us no time to prepare. That would be callous in the extreme. So I don't think it will happen for a while yet, several moons at least. I also believe more portents will appear as the time approaches."

"That's my sense too," Shamira agreed. "Of late, I've travelled astrally to hold counsel with priests and elders around the world. There's already an agreement in principle."

"For what?" This sounded interesting.

"A Mind Search, a gathering of the peoples of the world. We need to get ready for the deluge. We'll explore what we can do together, and how we can save as much life as possible."

"It sounds incredible," Akasha said. Shamira had been busy.

"It'll be held here in Samlios in your honour."

"I don't deserve that, but thank you all the same. When will it be held?"

"Needless to say, at the earliest opportunity. We must organise everything here and allow enough time for those who will arrive by boat. So it could be as early as one moon."

"So soon? You've put a lot of forethought into this." That was typical of Shamira, always a step or two ahead of everyone else. That was why she was the augur. The Mind Search was going to be a huge collaborative affair, right here in Samlios.

"I have to leave now," Shamira said. "I have to prepare for Irit's final rites in three days' time. Will you be well enough to attend?"

"Yes, definitely," Akasha said. How could she miss the funeral of a true legend of Samlios?

As Shamira opened the door to leave, Akasha plucked up the courage to ask her, "Who will be chosen to replace Irit?"

"It's a little early for that, don't you think?" Shamira said. "And I thought we'd dealt with that issue?"

"We spoke about it before Irit passed away," Akasha corrected her. "Now there's a need for a replacement – according to the Covenant of the Firstborn."

"I'm not even sure the covenant is still valid. Besides, no one can go though the reversal process to become fertile until the Solarii come and reinstate the Emerald Cavern."

"I see." Then Akasha had a bright idea. "Invite the Solarii to the Mind Search. They can repair the cavern while they're here."

"Yes, that's possible," Shamira replied. "We can put it to them. Now, I must leave or I'll be late."

Akasha was pleased about the Mind Search but she was worried about Shamira's offhand comment about the covenant. If it were no longer valid, how would the human race reproduce? She was no nearer to having a child; indeed, that prospect seemed farther away than it had before the great winds came. As she mused on her situation, she heard loud banging and sawing coming from the centre of the cloisters. There she found Tros, Uriah and a gang of men busy cutting up the oak of Samlios. How could they do that? The winds had felled the tree, but it was still precious.

"Stop! What are you doing?" she cried.

"We're not going to leave the tree here. We'll make use of every part of it." Her father knew how to placate her.

She turned to head back to her cell when Tros called out.

"You know you had that encounter with Jarda at the Step Well?" he asked.

"How could I forget?"

"Well, you remember during the great winds, we had trouble battening down the cloth to cover the well pool? The last time before your dance that we managed to get out of the cathedral was after half a moon. I remember that day – the winds were so strong we were forced to leave the cloth flapping around all over the place."

"What are you trying to say?" she asked.

"You'll never guess what we found when we got down there after the winds."

"No? Tell me."

"The cloth was fixed down by boulders and rocks and the pool waters were pristine. That's how we are able to drink the water straight away, without having to wait for it to cleanse itself."

"How did that happen?"

He looked coy, the face he wore when he had secret to impart. "I think the only explanation is that Jarda and the hybrids went down there and pinioned the cloth."

"How do you know it was them?"

"I found this embedded in the material," he said, holding up a piece of broken claw.

She held it up to the light. Curved and bony, it was a wolf's claw and no mistake.

"You think this broke off one of the lycans as they struggled to batten down the covering?"

"I'm certain of it. We found the stray amphorae the lycans took from you nestled at the base of the Step Well. It could only have been them. I think the hybrids saved our lives."

How was this possible? Were they that intelligent? Did they even care about humans?

"Can I keep it?" she asked, holding up the claw.

"Please do," Tros said with a smile.

"Thank you for telling me."

"There's one more thing," Tros said, as Uriah and the other members of his work gang gathered around them. "We look at a young lady like you and we see someone who talked to the great winds, who performed a sacred dance to them and they blew themselves to a stop. We see someone who has the ear of the divine. That's special. We rely on people like you to give us wise counsel about this flood."

"Tros," she replied, "you say such kind words." His affectionate pleas stirred her heart.

"We have something for you to remember us, and this moment," he said, as he took her by the hand, opened her fingers and pressed a pouch into her palm. The sparkle in his eyes and the softness of his gesture told her it was a precious gift. Whatever was in the pouch was small and oval. Her hands trembling with excitement, she opened it and picked out – an acorn. Even without asking, she knew where it originated.

She kissed him with utmost tenderness on the cheek. He blushed from ear to ear, and then turned to lead his men back to lumping logs. She turned and walked on. She put the acorn back in the pouch and deposited it in her shoulder bag with the broken claw. Every day was a gift, and today she'd received not one, but two.

CHAPTER 6

The Halls of Justice

Ensconced in his chambers, Horque had toiled through the night to co-ordinate the repair of the pyramid. The first night was always going to be the most fraught with pain and anxiety. His people had suffered from the slump in the rays of sunfire ambience. It was as if a demon had sucked the air from their bodies and then scourged their skin with heated stones and rocks.

The night-burn harmed not only the people, but also his intention to restore the pyramid's operation in three days. During the night, his men were incapable of any kind of sustained effort or movement. Even with the assistance of the ashlar for cutting though rock as hard as granite, and the irsution for lifting stones the size of elephants, the strain of removing the rubble and the boulders strewn across the pyramid field proved too much for them. The men worked on the more complex tasks of replacing the scored surface and the capstone as far as their stamina allowed, which wasn't much. One after another, they collapsed from exhaustion.

A cacophony of wails and screams ruptured the still night air. Despite the tightness in his chest and his itchy skin, Horque was determined to oversee the remedial operation and nothing, not even his own discomfort, would deter him. The impoverished operation of the pyramids had other repercussions, as he discovered when he returned to his residence. As he sat recovering in the water court, Tarsus made a confession.

"Master, we are also suffering because of the pyramid's malfunction," he muttered.

Now Horque remembered that the same thing had happened to the little people, some twenty years previously.

"See for yourself," Tarsus said, snatching the skullcap from his head and revealing a light fuzz of hair.

"I see," Horque said, feigning sympathy.

"And it's under the arms and in the groin." Tarsus let him know he was serious with the depth of his frown.

"I'll take your word for it," he said, shaking his head. What was all this fuss over a tiny shoot of hair?

"The hair growth is horrific," Tarsus explained, picking up on his air of disbelief. "To us, it's like going to sleep with fingers and waking up with claws in their place. Imagine that."

"Hair is no hardship," Horque argued. "The Solarii have a full head of the stuff."

"That may be," Tarsus said, jutting out his chin. "Animals have hair, feather and fur. So do the hybrids. Humans are hairless, or were, until the hybrid seed infected us. When the pyramids are working properly, the growth of the hybrid seed is suppressed."

Horque knew that. "We're trying to help. Suppress the hybrid seed. Release the Surge. Achieve that and we Solarii return to our doubles. We all strive for the same end."

Tarsus seemed satisfied with this mantra, and scuttled off to do his duties.

By high sun, Horque was feeling the beneficial effects of the sun's rays on his tired body. The new day brought a welcome respite from the aches and disquiet of the night, and his mood had improved significantly by the time Javian arrived.

"You found Berux?" he asked.

"Yes, he's under guard." Javian nodded, squinting in one eye.

"Good. Where is he now?"

"In the Temple of Ma'at, about to face the wrath of the vizier."

"Excellent," Horque said. "I will attend the court myself – I want to look him in the eye."

At the temple, he went to the judgement chambers with their high vaulted stone ceilings and long colonnade. There he sought out his mother, the Vizier Issa. The chamber was replete with magnificent regalia celebrating the first ever system of jurisprudence. Etched on the wall behind Issa's seat was an enormous white ostrich feather, the symbol of Ma'at, revered Goddess of Truth and Justice.

The smell of his mother's rose-scented perfume was a delight; just the right amount to keep away the tepid heats and stinking odours with which all Solarii were assailed. To reflect the seriousness of the charges, she wore her black judge's robes. Her vizier pectoral sparkled around her long, slender neck. While he could participate in the proceedings, she would have the final jurisdiction.

From the dais, Horque surveyed the court, front and back. He was aware of the throne-like seat behind him. Reserved for the pharaoh, today it was empty.

40

One day, he promised himself, he would occupy it. Below him was the scribe, Arar, and the Guardian of Justice, Lasec, who administered proceedings. As he took a seat next to Issa on a dais, Lasec bowed to him, but only just low enough to satisfy convention.

Lasec shouted, "Bring Berux in!"

"Lasec, you're presumptuous." Issa thumped her gavel on the desk. "How dare you flout my authority? Proceedings will commence when I command, and not a moment before."

"As you wish," Lasec replied with a scowl.

"It's not as *I* wish," Issa snapped. "It will be done as the law of Ma'at instructs, and I'll hear no more of your impertinence."

"Yes, of course, Vizier," Lasec said, his tone still haughty. "Shall I begin now?"

Horque intervened. "Despite the night-burn, we mustn't allow standards to fall. This case will be heard with all the normal diligence and discretion." He aimed a glare at Lasec. Lasec was the upstart son of Nimrod, the influential Steward of the Granary, with whom both he and his mother bore a seething rivalry.

"Before the goddess Ma'at, all cases are serious." Issa tapped the table with her fingers. "Now, let the case commence."

"Bring the accused in," Lasec repeated wearily.

Berux was led into the courtroom at the end of a leather leash, wearing a hangdog expression to match. He bowed low in supplication. His headdress was soiled and dishevelled. The night-burn had smeared his cheeks with a purple rash, and together with the withered left arm he'd carried since birth, he had the appearance of a ghoul.

The courtroom hushed as he stood in the dock.

"Let the pleadings and questionings begin," Issa hailed.

Lasec turned to Berux. "You're here to answer charges against you that you were absent from your duty at the pyramid field, a severe dereliction that led to the near-destruction of the Records Pyramid and jeopardised the survival of our people on Earth. This court will examine your guilt and then apply the appropriate correction according to the demands of Ma'at. Do you understand?"

Berux stammered, "Y-yes, I do."

"Now, for the scribe, tell us your name and standing."

"Berux," he muttered.

"Speak up so all can hear."

"I am Berux," he said, louder this time.

"What was your standing at birth?"

"My birth was anything but normal. I was pulled violently from my mother's womb and pronounced dead. Yet, as the embalmers prepared my tiny body for the journey to Du'at, the breath of the gods entered and revived me. But Anubis and

Osiris kept a piece of me," he added, pulling up his shirt to reveal the withered arm.

"You'll be going back to meet them very soon," Lasec sneered. "Once your guilt is established, your leaden soul will be taken to Du'at, weighed on the scales against the lightness of the feather of Ma'at, and disappear into Ammut's grasping jaws." Lasec opened and closed his mouth in a mock eating movement. "A fittingly horrific end for a man who's committed a horrific crime."

Lasec's words were disrespectful to the high standards and balances of Ma'at, and Horque reprimanded him. "The goddess Ma'at is immune to personal whim and the persuasion of the persona. You're supposed to be her representative, so remember that before you speak."

"We thank the protector for his timely reminder." Lasec's reply oozed disdain. Horque fixed him with a stare, but Lasec averted his gaze and continued. "I call Javian as witness."

Javian sat down in a small enclosure. One of his eyes had a nervous tic.

"Can you tell us Berux's whereabouts during yesterday's hybrid attack?" Lasec asked.

"Yes, I can," Javian replied. "Berux was absent from his post."

"He's guilty!" a voice shouted from the packed public area. Others stood up and shook their fists at Berux.

"It's all his fault!" another yelled.

When all fell quiet again, Lasec said, "May Ma'at bear witness that this testimony proves Berux's guilt." A self-satisfied grin flickered over his dowdy features.

Horque repeated his complaint. "Lasec, you're bringing Ma'at into disrepute. Sit down. Vizier Issa will take over the questioning."

Lasec threw him a look of venom and hatred that was almost tangible.

"Thank you, Protector," Issa said with her customary dignity. "Now, Javian, where did you find Berux? What was he doing during the attack?"

"I found him at his residence, engaged in a forbidden act."

"What forbidden act?" Issa asked.

"I found him lying with…" Javian paused and glanced nervously at Issa.

"You must tell us everything you know," Issa said.

"…A lady of the night."

"Javian," Issa replied, breathing a sigh of relief. "That's not forbidden. Many Solarii lay with them. Ma'at is not offended by our lust and sexual desires. We all know there are good reasons for the Solarii condition."

"I know, but that's not what I-I'm trying to say," Javian stammered.

"What *do* you have to say?" Issa asked.

"The girl," Javian said, fidgeting with his clothes.

"What about the girl?"

Javian wiped beads of sweat from his forehead. The eye with the squint was almost closed. He cleared his throat. "She was...not Solarii."

A sudden hush descended on the court. The scribe looked up from his papyrus. Lasec's mouth hung open. Berux hid his head in his hands. Horque could not believe his ears.

"Not...Solarii?" Issa repeated.

"No," Javian confirmed. "She was from the south, from Kush."

The auditorium fell as silent as the night.

"A Kushite. She was *human*?" Issa cried, raising her dark eyebrows.

Lasec lifted his hands in the air. The scribe's hand froze above the papyrus; a drop of ink dripped onto his pristine sheet and dribbled off the edge of the page.

Javian now had only one eye open. He cleared his throat. "Yes."

With that word, he had pronounced Berux's death sentence. Even Horque knew that.

Everyone started yelling. People rocked back and forth on their chairs, screaming obscenities at Berux and wailing like the goddess Ma'at herself had died.

"Quiet! I will have silence!" Issa cried, thumping the gavel. "This is a new and grave accusation. For a Solarii to sleep with a human is anthropophilia. The offence of anthropophilia is the crime of illicit sexual liaison between a Solarii and a human, a union forbidden in Solarii law ever since the Helios stung the daughters of men and produced the hybrids. Any union of a Solarii and a human evokes unwanted and unfortunate echoes of that original impregnation."

Horque took a deep breath. This crime had soiled something that until now had remained pristine. The world of the Solarii would never be the same again. No one had ever been convicted of this offence. It came as a severe shock to all who sat in the sultry atmosphere of the courtroom. A pall of stunned silence hung over the auditorium, broken only by the scratching of the scribe's reed brush on the papyrus sheet.

"Berux, do you have anything to say in your defence?" Issa asked.

"No, nothing," Berux replied. Discipline and conformity formed the corner-stones of Solarii society, so Horque hadn't expected him to say otherwise.

Issa smoothed her robes and asked, "What was the woman's name?"

"Petra. Her name was Petra."

"Javian, when you leave here, arrest the girl Petra," Horque interrupted. "Then pass her to the Semites. They can sentence her under their own laws. The crime of anthropophilia is as abhorrent to humans as it is to us."

"Thank you, Protector," Issa said. "Now, Berux, you're aware that anthropophilia is anathema?"

"Yes, I'm sorry."

Horque felt a pang of sorrow for Berux. The urge to conform was strong. Even in the anteroom to his own death, he couldn't bring himself to justify his actions, merely apologise for them.

"Your sorrow counts for nothing before the goddess Ma'at. Only the deed is judged."

"I'm not sorry for the deed, I'm only sorry I was apprehended – not like some others," Berux said. So, he was trying to break the shackles of his compliance.

"What do you mean?" Issa challenged him. "Do you have the crass impudence to imply that other Solarii have slept with humans? This is a grave accusation. Corroborate it or recant," she added, her voice stern with retribution.

"I can corroborate…nothing." Berux's voice sounded limp. "It's what I've heard from others."

"Hearsay is insufficient. No corroboration means no accusation," Issa said. Clearing her throat, she added, "Berux, you've been found guilty by this court of anthropophilia, the most heinous crime. Do you understand?"

Berux nodded twice. He screwed up his face in a thousand wrinkles of anguish and buried his head in his hands.

Issa touched the mole on her face, something she did when she was nervous. Well, this was nerve-wracking. "This infamous crime against Ma'at must be corrected and the contamination erased. Protector Horque is the wronged party in this affair. His pyramids are not working as they should, so he will decide on the restorative sentence."

Issa handed him the flail of justice. In a booming voice that echoed around the colonnade, he cried, "By the power of Ma'at invested in me, I declare that your punishment will be physical death and astral erasure."

Berux cried out in despair, a long, agonising denial. "No, not astral erasure! Why has it come to this?" His eyes bulged, tears streaming down his cheeks as he knelt on the marbled floor. "I have a wife, a family, a career, ambition, desires and appetites. I worked hard, rose through the ranks. I achieved more than was expected of me. The priapism is implacable. Every Solarii man suffers from it. The priests preach that we are born away from home with human bodies but with the fire of the sun in our souls. 'Wear beads of amber,' they say, 'seek out Solarii prostitutes'. Yet my case is severe. It hurts, the craving, the lusting. I couldn't stop the lust. This time, the girl was from Kush but others, even members of the Ennead Council, went with girls – human girls. Petra told me herself. I got caught while they hide behind their fine pectorals."

Those in the auditorium stood up and shouted at Berux, punching the air in disgust.

"Liar!" they cried.

"Fornicator!"

"Anthropophiliac!"

"Order!" Issa shouted, her shrill voice raising high about the hubbub. She slammed the gavel down on the desk until a semblance of peace reigned again.

"This is the Temple of Ma'at," she said unequivocally. "The Solarii Temple of Justice. Justice must be that: just ice, cold, blind and unforgiving."

The scribe had a question for Issa. "Shall I strike Berux's defamatory allegations from the written record?"

"That won't be necessary," she replied. "Let me remind you of the lore of erasure, to which Berux will be subject. Everything a person does or says deposits a tiny residue in the unseen realms of the astral light. During the course of a person's life, these residues accumulate into a complete, unbiased deposit, an astral record that survives the death of the physical body. Unless it is erased, this astral record will live on and inveigle others to commit anthropophilia. This further pollutes the astral light and unconsciously persuades more people to transgress with the same crime. Over the generations, this is how grudges fester between families, feuds between tribes, and why standards fall over the generations. Berux's heinous action has polluted his astral record, which must now be permanently erased from the astral light."

Issa smote the gavel down on the desk and glared at the scribe. "Is that clear?" she barked.

"Yes, Vizier," the scribe stammered.

"Berux, you will stand for the sentencing," Lasec instructed the accused.

Horque watched his mother's blue eyes narrow into icy diamonds. Her complexion was wan, the same white as the ostrich feather emblazoned on the wall behind her. Her voice had a metallic ring as she repeated the ritual words.

"Berux, because of the illumined astral light, this pollution has tainted your entire family. To correct this wrong, there must be retribution. Not only you, but also your wife and close family – your parents, all your children, your brothers and sisters, as well as your uncles and aunts, they must all must perish. This is the unalterable law of Ma'at."

Horque sighed. Ma'at was severe, but it was for good reason. Berux would pay a heavy price. Berux's accusations against the Ennead Council were scandalous. Yes, every Solarii had a rampant libido, with but none went with humans. That was unthinkable.

The vizier spoke to a hushed court. "Berux, you are to be taken to the Palace of Confinement where you and your family will be executed at rise-sun tomorrow."

Berux slumped onto the floor, prostrate. He lay there alone and unaided while Horque rose with a satisfied air of retribution.

"This is so all may bear witness as to how the pharaoh protects his people from pollution and corrects the balances of Ma'at."

CHAPTER 7

The Hill of Sighs

That morning, three days after receiving the acorn and the wolf's claw, Akasha felt decidedly odd. Her head itched all over. How could that be? She rubbed her palm across her scalp. She could feel…a light down. Was that…hair? How? Why? Hair growth. The next thing she'd be growing nails…and then teeth. She'd be an Eater. That was anathema. Animals had fur, claws and fangs. They were Eaters. Humans weren't animals. Nor hybrids. That was what marked them as unique, special and unfinished – hence the need for the Surge. She'd never experienced hair growth, not on her, nor on anyone else.

The light stubble on her head made her feel dirty. A wash, that's what she needed. Frantic, she grabbed an amphora, put on her shawl and followed the winding path down Temple Mount. The morning breeze felt warm on her cheeks. The streets, the cathedral grounds, the inn – everywhere was heaving with people mending fences, filling holes, repairing statues and assembling their market stalls. They'd cleared most of the debris. The only remaining testament to the winds was the tilt in the trees, all in the same direction, bowing low in awe to Mother Nature.

At the base of the pool, she found Big Qorus, the Green Elder, and Callisto, Tros' daughter.

"I'm so glad you're better," Callisto said.

"I'm here to wash," Akasha mumbled, heading for the pool.

"What's the matter?" Callisto asked. The Blue Elder always wanted to know what was wrong with people. So she told her.

"I've got…" The words stuck in her throat. This was harder to articulate than she'd imagined.

"What is it?"

"I've got hair growing," she said, lifting her skullcap. Her raised voice echoed around the cavern of the well pool.

"Oh, don't worry," Callisto replied. "It's affected everyone."

"It's new for you," Big Qorus said, "but folks like me and your father – the older generation – we've experienced it before. This is the third time it has happened to us. After a while, the growth recedes. You'll see."

"The Solarii promised to help us suppress the growth of the hybrid seed," Callisto added. "It turned out the emanation from their pyramids did just that."

"Are you saying something's happened to the pyramids?" Akasha touched the light down on her head to see if it had receded since she had last felt it. It hadn't.

"Exactly," Callisto said. "Somehow, they're not working as they should. The emanation is reduced."

What a relief. At least it wasn't just her. So this was the hybrid seed. What a scourge. She hated hair as much as the next person did. First the cleansing flow, then the prophecy of the flood, and now the growth of hybrid seed. This last moon had brought wave after wave of challenge and change.

"You said it's happened before. Tell me, what will they do next?" she asked.

"They'll build another pyramid. That's what they did on the last two occasions – first the Queen's about one hundred years ago, and the King's just before you were born, about twenty years ago. After that, the hair growth was suppressed, and eventually it receded and disappeared altogether."

"How long…do we have to put up with this?" Akasha asked, scratching her head irritably.

"It took them from one summer to the next to build the King's Pyramid," Callisto replied.

A year. She'd have to endure this for a year. The Solarii seemed to govern the important aspects of their lives: the Emerald Cavern, the ability to reproduce, and now the hybrid seed, the very thing holding back the greatest gift humanity had ever received – the Surge.

"What were you going to come and see me about?" she asked.

"I have a gift for you, but first I want to thank you for saving us all. We Samlios folk are simple. Those demon winds almost tore us all apart. You risked your life for us and for everyone on Earth."

Callisto bent down, pressing her lips against the centre of Akasha's forehead and prayed. "May your life be blessed and all your wishes fulfilled."

"You're too kind," Akasha replied.

"I can't quite appreciate the enormity of what you've done, so I'm going to tell you what it means to me. Because of your dance, I can walk in the healing gardens and smell the rose blooms. I can feel the warm earth beneath the soles of my feet. I can look forward to delivering the next baby in Samlios."

Secretly, Akasha hoped that it would be hers. "Thank you for saying so," she said.

"As I said, I have a gift for you. It is traditional to give it to a person after they've been in the Emerald Cavern, but you haven't been able to do that. Even so, I want you to have this," Callisto said, giving her a cloth purse the size of her palm.

As Akasha held it in both hands, a sublime sense filled the caverns of her soul. She opened the purse and drew out an unpolished crystal fragment, about the size of her fingertip. "It's..."

"...Your avatar: a nugget of blue emerald," Callisto said.

"It's beautiful," she replied, moving the stone between thumb and forefinger. She felt as if someone had handed her keys to the mysteries of the universe. "That came from me? During my birth?" She shook her head in disbelief.

Callisto nodded. "It's a condensation of the astral light ambience at your birth."

"I've heard of the avatar, I know everyone has one. It's such a marvel, isn't it?"

"It's one of the many things I love about midwifery and being a Blue Elder. Do you know how it works?"

"Do tell," Akasha said, reluctant to tear her eyes from the gem.

"Like everything natural, it's simple," Callisto said. "It happens in the same way that desert-dwellers collect water at dawn. They leave out a large funnel on which drops of dew gather in the cool night air. Eventually the dewdrops run down the neck of the funnel and collect in a bowl underneath it. In the same way, in the birthing chamber, a special casket condenses the astral light that was present at your birth, the astral attendance in which you were born. Instead of a pool of dew, you create a crystal. Mine was a yellow topaz, look!" She indicated the jewel she always wore around her neck.

"This is my dewdrop," Akasha said, and kissed Callisto on the cheek.

"I was there when your beautiful pale blue emerald was forming," Callisto said, as the dimple in her chin quivered with emotion. "Keep it close. It'll enhance you when you're low."

"I will. It's a treasure."

"Now," Callisto said, suddenly all matter-of-fact, "it's time for Irit's last rites."

So it was, from birth to death. Life was a strange and inexplicable journey.

With the pale sun high in the sky waters, Irit's cortege snaked its way to the sacred burial area on the Hill of Sighs. Everyone held her in great respect. Every citizen was there. Their wails of grief rose up like an offering to the Source, easing her passage back from whence she came.

Akasha walked behind Esther and Rocor the Gardener, Irit's mother and uncle respectively, until they gathered in a circle around a neat pile of rocks knee-high above the ground. Next to it was another cairn on which lay the body of Irit's father, Magril. They were obviously kin; both wore a look of undaunted pride. Apart from some rusting and sagging of the skin, Magril's face appeared as pristine as the day he'd died, over 120 years before. Akasha wondered at the preservative powers of the bright astral light, and its amazing ability to slow down the process of putrefaction.

Rocor stepped up to her cairn first.

"I'm no man of words," he said. "I'm a simple gardener who loves the rhythm and song of nature. So join me now singing Irit's favourite song, one last time, for her."

Samlios city, we live in her lee,
She is our ocean home.
We are made of air and sea,
And her mighty loam.

The whole community sung the revered song of Samlios, everyone in harmony. When they finished, Rocor placed a posy of white lilies on Irit's body, and gently bowed his head.

Akasha gazed at Irit's face, so soft, almost alive. She was sure she was sleeping, waiting for her astral body to return to her physical host. When it did, she'd awake and encourage folk to be kind and compassionate to the hybrids. But there was no awakening. She'd breathed her last.

Panion lifted his hands above his head. "We're here to celebrate a life, and to return the soul of Irit to the earth and her spirit to the Source. We all live in the shadow of a greatness never fulfilled. That is why we struggle to bring light where there is darkness. That is why we wait patiently for the release of the Surge, so that we may be nearer to the Source. Irit did that and more. She graced us by her presence and left us a legacy of maternal courage and humanity."

Akasha waited in silence, hearing only the sound of the waves breaking on the southern shores and the quiet passage of people as they paid their last respects with a dignified bow of the head. As she turned to leave, she caught the sound of a soft mewing. There, on the peak of Out Hill, was a lone lycan. Through wolverine eyes, he seemed to be aware of what they were doing, and he stared intently at Irit's cadaver. It was Jarda. He seemed to be crying, but surely not. A wolf with tears; how could that be? As the creature shuffled off down the far side of the hill, she noticed he had a bushy tail.

At that moment, Akasha knew two things: that Tros was right. Jarda had helped fix the cloth over the pool, and most astonishing of all, he'd come to pay his last respects to Irit. He was a brute, a creature of the forest. So how had he known of her demise, and the rites of passage?

CHAPTER 8

The Lore of Erasure

Horque was cold. The scourge of the night-burn wracked his body. Every limb felt stiff, every breath laboured. Despite it being delivered in the middle of the night, he'd responded to Berux's last request. It allowed him to escape from the fractious ambience around the pyramid field. Irex had failed to repair the Records Pyramid, heralding a second night of shortfall in sun-fire astral ambience. His people suffered all this pain, for want of a few rays of sunshine.

He and Marim walked through the dark city streets to the Palace of Confinement. From the Semite quarter came the second night bell, resounding over the city. From behind every door came cries of woe and despair. He ducked as an owl swooped low over his head. Dogs howled at the moon; cats screeched on the rooftops. Had the dread spirits of the underworld been roused from their deathly stupor and joined in the people's plaintive wailings? No, but it sounded like it. From beyond the palace, beyond the city, beyond Egypt, out in the cold depths of the universe, came the first distant stirrings of dawn, the last dawn for Berux and his family. But was this all Berux's fault? These were signs that pointed to a greater influence at play. Surely, the gods were displeased. It was Pharaoh Zoser's task to placate them and to intervene on the people's behalf, not incur their wrath. When this was all over, there would be a heavy reckoning.

While Marim waited outside, the cellar man led him down a gloomy corridor. The first birdsong chirped from afar, and it was almost sweet. Before entering Berux's cell, he paused to mentally plant the necessary protective astral symbols around his person. He was not going to catch whatever astral malaise had caused Berux's downfall.

The cellar man wiped his nose with the back of his hand, and chewed on a pellet of red gum. Horque walked past him and the cellar man slammed the door shut behind him. The smell of damp smacked his nostrils. The low ceiling made him feel closed in and aggravated his already shallow breathing. Berux sat slumped in the corner. A solitary glow lamp cast him in an eerie shadow. Hands on thighs, the condemned Solarii heaved himself up like an old man.

"Thank you for coming." His voice was hoarse, and his face pale and drawn.

"What do you want of me, Berux?"

"Protector Horque, I'm craven," Berux said. "I've suffered the travails of priapism. I've endured the stink of putrefaction on Earth and the emptiness of exile from our home planet, but it's all been for nothing."

"All of it, ejaculated," Horque sneered.

Berux shook his head sorrowfully. "I am to die. And because of the unforgiving dictates of Ma'at, so must my wife, my children and my family, all polluted by my crime. I was lured by lust. I surrendered to the pleasures of the flesh and became the first anthropophiliac." He screwed his face into a capsule of hate.

"Call for a priest to make your abject confessions. I don't want to hear them."

"I already have, but before he comes, I have a last request to make of you," Berux murmured, pleading in his voice. "My estate is worth salvaging. I need someone I can trust to dispose of it."

"I'm listening," Horque replied. He knew what was coming.

"At the pyramid field, I reported to you every day. You recently honoured me by giving me command over Dudael to search out the hybrids."

"Ha!" How could he mention that? "Your gross negligence allowed the hybrids into the pyramid field for only the second time ever. Under my watch. You say you've been honoured, but I've been humiliated by a Solarii – no, by an anthropophiliac. I'll need all the fortune of the gods to keep my position. I have only one salvation. You will be executed. Not only that, we're going to erase your *ka*, expunging your astral record, and every action you've ever made. I'm talking to a man whose life's worth amounts to no more than a puff of wind."

"Did you come to gloat?" Berux replied.

"No. I'm merely telling the truth."

"Then why respond to my request?" Berux asked.

"I didn't come for you. I came because it would offend Osiris to ignore the request of a condemned man."

"I have no one else I can trust," Berux continued. "You're a member of the Ennead Council, a Solarii of the highest integrity. Your mother is vizier. As Eye of Horus, Protector of the People, I call upon your protection. You're the ideal person to execute my last wishes."

"You're guilty of a crime so ignominious, even the gods view you with contempt. I doubt they'll let you into Du'at. Your goods and your estate are as polluted as you are. Don't prolong this ordeal because your end is nigh."

Berux winced. Perhaps he could see the early morning light creeping into the cell window, a splash of pale green luminescence on the horizon.

Horque stretched his tired limbs. His back to Berux, he stopped in front of the cell door.

"Don't go," Berux said. "My grandson is one of the few in my family who'll survive this bloody cull. He's innocent, and he deserves a fresh start. My dying wish is that my estate passes into his hands."

"Your estate is untouchable and of no value. No one would want to procure it," Horque said. "As a member of the Ennead Council, I'm prohibited from handling it, even if it's merely to pass it on to your grandson."

"Protector," Berux was insistent, "you can sanction the priests to exorcise the taint on my estate."

"Ask the priest yourself when he comes," Horque sneered.

Hugging himself, Berux rocked forwards and backwards, his face moving in and out of the pale dawn light seeping through the cell opening.

The sound of keys rattled in the lock and a moment later, the cellar man poked his head in. "The high priest," he announced.

The high priest was a squat man with a large nose and deep-set eyes, the blue of lapis lazuli. Around his neck sat a fine pectoral, replete with glowing faience balls.

"I am Cheiron," he announced.

"I'm honoured by your presence," Berux replied.

"Quite," Cheiron said, wincing at the stench in the cell. "Outside the birds are starting their morning chorus and the slanting rays of dawn will soon strike you down. Therefore speak now, or forever hold your peace."

Berux took a deep breath. "I want you to minister to me in my last moments," he said.

"There's nothing I can do for you," Cheiron replied, shuffling his feet as if he couldn't wait to leave. "You're guilty of a crime whose taint cannot be undone, not even by a priest of my calibre."

"I'm desperate to return to my solar double, my *ba*," Berux said, plunging to his knees in supplication. "Maim me, torture me, kill my physical body, but spare my soul, my *ka*. Don't erase it, I beg of you." Berux lunged forwards and tried to grab Cheiron's skirt. Cheiron dodged, and glared at him.

"You know the holy dogma that says life for a Solarii on Earth is merely a staging post," the priest replied. "When we die, we all want to cross the great Winding Waterway in the sky and make the final return home to the sun, a journey hazardous in the extreme. While a lifetime of dedication here can form a *ka* capable of making that crossing, the Twin Perils prevent us. The first is that we form a strong emotive attachment to the beauty of the Earth and her people. The second is that we commit some anathema or heinous crime that offends Ma'at. That, Berux, is how you've transgressed."

Berux was begging now. "Then have mercy on my wife and family. They did nothing wrong. It was I – and Petra the Kushite – who transgressed."

"You want mercy?" Cheiron shook with anger. "People want to feel the rays of sun-fire astral energy at night. You failed to protect the pyramids and keep them secure from attack. Ma'at cannot and does not tolerate failure. The goddess Ma'at does not countenance mercy, and she seeks only justice and correction. We are merely the instruments of her unbending will."

Horque listened intently to the high priest. The harmonies of Ma'at kept pollution at bay. The goddess was a harsh mistress, and his views and opinions and wishes didn't make one iota of difference in the grand scheme of things.

"Since the going down of the sun last night," Cheiron went on, clearly warming to his task, "my lungs are burning, my skin itches and my bones feel stiff. Because of your lust, the Records Pyramid has a gaping hole where the capstone resided and from where precious rays of stored sun-fire ambience have leaked out. It won't function until Horque can repair it."

"By then, you will be long gone," Horque added.

Still on his hands and knees, Berux banged his forehead against the bare earth.

"Stop that and stand up. You're a Solarii, not a coward," Cheiron reprimanded him. "You've been sentenced to physical *and* astral erasure. Your soul, and those of your family, will go to the underworld and feed the hybrid Ammut, the devourer of dead souls, eater of the unworthy."

Fireflies darted around the glow lamps in the chill early morning air. A moth burnt itself on the candle; a stray plume of smoke wafted upwards, dissipating into nothing.

"I have one last request," Berux muttered. "Purify my estate so it can be passed to my grandson."

"That can be arranged," Cheiron replied with obvious rancour. "The only way your estate and chattels can be cleansed of such a heinous crime is…by fire."

Berux went pale in the face, and bent double as if he'd been thumped in the belly.

"I've nothing more to do here," Cheiron snapped.

As he left, a cock began to crow, splitting the early morning vapours. The birdsong grew in both intensity and volume. The first sliver of dawn crept through the cell opening. For the pharaoh's people, the rising sun would bring a welcome respite. But for Berux and his family, it would bring a crushing end to their lives.

The cellar man thrust the door open. In walked the Guardian of Justice.

"It is time," Lasec said, a malevolent grin on his face that befitted his function as executioner.

Lasec hauled the terrified man out of the cell and down the corridor, halting at a pair of oval doors. Outside were a heap of discarded headdresses, skirts, shirts and robes. Amongst the jumble, there were even some pectorals and jewellery. Berux knew what to do, and with reluctance, he took off his clothes and sandals. Horque admired the symmetry of the Solarii creed that said one left life as one entered it: naked.

The Guardian of Justice pulled open the doors to the Court of Erasure. The distant pale stirrings of dawn shone through a large window opening. In the centre of the court was a plinth topped by a fearsome black diorite statue of a man with the head of a jackal: Anubis, God of the Underworld, Protector of the Dead. Clustered around him were a score of glum, dejected people: Berux's wife and the rest of his close relatives. They stared blankly into space, hardly bothering to hide their modesty. Only Evera, Berux's wife, looked up when the condemned man entered the court and threw him a glance full of daggers. As he staggered past her, she spat at him, her face contorted in a spasm of hate.

Horque peered through his whites to see into the astral. From what he gauged, the mercurial Lasec had conjured the required lethal mix of energies from the astral light. When the first emerald green ray of dawn slanted into the court and caressed the statue of Anubis, it would splinter into a multitude of smaller rays, like sunlight through glass, searing into each person, suffocating their bodies of breath and life. It was a good death. Any death that was quick was good.

"You'll also need this," he said and handed Lasec the Rod of Erasure, a sycamore club as thick as a man's forearm. Lasec ran his fingers over its elaborate jackal etchings and faience inlay. The man clearly relished his work.

Anyone caught in the chamber when the rim of the sun burst over the horizon would perish; this was not the time to loiter.

"Lasec, we have to leave. Dawn is upon us."

Lasec hurried from the chamber and the cellar man slammed the doors shut. All of a sudden, Lasec lurched back towards the doors.

"What're you doing?" Horque said, blocking his way. "You can't go back in there."

"I-I left the Rod of Erasure in the court," Lasec stammered.

A single terrifying scream split the air. A moment later, dawn struck, filling the court with a cacophony of blood-curdling cries. After a long and painful pause, the cellar man threw the doors open and Horque pushed past him. The stench of death was obnoxious. Berux and his family lay scattered around the court, their bodies still twitching as their *ka* left them for the last time.

"Protector, over here," Lasec called to him, pointing to a woman's corpse.

"That's Evera," Horque said. In her hand, she clutched the bloodstained Rod of Erasure. Her body lay next to her husband's, whose head had a gaping hole from which oozed a ghastly mass of blood and gore, the only visible sign that death had thrown a veil on the court.

"What happened here?" the cellar man asked, screwing up his face in confusion.

"It's obvious, she murdered him." Lasec chuckled.

"I don't understand. She knew he was going to die anyway. Why take the trouble to smash his brains out?" the cellar man asked as he scratched his scrotum.

"You obviously don't understand the joy of revenge." Lasec sighed in admiration.

That man has a black heart, Horque thought. "You left the Rod of Erasure in the court," he said aloud. "You were meant to remove it to prevent this kind of thing happening." He pointed to the crimson pool seeping out on the floor.

"I-I left the court in haste – because you told me to," Lasec stammered, a look of feigned surprise on his face.

"Clean it up," Horque said, spitting out each word, "then do your job. Astral erasure. Berux only. See to it."

Lasec grabbed the bloodstained Rod of Erasure and turned to the cellar man. "There he is." He pointed at Berux. The cellar man tucked the rod underneath Berux's neck so it formed a kind of wooden pillow of death. With the cold eye of an assassin and in one swift movement, Lasec twisted Berux's neck, snapping it over the rod with a loud crack. Berux's neck hung limp and twisted like a chicken's.

"Done," Lasec said, a malicious smile dancing on his lips. "You sure you don't want me to do the others? It's no trouble."

"No," Horque said. "Berux is the only one." Breaking his neck permanently erased his *ka* and the entirety of his record from the astral light: that way, his wickedness could never in the future influence someone else to do the same. The cleansing of Ma'at and the astral light was complete. That was a boon. Dealing with Lasec was not.

"Now," Horque said to him, "do you think you can organise their burial, or will you mismanage that as well?"

Lasec glanced at him and started lugging the bodies into a pile.

The stench of death in the court was overpowering, so Horque left the two men to their work. On his way out, he wondered whether he could curtain Lasec's worthless life in the same way as Berux's. That delightful prospect would have to wait for another day.

CHAPTER 9

Birthday Gift

A moon had waxed and waned since Irit's burial, and Akasha had been busy helping with preparations for the forthcoming Mind Search. With ten days to go, the tiny quay at Fishmouth Harbour was filling up with ships, cargo and people. Only the day before she had welcomed Savor and his entourage from the Land of the Clouds amidst a halo of pan pipes, dancing and singing. Today, she was on her way to the harbour again, this time via the long route along the western cliffs.

With the morning breeze fresh and cool on her cheeks, she noticed the path was scattered with the ashes of several different bonfires. She spotted a group of men in the distance erecting a beacon. At a conveniently safe distance from the fire, the men had built a log pile. Tros the Gatekeeper was the first to welcome her.

"Good morning, Akasha," he shouted, wiping his brow with his forearm. "And happy birthday."

She smiled, pleased they'd remembered. She wasn't accustomed to all this attention.

"Is it a score of years now?" Tros asked, doffing his cap to her.

"It is exactly that," she said.

"Come," he said. He grabbed her by the hand as the men made a ring around the half-constructed beacon and danced around it, singing the Samlios birthday song. At the crescendo, they jumped high in the air and shouted together on one great, "Hi!"

"Oh, I enjoyed that!" She felt her cheeks flushing, but the dancing was such fun.

"What do you think of our night beacon?" Tros asked.

"It's impressive." She cast an admiring glance. From the temple, she'd seen the flames lighting the moon-filled skies.

"We build a fresh one each night," Tros said, taking a slug of water. "They were your father's idea. Only a sailor would know the value of a beacon."

She felt a surge of pride for her father. Her memory flashed back to all those times, waiting on the quay with her mother, for her father to return from some far-off place. He would entertain them with tales of Mithrayzim, or Egypt as the Solarii called it, the Port of Irun, the Whispering Tower, the Gates of Gades, and the Land of the Clouds.

"And we've found a productive use for all the uprooted trees," Tros added.

"That's good," she said.

"Last night, our beacon guided another ship into harbour."

"Who was that?" This was news to her.

"It came in from the east," Tros said, pointing at a ship in the quay below.

"Yes. I recognise its pennants," she said. They displayed a mountain with a tower on the top of it. "That's the ship from the Pyrenes. That's Demos' ship, the *Crucible*."

"So it is," Tros agreed. "I admire all these folks, coming here across the seas. They've put their lives in peril to get here and left their loved ones at home. We all hope you'll resolve this flood business for us." The other men nodded their approval, murmuring respectful noises.

"I don't know for certain when the waters will fall," she said, "only that it will happen, sooner or later. We hope that in the Mind Search we can work out the best thing to do."

"So do we," Tros replied, and returned to his work.

The sun cast its pale rays on the turquoise sea, flecked by white waves. The ocean spread out before her on three sides: to the north, east and south. The great winds had wrought vast changes, rearranged huge quantities of sand and earth, dried out tracts of littoral land, and created new mudflats where the shoreline had receded from the Isle of Samlios. Providence had shined on them, because Fishmouth Harbour still had a navigable channel to the ocean.

Nearing the port, Akasha heard the shouts of men on the dockside as they unloaded the cargoes of silks and precious stones. The air tasted of salt and adventure. The ships' colourful bunting and ribbons fluttered in the stiffening ocean breeze. Gulls squawked as they swooped down over the waves.

She knew whom she'd find on the dock. In front of her, hauling a sea chest, was the avuncular figure of Demos the Pyrene. He was like a beach pebble, hardy, but worn smooth by the ravages of time. He had unflinching green eyes, a gaunt face, and legs fit for the most severe of seas. In perfect harmony with his craggy nature, he had a jutting jawline, a bent, broken nose, and a stump for a little finger on his left hand – the result of an accident cutting down the tall trees that grew on the great slopes of the Pyrenes.

"Demos, I hoped to find you here," she cried. He turned, and with a broad smile on his face, opened his arms to greet her. She felt safe in his huge embrace.

"Have you come to greet an old sea dog like me?"

"Of course, how could I not?"

"I heard about your dance and the dream vision, and that you were recovering. But now look at you and those rosy cheeks," he cried, squeezing them both with affection.

"I'm very well now. Tell me about your village. Did you find any striplings for me?"

"Looking for a man, eh? I'm afraid there are none available or even suitable for you," he replied. "Besides, the great winds buffeted everyone so much, no one's thinking about marriages and the like."

"That's a shame. Then tell me stories of the wide ocean. Did you see dolphins? Mermaids? Mermen? Or the Leviathan?"

"No, not on this voyage," Demos replied, his sea green eyes betraying a sadness.

"What is it?" she asked, concerned she'd touched a sore spot.

"The world. It's changing before our very eyes. Take the waterspouts: they appear out of nothing, great columns of water as wide as a city and as tall as the sky, swaying this way and that. At sea, they're as treacherous as a riptide. I've plied the seven seas for many a year and I've never seen the like before now."

"What do you make of it all?" she wanted to know.

"It's worse since the end of the winds," Demos added, adjusting his skullcap, which had nearly blown off in the breeze. "The *Crucible* was sucked directly into the path of a spout and we only just managed to evade it. I've seen enough to convince me that all these spouts are early signs of the coming flood."

"All the more reason to hold the Mind Search," she said. "We have to find the means to save ourselves. I refuse to be the last representative of a race tottering on the edge of extinction. I want to be part of a human race with a future."

"I agree, but we all need to protect ourselves against the apocalypse to come," Demos said. "On that note, I have something for you – on your birthday."

"Oh, you remembered!" she cried, wrapping her arms around him in a huge embrace.

"Shut your eyes and open your hand for me." She felt the weight of her gift as he placed it in her palm. "Now you can open them," he said, his voice soft and mellow as a buttercup.

There in her hand was a necklace with an exquisite white bone figure of a snake, coiled at the base and rearing up to strike, replete with hood and forked tongue.

"It's a cobra, I carved it myself," Demos said, puffing out his chest. "Do you like it?"

"Yes, it's wonderful. How did you know to fashion me a cobra?"

"I just did. Why do you ask? Is a cobra important to you?"

"The hooded cobra is my astral insignia."

"Is that so?" Demos said with a knowing smile. "Then it will work even greater wonders for you. Promise me you'll wear it and never take it off."

"I shall," she murmured, hastily fixing it around her neck. "How does it look?"

"It suits you, and it will protect you."

"From what? I've nothing to fear."

"Wear it all the same, for me?"

She nodded. She felt like she was walking on air. "I'm so pleased with this," she said. "Now, come and help in the cathedral. In eight days, the Mind Search begins and there's much to do."

CHAPTER 10

The Pectoral of State

Horque had long waited for this day, for the heliacal rising of the Dog Star, Sirius. A round moon, too, was propitious. He recited the Solarii Morning Prayer with extra enthusiasm before joining his mother in the water court. She looked splendid in formal attire, the vizier's pectoral shining over her lustrous skin.

"Today, my son, the Horque family will rule the Twin Ladies of Egypt!" Her eyes danced in the dull morning air.

Yes, today was the day he was to make the boldest play of his life, and stand as candidate for the throne.

"Pharaoh Horque," she said, enunciating each syllable.

"I like the sound of that," he said, his heart swelling with pride.

"Listen," Issa said. "Our efforts to deal with damage to the Records Pyramid sit favourably with the people. They see that Zoser has lost the confidence of the gods. How else could these terrible events afflict our beloved Egypt?"

He agreed. "Zoser's downfall began the moment the Taurus-faced Marduk sat astride the apex of the pyramid. He poured shame on us, on all of us."

"This is our opportunity," Issa said. "Zoser is finished but be wary of the other challenger, Nimrod. He stalks like a fox and has the cruelty of a hyena."

There was spite in his mother's words, but that was nothing new. Nimrod was her nemesis. Soon after Horque's birth, Genro, his father, had died in a freak accident. Nimrod was implicated but through his cunning, he'd evaded prosecution. Thus the grudge between the families was born.

"Mother, I know it."

"Lasec, his son, is the same," she retorted.

They were of one mind.

*

The Festival of the Gods traditionally began in the long shadows cast by the low-sun, and took place in the magnificent hypostyle court of the Temple of Amen, the scarab God of the Sun.

By the time Horque and Issa arrived, the lords and ladies of Upper Egypt and the nobility and aristocracy of Lower Egypt were all crammed onto the decking erected parallel to the two rows of gigantic columns. Semite servants drifted in and out of the mass ranks of the attendees, serving their masters and mistresses with iced water, prime Egyptian wine, warm beer and other refreshments. Fireflies darted in and out of the hundreds of glow lamps hanging on the columns. The Solarii wives were resplendent in colourful flowing silk gowns, white linen headdresses, and offset against ruby brooches, gold tiaras, turquoise necklaces and copper ankle torques.

As the malachite green disc of the sun disappeared below the rim of the horizon, Horque made his entrance into the temple, Issa on one arm and his beautiful sister Neferem on the other. The first person he encountered was the ambassador from the Land Between the Two Rivers.

"Greetings, Philo," he said, looking down at one of the little people. Mind, all humans were little, as far as the Solarii were concerned.

"Protector Horque," Philo replied, squinting up at him. "May your gods go with you and bring you success today."

"I intend that they should," he replied brusquely. These humans could be so bland.

"The Mind Search in Samlios, will the Solarii send an envoy?" Philo wanted to know.

"Shamira, the pythoness, sent an invitation," he confirmed, expecting Philo to be satisfied with that answer. He wasn't.

"The Emerald Cavern in Samlios needs repair," he pointed out. "Like many other places around the world."

"Is that so?" Horque remarked, feigning ignorance. "The new pharaoh will make the final decision on these matters. Should that be me, I wouldn't send one. There's a flood to prepare for and I wouldn't dispatch one my best men on a wild errand halfway around the world."

"That's a pity," Philo replied, and moved on.

Horque cast an eye around the festival. A row of scribes near the front sat cross-legged, papyrus in hand, ready to record the result. Sitting further back in the benches were human representatives from neighbouring cities and communities from the Northern Afri regions of Kush and Carthaginia and the Middle Lands of Attica and Hellas.

When it was time to begin, the high priest strode to the edge of the dais at the east end of the hypostyle court, its two rows of columns reaching high into the darkening water-filled skies.

"Great God Amen," Cheiron announced to a hushed audience, "we beseech you to help us choose a pharaoh for our Twin Lands, to govern the Solarii people with wisdom and in accordance with the law of Ma'at. Hear our prayer, Amen," he cried as he waved away a cloud of sweet, pungent incense that a temple servant wafted in front of him.

"Hear our prayer, Amen." The gathering repeated the refrain.

Cheiron opened a flat, rectangular box on the table to reveal the famous pectoral of state seated in its amber casing. Worn around the chest, it was a gold filigree necklace interspersed with six glass faience balls, which boasted extraordinary properties. Horque had seen them demonstrated on previous festivals. He looked through his whites to see pulses of astral energy surge in waves into the temple, hanging like violet and indigo drapes from the huge columns.

High Priest Cheiron lifted up the pectoral and presented it to the gods and the assembled audience. A look of wonder spread across them. The first challenger stepped forwards, and this was always the privilege of the existing pharaoh.

Cheiron asked him, "State your nomen – your commonly used name – and your prenomen – the name used when you're on state business."

Standing up tall, he announced, "My nomen is Zoser, pharaoh of the Solarii. My prenomen is Horemheb and I present myself with humility and honour."

Cheiron arranged the pectoral of state over Zoser's shoulders so it hung evenly over his neck and chest, with three glass balls resting over the heart area and the other three resting over his right pectoral. The high priest called for the servants to dim all the glow lamps, except those adjacent to the scribes.

With the sky waters circulating above, occluding the light of the stars and moon, darkness enveloped the festivities. Everyone stared at Zoser. For a moment, there was just darkness. Then the balls in the pectoral flickered. Was that light? The audience took a collective intake of breath as one of the faience balls flashed with its own luminosity. A colour appeared: at first a sombre green. Then it paled, spreading to the rest of the ball, until it glowed with a translucent emerald green. The other balls lit up; one glimmered pink, another a radiant yellow, a third sparkled with sapphire blue, a fourth glittered with gold. Soon all six balls were alight, shot against the background of the dark Egyptian evening.

The pectoral was alive and sentient, illuminated by the power of Zoser's astral connections to the gods. It was jewellery of the highest calibre, providing a true and fair assay of the spiritual capability of a Solarii man or woman to rule the nation of Egypt.

"Note the colours from each of the glass balls, their order, strengths and intensities," Cheiron instructed the scribes, who scribbled away enthusiastically.

Zoser sat down with a smug grin. The power and strength of the incumbent pharaoh's connections genuinely surprised Horque. But he could better that.

Soon he'd show it, as it was his turn next. He stood up, tall and proud. Fireflies danced around the glow lamps near the scribes. The astral light was so thick he felt as if he was walking through water.

"My nomen is Horque," he said firmly, "and my prenomen is Beremtha."

A premature ripple of acceptance swept through the ranks of the audience. The people's favourite he may be, but would he be the gods'? Though he couldn't say for sure just how much influence they did have. Either way, whoever succeeded the throne would be reborn into their new role; such was the power the gods conferred upon Pharaoh of Egypt.

The pectoral felt cold on his warm skin, then shimmered with bolts of astral power that shot into the chill of the evening like rays from a glowing sun. Silence reigned in this suspended moment, when the world of the gods was drawn into the world of men. Before long, the crescent of glass balls was lit up in a myriad of hues.

"The gods demonstrate their love of Horque," Issa crowed.

He sat down, his heart heaving with emotion, his eyes staring into the haze. Cheiron called the last candidate, the Steward of the Granary.

"My nomen is Nimrod, and my prenomen is Khufu," he proclaimed. Nimrod's chest swelled as Cheiron placed the pectoral over his broad shoulders. The scribes noted the brightness of the balls. Had Nimrod achieved divine favour? But Horque had achieved much. In the end, it lay in the lap of the gods.

"You've done all you can," Issa said warmly. "Arar will leaf through the pectoral parchment to make sense of the different colours, intensities and hues scored by each candidate. Soon he'll know the name of the new pharaoh."

While the chief scribe fretted, the Semite servants moved around the court, reigniting the glow lamps, until the great temple and its high colonnade were streaming with white light.

Horque could hardly breathe with the weight of the astral on his chest. As Arar walked towards the high priest, the atmosphere was equally thick with anticipation. Cheiron cocked his head to him and Arar whispered in his ear. With a solemn gait, Cheiron stepped forwards to the edge of the dais and raised his arms.

"Wonders of Egypt never cease," he proclaimed. "All bear witness to today's extraordinary proceedings. I present the new Pharaoh of the Two Lands of Upper and Lower Egypt, Holder of the Rod of Destiny and Keeper of the Orb of Power."

He paused and then declaimed, "Hail, Pharaoh Nimrod."

"Hail, Pharaoh Nimrod," echoed the reply.

The crowd erupted in cries of glee and applause, more in surprise than in praise of their new leader, and bowed low in beatific obeisance to him. Like great aurora, curtains of unseen power showered down on the new pharaoh, a telling acclamation from the astral light that Nimrod was indeed the most powerful spiritual guide of the Solarii people. At this, the apex of the ceremony, Horque could discern above his head the subtle outlines of the Red Crown of Lower Egypt and the White Crown of Upper Egypt in astral form, along with the short stub of beard protruding downwards from his chin like a thick, knotted rope.

He stepped forwards. "I am Nimrod, reborn as your pharaoh, chosen this day above all others by the great God Amen. I am the pontiff, the bridge, between him and you, and you and him."

The cheers of the crowd jarred Horque's ears. He couldn't believe what was happening. How had it not been him? How? What had he done wrong? How had he failed? The proceedings carried on around him, and he barely listened to Nimrod's words.

"It's my prerogative to choose my Ennead Council," the new pharaoh was saying. "All the posts in the Ennead Council will remain as before, with two exceptions."

Horque boiled inside with anger and frustration. How had Nimrod won? Why had the gods preferred him? He shuddered. His victory meant one thing: retribution. Nimrod would wreak havoc on the Horque family in any way he could. Issa glanced at him with her cold, fierce, lioness eyes. She knew it too.

"Lady Issa." The high priest called for her. She trudged onto the dais, her face hunched into a grimace.

"Pharaoh Nimrod has asked me to remove the vizier pectoral. Please lower your head," Cheiron commanded.

How could Nimrod do this? Issa had served the Land of the Sedge and the Bee with devotion and dedication, and her reward was an ignominious disrobing before the entire Solarii nobility. Trying to close his ears to the gasps of embarrassment from the crowd made it worse, as they screeched in his ears like the cries of a malevolent harpy.

Cheiron took the vizier pectoral, the coruscating light reflecting in its glass faience balls, and turned to Zoser, who bowed his head to receive it over his mighty shoulders. The deed was done. Neither Zoser nor Issa could refuse or even complain. Etiquette forbade it.

While Horque felt crushed and ashamed for his mother, Nimrod climbed on the pharaoh's throne, a self-satisfied smile quivering on his lips.

Cheiron made the next announcement. "Lady Issa is to be instated into the honourable role of Steward of the Granary."

A whisper scuttled through the crowd like a busy scarab beetle. This was a calculated act of political gamesmanship on Nimrod's part, which Horque saw right through. Nimrod had dumped Issa into a position that wielded considerably less political power than vizier. At least she retained her place on the Ennead Council where Nimrod could keep a wary eye on her.

Issa mustered a dark grimace, which passed as a smile.

As the giant Irex strode onto the dais, everyone hushed in anticipation of what was to happen next. After every important event, the high priest sent back to the solar doubles a clairvoyant transmission that traversed the sky waters and leapt like a starry jaguar across the inert space between Earth and the green planet behind the solar corona. Everyone, even Horque, felt pangs of homesickness on such occasions. It reminded him of home, of his separated double, and evoked the keen pain of his and his people's long exile. As Irex transmitted the tidings of Nimrod's accession, a poignant calm pervaded the evening gathering.

In the midst of this nostalgia, Issa murmured in Horque's ear, "I swear by the lioness Sekmet, Nimrod will pay for my humiliation. Ma'at will and must be reconciled."

With an almost imperceptible nod, he agreed. In their haste to leave Nimrod's ecstatic celebrations, Horque was about to walk away when Lasec yelled after him.

"Will the protector not stay to hear his next assignment?"

He froze. Rebuked by none other than a lowly Guardian of Justice – that was ominous. He felt the eyes of the world peer right into his soul.

"In ten days you are…" Lasec began, and then paused. He was toying with him. All Horque could do was grit his teeth.

"…To leave for the Mind Search in Samlios."

The crowd hooted its derision. Surely not that. Anything but a long trip away from Egypt. Who would protect his mother in his absence? By the gods, Nimrod had completely outwitted him. He felt weak and foolish. Crushed inside, he refused to show it. With a brusque nod of his head, he led Issa and Neferem away from Nimrod's celebrations. As they escaped through the crowds, still enthralled by the communication with home, Lasec taunted him again.

"Enjoy your trip!"

Horque winced but walked on with dignity, his determination shining like a crystal in the brilliant Solarii night. His moment of retribution would come. He could feel it in his Solarii soul.

PART 3

The Mind Search

CHAPTER 11

The Opening

Finally, it had arrived. The opening day of the Mind Search, the most important meeting ever held on Earth. With feverish anticipation, Akasha put on her best white dress. She touched the cobra figurine on her necklace and thought with fondness of Demos. His ship was docked in the harbour, alongside a flotilla of boats of all shapes and sizes, their pennants and flags fluttering in the ocean breeze. In the city, garlands of flowers and wreaths of yew and pine stretched from one side of the street to the other. Swathes of dark green holly leaves and braids of sunflower and daisy chains hung from the statues of the four archangels by the temple entrance. Purple bougainvillea and beds of flame red roses bedecked the portico of the Step Well. Such fecundity was testament to the Earth's regenerative powers, which in such a short period had recovered from the devastation of the winds.

Akasha joined the throng swarming towards the Crystal Cathedral. Samlios had never seen so many visitors. Every one of them had travelled the seven seas to be there, all drawn by her dream vision. What an astounding thought.

"Akasha." Someone called her name. It was her mother. Thera stood by the well, an amphora in either hand, a smile as wide as the ocean. Wherever there was water, her mother was never far away.

As they hugged, her mother whispered, "I'm so proud of you and everything you've done. First there was the dance of the winds, and now I hear Shamira has asked you to open the Mind Search."

"Yes, she has," Akasha replied, trying to conceal a shy smile.

"Tell us," Thera asked, beckoning others to gather round. "What will happen there? Will it help us survive the flood?"

"We hope so," she replied. "The most important thing is to secure as much safety for as many people as possible. After that, let's not forget the Surge – that sleeping giant of a possibility."

"We stand in its shadow," Thera replied. "What about the Solarii? Are they coming?" Her mother was evidently enjoying the opportunity to question her daughter in full view of her peers.

"I hope so. I want to see them close up."

"We all do," Thera said. "Look, I know you want to get to the cathedral but wait just one moment." Her mother grabbed her wrist and pulled her along gently. "I want you to meet Savor the Andean, ambassador from the Land of the Clouds."

Savor was tall and handsome with high cheekbones. He wore a wonderful red and white cape emblazoned with the sigil of his people, a jaguar leaping over a snow-capped mountain.

"I'm honoured to meet you," Savor said, bowing low. "Your name and reputation precede you."

"Such a striking costume," Akasha said with a brisk, open-handed gesture.

"Thank you," he said with pride.

"I must go. I'll see you both there," she replied, and danced up Temple Hill alongside those going to the cathedral.

Entering through the great door, she stopped in her tracks and her jaw dropped. Every column, arch, window and transept was decorated with bouquets of flowers, cones of pine, acorns and garlands of grasses, as well as exotic fruits, pineapples, passion fruit, bunches of figs – a true cornucopia of the earth's richness. The air was thick with incense. And the people – so many were crammed into tiers of seating set in an arc around the outside of the rotunda. Some were even on the upper gallery.

Demos the Pyrene swaggered in. He too was dressed in his national costume, a flowing red cape tied at the neck, and on his chest stood the motif of a tall, dark tower – the famous Whispering Tower of his village in the Pyrene Mountains.

"Look at my costume," Demos said, spinning around the lectern in the centre of the atrium, bringing a moment of light relief. The musicians stuck up a jaunty tune with pan pipes, zither and drums. There was a festive atmosphere in the rotunda, and why shouldn't there be?

Attendees had from come from as far away as Afri; others from the Land of the Clouds; many from the Middle Lands, all those places close enough to send representatives by sea in the limited time available. They mingled in the atrium, showing off their costumes, dresses and hats. The women were dazzling with their brooches, necklaces, bracelets and torques, a form of self-display newly borrowed from the Solarii.

A sea of faces, every one smiling, spread out in a half-moon shape in front of Akasha. Her body tingled from head to toe. The sight of those bright eyes, staring at her with expectation, cleared her head.

Someone waved to her and she waved back, despite not recognising the person. Everyone seemed to know her. She wanted to get to know them all, to thank them, to meet them and talk to them about hopes and passions. Behind the subtle mask of amicable smiles and the gestures of friendship, she couldn't help detect the scars of fear. Here for the first – and perhaps the last – time, people from different lands could meet and look each other in the eye with respect. The unsettling thought that few if any would survive the coming flood tempered the warmth of friendship.

At the entrance door, Tros stood erect as an oak. Behind him, the olive green sky waters, the hills of Samlios and in the far distance, the ocean shone like dappled glass. Tros hurried the latecomers to the last available seats. The court attendant finished delivering the incense. Shamira gave Akasha the signal to begin and she stepped forwards, arms raised. The background chatter stopped.

In that hiatus, she had that curious feeling of being in exactly the right place at the right time. It was her destiny to do this. It felt right.

Everyone knew of her dance and its profound effect on the winds, and they showed their spontaneous appreciation, touching the forefinger and middle finger of one hand onto the palm of the other, making a light percussive resonance so as not to disperse the gathering astral powers.

The ripple of applause continued until she cried out, "Greetings, people of the world. Welcome to the Mind Search. Let's begin with a prayer." Her strong voice resonated around the rotunda. "Place your hands in the position of the keeper bar, palm against palm, fingers against fingers, and repeat this short prayer with me: *Grant us the ability to listen to each other, and above all to heed the guidance of the most high.*"

"Thank you, Akasha," Panion said, taking over at the lectern. "Greetings, Mind Search," he began, leaning on his staff. "What we need today is to perceive our situation in full."

Demos the Pyrene twirled his cape in his hand and stepped boldly into the middle of the rotunda. "Like everyone else from around the world, I'm thrilled to be here," he said. "But one race is conspicuous by their absence – the Solarii."

A tremor of apprehension spread around the gathering, accompanied by a furious nodding of heads.

Panion took a deep breath and replied nervously. "They are coming."

"That's reassuring," Demos said, gesturing with his hands to appeal to the assembly. "But I have another question. What is keeping them within the boundary stele of Egypt? We're all here, yet none of us have the facility of their infernal flying machines."

71

Panion opened his mouth to reply but Demos had more to say. "Could it be that their sundials don't work on Earth?"

Some in the audience openly guffawed. Others snorted and still more laughed aloud. Even Akasha stifled a snigger behind her hand. Shamira stood up with a frown, and that soon hushed everyone up.

Eventually Panion regained his composure. "The Solarii will attend. They just haven't told us exactly when. They have a new pharaoh, so I imagine that's what's delayed them."

Quick as a flash, Demos countered, "I doubt that, because Philo was in Egypt for the inauguration and he's here. So why are they tardy? I'm no admirer of the Solarii, but even I can see that many of the decisions we need to make here will involve them in one way or another. So how we can begin without them?"

What had started so well had quickly deteriorated into a farce. How could Demos be so obtuse? In the end, Panion stammered, "We expect Protector Horque to arrive soon."

"Let's hope he does so before we've gone home," Demos barked. "And according to my experience of the Solarii, they work according to completely different timings to us. Hardly surprising for alien visitors."

Some of the audience rocked in their seats, clapped their hands, and stamped their feet, while others merely chuckled to themselves. Shamira stood at the lectern and everyone hushed again.

"Friends," she began, glowering at Demos, "we're better than this squabbling. This is the appointed time for the Mind Search to begin, and this is when we shall start. If we create an ambience of dissent, we'll never get the help we need from the astral light. We depend on its unseen power to grant us the gifts of insight and foresight.

"Look at it like this," she continued, "we have much to discuss about our own survival, with or without the Solarii. When they do arrive, we'll bring them up to date. In the meantime, let's begin for ourselves, because above all this is a human Mind Search, is it not?"

There was a general murmur of assent. The pythoness was gradually swaying them to her point of view. She pressed on. "It's important we start from the same place with the same understanding, so I want to describe our collective position. If you are familiar with elements of this story, please bear with me.

"Originally, there was one race on Earth: we humans. Now there are two more: the Solarii and the hybrids. These interlopers came to be here because the Source bequeathed us the gift of the Surge, the latest divine enhancement for the human race. He sent the Helios and the Solarii, angels of the sun, to deliver it to us. Clothed in brilliance and powerful in spirit, the Helios manifested here as hornets. They stung our maidens – against their will."

Shamira coughed into her hand. While Thera brought her a beaker of water, Akasha thought of old Irit lying on that cairn, the last of the maidens impregnated by the Helios.

"The offspring of this unholy union," Shamira went on, her voice increasingly defiant, "were a grotesque mix of animal, human and angel. Fathered by Helios and mothered by maids, this is the genesis of the hybrids who roam outside the gates of our cities in the lands we call Dudael."

In her mind's eye, Akasha imagined Jarda, Irit's hybrid son, standing on top of Out Hill, bold and proud. Wasn't it curious that the hybrids seemed to have grown and developed while humans stood still, stifled by the stasis of the hybrid seed?

"Their heinous act," Shamira went on, "upset the delicate balances of creation for which there had to be a heavy reckoning. The Solarii came to our rescue and bound the Helios beneath the valleys of the Earth. The Helios delivered the Surge to us, but in doing so, they also implanted in us the scourge of the hybrid seed, which prevents its flowering. Furthermore, the hybrid seed meant that, even when the father was human, our maidens gave birth to hybrids. Again, the Solarii conceived the Covenant of the Firstborn, to offer us as a race a means of fending off the horror of extinction. Also, this hybrid seed causes us to grow hair and nails, which is anathema to our ways and culture. The Solarii helped us overcome this through the sun-fire emanations of their pyramids, which suppress hair growth. For these reasons, we are extremely grateful to the Solarii."

Not for the first time, Akasha's mentor had impressed her. In a few short words, Shamira had turned everyone's appreciation of the Solarii around, but there was more to come.

"This is the tragedy of the hybrid seed, our situation today," Shamira continued. "Now I will speak of the future. Thanks to Akasha, we know the flood is coming."

"And that means we're all better off dead," Demos interrupted. He did have a way of catching people's attention.

"How's that? Explain yourself!" Shamira replied, removing her skullcap.

"Face the truth," he replied. "Whatever our preparations, the flood will deluge the pyramids, rendering them inoperable. On top of that, the priests in my village are prophesying that after the flood, the astral light will no longer be pellucid, as it is now."

"What's your point?" Shamira snapped. Was she losing her patience?

"Those fortunate enough to survive the flood may not be so lucky after all. With no astral emanation from the pyramids, and a dim and insulated astral light, there will be nothing to hold back the growth of the hybrid seed. With no covenant in place, all we'll be able to do is give birth to more hybrids. For humans, the flood is going to be an unmitigated disaster. I for one am thinking I'd be better off on the seabed."

This provoked uproar.

"How can you say that?" someone shouted.

"Outrageous!" another cried.

Demos stood quietly watching. He seemed to enjoy people's discomfort. With that resolute look in his eye, the one that defiantly stared down tempests at sea, he pressed on. "Good, I'm glad you see my point. We don't want to enter the new epoch as we are today. I want there to be a resolution to the tragedy of the seed, but it must come before the end of the flood. If not, I fear we'll never release the Surge in us and we'll be doomed to join the ranks of the hybrids."

A mood of heavy sadness weighed on the Mind Search, who muttered and mumbled amongst themselves, and shifted uncomfortably on their seats. Eventually, Demos sat down, to the accompaniment of an ironic ripple of applause.

"Yes, well done, Demos," Shamira said. For a moment Akasha thought her mentor was being sarcastic, until she added, "You've laid bare the truth of the matter. While I would have softened its sharper edges, I agree with you. The future's bleak. There's no way round it."

Shamira was always surprising her. She continued to cut swathes through the truth.

"The Solarii are vital to these proceedings. Once they were angels, lighter than a shadow, marauding through the astral light faster than thought. Even as humans, they possess huge astral power and can bring about changes of which we can only dream. How else could they have given us the Covenant of the Firstborn? I, too, keenly await their presence. While we tarry, we can achieve much together. Akasha, tell us what's planned for this evening."

"Yes, yes," she stammered. Most of what she'd heard wasn't new; it was just that it had exploded her expectations of a friendly and genteel gathering. Her head was spinning like a whirlwind and she just about remembered the plans. "Tonight we'll gather in the amphitheatre for a night around the fires. We're going to tether the threads of today's Mind Search."

That was the end of the first day. As people streamed out of the Crystal Cathedral towards the southern beaches and the amphitheatre, she trudged along with them, under a spell of confusion and shock.

What had happened after the opening? Shamira had spoken of the tragedy of the seed – which felt like she was describing an abyss. Demos had taken them to the edge of that abyss and invited them to stare into it and reap the unconscionable truth of their situation. With a huge smile on her face, Shamira had pushed everyone into it. Yes, that about summed it up.

Akasha felt lost, helpless, falling headlong into the abyss.

CHAPTER 12

Around the Fires

Numb and cold, Akasha trudged down the cliff path to the amphitheatre. Without the Solarii, it was impossible to resolve the tragedy of the hybrid seed before the onset of the flood. Shamira must have guessed the reason for her inner turmoil, because she put a consoling arm around her shoulder.

"You won't solve this one on your own," she said. "That's the purpose of the Mind Search, to bring us to a collective agreement regarding our situation. Perhaps then we'll see the way through."

Akasha nodded.

"You've prepared for this night, so go and make it happen," Shamira added with a smile.

Tros was at the base of the path to greet her. "As you instructed, the fires are ready to be lit," he said. There were three huge bonfires on the floor of the amphitheatre. Akasha loved this place. As a child, she'd spent whole days on the seashore collecting shells and then she'd climb up to the stage where she'd listen to them whisper in her ear; tell her secrets about herself, her parents, her friends and the world.

The panorama from the amphitheatre was breathtaking. It overlooked the vast expanse of the southern ocean, where schools of dolphins dived and played, and the ocean's white-capped waves broke rhythmically on the shore, dancing to the beat of the crystal sky goddess.

"Yes, light the fires," she said. Tros was the gatekeeper, and one of the gates he kept was the Gate of the Veil, the subtle curtain between the astral and the incarnate. He was a fire-bringer. He busied himself with the task of lighting the first one. She looked through her whites to see what he was contriving in the astral. Out of his index finger, he directed a slender lance of crimson energy into the tinder at the base of the bonfire. The lance seared through the astral light like a beam of sunlight emerging from behind a cloud. The tinder glowed and throbbed until a thin red flame flickered in the physical realms. Out of the unseen realms of the astral light, Tros had brought the fire that warmed, purified, and gave the sublime gift of light. The fingers of flame reached out along the twigs and branches. As the golden flames licked the wood, devouring it, Tros stepped back to admire his handiwork.

As always, the honour of water bearer fell to her mother. Thera seemed to have cajoled half the population of Samlios to draw water from the well, and the other half to bring it down the cliff to the three fires. For his part, Uriah had posted any other folk who were spare to hold the glow lamps along the path, around the amphitheatre and even along the southern beaches. In the darkening night, the trail of lanterns looked like a great coiling snake of light.

Akasha sat by one fire, Panion and Shamira by the others. One by one, the people attending the Mind Search sat down cross-legged by one of the three fires. Soon enough, each of them were chattering away to their companions, sharing stories of their adventures and voyages to arrive at the Mind Search.

Demos sat next to her on one side. On the other side was Philo the Babylonian. His yew green eyes danced around in their sockets, observing everything. He had something of the fox and the scorpion about him: wily but tough.

"How was your journey?" she asked.

"As long as the road and as fluid as the sea," he replied. "I came via Egypt, where I saw the new pharaoh installed."

"What do you think of the Solarii? Are they as cunning as Demos implies?"

"They've always been straight with us. I don't know where he's got his suspicions from."

Well, that was interesting. The others sitting around the fire grunted in assent.

"What did you think of Demos' augury about the aftermath of the flood?" Akasha asked.

"Alas," Philo replied, as the flames cast him in an eerie light, "his insight agrees with the deliberations of our high priest in Babylon."

If Shamira wouldn't tell her, she'd ask Philo. "What exactly do they foresee?"

"The astral light will grow dim," Philo said, "like a candle flame reaching the end of the taper. In that situation, not all our wonderful astral gifts of clairvoyance, telepathy, distance healing, will endure. Worse still, they claim that any survivors of the flood will degenerate into dullards and brutes like the hybrids, ushering in an epoch that will be shredded by barbarism, war and cruelty."

"That's wrong." How could he say that? These priests and their galling philosophies made her mad. "I'm responsible for my actions. The astral light is persuasive, but so are my peers. In the end, I have free will, to choose what path to follow or what decision to make. I'm not a puppet whose strings are pulled by an omnipotent astral light, and I never will be."

The words that had just come from her mouth sounded different to the ones she would have said previously in similar circumstances. Here she was talking to two older, respected men, Demos and Philo, who would normally be making these comments to her, rather than the other way round. Something profound was speaking to her and she was listening to that voice. Philo, Demos and the others around her bonfire were spellbound, their mouths agape, hanging on her every word. While the old Akasha would have felt shy, the new Akasha felt thrilled.

"Demos," she said, turning to her friend. "Earlier, you kicked up a sandstorm about the tardiness of the Solarii. I hope you've had time to change your mind."

"No, I haven't," he replied, as stubborn as ever. "My doubts about them run deep and I'm still not sure they'll come. They have a far greater task ahead of them than attending this Mind Search."

"What would that be?" This sounded ominous.

"The Solarii are caught on the horns of a dilemma," he told her, "one of arrogance, the other of complacency. Many years ago, when they were building the Pyramid of Records, the bull-faced Marduk led an assault of hybrids against it, which they repulsed. Then they surrounded themselves with fierce astral shields and flew their Horus Wing craft to keep the hybrids at bay. They were safe. History would never repeat itself, or so they thought...until two moons ago, when it did. For the Solarii, it was utter humiliation, not least because it was Marduk who led the attack. But this time, the bull-headed hybrid paid for his temerity with his life. And Zoser paid for it with the pharaoh's throne."

"How do you know all that?" she asked.

"Philo told me," Demos replied. "He was there."

"Every word of it is true," Philo said, nodding his head.

She needed to understand the Solarii and Demos was more prepared than Shamira to talk candidly about them. She probed deeper. "What's bringing all this about?"

"I think it's because the astral light is fracturing, breaking down. The astral light has its fingers in our souls and our hearts and our minds every moment of every day. It's the same for the Solarii. They may be aliens, with souls forged in the ice-cold astral fires of the sun, but they've adopted human form and so they are subject to the Earth and her astral light as much as we are."

He paused. Tros loaded their ebbing fire with more logs, which spat sparks into the still night air.

"So what are you saying?" Akasha was struggling to understand. "That the Solarii are in trouble?"

"They've been in trouble since the Helios failed to properly deliver the Surge,"

Demos said. "If they don't resolve the tragedy of the seed, they'll die a watery death on Earth, something that's anathema to them. That's why they're desperate to return home. In my reckoning, the flood provides them with exactly the opportunity and motivation they need to end their long exile."

The groups sitting around the other two bonfires had stood up and were preparing to walk back up the cliff path.

"Hear me out," Demos pleaded. The spluttering flames lit up his features in alternate light and dark. "I distrust the Solarii," he said, as his words took on an ominous edge. "They have their own aims and purposes. For instance, what about this Mind Search? I wouldn't be at all surprised if they'd tried to persuade you to hold it in Egypt."

"Why, yes, they did. Shamira told me. How did you know?"

"A good guess," Demos admitted. "I know a little of how they think. Why would they come here?"

"Because we invited them?"

"No. If they do turn up, it'll be to examine you," Demos said, pointing at her.

"Me?" she replied, taken aback. "Why me?"

"Because of your dance, you're renowned the world over. Think about it: a young girl brought the destructive power of the great winds to a shuddering halt. That was some feat. That took astral skill of the highest order. You can see why the Solarii would want to take a closer look at you, in case you pose a threat to them."

"I see." She had not considered that. Was she being naive? She began to think so.

"If they succeed in resolving the tragedy of the seed and releasing the essence vitamins of the Surge in us, I fear they'll leave us a few parting gifts. I can feel it in my old sailor's bones."

"What kind of gifts?"

"I don't know. It's just a feeling. Look, everyone is leaving to go back to the city. I must find your father... Ah, there he is," Demos declared, as he headed off to speak to Uriah.

She should have taken Demos more seriously. He spoke the truth, and it shone like a beacon into the night skies. There was more to the Solarii than she'd imagined. Were they manipulative and overbearing? When and if they arrived at the Mind Search, she'd make up her own mind.

CHAPTER 13

The Fragile Harmony

Early the next morning, Akasha sat watching the sea of faces in front of her in the cathedral rotunda. Their shoulders hunched, they wore bags of weariness under their eyes. They had left some of their sparkle in the embers of the bonfires. She fingered Demos' cobra amulet as she watched the stragglers take their seats. Thera and her water-carriers handed out beakers, trying to revive the people's spirits. Shamira caught her eye, and it was the moment to start.

"Greetings, everyone," she said.

"Greetings, Akasha." The response came like a voice of many strands.

"I see we've started to comprehend the enormity of our situation," she admitted. "Let's return to the pressing questions. How do we survive the coming apocalypse and its aftermath, and how do we release the Surge?"

Savor the Andean walked to the lectern and turned to greet the assembly. Whenever she looked at him, she heard the haunting melodies of the zampona, the pan flutes that Savor had played around the fires the night before.

"We Jaguar People," he said, "are loyal servants of the Source. In the lofty mountains of the Land of the Clouds, we have built sanctuaries and holy temples to host the highest and finest parts of the astral light. See the benefits. Look at me: I'm as old as the hills but my skin shines like that of an angel and I'm as fit and wiry as a sapling."

He was right: his eyes and face wore a ridiculously healthy pallor.

"To escape the flood," he went on, "climb the foothills into the Jaguar Mountains. If you live in the Land Between the Two Rivers, go to the Zagros Mountains. If you are close to the Pyrenes, join Demos. Wherever you are, go as high as you can."

"That's a good idea," someone cried from the audience. It was Akasha's father.

"Uriah, speak to us," she said.

"I have another proposal, as simple as Savor's," he began. "I'm going to construct a boat. It will offer safe refuge to all men and have ample room for Earth's little creatures. That way, they too will have a future. Who would want to live in a new epoch without the sweet song of a nightingale, the trumpet call of an elephant, or the buzz of a bee?"

The applause was rapturous. Everyone rose to their feet. Akasha was so proud of her father. Thera held his hand and lifted it high in a joint salute. Savor picked up his magic pipes and played a celebratory melody to enrich the joyous mood. People were off their seats and in a moment of spontaneity, swayed and danced around the rotunda.

This was a moment of release, a high point of the Mind Search thus far. Everyone turned to face the future, together and in harmony. All day long, the discussions were animated and fervent, until later in the afternoon, Shamira brought the Mind Search together and declared, "Now there is a special address."

Tros emerged into the rotunda carrying something heavy and bulky in his arms. It had a black cloth draped over it.

"What have you got there, Tros?" someone quipped.

"You'll find out soon enough," he said, placing it on a plinth in the centre of the rotunda.

Shamira gave him the nod and he removed the cloth to reveal an exquisite statue, carved from amber-coloured marble shot with pale blue veins. The bust was of a woman of the orient, with high cheekbones, a clear brow and a strong jaw. Akasha could even see small folds in the skin under the eyes and crinkles in the ear.

"May I introduce you to Li Ching from the Land of the Yellow River, who will today talk to us from afar," Shamira said. "Like many others, Li Ching was desperate to attend the Mind Search in person but was prevented by the huge distances involved. Arka has sculpted this statue of her and it will act as an anchor to her dream body. Lady Li Ching, please address the Mind Search."

Looking through her whites, Akasha saw a still blue flame appear in the astral clouds above the head of Li Ching's bust. Small droplets of the flame fell onto the head, bathing it in a blue vibrancy. Soon enough, Li Ching's face on the statue was ablaze with an azure flame that did not burn.

The eyelids on the bust opened. The face was alive with warmth and colour, a real person with water coursing through her veins. The hardness of the marble gave way to soft folds of flesh.

"Greetings to the Mind Search."

"It spoke," someone said.

Someone else shushed them. Akasha could have heard a mouse squeak, it was so quiet.

"I am the Lady Li Ching," the bust said as the chamber filled with her warm yellow presence. "Greetings to Panion and Shamira, old and trusted friends," she continued. "I speak to you on behalf of the women of Cathay. We worry about the aftermath of the flood. Our priests believe the astral light will dim, rendering useless the pyramids and Emerald Caverns alike. We fear the Solarii will bequeath us their sexual rampancy on us and we'll end up mating like animals on heat. After several generations, we would face having as many children as pebbles on the beach."

Akasha had heard these fears voiced before, and now everyone else had. A hushed silence fell on the Mind Search as Li Ching went on.

"We must find ways to prevent the hybrid seed from appearing in us, and in our children. That way, after the deluge, the human race will be clear of it for evermore. That way, the Surge can flower in us all and we can rejoin our true purpose. I commend these words to the Mind Search."

Li Ching's soothing presence receded from the room through the astral portal of the statue that after a while returned to resemble a moribund piece of stone. Shamira stood beside the bust.

"We send Li Ching our warmest greetings and thank her for her wise words. Now let us gather outside and pray for the arrival of the Solarii."

Demos shot to his feet and wagged his finger at the assembly.

"I will not pray for their arrival," he scoffed. "The day grows late and still there's no sign of the aliens. I tell you, they're not coming."

He looked demented. What was wrong with him? Why such hatred? Such venom?

"Without the Solarii," he added, eyes blazing, "this Mind Search is a ship with its rudder stuck, endlessly turning in circles. To face the unknown danger of this flood, I sailed across the sea, avoiding the waterspouts on the way. I left my family at home and I need to go back and protect them. My ship is sailing. Who's coming with me?"

What was the man thinking? How could he place his own feelings above the needs of the fellowship of humans? The Mind Search had barely started on the contentious issues facing them, yet there was Demos advocating an abrupt end of it. Akasha wanted to grab him by the shoulders, shake him, and drive out all those capricious desires from him. She had dealt with her urge for a child and sacrificed her personal wishes for the common good, so why couldn't he? Alas, Demos wasn't alone in rupturing the fragile harmony in the Mind Search. His followers dreaded the flood, and his heated words fanned the flames of their insecurity.

The sounds of a thousand feet shuffling across the atrium floor drowned out her troubled thoughts. Which way were they walking – to join her and Shamira for their prayer, or Demos' rump contingent who were leaving the Mind Search?

CHAPTER 14

The Return

Akasha stood by the entrance door outside the cathedral, hoping and waiting for the congregation for evening prayer to form. In the cool of the gathering gloom, she rubbed her hands together, wondering how many, if any, would join her, or even if the Mind Search would convene tomorrow. How had it come to this after just two days? The wait was agonising. All their hard work and preparation, hopes and plans, would they amount to anything? Or would they disappear back into the astral light?

Philo the Babylonian emerged from the Crystal Cathedral, into the fading evening light. Without a backwards glance, he headed straight towards her, Shamira and Panion. At least *he* was loyal to the cause. Behind him was Savor the Andean. Further back was a line of people, heads bowed, shoulders hunched. Philo, Savor and the others arranged themselves in a crescent ready for prayer.

Akasha put her hands behind her back, one hand gripping the other wrist, while she choked on tender emotions. She sneaked a glance inside the cathedral, hoping to catch a glimpse of the traitor Demos. There he was, gesticulating like a madman. His voice boomed around the cathedral vaults, stoking the fires of their distrust of the Solarii and haranguing the people to leave.

Shamira whispered in her ear. "Stop frowning."

Easier said than done. Everything was falling apart. Demos was leading the people away, with only a rump remaining. That would never work. The Mind Search would end before it had even started.

Shamira carried on as if it was any other day, and recited the vespers. The people with them responded tentatively, seemingly distracted by the goings-on with Demos. Akasha mouthed the prayers, which ascended skywards but had no wings to fly higher. How could the people leave prematurely? They should see it through to the end, no matter what happened.

As the green disk of the sun slipped below the horizon, from behind her came the sound of marching feet. Demos, head high, chest out, stomped past her and set off at a frantic pace up the slope of Port Hill. He was heading for Fishmouth Harbour. He was really going to leave. The rump followed him like tame animals, some whistling and skipping. As the line of men and women filtered past them, the ones in the middle, and even more so the ones towards the tail, appeared agitated and uncertain. The stragglers at the end of the line dawdled and lost ground on those ahead of them. Then they lost their nerve. Surreptitiously, they crept out of the line and joined those attending prayers, where they were welcomed like long-lost sheep.

The main rump continued to trudge up Port Hill after Demos, their shadows dancing on the hillside. Many carried glow lamps, and in the gathering dusk, the line of people formed a snake of bobbing lights. A murmuration of sparrows swooped in the sky above them and in the cool evening air, landed on a bent tree on the hilltop. Even their sporadic chirps seemed to have a shrill ring. Nothing was going right and Demos was quitting. Akasha swallowed her disgust. Shamira tapped her on the shoulder.

"Am I frowning again?" she asked.

Shamira shook her head. "No, but the evening prayers have finished."

With most of Demos' contingent over the far side of the hill, the people rose from their prayers but their legs appeared rooted to the ground. They had nothing left in them to give. Alone and empty inside, it was as if a close friend had suddenly and unexpectedly died. The quiet of dusk surrounded them like a thick blanket. A light breeze off the ocean smelt of salt and far-distant places.

If someone were to ask whether she was living her life in the shadow of the apocalypse or in the light of divine grace, at that moment Akasha knew which it would be. Mentally, she combed through the proceedings of the opening two days, desperately trying to find out where it had gone awry. Weighing it all in the balance, there was no way forwards. The abyss between the two parties would take the remaining days to bridge. To continue with the Mind Search was futile. The flood would kill them all. In a moment of pique, she ripped the cobra necklace from her neck. She was on the verge of throwing it away when she heard a muffled shout. Distracted, she shoved it into her basket of herbs. The noise sounded like a distant siren. She heard it again.

"Helloooo!"

The cries were coming from Port Hill. She screwed up her eyes to look into the dusk. There was a host of silhouettes on the crest of the hill, next to the tree. They were shouting something but they were too far away for her to make out what they were saying. More folk appeared on the hill. Demos' contingent was striding back towards them.

There were more shadows by the tree and more cries, which were growing vociferous. Amongst them, she heard Demos' stentorian tones, and Akasha didn't know whether to laugh or cry. Either way, the old sailor was returning. Why? Was someone chasing him? He was nearly halfway down the hill now. She could barely see him, but she could hear him. The shadows and shapes in the dusk were confusing, like the vague, swirling mists of energy she saw when dream travelling in the astral light.

"Look up. Look in the sky!" he was saying.

Where? Everyone looked up, scanning the darkening sky, peering towards the hill. Was it a portent? Was it the beginning of the flood? Akasha realised what it was. There were four twinkling lights on the eastern horizon, too low to be stars.

"What are they?" Shamira cried, her voice raised and excited.

The spots of light grew larger. Whatever they were, they were heading their way. Against the backdrop of the olive green sky, she could just make out trails of white smoke behind the four specks. This was extraordinary. This was redemption.

Demos was leading his contingent back to them. The outsider had returned. The specks in the darkened sky became clearer as they approached. They were flying chairs. Seated in them were huge men.

"The Solarii," Akasha blurted out, unable to contain her joy.

"That's what I've been trying to tell you," Demos said, as he slumped on the ground, puffed out from walking so fast. The rump was right behind him. From the vantage point of the summit of Port Hill, the same hill that had obscured her view of their approach, Demos had seen the Solarii flyers emerge out of the eastern horizon and turned back. Falling into the arms of their companions, the two groups embraced like long-lost friends. Many broke down with the emotion of the reunion. Others knelt on the ground and cast a soulful eye towards the approaching Solarii flyers.

"Welcome back," Akasha said to him, overcome with relief. "We missed you."

"We must give thanks," Panion said.

"Then thank Tros," Demos replied.

"Why's that?" Panion wanted to know.

"The flames of Tros' beacon drew the Solarii here through the long evening shadows," Demos said, shaking the gatekeeper warmly by the hand.

Tros' eyes glowed as bright as his bonfire. "Yes, I lit the fire," his voice boomed, "but it was your father, Akasha, who conceived the idea of the clifftop beacons."

Uriah bowed low and lapped up the imaginary applause, and everyone collapsed in hysterics.

"The Solarii are here!" Akasha cried again, as if to make sure it was actually true. The thought of seeing these legendary beings thrilled and frightened her in equal measure. The four craft hovered above them, making a low growling noise, like the sound of the tide coming in when heard from afar.

Salvaging her presence of mind, she turned to the gatekeeper. "Tros, the only ground even enough for the flyers to land is right where we're standing."

Tros and his men ushered the crowd back. Shoulder to shoulder they stood, like a great thicket of people, gazing upwards, with a large circular space in their midst. The bonfire spat sparks into the night air and lit the area where the flyers could safely land.

Cubit by cubit, the four craft lowered towards the earth, into the waiting ferment. With strange hisses and a loud thump, the flying chairs touched onto the ground, enveloped by clouds of white smoke and dust thrown up by the machines. Akasha turned up her nose at the acrid tinge of sulphur.

"Better late than not at all," Demos grumbled. He would, wouldn't he?

The news spread rapidly, swelling the crowd. Human visitors were rare enough, but Solarii guests were virtually unknown. As the vapour clouds and dust dispersed, the Solarii flyers unstrapped themselves and stood before their craft, encircled by a feverish and emotional crowd. Akasha gazed up at the Solarii. They were here. They'd actually arrived. Surely, it was a sign that all would be well. Despite Demos' reservations, she wanted to trust them.

Three of the Solarii turned towards a fourth, a tall man with an angular nose and strong chin. That turned out to be Protector Horque, confirmed when others called him by that name. He barked an order in a deep, slow voice and two of them moved back to tend to the flying machines. They were as tall and imposing as trees, and Akasha didn't know if she was more afraid of them, or their strange machines.

The protector spoke briefly to a fourth Solarii, whom he addressed as Khephren. Horque stared at Akasha, Shamira and Panion, then slowly turned full circle until he'd scrutinised everyone in the crowd. Akasha guessed he was looking at them all through his whites, measuring the astral of the city and its people. My, he was thorough. Demos had warned her.

The protector was the focus of everyone's attention, including hers, which wasn't surprising, because he wore this cloak of authority and carried himself with a regal bearing. He carefully peeled off a kind of skin-coloured covering over his fingers and hands. She assumed they were some sort of protection from the cold when flying. With the gloves removed, she looked at his fingers and could have sworn there was something odd about them. The other three flyers were the same. Yes, they all had four fingers and a thumb. No, it wasn't that.

Then she realised. Her eyes opened wide and she whispered in Shamira's ear, "Their fingers, they're not like ours. They're – all the same length."

Shamira nodded.

These Solarii really were an alien people.

There was another surprise. Two smaller men, human in size, appeared from behind the bank of flying craft and joined the Solarii men. Akasha assumed they were Semites, since it was common knowledge that the Semites were in voluntary service to the Solarii. Panion seemed to recognise one of them and gave him a warm greeting. His name was Tarsus, but who was he? Apparently, he had once lived in Samlios, and long ago emigrated to Mithrayzim.

Amidst the heady emotions of arrival and homecoming, at least Big Qorus retained his presence of mind, because he announced with considerable gravitas, "I am the Green Elder of Samlios and I welcome you, Protector, and your entourage. Now, if you would be as kind as to—"

"*Only* the Green Elder to welcome me?" the protector said loudly. Who else was he expecting?

"If it pleases Your Excellency, your formal welcome from all the five secular elders and the rota of three religious leaders will take place at the Mind Search tomorrow," Big Qorus hastened to explain. He was showing deference all right, but too much.

The protector nodded curtly and said with a perfunctory air, "These Horus Wing craft must be secured. Marim, Lasec, see to it."

"Can we help?" Big Qorus asked, as he approached the flying craft.

"Wait. Stay where you are." The protector held his arm out, preventing anyone from approaching their precious machines. "Don't touch them. My men will do this task."

Akasha puffed out her cheeks. The man's voice was full of disdain. He was obviously accustomed to deference and obedience.

Big Qorus backed away.

Her attention turned to the four flying machines, as much objects of curiosity as the Solarii. She'd never seen anything like them; machines barely existed in human culture, although the nascent Surge had promoted the invention of instruments and tools. The nearest thing they had to a machine was the glow lamp, their one source of light, but glow lamps didn't glide through the air like a bird at the will of its flyer. By contrast, the Solarii had built machines such as their infamous solar furnaces and the tools to construct them, notably the irsution and the ashlar.

She took a closer look at these flying machines. They had landed in a perfect line and that told her a lot about the fastidiousness of their owners. The four machines were so similar to each other, she imagined they had a template somewhere and simply hewed another machine out of a granite slab whenever they needed one. Each one was as sleek and subtle as a black panther. The smooth sculptured stone reflected the lithe orange-yellow flames from the bonfire. The driver and passenger sat back-to-back. She supposed the network of pipes that ran from the top to the bottom along the sides of the craft carried the effluent, the trail of grey-white smoke she'd seen on their arrival.

The crowd surrounded the two Solarii Horque had called Lasec and Marim, who now did something quite extraordinary. Suddenly, all four machines sparked into life and began to shudder and vibrate. No one had touched them. If that wasn't frightening enough, each craft let out a small puff of white smoke, lifted off the ground and hovered on their own accord, as if suspended by an invisible hand. They emitted a low drone as a backdraught of air stirred up the dust. Partly out of surprise and partly out of fear, everyone took a step back.

Big Qorus tried to impose himself. "Tros, please show our guests where they can store the machines, in the annex at the back of the cathedral."

"No! Show us to our quarters," the protector insisted. "The craft will be stored there, with us."

"In that case, please follow me," Big Qorus replied. "Protector, it is my honour and privilege for you all to lodge in my quarters."

Tros stood next to Big Qorus, and they both held glow lamps as the party set off. Behind them came Protector Horque and the other three Solarii, accompanied by the machines. The crowd parted to let them through, looking on in awe as the machines moved together like trained animals. Tarsus and the other human servant scuttled behind them.

Once they were out of sight, Akasha and Shamira invited the Mind Search to return to the amphitheatre bonfires for a dual celebration: Demos and his rump had returned to the fold and the Solarii had arrived.

Something else was stirring in the night air. It hovered nearby, out of her grasp but within her reach. It was a feeling of excitement like never before. This protector and his Solarii connections could help. He would play a part in the release of the Surge. She didn't know how, but she intended to find out.

CHAPTER 15

The Meeting

By the middle of the evening, the bonfires had almost burnt out, as had the excitement of the day. The earthy smell of burning wood hung like a cloak in the sultry summer night air. Akasha sat beside Shamira and Demos. Shamira pleaded with her to welcome him back and in the end, she had forgiven him. As they chatted, she touched her bare neck. It felt strange not having the cobra necklace there. Where had she put it?

Shamira spoke with an air of triumph.

"Tonight, we celebrate. We're more than groups of individuals, villages and tribes. We are one people joined together in the astral light by invisible gold and silver chains of speech and communication. So let us give voice to the stories of our lives. Let us dedicate this night to the human story in each of us. Come, I invite you all. Who will go first?"

As Savor was about to start, a figure emerged out of the shadows, to be illuminated by the glowing embers of the fire. He took another step forwards and the warm light from the fire shone up into his gaunt face. It was the lanky Qorus.

"Pythoness, I'm sorry to interrupt, but I have news of the Solarii," he said.

"What's the matter with them?" she asked with a concerned air.

"They're all right, but one of their Semite servants is sick."

"Akasha, bring your herb basket. We're coming."

Akasha would have loved to stay and listen to Savor's story, but something tugged at her soul.

"I'm ready," she said.

She stepped away from the warmth of the fires, into the near-moonless night. Big Qorus led the way, holding a glow lamp. All was quiet as the trio walked back from the old amphitheatre, up the hill and into the heart of the city.

She was excited and nervous at the prospect of seeing the Solarii close up. Now she could make her own mind up about them. The ringing of a bell pierced the silence of the night.

"All's well, at second quarter."

It was the city guards, calling the quarters of the night. The stentorian sound of their voices set off the local canines in a raucous round of yapping.

"I must warn you," Shamira said as they approached, "don't get distracted by Protector Horque."

"Why? I've already met him."

"These are different circumstances."

"How are they different?"

"We're going to their residence," Shamira said. "Already they will have summoned their astral protections and insignia into the chambers, which will bear the authority of their astral light. Please remember the reason we're going there, which is to offer care for their manservant."

"Panion seemed to know one of them – Tarsus?"

"Yes, that's right. He's well loved in Samlios and remembered for his brave fight against the Helios. But that was long ago. Now he lives and serves the Solarii in Egypt."

"I see," she said. If he'd lived there all that time, he must know a thing or two about them. But that wasn't Shamira's primary concern.

"And mentally erect an astral shield around your person before we enter," she said.

Shamira had already briefed her on how the Solarii possessed powerful astral arts that could divine a person's heart and soul unless they protected themselves. That was all very well, but was Shamira becoming as suspicious and cautious as Demos?

Big Qorus banged his fist on the oak door. Footsteps echoed in the inner corridor. The door swung open and a giant silhouette filled the entrance. He was so tall, he cast a long shadow over them. Akasha took an involuntary step back.

"I am Lasec, Guardian of Justice," the distinguished-looking Solarii declared.

"I am Shamira, and this is my assistant, Akasha. We've come to help your manservant."

"This way," Lasec said, while insisting Qorus wait outside. He made them wait in the antechamber while he disappeared into the main chamber.

Akasha's breathing grew quick and shallow. A knot formed in her stomach. Cramp? No, please, not now.

Protector Horque's deep voice resounded through the antechamber.

*

89

Although it was late, Horque was awake. Benjamin, Khephren's servant, was ailing. It would be an unnecessary inconvenience if he were to be ill during the Mind Search. Benjamin was human, so Horque had called for a human to heal him. Besides, it provided the ideal excuse to meet the famous pythoness at close quarters, to assess her fearsome reputation and that of her apprentice, Akasha, who since her dance of the winds had rapidly acquired a reputation of her own.

"Lasec, show them in," he bellowed.

The coldness of the alabaster floor ran along his bare feet and up his ankles. He sat upright in a high-backed wooden chair that fitted his size to perfection, and fingered the mother-of-pearl and turquoise inlay in the hawk motifs on the uprights: open beak, claws taut and wings wide. He'd requested this motif before arriving and the pythoness had kindly provided it. How odd that they should welcome him with a mere Green Elder when he'd expected the High Priest. No matter, Samlios was an old Solarii city. The Helios had built it for the humans long ago. Because of its interior structural harmonies, he felt relatively at ease in its vaunting domed architecture.

Outside, an owl screeched. Inside, a cool breeze blew through the open colonnade, lifting the gold-yellow curtains through which the two women made their way into the chamber and sat on two vacant chairs opposite him.

"Khephren, we'll finish our game later," he said. He enjoyed the Intricacies of the Foxes and Hounds principally because its thirty-two pieces and thirty-two spaces provided for an enthralling game of seemingly endless possibilities. And he was good at it, especially when playing black. After all, he was the black hawk. It would provide a welcome distraction from the tedium of the Mind Search. He hadn't wanted to come. Nimrod had given him no choice.

In the mood for playing games, he wondered if his guests knew the common name for the two kingdoms of Upper and Lower Egypt, so he asked, "Ah, the two ladies, just like our Two Ladies in Egypt."

"Yes, but we're not Egyptian," Shamira replied, clearly no one's fool.

"No, not yet," he murmured ironically to himself, and then added loudly, "So you've come at last."

"We came as soon as you requested," the pythoness replied. "It was a shame you weren't able to do the same when invited to the Mind Search."

"We came when we came, now we are here," he replied ambivalently. "You may address me as Protector Horque."

"And I answer to Shamira, High Priestess and Pythoness of Samlios," she rebuked him – again.

He measured the pythoness, her astral abilities – they were broad and versatile. She could be a formidable foe or a potent ally. He liked her; she had heart and courage and was uncompromising. Just like his mother.

"This is Khephren, our healing priest," he said.

"And this is Akasha, my apprentice."

He detected a deep pride in her voice.

"You're the dancer?" He shifted his attention to Akasha. She was fidgeting. Was she nervous? Looking through his whites, bright lances of power shone in her emanation, no doubt the astral crystallisation of her dance. She was a lady in waiting, he concluded, mildly impressed.

"The introductions are over," he said. "Khephren's servant is hot and water drips from his forehead like a stream. The local spirits dislike him. It's the Samlios air. It reeks of the underworld."

"There are dried and fresh flowers for you," Shamira said, pointing to the petals and bunches of flowers spread around the chamber perimeter.

"They are appreciated, as is the chair. Thank you." He could be gracious if he chose to be. "Lasec, escort the ladies to Benjamin. Pythoness, you will do something to help him." He softened his brusque manner out of a grudging respect.

The moment she stood up, Akasha felt light-headed and her head spun like a whirlwind. She grabbed the armrest to prevent herself from stumbling but thankfully, Horque was too engrossed with Shamira to notice. That was odd; why should she feel like that without warning? She dismissed the thought, instead searching through her herb basket to divert attention from her discomfort. She sat back up again, clutching a length of string she'd found. Something gnawed at her soul.

Horque and Shamira were still conversing. She glanced at his hook nose and intense eyes. His shoulders were broad and square. Apart from his lips when he spoke, he barely moved a muscle; he sat statuesque, radiating imperial majesty. She could not explain how or why, but she felt under his spell. It was as if she had to submit to his control. How could he manipulate her, without saying or doing anything?

She nervously plucked the piece of string from her herb basket and threaded it through her fingers. Without realising what she'd done, she'd picked Demos' rearing cobra necklace from it. A flood of tiresome memories surfaced, about Demos deserting the Mind Search, and she shoved it back in the basket.

She heard her own name mentioned, and then her dance. Yes, it stilled the winds. That didn't appear to impress him, or if it did, he concealed it well.

Now he's scrutinising me in the astral light. I can feel his piercing gaze on me. Shamira warned me: they probe, they're intrusive. What does he think of me? What does he think of us? Does he have any feelings? He doesn't show any. With those fingers all the same length, he is strange. He travels from Egypt to talk to us, then presents a façade of granite. How do you communicate with a statue?

She followed Shamira towards the door of the chamber, Lasec leading the way. Looking back at Horque, she realised how eerie and incongruous the Solarii really were. The dim lighting and the sudden and unexpected potency of the moment caught her off balance and she stumbled. With a heavy thud, she hit the stone floor, scattering the contents of the herb basket across the alabaster tiles.

Shamira was by her side in an instant.

"Are you hurt?" she asked.

Akasha grimaced and shook her head. She sat up and rubbed her knee. Shamira put the herbs back in the basket. All the while, Lasec stood by the entrance, haughty and tight-lipped.

She felt her face flush. Horque was staring at her. He sat high on his throne, bristling with certainty and purpose. His black eyes peered right through her like she was invisible. He was looking at her through his whites, into the inner recesses of her soul. She felt naked. Her astral shield was woefully inadequate against his armoury of astral powers. Propping herself up on the cold floor, Akasha thought she detected a wry smile flicker across his lips.

"Come, there's nothing broken. Take my hand," Shamira said reassuringly. Marim emerged from the shadows, speaking in hushed tones to Horque. The two Solarii seemed unaware that, because of the domed acoustics of the chamber, she could hear every word of their conversation.

"Excellency, these little humans make big fools of themselves," Marim whispered.

"So it appears," Horque replied. "You prepared the astral atmosphere in the chamber as I requested. The dim lighting helped me see through my whites with crystal clarity, revealing all their astral connections. Now I'm well informed of their motives."

Now she understood why she'd felt light-headed and uncomfortable. Demos had warned her, and she'd prejudged the old sailor. The Solarii were as slippery as snakes and to outwit them, she'd have to stay sharp and alert.

Lasec and Khephren led them to an annex where Benjamin lay in bed, Tarsus by his side.

"Before leaving Egypt," Khephren told them, "I administered the usual medicines for the journey but they haven't worked – at least not for Benjamin." His tone was almost apologetic, which quite surprised her, considering Horque's arrogance.

"Tarsus, are you sick as well?" Shamira asked.

"No," Tarsus replied, with a glowing smile. "On the contrary, I haven't felt as good as this since the last time I was in Samlios."

"Well, it is your home, isn't it?"

"It is," Tarsus said. "Or rather, it was."

Shamira turned to Benjamin and examined him. His forehead and body were moist with sweat and his unpleasant odours filled the room. To mask them, Shamira picked out some sweet-smelling herbs and garlic bulbs from the basket and laid them on the floor.

"How are you feeling?" she asked.

"Tired," Benjamin replied, "and weak."

"I see," Shamira replied softly. "Have you drunk our water?"

"Yuck, it tasted horrible."

"Yes it will, and that's why you feel like you do. Your body is accustomed to drinking the waters of the wells in Egypt. Here the emanation of the land is different – making the water taste different. Did you bring a clod of Egyptian earth with you?"

"No, why should I do that?" He struggled to sit up.

"Your soul grows accustomed to the nature of the astral light of the land where you live or were brought up. That's why Tarsus feels at home here. When you go on a journey or physically leave that land, it registers the absence as an ache. Hold a clod of earth and it will soften the homesickness."

Benjamin nodded and coughed again.

"Can you help him?" Khephren asked.

"I have a potion which will ease his discomfort. Akasha, use the herbs I told you about earlier and make a draught for Benjamin."

Shamira repeated her request more firmly when Akasha did not reply. "Do as I ask, Akasha, and pay attention."

"I'm sorry," she replied. "I was only half-listening." She delved into the herb basket and with quick hands, mixed and administered the potion.

As they left, they found Qorus waiting for them. With every step, Akasha heard his sonorous voice. As they reached Temple Mount, the guard's call of the third quarter of the night rang out over the rooftops.

A while later, Akasha heard the fourth quarter. Dawn was breaking and she was still awake. She couldn't shift her mental image of a huge, powerful man – the Solarii protector.

CHAPTER 16

The Isis Address

When she awoke the next day, Akasha searched everywhere for Demos' necklace. Wracking her brain, she remembered taking it off in a moment of pique at Demos' antics at the Mind Search, then finding it later in her herb basket. After that, her recollection was hazy.

The third day of the Mind Search was calling her, and what a brilliant day it was. Samlios bathed in the warming rays of the sun. Not a breath of wind disturbed the peace that had descended on the Five Hills. The ocean was as smooth as glass.

Inside the rotunda, the cathedral was packed. In honour of the Solarii, Thera had decorated the chamber with chains of yellow and gold summer flowers and placed containers of fragrant rose water around the perimeter. Unfortunately, none of it was enough to placate Shamira and Demos, who had already locked horns.

"This marvellous weather shows how much the people are encouraged by yesterday's events. Their hopes are sky high," Shamira was saying. "This is the day we've prayed for, the day the Solarii shall speak."

"I'll wait and see what they say," Demos said, managing a rueful smile. "I'm sure they'll spring a surprise on us."

"You're a sceptic, Demos," Akasha told him. "But now I understand why. Last night I saw for myself how strange and different they are to us. Yet they live on Earth as we do, they breathe the same air, and their souls absorb the astral light as ours do. They have wants and desires, even though they may be sometimes at odds with ours. The only difference between you and me is that *you* don't trust them." She shook a finger at him, half-serious, half-playful.

"And you do?" Demos scoffed. "There's more to it than that. Simply because they bear more than a passing resemblance to us, we assume they are the same as us. They are not. They are aliens, and do not ever forget it. They do not think as we do and that makes them inscrutable and incomprehensible. They want to end their exile as soon as they can and they'll do anything to bring that about."

Demos was a lovable rogue and proud of his individuality. He wasn't going to back down or change his views. Akasha planted her hands on her haunches and replied, "As you said, we'll see."

"The Solarii will arrive soon," Demos replied and shuffled off to his seat. As a parting remark he added, "Oh, mind you put your necklace back on."

They all wanted to witness the Solarii, and absorb the emotions of this historic day. Every man and woman perched on the edge of their seat. A thousand heads strained to catch an early glimpse of their renowned visitors.

As Horque came into view, the crowd let out a collective gasp of amazement. The four Solarii walked across the atrium as if they had just thawed out. Hands stuck by their sides; only their legs moved as they walked, taut and wooden. The flap of their sandals on the marble flagstones echoed around the vaults, one sound, four steps, synchronised. It was even more eerie because they ignored the awestruck audience around them.

While the four aliens sat down, Tarsus stood next to Horque and Benjamin next to Khephren. Seeing Benjamin, Akasha assumed the healing potion must have worked.

"Let us show a warm welcome to our Solarii visitors," Shamira cried. Animated applause shot around the massed ranks. While Shamira introduced the Solarii to the five elders and three of the rota, Akasha once more took the opportunity to study the enigma that was Horque. His bearing was so regal. He wore a traditional Egyptian cloth skirt, the broad protector pectoral, and copper ankle and wrist clasps. The rays of the sun streamed through the crystal roof and in the bright light, she noticed a fleck of his black hair protruding from beneath his linen headdress. He was as stone-faced as the statues of the archangels outside the temple. Demos was right again. The Solarii were as difficult to read as their hieroglyphics.

"We await the Solarii ideas for how we may all survive the flood and how we may rectify the tragedy of the seed," Shamira said.

This seemed to revive Horque. He slapped his large hands on his thighs and pulled himself erect. His massive frame towered above everyone. The Mind Search waited.

"I am Horque, envoy of Nimrod, Pharaoh of the Twin Lands, and I am here to deliver his reasoned terms to you." His voice sounded as far away as the look in his eyes.

Akasha listened intently to every nuance, trying to divine what he was about to propose. Reasoned terms – what did that mean?

"We offer the hand of friendship to our human companions," Horque said flatly. "We have imprisoned the Helios beneath the valleys of the Earth. We have given you the Emerald Caverns and the Covenant of the Firstborn. We have build pyramids to suppress the growth of the hybrid seed in you. All these things we have done to help you. Now we will deliver the elixir of the gods, the Surge."

He turned his head, expressionless. She wondered if he was deliberately intimidating, or if this was his normal craggy and officious manner. The glass balls on his pectoral glowed with a golden hue, indicating the nature of the astral energy at play. Whatever it was, it made her bones ache and her limbs feel like granite.

"Our races may be separate," Horque continued, "but our fates are entwined. The flood is coming. To you, it is a threat. To us, it's deliverance. The pantheon of gods has sent this deluge to expedite matters on Earth. When our exile finally ends, we shall leave many legacies, one of which will be to the Semites, who will be rewarded for their honourable and dignified service to us. Our superior astral powers have enhanced their seed, so that in the future it will prosper over all others. But I speak of things that are yet to pass."

Was he implying that the Semites were the most fit to take on the Surge?

"Now I shall deliver the pharaoh's proposal," he said. "When the waters fall from the sky, the pyramids will be swamped and will cease to function as solar furnaces. Without the pyramids, we will perish. Without the pyramids, the hybrid seed will become active in humans and humans will degenerate. Therefore, we must return home before the flood ends. For this to happen, we must remove the hybrid seed in humans to allow the Surge to flourish."

That sounded something like what she'd expected to hear.

"The goddess Isis is mother of the Solarii," Horque continued. "She foretells a new race, one in which the hybrid seed will never again appear, not even as an atavism. The seed of the new race will be stable and fixed, generation after generation, and will not give rise to the hybrid."

This was the foundation stone of the pharaoh's proposal: a new race. How would it come about? What would happen to them, the existing humans? And who was this Goddess Isis? The Solarii may worship her, but humans didn't.

Horque delved into Solarii legend. "Mother Isis found and brought together the scattered body parts of her beloved husband Osiris to create a new birth, the child Horus. In the same way, this seed will combine the remnants of the human with the best of the Solarii in a formidable and all-conquering new race that shall be known as the seed, or Genes of Isis."

The last phrase sounded like a mantra repeated endlessly in the vaulted temples of Karnak, Thebes and Jizah. Akasha had a premonition about what he was going to say next and something screamed deep within her.

"Humans, listen to reason." Was Horque pleading with them? "The Solarii seed is clear of the hybrid strain. Let humans bring forth a woman who can sustain and nourish the Solarii seed. Between them, they will produce the first children of this new race. The progeny of the Solarii father and human mother will be the Genes of Isis, or Genesis. This is how the Surge will flower in humans. This is how the new human strain can survive and prosper in the aftermath of the deluge. This is the pharaoh's proposal. As it is spoken, so it shall be done."

Unbelievable. He was proposing anthropophilia! She suppressed the urge to vomit and put her head between her knees. She felt like the life force had retreated inside her and been tethered in some dark, forgotten abyss. She managed to look up, her head spinning with nausea. Around her, the chamber sat in stunned silence. Their faces were pallid, their expressions scarred with fear and loathing.

She expected there to follow a stern condemnation of the pharaoh's absurd proposal. The people of the Mind Search were coming around, as if awaking from a nightmare, staring blankly into the empty air. She swallowed her bile and stood up. At the same moment, Horque rose too.

"I shall return at high sun tomorrow to hear your agreement," he announced. "Then I will go back to Egypt."

He led the Solarii deputation out of the Mind Search, each slow step followed by thousand pairs of eyes. Akasha was stupefied. The pharaoh hadn't made a proposal at all. He'd delivered an ultimatum, and the most horrific one imaginable.

CHAPTER 17

Visitation

The Mind Search reconvened at dawn. Somehow, they had to conclude their deliberations and reach some sort of a decision before the sun disc had risen to its apex.

Akasha sat in the rotunda, eyes heavy from lack of sleep. She listened to the proceedings and tried to make up her own mind. All her unanswered questions boiled down to one – why on earth was the pharaoh proposing a union of a human and a Solarii? Had he gone mad? Could he really expect humans to breach the dam of the oldest taboo of them all? Then again, they couldn't allow Horque to return to Egypt without some sort of an agreement.

In her personal situation, she had so many conflicting desires with which to contend. The Solarii were not going to repair the Emerald Cavern. There was no point. In the aftermath of the flood, the caverns would go the same way as the pyramids. She found herself in the cleansing flow, so she was ready for motherhood, yet she, like every other human, would rather die than agree to marry a Solarii. It was impossible to make the right decision in the midst of such emotional turmoil. If only there was a sign to help her make up her tortured mind.

The pharaoh's proposal had sown discord amongst the Mind Search as well, with Demos leading the ranks of the disaffected.

"It's anathema," he said. "When they first arrived on Earth from the sun, the Solarii were assistants to the Helios. They were kith and kin. I tell you, they can't be trusted. They're tainted by association with those renegades."

Reluctantly, Akasha had to admit his stance was convincing.

Then there was Shamira. She was a stickler for the rules and if anyone were to forbid the contravention of the taboo, it would be the pythoness. Yet during that fateful morning, her words once again surprised everyone.

"I've pondered the pharaoh's address," she began. "It's clear we've reached a turning point in the luminous path of the human race. Let's make this decision without emotion or undue persuasion. If we refuse pharaoh's idea of a Solarii-human marriage, what will happen? In the aftermath of the flood, we'd be on the slow path to degeneration and eventual extinction."

Now Akasha was worried.

"We have no alternative," Shamira stated, "but to accept the Isis address."

Akasha was stunned at Shamira's conclusion, not least because it sounded like the reasoning of a Solarii.

To the Mind Search, Shamira's pragmatic approach was as unexpected as it was unpopular. People stamped their feet, as if stamping on her words. Yet there was no opportunity to counter her arguments. The sun rose higher in the sky. A silence fell on the assembly like a pall, filling Akasha with a sense of impending doom. Shoulders slumped and heads bowed. The sun shone through the transparent dome of the Crystal Cathedral.

It was high sun.

The sound of slow, heavy footsteps broke into the chamber like claps of thunder. Stern and deliberate, Horque entered the atrium.

"Well?" he demanded. "What is it to be?"

"Protector, the Mind Search is divided," Shamira admitted. "This is a complex and emotional issue of the highest importance to the human race. The pharaoh is asking us to violate our greatest taboo. Obviously, we can't do this lightly. We ask you to tarry a little longer."

Horque sniffed the air, and frowned. "Pythoness, this is unacceptable. The Solarii also have to prepare for the deluge, and anthropophilia is equally taboo for us. I am Protector of the Pharaoh and His People and must return on time."

"Wait," Akasha said, reaching out a hand of friendship.

Horque was about to walk out into the midday sun when she added in a plaintive tone, "Have you ever had to overcome your greatest fear?"

Horque paused. That question seemed to irk him. He turned back to face her. She returned his gaze, eye to eye, soul to soul. In that moment, something passed between them, something magical, unique; a mysterious desire, a precocious kindling.

Often, the smallest of acts can summon the greatest of things.

Out of the astral light, a speck of luminescence appeared. In the space between her and Horque, it grew into a revolving ball of brilliant astral fire, then spiralled into a cone of power. Curtains of white and silver energy rained down on them. Shimmering lights manifested first in one corner, then in another part of the cathedral's crystal wall. Gradually, the drapes of astral luminescence coalesced into pairs of eyes; everywhere, eyes.

Akasha's ears were ringing and the palms of her hands were mottled, sure signs of the presence of the astral illuminati. Around the walls were pairs of eyes with silver-white brows, white pupils and deep blue irises. Streaming from them were silver tears that cascaded onto the cathedral floor. No, they weren't tears, but a threefold ray emitted from the iris, vertically downwards, like a lotus. The eyes peered at the Mind Search and – she couldn't believe it – at her and Horque.

She felt natural, at ease in herself beyond anything she'd ever felt before. Even the nagging, doubting demons quietened in her. In the midst of a sensation of a glorious well-being, she heard the soft voice of her own spirit.

"Who – what are you?" she whispered.

A voice replied with crystal clarity.

We are the Watchers, scouts of the Source.

She was in the presence of the divine. She felt as high as the cupola; her being spread its astral wings over the whole city. The brightness between her and Horque condensed into the shape of an oval rod of brilliant gems, suffused with a cool, spiritual glow. Then a shimmering astral curtain of vibrant silver appeared on the crystal wall opposite them. A shape manifested on it; a glyph. And another. They were words. Some kind of writing appearing on the wall, holy in glyph, drawn by an invisible hand:

This is the time of necessity.
The Surge is paramount.
We proclaim the union between a twice-born Solarii
And a fair maiden daughter of man.
Let the return be signed by the blue bow.
Willing. Watchers. Waiting.

The sacred glyphs formed on the wall in a living, breathing dictum. After a few moments, they dissipated back into the astral light. Akasha received the wisdom of the Watchers' edict as a knowing certainty, and she knew that everyone else present in the auditorium had received the same epiphany. She took a deep breath and glanced around the chamber. Everyone sat in awed silence, their eyes shining like suns. The atmosphere was thick with astral power.

"So be it, let it be done." Horque spoke the words so softly that she wondered if someone else had articulated them.

A lance of astral power was coming out of her eyes, a brightness unconfined. This was a miracle. As the Mind Search was about to break asunder for a second time, the Watchers had delivered their edict, kindling genuine hope for the future of the human race. And she would be part of that.

She joined the people of the Mind Search in a song of praise to the Watchers, celebrating their grace and grant and spiritual beneficence. She was delirious with happiness. She never wanted the moment to end.

Part 4

Exodus

CHAPTER 18

Diaspora

Warmed by the rays of the morning sun, Akasha shuffled through the crowd on the dock. The ocean waves breaking against the quayside sent cascades of surf into the air, in which the vibrant arc of the rainbow appeared and then disappeared. The smell of salt from the spray pinched her nose. Thick ropes tethered a score or more ships to their mooring stations. Their crews shouted at each other in amiable competition, each one trying to make their ship ready for the ocean voyage before the other. A light easterly wind carried the scent of adventure and the promise of home. Gulls squealed and wheeled in the air, high above the throng of people on the quayside.

She turned back to look for Tros.

"Keep up," she admonished him.

"I'm doing my best, but these people on the quay are as close as blades of grass," he complained, elbowing his way through the crowd.

"Stay close by. I can't pass the herbs and sods of earth to the people when you and my basket are nowhere to be seen."

Tros nodded. "This is going to take another miracle."

"Why's that?" she asked.

"To find so many places on so few ships," he said, laconic to the last.

"Can't be helped," she replied. "They voyaged from far and wide to attend the Mind Search. It came to a spectacular end and now they all want to go home and tell their families and friends what's happened. It's only natural."

"That may be," Tros said grumpily, "but I never imagined they'd be joined by every last man, woman and child in Samlios."

"That's true," she admitted. "Then again, we did advise everyone to vacate the lower ground. No one will be left behind to drown."

Tros had been on the docks since first light and Akasha was impressed with his huge capacity for hard work. In that respect, he reminded her of Horque, although the protector was more imperial and majestic than Tros could ever be. Akasha's first morning call was to Qorus' residence, where she'd hoped to retrieve her missing cobra necklace and see the protector one last time. But she was disappointed on both scores, as the Solarii party had slipped away at dawn without ceremony. She'd searched for the necklace in the chamber, but all that remained were fond memories of Horque's ubiquitous presence.

On the docks, the mass of people milled around the quay, pulling baggage carts and carrying sacks of clothes and other belongings. Out of the crowd emerged Callisto's stocky frame and full-moon face. A look passed between them that carried a thousand unspoken words, and then they embraced in silence.

"I'd never have imagined that we'd desert old Samlios," Callisto said with dewy eyes.

"I know it's an awful wrench, but the alternative isn't worth contemplating."

"It's not only the city. It's the temple, the cathedral and the Step Well we'll leave behind, it's also our ceremonies and way of life. I've enjoyed my time here as Blue Elder, yet now I have to say goodbye to all those people I healed, and the children like you who I delivered over the years. But do you know what pains me the most?"

Akasha shook her head.

"It's my mother's open grave. The raging floodwaters will wash away her remains, which will simply rot on the seabed." Callisto's chin quivered with emotion.

Akasha knew that this opposed their traditional rites, where the corpse was left on a cairn in the open. The pellucid astral light slowed the rate of putrefaction, so corpses endured many years in pristine condition, allowing friends and relatives to celebrate birthdays on the Hill of Sighs as a remembrance of the person's life and good works.

For once, she felt helpless. What could she do? In the end, she gently rubbed the back of her hand against Callisto's cheek. The two of them stood by the edge of the quay, sharing a moment of grief for a lost city and a dead mother, surrounded by the bustle of hasty departure and the discordant strains of an uncertain future.

"Here, after all your kindness to me, I've something to give you." Akasha delved into the herb basket and pulled out a package held together by flex. She pressed it into Callisto's hand.

"What is it?" Callisto eyes lit up as she untied the knot to reveal a concoction of green-leafed herbs, a water snake amulet and a round sod of reddish-brown earth.

"They'll help with the journey," she said. "The herbs and the amulet will ward off seasickness. When you're homesick, grasp the sod of Samlios earth in your hand."

"Thank you," Callisto said, pressing her hand warmly.

"Whose ship are you sailing on?"

"On Philo's," Callisto replied, holding out her hand to the Babylonian. Akasha could still see the glory of the Watchers' presence in them both. Their skin shone and their eyes were as bright as jewels.

"Take care of our Blue Elder," she said to him.

"I will," Philo replied with confidence. "I'll find a place for her in the great Tower of Babylon. Tros is coming too."

"There's another reason I'm going there," Callisto said, with a knowing nod. What was this all about? "In due course, I'm hoping to be called upon to use my midwifery skills."

Akasha was bewildered. "For that to happen, someone would have to be with child. How could that be?"

"The gardens, Akasha," Philo interjected, his yew green eyes dancing with delight. "The Hanging Gardens of Babylon. How could you forget?"

She was still bemused. "What? Are you thinking that the pregnant human mother, 'the fair maiden', will end up in the Hanging Gardens?"

"Where else would she go?" Philo exclaimed. "It's traditional. Mothers-to-be spend the period of their pregnancy in healing gardens. Mine did, did yours?"

She nodded. "Of course."

"The Hanging Gardens are the best kept in the world. Masco sees to that, he's a wonderful gardener – though obviously not as good as your Rocor," Philo went on, his face animated. "Once she falls with child, it'll be the most natural place in the world for the fair maiden to go."

"Why, yes, I suppose you're right." Akasha hadn't thought of that before, but Callisto and Philo had shown unusual foresight.

"So when will we see you there – in the gardens – Akasha?"

What was Callisto talking about now?

"Me? I'm going to sit out the flood in the Whispering Tower. Why would I go to Babylon?"

"No, you can't say that. You can't ignore your destiny," Callisto replied, with mild rebuke. "It's time you admitted that you, more than anyone else, have shaped your life for this opportunity. You're the only maiden in the cleansing flow, and the only one can conceive in the short time available. All the other maidens have absorbed the emerald rays. They're infertile, and couldn't become fertile for at least two years. Likewise the men. The human race doesn't have two years. Whether you like it or not, you're the Watchers' fair maiden."

Oh. My. Lord. Callisto was right. Akasha stood on the quay, frozen to the spot.

All morning, people had milled around her, touching her elbow with reverence, pausing to congratulate her, bowing with respect, and she'd not even wondered why. Then she remembered her dream vision, the one she'd experienced after the dance of the winds. She was destined to preserve the human race, but surely not like this?

"I thought it would be someone else, not me," she stammered. "Besides, I *can't* marry a Solarii."

Did she mean that? Since the Watchers' visitation, events had unfolded with immoderate haste, and now she needed to revisit that decision.

"Our ship is leaving, but you must promise me you'll accept the union."

"I will try."

As Callisto stepped back, she said, "Until Babylon, then?" Then she turned into the crowd, and was gone.

Akasha frowned. How was this possible? Was she really such a dullard, the last to realise what everyone else already knew? No one had envisaged that events would unfold as they had. As she struggled with her inner demons, a craggy voice boomed across the dock, "Ak-ash-a!"

Peering through a cloud of spray, she recognised the silhouette of her old friend Demos, waving at her from the deck of the *Crucible*.

"There you are. I've been looking for you. I want to see it," she yelled back. Like many others, she'd heard he'd received a wonderful healing from the presence of the Watchers. She climbed the gangplank. He gave her a warm hug, and his skin smelt of the ocean waves.

"Let me see it," she exclaimed again. It wasn't a dream, and she wanted to see real evidence of a miracle. Demos smiled and held up his hand. Where once his little finger had been a short stub, it now boasted its full complement of three phalanges, which he wriggled like a piglet's tail.

She beamed. "It's true then. The pythoness told me about it."

"I feel so humble," Demos said. "The finger re-grew. The healing power of the Watchers has regenerated it. I'm whole again."

The crew gathered round, making admiring noises.

She repeated Shamira's advice for all to hear. "The angels might return. Until that day comes, let's hold them in awe."

The remembrance over, Demos insisted everyone got back to work.

"And you," he said, "follow me to your cabin."

When they got there, she slumped into a chair.

"Something's wrong. What have I done now?" Demos asked.

"Nothing, this time it's me. Everyone seems to think I'm the fair maiden, and set for this union, but I'm not sure."

"It's for you to decide, in your own good time. Now I must return to the bridge," Demos said as he closed the cabin door behind him.

He was right. She had to think it through on her own. The emotions and grief of the diaspora from Samlios made it difficult to think straight. She kept replaying the Watchers' visitation, and those eyes, staring right through her, so soft, so gentle and kind.

Part of her accepted that it was her destiny to be the mother of a new race, but another part of her fought against it like a feral cat. The mother of the new human race – she pinched herself at the thought. What about the fate of the old human race? People were saying that after the flood it would flounder in the dim astral light, and degenerate into a sad extinction. That was utterly unacceptable to her.

Here was an opportunity to fulfil her dream of motherhood, but with a Solarii? That wasn't how she'd envisaged it at all. Growing up, she'd learnt that sexual intercourse with a Solarii was a vile thing, worse than eating human flesh or defiling a sacred place. It echoed the tragedy of the seed, when as hornets the Helios stung Irit and the daughters of men against their will. Yet the Watchers' edict removed that prohibition. In the secret mansions of her soul, she still harboured the relics of the taboo.

What about the hybrids? What would happen to them when the flood came? And why were the Solarii and the hybrids perpetually vying with each other? Even the humans kept them at bay, erecting astral shields. She'd been brought up to fear them. *They're dangerous and unpredictable* was the mantra, though Jarda was anything but. He was canny and helpful. If anything, the Surge had appeared more in the hybrids than the humans. Now the Watchers had revoked the taboo, humans could make a fresh start with the hybrids – meaning she was free to help them survive the flood.

Then there was Protector Horque, a Solarii whose nobility seemed to transcend the taboo. From the moment she saw him striding out of that vapour cloud outside the cathedral, she'd felt an abiding affection and admiration for him.

She conjured him in her mind's eye. She liked the way his long earlobes protruded from his headdress. Oh, and that hook at the end of his nose, didn't it give his face a hawkish appearance? And his fingers? At first, she despised them; now she thought they were quirky and well, *different*.

If she couldn't choose him, perhaps he could choose her. She was sure he liked her. He hadn't made any everlasting declarations of love, but the Solarii didn't overtly display their feelings. There had been hints. When she'd gone to attend to Benjamin, and she'd stumbled on the floor, she'd sneaked a glance in his direction and there'd been a glint of emotion in his eye. In the Watchers' presence, he'd softened towards her, or so she'd imagined.

Then again, the Solarii could select Horque as their 'twice-born' groom. How was that possible? Everyone was born once, so this twice-born must be an attribute peculiar to the Solarii. Perhaps Horque was already twice-born. She didn't know. She sighed. The ramifications were too awful to contemplate.

"I'll stay out of it altogether," she murmured to herself. "I'll wait for another man. Someone else can volunteer. I'm a maiden, but it's not fair. It's not me."

CHAPTER 19

The Market Square

Arms folded, head held high, Horque stood on the deck. As the blue-green waters lapped against the barge, downriver a crocodile slunk into the river and glided towards him, menacing eyes above the waterline. After Samlios, everywhere eyes. Despite that, he held a grudging admiration for crocodiles. They were natural hybrids, as much at home on land as in water. Unlike the crocodile, he couldn't swim and had a morbid fear of drowning. He couldn't wait get off the barge.

A cry from the oarsman interrupted his contemplation.

"Make fast, fore and aft," he shouted to the men by the mooring bollards. The crew threw out the heavy securing ropes and the barge shuddered to a halt. On the quayside, an officious-looking man with a pallet and a scribing feather emerged from a rough wooden shed and limped towards the barge. Adjusting his headdress, he steadied his quill above the papyrus and cried in the general direction of the barge.

"Port of origin?"

"Karnak," Marim shouted back.

"Cargo?"

"I'm the cargo," Horque declared.

The man on the quay bowed reverently. "Protector, no one told me. They s-said you were in S-Samlios."

"I was. Now I'm here, waiting to disembark." The men lifted the gangplank into the air and dropped one end onto the barge.

Before he stepped onto it, Marim called to him.

"What are your orders regarding these?" he asked, lifting a flap of the canvas sheeting to reveal four Horus Wing craft, lying on their sides like lifeless lumps of black stone. They'd flown the craft without problems from Samlios for an audience in Karnak. With his report to Pharaoh Nimrod complete, Horque had wanted to return to Jizah, but the mental nexus failed to work on all four craft. He wasn't going to walk from Karnak. A crocodile could have swum faster than this barge.

"Take them to the Temple of Horus," he said. "The craft must be ready for the forthcoming voyage to the Whispering Tower." Before leaving Samlios, he'd arranged with Shamira to meet her there with the 'fair maiden'.

"Yes, Protector," Marim replied.

Horque strode down the gangplank. The solid ground felt good beneath his feet. He was a flyer, not a sailor, and three days of travelling downstream from Karnak along every twist and turn of the river had been tedious enough. With Tarsus carrying the luggage behind him, he set off down the well-trodden path.

They reached the edge of the market, which in the normal course of events would be bursting with Semite servants shopping for their Solarii masters, berating and bartering with the stallholders, and with Solarii going about their business. Today, though, stray dogs sniffed around the deserted stalls in the surrounding streets and alleys.

He entered a narrow street lined with more unmanned stalls. Near the end of the lane, a thick cloud of grey-white dust particles billowed like a sandstorm from the stonemason's yard. Emerging on the other side of the cloud, Horque wiped the dust from his face and shook his headdress. The limestone dust tasted acrid. He reached into his pocket for a cloth and as he walked on, Tarsus called to him.

"Protector, this fell from your pocket," his servant said, bending down to retrieve a silk cloth.

"Don't touch it," Horque barked, recognising it straight away. He picked it up, opened the leaves of the cloth, and breathed a sigh of relief. Then he placed it back in his breast pocket and patted it twice. He needed this particular item, and he didn't want anyone else to touch it.

A long line of Semite servants carrying bags and luggage passed in front of him, blocking his path and forcing him to wait. A rich palanquin was coming: he could smell hints of rose fragrance, a deliciously arresting perfume, before it arrived. Four burly men in flowing white robes carried the chair, which had an elaborate awning to protect the woman inside from the prying glances of the masses. Through a small opening, he caught a glimpse of the Solarii woman. She reclined amongst a liberal sprinkling of laced cushions. Catching his eye, she shut the awning with haughty indifference.

As Horque looked away, his eyes met those of a young Semite girl who held the train of the awning. Her rounded face made him think of the full moon. Her tawny eyes had such a bright glint to them. She had a long, slender neck, a dancer's neck found in women with great poise and elegance of movement. She threw him a smile of such innocence that he took an involuntary step back.

He held out a hand and cried out, "Akasha!"

The girl threw him a look of fleeting surprise as she followed the palanquin around the corner. The remaining Semite servants passed in front of him until they too disappeared from his sight.

His heart raced and his face burnt. Feeling light-headed, he leant back against the wall, trying to gather his thoughts. A sudden longing to see Akasha swamped his mind. It was an ache he'd never felt before. These were feelings, unusual and alien.

The tawny-eyed girl was a Semite servant. That was what had made the likeness so close, and why her swarthy looks had affected him. Besides, Akasha was from Samlios, so what demon of coincidence had conspired to present him with a Semite girl who resembled her like a twin?

With his back hard against the wall, he glanced down at Tarsus, who stared back. His servant's face was blurred and hazy, like in a dream. His mouth was opening and closing but no sounds came out of it. In slow and gradual succession, his senses returned and Tarsus' words faded into his hearing.

"Are you all right? What's the matter?"

"I…I just need to catch my breath," Horque murmured.

The lingering smell of the woman's perfume stung his nostrils again, rousing him from his stupor. How did he make sense of this sudden feeling for Akasha? There was a real passion, yes. When he first saw her double, it was as if he had stepped over some invisible boundary in himself. He felt warm, vibrant and jubilant. The emotional connection between him and Akasha was unlike anything he'd ever felt in his life. He knew about living; he was discovering loving.

All was not well in the main market. A crowd of jeering Semites surrounded two Solarii, who were standing back-to-back on a dais. Arar, the head scribe, was one and Irex, the giant, was the other. Javian and some other Solarii guards stood watchfully around the perimeter of the market. Horque drew alongside Javian to listen.

Scroll in hand, feet shuffling nervously, Arar appeared to be making a proclamation, which the Semites' heckles were drowning out.

"We'll never survive now," one called out.

"They've betrayed us," another cried angrily.

"This is the sacred decree of Pharaoh Nimrod. Semites, heed it well," Arar shouted. "Long may you live under the pharaoh's mantle."

The crowd hissed and booed. They clearly did not like the decree.

"What was the proclamation about?" Horque asked Javian.

"The Semites asked the pharaoh to provide them with safe haven from the flood, or else release them from their service so they can find somewhere for themselves. The pharaoh has refused. We need the help of the Semites to survive the flood," Javian replied. "You can see it's enraged them."

Horque had suspected as much. The Semites were a difficult people to deal with, but they were honest and hard-working. At the very least, they deserved a modicum of assistance from their Solarii masters. If he'd been pharaoh, he'd have granted it.

When he'd met the pharaoh three days previously, Nimrod had failed to inform him of this proclamation, and that was a deliberate slight. Horque was protector, why hadn't he been told? To find out from a mere underling was humiliating.

The Semites shouted their opinions.

"Abandoned to the flood, we're no longer welcome here. Let's leave. Now!"

The crowd roared its approval until a Semite woman reminded them that they could not.

"The astral shield," she pointed out. "It keeps the hybrids in Dudael, but it also keeps us in Egypt. We're stuck here."

That reminder incensed the already ugly crowd. Someone threw a vegetable at Arar, which hit him on the shoulder and dropped down by his feet. Arar kicked it off the podium and it struck the Semite woman in the eye. This act was a spark to dry tinder. The crowd bayed at the scribe like a pack of hyenas. Suddenly it was raining rubbish as they threw whatever they could lay their hands on at him. With no cover on the podium, Arar and Irex crouched, covering their heads with their hands.

No matter how much Horque sympathised with the Semites' plight, this was an offence against Ma'at.

"Come with me," he barked at Javian, and pushed his way through the crowd.

As he arrived at the platform steps, a stone thrown from the crowd hit Arar in the face and a trickle of blood oozed from his lip. Irex unsheathed his ankh. Holding it by the pointed end, he used it as a healing device to seal the cut on Arar's face. No sooner had he finished than he reversed his grip on the ankh, now grasping it as a weapon by the looped end, and took aim at the heart of the crowd.

CHAPTER 20

Ocean Voyage

Arms outstretched, Akasha hung over the stern of the boat. She felt surrounded by the vast expanse of ocean, pale jade in the morning light. The wind whipped up a spray that splashed against her face and arms. The boards creaked and the sails flapped against the rigging in the cool, refreshing breeze. The crew exchanged friendly cries as the ship made headway towards the Port of Irun and their eventual destination, the Whispering Tower.

Although sad to leave her home, she felt elated by the stark beauty and constant ebb and flow of the ocean. The lore of the sea had shaped Demos in a way she was only just beginning to appreciate. Now she knew what caused that effervescent glint in his eyes. The sea had etched its ways on him. In return, he'd surrendered to the high and wise and mighty in its ways, which became his ways in a different kind of union.

Despite the ship pitching and yawing into the seas, she'd rapidly acquired her sea legs, even though their self-enforced exile from the Isle of Samlios was only four days old.

A whistling, singing sound caught her attention. Demos pointed out a pod of fifteen dolphins playing and dancing in the wake of the ship's bow wave, making a series of high-pitched clicks.

"Look!" she cried. The creatures leapt from just behind the bow wave, hung in the spray in the air and dived with aplomb back into the water just in front of it. As if in rapturous applause, the rest of the pod made loud clicking and whistling sounds. They all joined in the fun, leaping and playing follow-my-leader, swimming with ease alongside the boat and diving under it and reappearing on the other side with a momentous leap into the air, twisting and turning in delight at their acrobatic skills.

"I love their sense of freedom," Demos enthused. "The way they belong to the sea, and the way the sea belongs to them."

Demos had ushered her through an invisible door in the great mansion of her life, revealing a new room.

"I want to belong to something like they do, and like you do," she told him. "I want to belong to something that gives as much joy. I want to join the purpose of my life. It must give you such strength to know yours."

"I thought you'd already done that?"

"I know everyone thinks that, but I still have doubts."

"There's no room for doubts. You can give the human race a future. All you have to do is to volunteer for this union with a twice-born Solarii."

"I know...but there's the taboo."

"No," he said. "There's no taboo. The Watchers have washed it away. It doesn't exist anymore. What you have to do now is remove it in yourself."

"I'm trying," she murmured.

"I was present when the Watchers endorsed a union between a twice-born Solarii and a fair maiden."

"What do you mean?"

"I mean that the precise moment the Watchers manifested in the cathedral was most telling. The Watchers are a divine agency, they inhabit the highest and brightest part of the astral light. They are the illuminati. For them to appear anywhere on Earth, they have to be summoned by a special need. You called, and they responded."

"Me? When did I call for them to come?" She furrowed her brow.

"Something high and unique passed between you and Horque. Everyone felt it and saw it though their whites. Everyone except you, that is."

"It was a glorious feeling, one I'll never forget." Akasha sighed at the memory.

"I'll tell you what happened, because you don't seem to have realised. The Watchers came when a feeling of genuine love passed between a human woman and a Solarii man. It was a rare and sublime passion. In that moment, the taboo was finally and irrevocably broken. They didn't endorse a union of any Solarii and maiden: they endorsed you and Horque. That's the union the Watchers want."

She was speechless. Demos' words had shaken her to the depths of her being.

"Think carefully about what I've said."

Demos was right – as usual. Her heart fluttered like a butterfly's wings. Her and Horque. It was possible then, especially if the Watchers had said so.

The seas were getting choppy and the dolphins' whistles reached a crescendo. It was as if the dolphins were trying to tell them something. Fists clenched, Akasha stood in silence. Frustration stewed inside her. She was desperate for a child, yet the only way was with a Solarii.

"These issues are woven thick like a rope," Demos said.

She nodded.

Demos sucked on his breath. "The singing and the whistling, they've stopped. The dolphins have vanished."

"No, they've just gone below the waves," she replied, casting a wary eye across the heavy seas. "They'll return in a moment."

"No," Demos was adamant. "There's a gale blowing." His face darkened. "I've seen this before."

"Where? When?"

"It's dangerous for you to stay on deck. Please, go to your cabin."

"Tell me. What is it?" she insisted, but he was already leaving.

"I must get to the bridge. Get below, now. I'm ordering you."

The sails beat against the timber masts. Akasha's stomach plunged and rose with the rough swell. She swallowed hard on a dry throat. On the horizon, she saw a long finger of dark cloud descending from the sky waters. It danced in the air, swaying first one way, then the other. The finger of moisture thickened into a swollen arm, reaching down from the sky waters to the surging seas below.

The winds whistled through the rigging. Near the bridge, Demos shouted orders. The low tolling of a bell rang through the ship, urgent and insistent, and the crew swarmed onto the deck. Some clambered up the rigging; others pulled hard on ropes and tackle.

A wave crashed against the little ship and covered her in a fine film of vapour. The skies had darkened: she could barely see her hands in front of her. The brooding cloud on the horizon had broadened into a murky funnel.

The waterspout raised the hackles on her neck. There were footsteps coming her way. Searching for somewhere to hide, she slid down inside a large rope coil. Demos hurled more orders at the crew, his gruff voice rising and falling amidst the billowing wind and rain.

"Batten down the hatches. Prepare for the fight of our lives."

Men clambered up the mast, unfurled the remaining sail, and changed the tack of the others. The spiral of winds was sucking the ship into its fatal grasp. Akasha burrowed down in the rope hollow and peered anxiously through the slits between the ropes. The waterspout was a huge, spinning column of water. The waves were larger, higher and deeper, as they rose and fell to the rhythm of the twisting winds around the base of the funnel.

Her stomach ached from the swell. She should have followed Demos' orders and gone to her cabin. Too late: now she had to stay where she was. Her hands shook, partly from cold, mostly from fear. The howls and whistling of the wind muffled all other sounds.

An ocean swell tipped the top of the rope coil over her. It was saturated and heavy. She struggled to lift it off her. The waves hit the ship broadside as more ropes uncoiled and buried her. The deck tilted one way, then another. There were the creaking sounds of barrels, tackle, ropes, cargo, crew, anything not battened down, sliding backwards and forwards across the deck, crashing into each other, smashing into the wooden railings.

Another huge wave crashed against the hull, drenching her in freezing spray and foam. The rope hollow acted like a bucket. In a flash, the swirling torrent deluged her, forcing her against the side, banging her chin. The waters rose over her. She swallowed a mouthful and spat it out. Trapped by the ropes on top of her, she was drowning. Then suddenly the waters drained through the slits in the rope coil. She gasped for air, for life.

"Help me!" she yelled. But could anyone hear her above the roar of the tempest?

Her body convulsed with the cold and the wet. Her eyes stung with salt. The sodden ropes bore down on her legs and chest, stifling her breathing. Fear sucked the breath from her. She felt the cold stare of death upon her soul. She felt like an unborn child in a womb, roped by an umbilical cord and drowned in waters. Suspended in a giant vortex, she felt her life ebbing away, drop by drop, with such ease that it felt like the greatest kindness anyone could ever do to her, and the simplest thing in the world to accept. It was so subtle and painless. It was liberating.

It was the ultimate choice – live or die. She could leave this world or stay and fight for her life, and for the human race.

CHAPTER 21

Promise and Compromise

Irex was about to unleash the ankh weapon when Horque pushed down on his forearm, forcing it to the ground.

"Sheath it," he hissed.

Irex obeyed.

"Semites," Horque roared, trying to win their attention. "Listen to me!"

The marketplace hushed. They'd witnessed him lower Irex's firing arm and save Semite lives. He'd earned a respite, but not for long. In Samlios, he'd learnt how not to deal with humans. There was no point going in head first like a hippopotamus. Far better the cunning of a fox and the guile of the owl.

A Semite man broke the silence.

"The pharaoh has disowned us. We're nothing to him. We're finished with Egypt."

This rallying call promoted a ripple of support until a woman urged quiet. "Protector Horque's returned from the Mind Search," she said. "He's talked to humans there. Let's listen to what he has to say."

Horque turned full circle, trying to impose his presence on the crowd. A thousand pairs of confused, defiant eyes stared back at him from beneath a sea of skullcaps. Whatever happened, he had to prevent the Semites from leaving Egypt. The Solarii depended on their labour and domestic service. Without it, the Twin Lands would cease to function.

"Semites, nothing can change the pharaoh's decree," he cried. "So why not find other ways to survive the coming deluge?"

"Such as?" the women shouted.

"Building a sea craft. You can sail into the next epoch."

There were murmurs of agreement, and the furious nodding of heads. At the

119

base of the steps, Tarsus called up to him, "That may be, Protector, but will the pharaoh grant us leave to work on a boat?"

"You don't need his permission," he replied, "because you have mine. I offer you this contract in the name of the Egypt and the pharaoh, and it shall remain in force as long as I live. In this matter, my word is his word."

He waited as a ripple of whispers rustled across the crowd. Tarsus shouted back, "Will anyone be punished for today's indiscretions?"

Horque was that close to achieving his goal.

"Loyal Semites, I offer all of you immunity from prosecution for any offences committed today. In return, you must pledge to stay in Egypt and build a sea craft. Accept this deal, lay down your anger, and return to your homes in peace."

A ripple of applause broke out and the crowd started to disperse. His aim achieved with no bloodshed, Horque resumed his journey home. Tarsus followed in silence, wearing a determined look that spoke of both fright and elation.

Even so, Horque felt conflicted. He'd prevented the slaughter of loyal Semites and halted their mass exodus from the Twin Lands. The end was laudable. It was the means that troubled him. The gross irreverence of the Semites had disturbed the peace of Ma'at and deserved the stiffest punishment. Under normal circumstances, he would never have stayed Irex's hand. So why had he? Compassion? What was that to a Solarii? Was he going soft? No, it was simple expediency. Without compromise, there was no future.

There was more. He had feelings for a human woman. That was potentially catastrophic. Beguiled by the soft, human qualities of mercy and meekness, he would lose his Solarii nature. If he did, he'd fall victim to the first of the Twin Perils, a soulful attachment to the beauty of the planet Earth and her people. At the moment of death, the attachment would prevent his soul from crossing the Winding Waterway.

Despite such a dire threat, an early sense of love stirred in him, like a bud forming on a spring flower. He'd never before experienced such tender feelings. This excitement and head-spinning frenzy were far from the stern rigour and unbending stoicism to which he was accustomed. He reminded himself of who he was. I am Horque, Eye of Horus, Protector of the Pharaoh and His People, Guardian of the Pyramid Field. Holding up his fingers, he stared at them. They've not changed. They're still all the same length. I am Solarii. That was how he had been born and that was how he'd die.

Finally, he reached his residence. Pausing outside, he uttered a silent prayer of thanks to Isis for seeing him home safely. Then he strode through the gates and breached his own threshold for the first time in seven days.

The familiar smells, colours and objects filled his mind with an exquisite sense of satisfaction. This was unusual; in the normal course of events, he felt no twinge of emotion. His home was a place to lay his head, not a shrine for living. Entering the water court, he looked at it as if for the first time – the stark beauty of the four hawk-headed statues of Horus, the elegance of his carved chair with hawk motifs, and the soothing comfort of the cool alabaster floors.

His mother looked majestic, wearing a black sapphire necklace that matched her black locks. Her first question was straight to the point.

"Who's this twice-born?"

"The pharaoh. He's the groom in this surprising union," he replied.

"I could've told you that would happen." She was full of her usual self-assurance. "How did it come about?"

"Cheiron pointed out that Nimrod, following his victory in the Festival of the Gods, became the pharaoh and a god. His ascension to the throne is akin to a rebirth."

"Making him the twice-born. How convenient." Issa frowned. "And the humans' 'fair maiden'?"

"I'm to collect her from the Whispering Tower."

"I trust the bride they send us will be strong enough to bear the Solarii seed," she said wryly.

"She will be. There's only one able to produce a child before the deluge."

"How is she named?"

"Akasha, and on my way here I saw a girl in the market who resembled her."

"What is she like, this Akasha?"

"She's young, confident and decidedly capable. Here, I'll show you." He pulled out the silk cloth from his pocket and placed it on the table. Opening its leaves, he revealed a white bone amulet, styled into the form of a cobra with its coiled body, forked tongue and open hood. "This is hers," he declared, with an air of triumph.

She took it in her hand and closed her eyes. After a while, she raised her eyebrows.

"The owner of this necklace has a destiny that's entwined with yours, which you well know. That is why you are attracted to her – you can't help yourself. Now she is promised to Nimrod. When you travel to the Whispering Tower, do not be distracted in the execution of your duty."

His mother was right. There was more at play than his personal feelings. Destiny? What destiny?

"In the astral light, much is clouded by the uncertainties of the times," she added. "Ever since I heard of it, I've contemplated the Watchers' edict. And from it, I've conceived a great venture for you."

"For me? What is it?" A Sekmet priestess, his mother's astral arts were as good if not better than Cheiron's, who was the chief astral master of the court.

"It's too early to say." She shook her head. "First, I need to fashion the future. Then I will reveal more of it to you."

As she stalked from the court, he wondered what she was going to conjure, but soon his weary thoughts drifted in and out of the events of the past seven days. Ever since he'd planted his foot on firm ground that morning, it seemed he'd succumbed to a maelstrom of events, ending with his mother coaxing out of him the true extent of his burgeoning feelings for a human girl.

The bone cobra necklace: that was where it had started, and that was where it ended. That morning he'd guarded it with his life. Now he wished he'd left it where he'd found it.

Other than that, the Semites were on the brink of rebellion. The Solarii needed a miracle to meet the Watchers' requirements to end their exile. The deluge was imminent. In six days, he'd travel to the Whispering Tower to collect the fair maiden.

He pulled himself up out of the chair and walked out of the court, leaving the cobra necklace on the table.

By the will of Horus and with a little help from his mother, he'd rise above it all.

Chapter 22

The Rebuke

The ropes bore heavily on her chest as the rain lashed down. She was trapped, frozen, and sodden from head to toe. She swallowed mouthfuls of water as the level rose, then fell.

"Akasha!" Someone was calling her name. She saw lights above the rope coil.

"Here!" she cried, wincing with the effort.

A woman's voice shouted, "She's under the ropes. Quick!"

A hand reached down and lifted the rope bundle from her battered body.

She blacked out.

Akasha awoke, groggy and aching. A man with a distinctive salty smell was carrying her in his arms down a murky corridor. Through a film of pain, she opened her eyes. Demos cradled her like a baby and laid her down somewhere soft. Shamira gently held the back of her neck and dabbed a damp cloth over her face.

"Are you all right?" the pythoness asked.

"Yes, I think so." Akasha flinched as she moved her chest and lay back down again.

"Lie still." Shamira's voice was full of comfort.

"What happened?"

"A water spout," Demos said. "Ever since the great winds, they appear so quickly. This one almost swallowed us whole and spat us out the other side."

"It was Demos' expert seamanship that saved the day," Shamira added. "What damage did we suffer?"

Demos wiped his forehead with a kerchief. "Apart from shipping a lot of water, the little damage we sustained can be repaired, with good will and strong intent."

"A bit like me, then," Akasha said.

At least Shamira smiled at her attempt at self-effacement. Demos was less impressed.

"Oh, and I realised something about the dolphins' cries and whistles," Akasha said. "They were trying to warn us about the water spout."

"Aye." Demos nodded begrudgingly. "You may be right on that one. But my crew got us through this escapade by following my orders, which is more than I can say for you, young lady."

She managed a coy look in advance of the rebuke she knew was coming.

"You ignored my order to go below decks and you nearly paid with your life," he said, his voice a mix of despair and worry. "When you're on board my ship, you will follow my orders – and never take refuge inside a rope coil again. If the top of it slides off, it can crush you or shear off a limb."

She nodded. "I promise."

"Good, that's done with, then." Demos stood up to leave. "Now, I'm going to sail this ship to the Port of Irun in six days. Don't doubt that for a moment."

As Demos passed her bedside, Akasha grabbed him by the wrist and looked him in the eye.

"I'm sorry, Demos." She had to admit she was wrong and he was right – again.

"And so you should be," Demos said, emotion getting the better of him. "I was very worried about you. I love you like a daughter. You're not only important to Shamira and me, you're important to all of us. Don't play with your life. It's not yours to play with."

"I'm beginning to realise that," she said, while wondering how the right kind of rebuke could make a person feel better.

"You must get some rest," Shamira said.

Her eyes closed and she fell into a dream. A round moon cast long shadows over a desolate landscape. Alone and frightened, she followed a winding road towards a solitary tower. As she was about to enter, a flash of lightning struck the tower, engulfing it in orange flame. She rushed on, past the flaming tower until she reached the edge of a precipice. Siren voices beckoned to her from the abyss.

"Come, leave the pain and injustice of the world behind."

She was tempted. She could end it in a moment, a breath. Life was so confusing and death so simple. In the midst of the maelstrom, an inner voice called to her, "Your life isn't yours to throw away. Fulfil its great promise."

Girding herself, she turned away from the abyss and retraced her steps, past the stricken tower.

When she awoke, she felt a fresh vitality coursing through her veins. That life-affirming act filled her with strength and fortitude. The Surge was paramount. That was the Watchers' edict. Regardless of her personal feelings, she resolved to do whatever it took to rescue the Surge, and with it, the human race.

CHAPTER 23

Mother of the Future

Six days later, Akasha stepped off Demos' ship into a wall of rapturous applause from the townsfolk of Irun. Colourful flags and pennants decorated every nook and cranny of the tiny port. Surrounding her on the quayside, the boisterous crowd threw their skullcaps in the air and cheered her with wild abandon. How did they even know who she was? But they did, and they weren't shy in their welcome. People patted her on the back and pushed bouquets of flowers into her hands. They were not only with her in spirit, they'd resolved to join her and Demos in their trek up to higher ground.

Those six days since the rope coil had been especially productive. The incident had drawn a shroud from her eyes, allowing her an uninterrupted view of her life, which now felt connected to a promising future. Her close brush with the spectre of death hadn't shaken her resolve. On the contrary, after Demos' talk, she was determined to take her place alongside Horque in the union ceremony.

Soon after disembarking, they began the long trek to the Whispering Tower and the High Pyrenes. From the mountain plateau, the sky waters appeared menacingly close. The mass of water was almost still, with little or no circulation. Akasha peered up into the muted reflection of her own world and its shimmering palette of colours: brown-specked hills, emerald green forests and the copper yellows of the plain. She was staring at a gigantic floating mirror.

"Welcome to my land," Demos said. He made a sweeping movement with his hand that introduced the flat terrain, and beyond that a vista of snow-capped mountains and broad, plunging valleys that surrounded the plateau on all sides.

"Look over here." Demos pointed at a tower some distance away, its peak shrouded in low mist and cloud. "That's the Whispering Tower, my home."

125

As they approached, the mists cleared to reveal a spindly tower that reared up like a granite finger towards the sky waters. The fresh mountain air was invigorating.

"It's a sight to behold!" She'd never seen the like of it, though she'd heard talk of it. Just before they reached it, Demos showed her another village on a second hillock, several leagues farther on, which he called Avesta.

A group of people emerged from the village at the base of the Whispering Tower. One of them waved and yelled. "Father! Father!"

The resemblance was obvious: the burly physique, the bright look in the eye, the craggy chin, and even the same exuberant, overbearing manner.

"Tamir," Demos called out. "Let me see you."

While Demos embraced his son, the villagers welcomed the others in their party, their cries filling the afternoon air with the warmth of safe homecoming.

"Please show our guests to their quarters," Demos said, his green eyes shining with joy. "When everyone's rested, we'll meet and parlay."

This was no time to rest. At once, Akasha turned to Tamir and asked him to take her to the top of the tower.

"You youngsters, remember this is no ordinary tower!" Demos shouted after them.

But they were gone, climbing the scores of steps to the pinnacle. On each landing was an opening that gave onto the outward vista, with fleeting glimpses of the mysterious Avesta and the surrounding mountains, the green swathe of the plateau, and the ocean beyond.

Enjoying walking up the spiral stairwell, Akasha felt goosebumps on her skin as they reached the higher, chillier parts of the tower. Soon enough they attained the summit, a round gallery enclosed by a crenellated parapet. In the centre was an enormous bell, dark as the colour of earth after rain, its surface as smooth as a placid mountain lake. But her main impression was one of profound stillness.

Tamir walked her over towards the edge of the parapet and they stood next to an opening. She felt giddy just standing there, hardly daring to look down. Holding his hand, she ventured near the opening and peered downwards. The drop seemed to go on forever. There were even wisps of cloud below her. Circling the tower was a murder of crows, their raucous squawks an intrusion from a nearby hostile world.

High, fluffy clouds mingled with snow-capped mountains that strode into the horizon like frozen giants. The jade-green sea looked like a pond. A sublime sense of freedom snaked up her spine.

Behind her, someone spoke. Akasha swivelled round, but there was no one there. Then to her right, someone else said something; again, she turned, but there was no one. There were many voices, speaking in a jumble of words and phrases. It reminded her of holding a conch shell to her ear. Yet this was the tower, and there were only the two of them here. She was confused, and her confusion deepened when Tamir grinned at her.

"What's happening?" She frowned. "I hear murmurs, people speaking in faint voices. When I look around, there's just a row of empty seats around the parapet."

"That's the mystery of the Whispering Tower." Tamir bent close to her and spoke softly. "From this gallery, they say you can hear fragments of every conversation in the world."

Although deeply impressed with the tower, it had set off a different train of thoughts about high places. Savor the Andean had said they were nearer to the Source. Akasha's thoughts were slow enough for her to glimpse the gentle flight of their passing shadows. Her soul whispered to her. It wanted her to stay here, not just for the near future, but forever.

She had to survive the flood somewhere. Here she felt protected. She was tempted to stay, but she'd promised to marry a Solarii. What to do? Where to go? It was all so confusing.

Across the plateau, she noticed a flash of movement – white and tawny – in the adjacent village, Avesta. It was a bird, or was it?

"Tamir?" she said, alarmed. The bird glided around the base of the tower in a wide circle. Its broad wings caught the updraught and it spiralled towards them.

"Don't be scared. It's only Strata," he said.

"Strata? It's a hybrid?"

"*She's* a hybrid. Avesta is the bird village."

"I should've known," she said.

Strata reached the height of the tower and glided with serene power above them. She was a magnificent eagle, with tawny-white feathers on her wings, mighty talons, and markings on her breast. With the head of a human woman, she had beady eagle eyes and a crooked beak, high cheekbones, a dark complexion and pointed ears. Tamir waved at her and the hybrid bird tipped her wing, and then soared on an updraught and disappeared into the misty clouds.

There were lycans in Samlios, but a bird hybrid was something new. Besides, Strata was friendly and it was clear she was a good neighbour to Tamir and the villagers.

Akasha turned back to the gallery to find people coming through the door and taking their seats around the edge of the parapet. Demos and Shamira commanded the centre.

"Welcome, everyone," Demos said. He told them all about the Mind Search: the wonder of the Crystal Cathedral, the propitious arrival of the Solarii, the pharaoh's proposal and the miracle of the Watchers' visitation.

Shamira spoke with her customary authority.

"Friends," she began. "The Watchers' edict endorsed a union between a twice-born Solarii and a 'fair maiden daughter of man'. We have agreed a bride to represent the human race. I'm honoured to present Akasha of the dance of the winds."

The audience cheered and burst into rousing applause. All eyes on her, Akasha joined Shamira at the centre of the gallery. Her heart was racing. She felt awed by the audience and the glory of the setting: the tower, the sky waters, the whispering and the plateau.

The admission she was about to make was deeply significant, not just for her, but for the future of the human race. A little voice whispered in her ear, words Shamira had once told her.

We humans never fully comprehend the significance of our acts until much later. Through the fullness of time, we can reflect in the evening light and see the shadows of the events in which we've participated.

There were no shadows here. This was real. This was in the full light of day. Everyone bore witness. At one of the highest points in the world, nearest to the Source, perhaps he'd hear her admission.

Around her were her friends, expectant and ecstatic. Shamira held her hands in prayer. Uriah's face glowed with happiness. Thera clapped her hands with joy. Old man Panion mumbled to himself. Demos was as inscrutable as ever, staunch and robust in his support. If only Tros the Gatekeeper and Callisto could have attended, her circle of joy would have been complete. She'd filled all of these people's lives with the mystery and grace of her life and they'd reciprocated in kind. They were her kind, her companions through life. They would stand by her. Because of them, she felt as immovable as the mountain and as indestructible as the Whispering Tower.

The adulation of the people around her shone out of their eyes. A human-Solarii union meant continuance for them, for their kind, for humanity. Something ancient coursed through their veins. Yes, this moment harked back to the very beginning, when the child of man took its first faltering steps on Earth. Her admission was part of that long, arduous, but joyful journey, the epic human saga. That was what wanted continuance: the human who was as old and primordial as the Earth. She, Akasha, would give it.

"I accept this great honour. I stand here before you as a willing and able volunteer, to marry the twice-born Solarii, whoever that may be. The Watchers' will be done."

The background murmurings went quiet. All was silent. Even the sky waters stopped rumbling.

"The whispering's ceased," Shamira said, startled.

"I never thought I'd see the day." Demos arched his eyebrows. "Garios, my father, once told me it can happen, but it's never done so in my lifetime. The tower can, he said, not only receive words and phrases but in rare circumstances, transmit them as well. Akasha's admission has been sent on angels' wings all around the world, to anyone with ears to hear."

"Your commitment is clear for all," Shamira confirmed.

The audience stood up as one and cheered. Tamir and Thera went round each person with an amphora and filled up their beakers with water.

"The liquid in your beakers is sacred water," Demos explained. "We garnered each drop at dawn from the sky waters and retained them especially for this wondrous occasion. Because, my friends, we're about to celebrate a betrothal made in heaven by drinking the dew of heaven.

"A toast to Akasha, mother of our future!" Demos cried.

"Mother of our future!"

CHAPTER 24

The Gates of Gades

For Horque, the six days since the fraught incident with the Semites had passed like clouds scudding across a windswept sky. News of the mercy and compassion he'd shown reverberated amongst Semites and Solarii alike. Then the rumours came that he'd returned from Samlios a changed man and was now an avowed Semite sympathiser. More damaging still was the accusation, which no doubt could be traced back to Zoser or Nimrod himself, that by agreeing to allow the Semites to build a boat he'd flouted the pharaoh's decree.

Alarmed that this wave of slurs might culminate in some gratuitous act of revenge, he was relieved that by the morning of his flight to the Whispering Tower, nothing had transpired. Even his mother was wary.

"My son," Issa said, "be careful on this voyage. I fear the worst."

"Fear nothing. I've been to Samlios and come back," he said. "The Whispering Tower is closer, the journey less hazardous. I shall return. I promise."

"Then go with the speed of Horus," she said, "and bring back the pharaoh's bride."

Everyone in the world knew that was Akasha. He tried to be indifferent to this fact, but on hearing her name next to that of the pharaoh, a drop of disappointment bled from his resolve.

He made his way to the Temple of Horus, where his own craft and the other three damaged ones were undergoing repair. In the outer temple precincts, Marim, Khephren and Lasec were standing in animated conversation. As he approached, they neither noticed him nor turned to greet him, which was unusual. Under normal circumstances, Solarii hearing was as acute as a hyena's on a still night. When they eventually saw him, Marim and Lasec shuffled to uneasy attention.

"Protector, greetings," Marim exclaimed. "Are you here to bid us farewell?"

"No," he replied, shaking his head. "Why are you surprised to see me? Aren't you accompanying me? Your three craft are ready for flight. So where's mine?"

There was an awkward pause. Marim stared at the ground, showing appropriate contrition.

"There was a message," he muttered, clearly embarrassed.

"Tell me," Horque growled. He smelt something rank. This was either Nimrod's work, or that of his minion, Zoser.

"Your Isis authority to travel to the Whispering Tower has been revoked," Marim said.

"I see." Horque grunted. He couldn't cross the boundary stele of Egypt without the authority of Isis, the Goddess of Travellers. "The Isis Pass was only granted ten days ago in Karnak. This is an unprecedented turn of events."

"That's what we were discussing," Marim replied, shifting uneasily.

Words were portals of power that could allow or forbid, promote or deny. They were exact and definite, like the sacred spelling of a hieroglyph. He replayed Marim's words in his mind and asked, "Which seal did the message bear?"

Marim appeared to be trying to remember. "Why is that important?"

"The pharaoh issued the Isis authority to me, so only he, and not Vizier Zoser, can revoke it."

"I-I," Marim stammered.

"Let me remind you of the code. Should you err in a matter such as this, it would constitute an offence against Ma'at. Lasec will remind you of what happened to Berux, in case you've forgotten. So I ask you again, what was the seal on the message?"

"I'm trying to recall." Marim's legs were trembling.

"If the message bore the seal of the crossed crook and flail, I am the pharaoh's loyal servant and will accept his revocation. If it bore the seal of the office of the vizier, then I shall respectfully decline the order and proceed with the voyage as planned. Therefore, I ask you for a third and last time, which seal did the message bear?"

Marim wiped a bead of sweat from his forehead. Under such duress, he appeared to be struggling to recall.

"Protector," Khephren intervened, a balm amidst the storm, "I saw the message. It bore the seal of the white feather."

"Yes, yes, I remember now," Marim said. He sounded elated that he could finally acquit himself properly. "It did. I can confirm that."

"That's what I thought," Horque said.

"By Horus, I'll deal with Zoser and his pathetic message on my return. In the meantime, bring out my craft. I'll brook no further delay." He waited under the thin shadow of the temple housing as Marim went inside. A short while later, Marim returned.

"Excellency, the repairers have fixed three of the craft."

"I can see that. They've had six days to do so. Now where's mine? Bring it out. Now." He struggled to stop his temper from fraying.

"Excellency," Marim replied, cowering, "on receiving the message, they stopped the final repairs. The craft is ready to fly, but it lacks fine-tuning. To fly it in such a state would court bad luck."

"Pah! Luck is a phantom that lurks in the shadows. The true light of Ma'at burns it off. Do not talk of luck again."

"Y-yes, Excellency." Marim failed to hide the reluctance in his tone. He fingered his sacred amulet, mouthing silent prayers and imprecations.

"We must leave," Horque said. "Prepare the craft."

They were soon in flight, Horque in the lead, leaving behind these ridiculous political machinations. They reached the wide expanse of the Middle Sea and followed the coastline westwards. Below him were the smooth contours of the land; low, rolling hills sprinkled with sparking rivers, while herds of wild animals crossed verdant plains. Such fecundity.

He spotted the Gates of Gades, marking the point where the land of Afri to the south kissed the Great Northern Continent. On either side of the narrow channel, the Solarii had long ago built an obelisk, tall, slender needles of limestone, full of carved protective hieroglyphics. Their copper and zinc sleeves reflected the rays of the sun, creating a curtain of astral energy between the two obelisks that extended far beyond them. This curtain was the invisible barrier that prevented any prowling hybrid from intruding into Solarii territory, and was part of the many shields and protections around the world that confined the hybrids to Dudael.

As they turned north towards the Pyrenes Mountains, a piercing scream and a searing flash of light rent the air. One of the predatory hybrid birds had ventured too close to the astral curtain and paid for the mistake with its life.

As it vaporised against the astral shield, a burst of luminescence struck Marim, whose craft plummeted out of the sky like a stone. Horque followed him down, the two craft tumbling earthwards, neck and neck, vapour trails spiralling behind them. The ferocious rush of air tore at his face. His stomach ached, and he swallowed down his own vomit. A copse of trees shot into his peripheral vision. The ground was approaching fast. He must pull out of the fall soon, or perish. He had to save Marim.

He summoned every iota of the power of his mind to take control of his deputy's craft. With sheer strength of will, he brought both craft to a shuddering halt in mid-air. His craft tipped over and he faced the ground. Only the leather straps kept him from a fatal fall.

Slowly, he righted his craft. Next to him, Marim rubbed his eyes. Relief and fear gripped Horque in equal measure as he felt something brush against his feet. A swathe of greenery shimmered below him. Leaves and twigs. His craft was hovering above the crown of a tree.

With a nod of thanks, Marim took back control of his own Horus Wing and guided his craft to rejoin the other two flyers. Horque remained hovering above the tree to say a quiet prayer to Osiris and Anubis, dread Gods of the Underworld. You won't claim me yet.

Barely a stone's throw in front of him, where the bird hybrid had been vaporised, was a small rent in the astral shield. Just behind it, on the other side, a flock of birds was marauding. They were no ordinary birds, but rapacious hybrids, a glut of terrible aerial monsters with broad, strong eagles' wings, talons as sharp as a lion's, long, thin mouths and sharp, cutting teeth. Suddenly, the flock dived towards the rent, squeezing through it like malevolent children emerging from the fertile womb of a demonic mother.

Before he could take evasive action, the screeching flock was upon him, full of raucous fury. With a death-defying cry, the first killer smashed into the side of his craft, severing the exhaust system, releasing a grey-white gas cloud into the atmosphere. The shock tore through Horque's body, a wave of mind-numbing pain. Shunted sideways with great force, the leather straps seared and burnt the skin of his chest.

The monster rammed his craft, shoving it headlong through the air. The straps snapped. The force of the movement threw him into the air, turning and twisting. Smoke billowed, stinging his nostrils. His mind was shredded, his body hot like fire. For an instant, he hung in mid-air, suspended between dear life and grim death.

Below him, a gigantic explosion billowed up from the ground as his craft smashed into the earth. A plume of red fire shot into the air, scorching his back. The pain was excruciating. As he reached the zenith of his arc of upward movement, a second bird smashed into him, its mouth agape, tearing his flesh with its open jaw. Then a third buffeted him with its forehead, gouging his helpless body.

Plunging headlong, he spiralled downwards. Accompanying his fall were the cacophonous sounds of the birds, crowing and screeching their triumph. As his body thumped into the unforgiving earth, Beremtha, his astral insignia, jolted out of it and took flight to the dread caverns of the underworld.

CHAPTER 25

The Whispering Tower

Soon after the toast, Akasha noticed three specks on the horizon. Was that the Solarii approaching?

As they neared, the specks changed into long vapour trails. Her heart leapt. Demos and Tamir set off down the stairs to greet them. The three craft glided to a standstill at the base of the tower and their flyers emerged amidst a haze of smoke and dust. She was sure one of them was Horque. The long climb up the stairs would take forever.

She'd longed for this moment. All those nagging doubts about the hybrids and irritating objections to the union had gradually dissipated like mist in the glow of the morning sun. In Samlios, there hadn't been the opportunity to deepen her relationship with Horque. Here she'd have him to herself, and could stare into his eyes for as long as she wanted.

The human race needed this fresh start. Up to now, a plunging chasm of mutual distrust separated the two races, broadened further by the tragedy of the seed and the taboo. From now on, a new human race would be born of a wondrous love that reached across that chasm, a race that would endure for as long as angels strode the Earth. Now that chasm had narrowed to a small divide, a tiny gap that could be breached by the simple act of holding hands, a prayer, or a genuine look of affection. She understood that love was the most subtle adhesive of all, for at once it could unite friend and foe, angel and demon, human and Solarii. In truth, love was a miraculous substance and a wondrous gift.

She paced the ramparts, kept her eyes fixed on the stairwell door. When would he come? The sound of his steps echoing in the stairwell was like the hymns of angels singing in harmony. As the door opened, her heart missed a beat. It was Demos.

The Solarii who followed him lowered his head beneath the lintel. Assuming it was Horque, Akasha stood before him. As he straightened, she realised it was Marim. The others were Lasec and Khephren.

Where is he?

Tamir brought up the rear and closed the door behind him.

What was happening? Her head was cloudy with emotion. Why did the Solarii all wear glum expressions? Why did Marim look and smell like he'd walked through a blazing fire?

"Something's happened," she blurted out. In that instant, her hopes and expectations emptied into the void. She slumped down on the floor, her head in her lap, and her hands on top of her head. It could not be. Inside her skull, she screamed long and loud.

While Marim told the story of woe, she didn't know whether to block her ears or open them. He told of Horque's bravery, of how he'd tried to save him from the marauding hybrids, which had then turned and mauled the protector. As they sought to rescue him, the dread creatures had attacked them as well, preventing any immediate search for his mangled body.

She had to know. She dared to ask the question on everyone's lips.

"Is he dead?" Her voice trembled.

"Not even the protector could have survived that attack, Lady Akasha." Marim's voice ached with grief and sorrow.

Thera put an arm around her and she buried her head in her mother's bosom.

"He was a great Solarii," Marim said, "whom I had the honour to serve for many years. He was a hero who died performing his duty."

Shamira rose to speak. Her chin was trembling, a rare sign of emotion.

"This is a dark foreboding for the future union of our two races," she said. "The hybrids are confusing. They're savage to the Solarii but to humans they can be kind and affable. We offer our condolences to the Solarii for the protector's tragic death, but most of all to Akasha, who has lost her groom."

There was a moment's silence.

"Lady Shamira," Marim replied, "there must be some mistake. Protector Horque was not chosen as the Solarii groom."

Now Akasha felt the sorrow of disappointment, as well as grief.

"Not...Horque?" Her words echoed in the distant recesses of her mind, as if she'd summarised the wretched situation with inadvertent clarity.

"No. Pharaoh Nimrod is the twice-born Solarii. He is to be your groom," Marim confirmed, coughing into his hand.

"The pharaoh." She gasped for breath. "I don't understand. Demos, you said, the Watchers..."

Demos' face dropped like a heavy weight.

"Despite this tragedy," Shamira said, "the union must proceed. The human race must salvage a future."

"And the Solarii must too," Khephren said stiffly.

"My duty is to follow the protector's last orders," Marim said. "I am to bring the Lady Akasha back to Egypt. On the way, we'll have the unpleasant task of returning to the site of his brutal murder. We'll need to find his body and bring it back to the Horque family for the customary embalming and burial. Make yourselves ready, all who would accompany us."

"I don't want to marry the pharaoh. I want to marry Horque!" Akasha cried. The thought of marrying the pharaoh, a Solarii she'd never even seen and never wanted to see, made her feel sick.

"Horque is dead, Akasha," Shamira replied. "Grieve for him, yes, have tears for him, but Marim is right. We must fulfil Horque's orders and wishes. Otherwise, we dishonour his life. He came here to collect you. He would want you to come with us. You must be strong now. At least, let us retrieve his body, go to Egypt, and help his family bury him with honour. Then we'll see what's best to do."

Akasha's eyes were moist with tears. Horque was dead, and she wanted to die too. This eddy of emotion was spinning her around. She couldn't think straight. She tried to listen. Marim was talking to Shamira, saying something about the voyage to Egypt.

"We have four places for passengers," he was explaining.

"Then Akasha, her parents and I will return with you," Shamira concluded. "Is that what you want, Akasha?"

She looked at Shamira and a cascade of thoughts clamoured for attention. Shamira's question was another gate through which to pass. She could always refuse, and decide to stay with Demos and Tamir at the Whispering Tower. No one would force her to leave. The question was, if she stayed, would *she* respect herself?

Before receiving the news, I'd found a way through the labyrinth of the taboo. I knew I could love Horque, that he could be my prince, my protector. Yet that only worked if he stood by my side in the union ceremony. I can't marry anyone else.

His death is so sudden, so unexpected. And at the hands of the rampant hybrids. Why did it have to happen now, after I'd settled to marrying him? I can feel the pangs of conscience gnawing at my soul, even more than the grief. I want to stay, though the subtle strings of destiny draw me to Egypt. I'll gird myself. I'll see him buried with dignity.

Wiping away a tear, she murmured, "Yes. It's what I want."

"Then we must leave," Shamira stated, a look of fierce pride on her face.

Shamira lifted Akasha on one side, Thera on the other. They were her supporters, her rock. They helped her down the scores of worn steps, each one a supreme effort of will and a pang of sorrow.

Horque would want her to find his body, bring the pieces together and make him whole again. She would bury him with full rites. Shamira and Marim were right: he would expect – no, demand – that of her. That gave her the morsel of courage she needed to take the next step, and the next, until they paused on the first landing. She felt numb, and frightened, but determined to go on.

It was a long way down to the bottom. The stairwell was suitably dark and gloomy for her to hide her distress and confusion. She remembered something Shamira had told her.

Regrets are the bindweed in the garden of your life.

She understood. Before now, she'd never had any real setbacks, or suffered enough to have regrets or even pity herself. She resolved to be fair with herself, to be pleased about being alive and to share and value the good times with her friends and family. On the *Crucible*, she'd chosen life and now she'd reaffirm that choice. They paused on the penultimate landing and she delved into her herb basket, pulling out a cloth purse.

"What's that?" Shamira asked.

Akasha held up a nugget of blue emerald. It pulsed with a bright translucence that lit the twilight of the tower, filling her with its gentle power.

"Your birthstone," Thera cried, her blue eyes sparkling with delight.

"Callisto gave it me as a parting gift," she said, walking down the remaining stairs unaided.

The whole village had gathered by the Horus Wing craft. She had one farewell to make, and looked for his bright eyes and stubborn chin. She soon found him.

"Demos," she cried, giving him a swift, emotional hug. "I fear we'll not meet again."

"Me too." He nodded. "I wish you'd kept my gift. It was for your protection, remember?"

"I do," she said. "I mislaid it when we went to visit the protector at the Green Elder's residence. I thought Horque might have found it and would return it to me when we met again. Now…" She choked on the rest of the sentence.

"You *are* the cobra. The necklace is incidental," he said. "I'll never forget the quayside in Samlios, the Mind Search, and that huge water spout and the rope coil. We may part but we're bound forever by shared memories."

"I've learnt from you too," she said. "You've shown me it takes courage to say what you really think, even if it means swimming against the tide of opinion."

She climbed into the passenger seat in Marim's craft. The remaining farewells were as swift as the take-off, and soon the three Horus Wing craft headed south to the Gates of Gades.

CHAPTER 26

The Basilisk That Slays

It wasn't long before the glimmer of the Gates of Gades shone before her. Nearby, Akasha noticed a thin plume of smoke snaking up into the late afternoon air. Marim had seen it too, and he directed the craft towards it. Soon enough, she spotted the source of the smoke: the tangled remains of Horque's craft. His body couldn't be far away.

"We need to find his remains soon," Marim said. "The Horus Wing craft are powered by the warming rays of the sun. Once it sets, the craft have only a small reserve."

Marim hovered over the area to make sure the hybrids had disappeared. There was movement on the ground. He landed some distance from the wreckage and they took cover behind a large tamarisk bush.

"The pyre is what they fear the most. They'll scatter at the merest whiff of smoke." Marim chuckled to himself, as if relishing taking revenge on the hybrids.

"No need for that," she replied. "The hybrids only attack Solarii – they don't harm humans. My father can approach them."

Uriah made ready to approach the hybrids, but Marim was adamant.

"No. Nothing must jeopardise your safety. I can't permit any of you to approach these murderers."

"All right, use the fire then," Shamira agreed.

They wrapped twigs into a torch that Marim threw towards another tamarisk bush. The flames spread across its spindly leaves like liquid. The engulfing fire shot sideways and lit the tinder-dry grasses and bushes nearby. Soon the hybrids beat a hasty retreat, their hooves thumping the ground like drums and leaving behind a billowing cloud of dust.

"I'll scout around the area," Marim murmured. "Don't move from here."

Marim edged towards the burnt-out tamarisk bush, concealing himself behind the rocks and vegetation. When he was nearer the crash site, he clambered up onto a rock and waved them on.

As they set off to join him, there was a flash of fur and fangs. A huge bear hybrid leapt at Marim and knocked him off the rock. The hybrid's vicious snarls and growls mingled with Marim's cries as it slashed at him with sharp claws and killing fangs.

Shamira was at his side in an instant. Bending her head back and exposing her neck, she unleashed the strangest cry Akasha had ever heard. It was a prolonged, low-pitched growl, like a primeval animal. It made Akasha's skin crawl, and it distracted the hybrid, which turned away from Marim and lumbered towards the pythoness.

Drops of blood oozed from its sabre-like fangs as the creature ground to an abrupt halt, as if it had hit an invisible wall. Looking through her whites to find out why, Akasha saw two rays of searing astral fire beaming out of Shamira's eyes. The pythoness fired bolt after astral bolt into the hybrid, until in an ugly spasm it toppled over in a heap of fur and flailing limbs. Clutching its throat with both paws, it gasped for breath. The creature's face turned pink, then crimson, then a deeper shade of purple. Shamira was squeezing the life out of it. Its body twitched and writhed, then heaved one last agonising sigh.

Akasha had never seen Shamira kill any living thing. The pythoness had taught her that all life was precious. Of course, Shamira had an armoury of astral powers – she was the Basilisk That Slays. Yet to kill a hybrid in that excruciating manner and save the life of a Solarii was shocking to Akasha, exacerbated by her tender emotional state.

Marim had scratches on his throat, face and shoulders from the beast's claws and fangs. Khephren and Lasec searched for the protector's remains and before long, they returned with the news that they had found them and stored them on the craft.

"Look what I found amongst the wreckage." Khephren held up a shiny, metallic object about the size of his forearm, but with an unusual shape.

"What is it?" Shamira asked.

"It's an ankh." Khephren wiped the dirt and ashes from its silvery surface. He handled it as if he were touching a live object. Then he held it up for all to see. It was T-shaped, with a hook or noose above the junction point.

"This is a parting gift from the protector," Khephren stated with a solemn air. "To find this in the debris of his craft is an omen. It's a sign the protector still influences events on Earth, even though he's crossed the great waters and entered the Field of Rushes."

"What can it do?" Shamira wanted to know.

"I'll show you," Khephren said.

Marim's scars were deep, his flesh like shredded parchment. Khephren held the healing tool by the sharp end. Akasha looked through her whites to see an emerald green force pulsing out of the looped end, emitting waves of soothing balm. Khephren held the ankh a few cubits from a gaping tear in Marim's shoulder. The ankh transmitted an astral healing force deep into the wound. The two ridges of open flesh closed before her astonished eyes. Soon it was just a broad scratch on the surface of his skin.

Once Khephren had finished, Marim gave a thin smile and slumped back against the rock. He was pale and evidently still weak.

"Are you fit to fly?" Khephren asked.

Marim nodded.

"Good, then we must leave immediately."

Marim had served with Horque for longer than Akasha had walked the Earth, so it must have been hard for him to continue to perform his duty in these tragic circumstances. Whatever anyone else thought, these Solarii were singular in mind, as devoted to each other and their purpose as humans, if not more so. They were slowly earning her begrudging respect. And the Solarii clearly weren't so awful if they possessed a tool like this healing ankh. Akasha and Shamira strapped themselves into Khephren's craft, which set off into the early evening light.

During the flight, Akasha struggled to keep her own demons from running amok. She must have badly offended them – how else to explain the catalogue of misfortunes that had befallen her? While rogue hybrids had murdered her dear Horque, the ones she had encountered – like Jarda and Strata – were tame and friendly. Then she witnessed her mentor, the Basilisk That Slays, slay a hybrid to save the life of a Solarii. Everything was upside down. In the midst of her confusion, she again drew strength from her blue emerald avatar.

Who was the pythoness? What other secret powers did she possess? Akasha opened her eyes wide: she was such a sluggard. Now she understood. Pythons were constrictors, snakes that killed by suffocation. Shamira's titles – the Pythoness, the Basilisk That Slays – were not titular at all. They were real, and earned. And to kill to defend another life was just and fair.

The light was fading. But it was growing lighter, not dimmer as they approached Egypt. How was that possible? Up ahead, she saw the reason: three sources of radiant light, each shining with an inner luminescence like those of fireflies, only a thousand times brighter and more powerful. Their size was monumental: Solarii-made mountains of stone, smooth, shiny and immense. They hummed with a colossal astral potency. Next to them was the black granite Sphinx, the mysterious hybrid lion with the face of a maiden.

Egypt was a new beginning. Any talk of a union could wait until she'd honoured the Solarii with whom she'd fallen in love. His last rites were her first priority.

She pulled the shawl over her shoulders as Khephren landed the Horus Wing craft. In a swirl of smoke and dust, she stepped onto the ancient soil of Egypt, the Land of the Two Ladies.

PART 5

Ten Days

CHAPTER 27

The Invitation

Akasha's limbs ached as she forced herself up from the chair. She paced up and down on the alabaster floor and peered into the upper reaches of the large vaulted chamber.

"Can someone let us outside?" she cried. "I've studied this frieze for four days now and I still can't make any sense of it." She threw her hand in the air, as if to make the shape of one of the symbols, then let it drop limp by her side.

"Khephren asked us not to leave without an escort," Shamira said. "We can't just go anywhere we want to. We are his guests. We are visitors in Egypt, in their land. They have their customs, and we need to abide by them."

No, that was not right at all. "We are their *honoured* guests," Akasha replied. "Visitors? Their land? How can we be the visitors? They are the visitors on Earth, not us. And it's not their land. It's the land of the Semites, the land of Mithrayzim. The Solarii appropriated it and named it Egypt. Humans were here long before they were, and we'll be here long after they've gone."

She reached up towards a window opening.

"Look. I can't even reach the opening, let alone see out of it," she complained. "These four walls are crowding in on me."

After all her trials, she was in the heart of the Solarii civilisation. If she was going to understand these strange and exotic aliens, Egypt was the place to do it. Directly outside her chamber were the high perimeter walls of Khephren's residence. The rich and varied sounds of the street sellers, of mothers and their children, and the general bustle of daily life drifted into her chamber. She was that close to Solarii life. In the evenings, the wind changed direction and brought the smells of cooking and maudlin sounds from the city, those of the zither, the flute and the drum as the Solarii gathered and sang of their homesickness, and their yearning to end their exile.

There was a knock on the door. She leapt up to open it, hoping it was someone to release her from this unexpected incarceration.

"Tarsus," she said. "Welcome."

She opened her arms to greet him. Finally, another human, a friendly face: someone she could talk to and not end up with a crooked neck. And he was close to the Horque family.

"Lady Akasha, my condolences," Horque's old servant replied, bowing reverently to her.

"How are you and how is his family?" Shamira asked.

"I am still grieving, like the Lady Issa and Neferem. This morning I've been to the court to deliver a papyrus to the pharaoh, and now I'm here to give this to you." He handed Akasha a scroll tied with a white ribbon. It bore the seal of a black hawk; wings spread wide and glaring eyes.

Opening the scroll, Akasha saw a series of neat columns of markings and glyphs. "These hieroglyphics don't mean anything to me," she said. "What do they say?"

"We'll ask our host to translate it for us," Shamira said.

"Absent host, more like. We've hardly seen Khephren since our arrival."

There was another knock at the door, and Khephren walked in with Marim. Marim looked stronger and rested. The only sign of his scuffle with death was a blotchy rash in the centre of his forehead.

"That hybrid gave you a severe mauling, but here you are, hale and hearty," Akasha said.

"The pantheon has smiled on me, and Khephren has aided my recovery," Marim replied, matter-of-fact. "I cannot stay long. Before I go," he turned to Shamira, "I wanted to thank the gods for sending you to save me from the hybrid."

"I did what I thought best," she replied. "Where are you going?"

"I have duties to perform," Marim replied, his face expressionless.

"That's a shame," Akasha said. "You knew Protector Horque well. I hoped you could tell me more about him."

"This isn't the moment to speak," Marim insisted. "Horque has travelled the Winding Waterway to the Field of Rushes. Now, I must depart." He crossed the threshold and closed the door.

Shamira turned to Khephren. "Tell us about the Solarii customs regarding these matters. It's important we're conversant with them. We don't wish to offend anyone."

"I understand," Khephren said. "The law of Ma'at prohibits any marriage from taking place in a period of mourning for an important personage such as Protector Horque. Indeed, the pharaoh will only announce the date of the union after the funeral."

146

"I see," Akasha said. She supposed she had no choice but to abide by these customs.

"There's one more thing." Shamira handed him the papyrus. "Tarsus has just delivered this from Issa. Can you tell us what it says?"

"It's an invitation to visit her house today. No doubt she'll inform you of the funeral arrangements."

At last, an opportunity to leave these four walls. Akasha stood up and smoothed down her dress.

"We accept," she said. "I'm ready."

CHAPTER 28

The Negotiation

The four black diorite statues manned the corners of the water court like sentinels of the underworld. A breeze ruffled the surface of the water in the pool. The deep silence was as thick as night, even though the green sun bathed the court in its gentle afternoon rays. She'd prepared herself as thoroughly as she'd prepared the court. She, the lioness, was on the prowl.

"Sit down, High Priest," Issa commanded. Cheiron obeyed. She'd never quite understood the priestly regime. The people coerced and persuaded the priests, not the other way round. With Cheiron in her house, her senses were on high alert. She knew why he was here. In fact, she'd expected him earlier, but she didn't want him sniffing around for long. She had urgent business to attend to. Besides, he was not the halfwit he made himself out to be. Underneath his jet black priestly robes and elaborate emblems of office stalked a calculating man, but a man nonetheless, a man susceptible to beautiful women.

Issa wore a long white gown and a white veil over her shoulder-length locks. She noted with pleasure that he inhaled her rose-tinted perfume and glanced every now and again at her ample cleavage. She knew how to persuade and coerce.

"Are we alone?" It was half-question, half-statement. From half a man, she concluded.

"Of course." She spoke curtly, annoyed that he should ask. She'd sent Tarsus to deliver two invitations, while Fryme had gone to the market to obtain a quantity of hyssop. "I'm suspicious of the Semites," she added. "My servants keep disappearing for long periods."

"That's because they're occupied with their boat," Cheiron said, adding with bite, "remember? The one your son granted them permission to build?"

"Have you come here to gossip about Semite servants?"

"No, not at all," Cheiron said, shaking his head.

"Then state your business," she growled.

"For four days, Horque's cadaver has lain in peace in the embalmers' burial vault. That is where I would have expected it to stay until the day of his funeral. This morning you removed it, depriving it of the astral protections there and exposing it to the loathsome fiends of the underworld who will feed on any of his wrongdoings. I've come to take it back."

"You won't do that," she snarled. How dare he come into her lair and make demands on her son's body? "It's better protected where it is. The embalmers had already cleansed his corpse with natron salt and embalmed it. I have ritually purified it. I myself will intone the Declaration of Innocence over his body, and these words will be like incense to Anubis and Osiris. They will allow him to pass the weighing of the heart." She knew when and how to use her claws.

"I'm sure that's all in order," Cheiron replied, clearly trying to remain calm. So, she had rattled him. "But the embalmers informed me you refused to let them remove the soft organs, thus preventing the body from being mummified," he added, looking down his nose at her in that annoyingly patronising way.

"As a mistress of the Sekmet arts," she countered, "I'm proficient in handling the dead and shall personally observe all the ritual proprieties. Who better to prepare my son for his final spiritual sojourn than his own mother?" That argument should convince him. She didn't want him to suspect the real reason she wanted to keep the body intact.

"I understand," Cheiron replied. "You'll be aware that the pharaoh has granted your son a full state funeral, to take place after the assize trials in the Temple of Ma'at, on the tenth day after his death."

"I'd have expected that for a member of the Ennead Council," she said. "If there's nothing else, we both have work to do. Six days pass quicker than a sparrow in summer." She wanted him to think she was fully compliant.

"Wait. There is another matter." Cheiron pulled out a papyrus scroll, which bore her own emblem. Earlier the same day, she'd asked Tarsus to deliver it to the pharaoh. It threw her momentarily, because she'd anticipated Nimrod would summon her to the temple to discuss it. Evidently, he'd thought otherwise and sent Cheiron.

So be it.

"I see." She sat back down with a ruffle of her silken gown. "I need to know with whom and with what I'm dealing here. Did Pharaoh confer you with full negotiating powers?"

"Yes, I'm the pharaoh's envoy," he replied. Another smug smile.

This was the moment to use her feminine guile. She leant forwards to reveal just a glimpse of her plunging cleavage, which Cheiron gazed at with guilty voracity. She knew he'd never been at ease with women, in particular with beautiful, seductive women like her. He was dazzled by her elegance and carnal sexuality. Although he was married, he'd done so more out of political conformity than any genuine feelings. His wife had told her so. All he knew about was the pantheon. He could appease the gods, cajole them, sacrifice to them, even bargain with them, but to do those things with a woman was an entirely different matter.

Cheiron looked away briskly and coughed into his hand.

"Good, then we can begin," she said, revelling in his discomfort. Hawks taunted mice, just like cats. "That means you've read my missive, in which I warn against the choice of the pharaoh as the *true* twice-born."

"It was bold of you to do so," Cheiron remarked. "Many would have baulked at challenging an incumbent pharaoh, especially over such an important matter. Instead of sending me, he could have dispatched his elite guards to conduct you to an ignominious end in the Palace of Execution."

"That may be so, but he didn't. He sent you instead." She'd weighed her chances before sending the missive and been proved right. "This matter is crucial to our people. If Pharaoh is not the true twice-born and he marries the fair maiden, there'll be no undoing the union. It will be too late to try another twice-born. I believe there are misgivings about the pharaoh."

Every nerve fibre tensed. The lioness was stalking her prey. She had to lure him in a little more before she pounced. He fiddled with the ruby ring on his finger.

"Your epistle alarmed the pharaoh," he said eventually. "He's responsible for his people and he wants them all to end their exile on Earth and return home. I agree we must get this right. If he isn't the true twice-born, then who is?"

She allowed a thin smile to play on her lips.

"I can't say."

"That doesn't help your cause. If and when this mysterious person appears before us, how will you prove beyond doubt that he's the true twice-born?"

"When the time comes, there will be no doubts. The true twice-born won't be my choice. The pantheon will confirm him by an incontrovertible sign."

"I'm sure they will," Cheiron said, patronising again. "Where's the sign? Without it, why should we believe you?"

He was insufferable. She had to negotiate carefully, subtly manoeuvring him into position.

"Only the gods can produce the sign. I can't control them, and neither can you. Reflect a moment. If I'm right and Pharaoh continues this union with the Lady Akasha, there'll be no return home and we'll all die a horrible death down here. Can you afford to take that risk?"

Cheiron nodded. He was coming around to her way of thinking.

"The sign will appear when the gods are ready, and not before," she said. "Have I been wrong in the past?"

"Not that I can remember," he said pensively. "Assuming you can deliver the true twice-born, what are your demands?"

She paused to savour this moment of power. Since Nimrod had deposed her as vizier, she'd waited for her opportunity and here it was. The lioness pounced.

"There are two."

"The first?" Cheiron sat upright.

"I want the emblem of the white feather back."

"That's not possible. Zoser is vizier."

"Then remove him."

"Only Pharaoh can do that, and I doubt—"

"Then you'll need to persuade him," she interrupted. "You're the high priest. Help him see the truth of his situation."

"I'll try," Cheiron said, in a tone that chilled the embers of her soul. "Though I should warn you, should you fail to deliver the twice-born, should this sign of the gods be wrong or ambiguous, you'll forfeit your life, your estate, your dynasty, everything."

She puckered her lips and fingered the black sapphire necklace. She was in her own house, surrounded by her own astral ambience. No snippet of a priest was going to intimidate her.

"That's how you know I'm serious about this," she said. "The nymph Akasha is already in Egypt for the union. The flood is imminent, we know not when."

"Then find and deliver this twice-born – soon."

"I will." Her dark eyes blazed in defiance. "Do you believe me?"

"I don't know," Cheiron said.

That was enough. She'd inserted a modicum of doubt in Cheiron's mind. At least Pharaoh would take her demands seriously.

"My second demand is for Pharaoh to reveal to me his god name."

Cheiron opened his eyes wide in disbelief.

"A god's name is between the person and their god. You ask too much."

"Then let him marry Akasha and endure the outcome," she said. The lioness bared her teeth.

He swallowed hard. "I'll put your demands to Pharaoh."

"Do that, High Priest."

"When will you deliver?"

"In six days, on the day of Horque's funeral." Of that, she was certain, or least she had to sound so.

"How?"

"Don't worry about that," she promised. "I'll present the twice-born to

Pharaoh and court alike. You'll all see the sign."

"The pharaoh won't marry before Horque's funeral. So deliver on your promises in six days or suffer the consequences. So be it. Let it be done." Cheiron uttered the fatal words that sealed the agreement in the astral light. As he got up, his knees creaked, divesting him – as far as she was concerned – of his last cloak of dignity. Clearly angry at being ensnared in her web of intrigue, he stormed out of her house.

Her first reward: an end to the shame she'd endured after her demotion to the Steward of the Granary. She was Vizier Issa. That was where she belonged.

Her second: the power to shape the leadership of the Solarii. Armed with the pharaoh's god name, she would control the destiny of Egypt and wield the mace of power. For herself, she would save her people from ignominy.

CHAPTER 29

The White Ribbon

As Akasha and Shamira walked out of the front gates of Khephren's house, Javian and Irex were waiting for them. Javian had a ruby rash on his neck and lower chin, similar to the one she'd seen on Marim's forehead. Were the Solarii ill? Why couldn't they use their ankhs to heal themselves? Before she could ask him about it, Irex addressed her.

"We are your guard and will escort you to your appointment."

"Guard? From whom? From what?" Irex was a giant, and he harboured something of the hyena in him.

"It is the law of Ma'at," Irex said. "The pharaoh's family is protected at all times. You *will* follow us."

"We *will*? Do you know you are talking to the pharaoh's bride?" Akasha jutted out her chin. She would command their respect. Both men bowed low, mollifying her growing pride.

"You will address me as *Lady* Akasha," she said, with as much pomp as she could muster.

"This way, if it pleases m' lady," Javian interceded.

Akasha and Shamira followed the guards into Jizah. It was her first opportunity to see the Solarii city and people at close quarters. The monumental scale of their temples and obelisks was awe-inspiring, and she felt small and insignificant beneath their huge colonnades. The people were a different matter; they looked all the same to her, with their long, pointed heads and imposing figures. They dressed all the same, in their standard garb of cloth headdress, skirt and leather sandals. She'd expected the fantastic, the fiery and the flamboyant. She was disappointed.

Irex stopped opposite a house with a pair of sturdy oak gates set in the high perimeter wall. Engraved into the stone lintel above the gate was a hawk in full cry; beak open, talons spread. Its menacing eyes stared right through her. Akasha hunched her shoulders as a shiver ran up her spine. This must be the Horque residence.

"This is the house of Lady Issa," Irex confirmed. "By the rules of Ma'at, we are forbidden entry, so we will wait for you here, outside the gates."

She marched up to the gate, and noticed a white ribbon tied to the door-knocker, the same as the one on the scroll. Taking her by surprise, the gate swung open and a hooded Solarii brushed past, nearly knocking her down. Before she could get a good look at him, he had disappeared around the corner.

Tarsus was standing just inside the gate.

"Ladies, welcome. I've just returned myself," he said.

"Who was that Solarii, in a cloak as black as his looks?" Akasha asked.

"Cheiron, the high priest," Tarsus whispered, a note of awe in his voice.

"He almost split me in two."

"I'm sure he didn't intend to." Tarsus gestured for them to enter.

"What's the meaning of the white ribbon?"

"White is the Solarii colour of mourning," Tarsus explained. "The ribbon signifies to the community that the household has suffered a recent death. Their ethical code, the law of Ma'at, forbids any Solarii other than priests and close family members to cross the threshold of the house in mourning. That's why your Solarii escorts remain outside the gates."

"I see. Yet *we* crossed the threshold," she said.

"Humans can do so, on or after the fourth day after the death," Tarsus explained.

"So the rule is different: four days for humans and ten days for the Solarii. Are we lesser than them? Are they greater than us?" She flicked her finger under her chin. These blatant distinctions angered her.

"It's not like that." Tarsus sounded defensive.

She was about to voice her opinion when Shamira gave her one of those intimidating glances that stopped her in her tracks. She was in a house of mourning with a grieving mother and this, on reflection, wasn't the best time or place to conduct an inquest into Solarii law.

Therefore, Issa's invitation to them had come on the fourth day after Horque's death, the earliest possible opportunity she could have given it. Why the undue haste? Akasha felt she was missing some important fact. Either that or she was an unwitting participant in an elaborate game in which Issa was at the heart.

They stopped by an arch that opened onto an uncovered water court. It was late afternoon and the wind from the river was warming. In the centre of the court was a rectangular pool, covered with pale blue water lilies, with a majestic fountain as the showpiece. The atmosphere was heavy.

In each corner, a sullen hawk-headed statue glared out of the gloom, as if asking who dared disturb their peace. The statues' eyes, inlaid with mother-of-pearl, gave them a lifelike luminosity that made Akasha shudder; even more so when she realised that they were hybrids, half hawk and half human. This, she found, was a huge contradiction: the depiction of a hybrid at the core of a household whose lives had been destroyed by hybrids. The world was upside down again.

While she waited, a human woman approached Tarsus and whispered something in his ear. Then she entered the water court and handed a small package to someone out of her line of vision.

The unseen woman said, "Thank you, Fryme. Is it all there?"

"Yes, Lady Issa. All that you asked for," Fryme replied.

Fryme then left and Tarsus announced them. "The Lady Akasha, and Shamira the Pythoness."

Akasha heard a rustle of clothing and soft footsteps. Out of the shadows emerged a tall, elegant Solarii woman. Her heart melted as she saw the resemblance between mother and son.

"I am Issa," the Solarii woman said. Dark and mysterious, her sharp blue eyes seemed alert to every nuance and subtlety. "And this is Neferem, my daughter," she added, with a gesture towards a divan behind the water pool. A Solarii woman rose from it and acknowledged them with barely concealed indifference. Her eyes were melancholy as she glided over to the water pool. She rested her cupped hand on top of one of the blue lilies and filled it with water. Opening her fingers and letting out a prolonged sigh, she let the water dribble out of her palm and back into the pool. Witnessing Neferem's poignant cameo, Akasha felt a chill astral wind run through her own soul. All creatures – humans, Solarii, angels, even hybrids and animals – drew life from the great pool, and for a short while made insubstantial ripples on its surface. In the end, everything drawn from it would be returned to it, replenishing the greater pool for the next generation.

"So it is, so it always will be," she whispered to herself.

"Is she all right?" Shamira asked.

"She's distressed by her brother's death," Issa said, in a matter-of-fact way. She turned to Akasha. "You met my son in Samlios."

Akasha was unsure if this was a statement, or a question. "Yes," she said. "Did you want to talk about Samlios?" What she really wanted to know was why Issa had invited them with such undue haste.

Issa shook her head. "My son told me that you'd impressed him, and that was rare indeed."

"I see." She almost swooned on hearing those few sweet words that confirmed his affection for her.

"I wanted to look you in the eye and find out how you felt about him, but why did *you* accept my invitation?" Issa asked her.

From her heart she replied, "Your son meant a lot to me. I wanted to pay my respects to you."

"That's all I wanted to know," Issa said, delving into her bag.

"Also, I wanted…" Akasha paused and cleared her throat, "to ask you if I could have something of your son's, as a token of what might have been. But I'm not sure the Solarii have such practices?"

"We didn't, but we do now," Issa confessed. "Since the Casting of Shadows, a dewdrop of sentimentality has crept into our otherwise robust and traditionally disciplined way of life. In response to your request, I can give you something more than a token." Issa held up a small necklace with an arching cobra motif.

"There it is!" Akasha cried, and swallowed hard on the lump in her throat. The flood of memories rushed back. She and Horque had been so close, yet so far apart. The necklace was a symbol of their ephemeral union.

"Thank you, Lady Issa," she said.

"Horque tried to return it to you in Samlios, but he missed you. He left it here before departing for the Whispering Tower."

"I will cherish it," she said. So Horque did care for her. She had known it all along. She felt that same bittersweet emotion. The lump in her throat grew larger.

The four women sat in silence, sharing a common sadness at a loss of a great and mutual friend.

Shamira glanced at Neferem and asked Issa, "Will she recover?"

"In due course. She objected to you coming here so soon after Horque's death. We have our customs. It is a moot point whether I should have tarried longer before inviting you."

"We'd like to attend the funeral and pay our last respects to Horque," Shamira said.

"Of course. We'll keep you informed of all the arrangements." Issa's tone was dismissive, as if it was of no importance to her whether they came or not.

Why did Issa betray no trace of emotion? Was that the Solarii way? Surely, she must be grieving for the tragic loss of her son. So why was she hiding her feelings?

"Lady Issa, I thank you for the invitation, and the cobra necklace. You have no idea what it means to me," she said.

"Oh, but I do, Akasha, I know exactly what it means to you."

"I think we'd better go," Shamira said.

"Tarsus will see you out," Issa said.

As they left, Akasha again felt the conflicting emotions of a love that had blossomed but had no time to flower.

CHAPTER 30

The God Crucible

The moonlight flooded through the window but Issa was still awake. Once the street cats grew tired of fighting and the hyenas and foxes stopped scavenging, she roused herself and began her descent. Clutching a glow lamp in one hand and Fryme's package in the other, she crept downstairs and stopped in the middle of a corridor, beside a section of wall that would have appeared unremarkable to anyone else. She knew otherwise.

A few words, an arcane utterance, followed by a shimmer of light and the astral curtain disappeared, revealing the secret door. She stepped through it, into the corridor beyond. She was going to the God Crucible, an occult chamber beneath her house. Its astral protections were such that no one, not even Cheiron, suspected its existence. Her breathing was shallow. This was the outer point of no return.

Her glow lamp threw long shadows down the narrow, sloping tunnel. Divided in two, it had steps on one side and a slanting ramp on the other. In front of her on the ground was a piece of white bandage, accidentally torn off the partially mummified body of her son, which she'd dragged down the ramp before Cheiron had arrived. How heavy he had been. They didn't call it a dead weight for nothing. She could still smell the musty odour of the dust particles she'd dislodged.

At the bottom of the ramp, the tunnel gave way to a dome-shaped chamber, the God Crucible. Her son's cadaver lay on a bench, and she ran her hand over the embalming bandages. Beside it was a second, vacant bench. There, she would lie during the ritual she was about to perform.

The Anubis embalmers had washed Horque's body, encased it in natron salt, and mummified it according to all but one of the traditions of the jackal-headed god – the exception being that they had not removed any of his organs. On his

157

chest, she laid a scarab pectoral, and into his mouth, she placed a length of straw.

Opening Fryme's package, she fingered the dark green leaves. She'd used hyssop many times before and had grown to enjoy its astringent odours. Deftly, she worked the herb into a paste and poured a droplet onto a wafer. Before lying down on the bench, she reread the hieroglyphs on the wall: *The Spell of the Gods* and beneath that, the warning, *Use me wisely, lest I turn and rend thee.*

This ritual was the ultimate. It was life and death. She had to be dedicated and fulsome, lest the warning would apply to her. She replayed every detail of the ritual in her mind before preparing for the trance. The timing was of the essence: the ritual had to be conducted on the night of the round moon and completed by the rise of the sun.

Carefully, she adjusted the aperture on the glow lamp so the amount of light hovered on the twilight between astral and incarnate. Lying on the bench, she placed the wafer beneath her tongue, relishing the minty bitterness of the hyssop as it suffused her being. Slowly, mists and vapours of the astral veiled her eyes.

She drifted in and out of consciousness, as her *ka* eased out of her physical body, until she crossed through the veil and entered its natural domicile, the huge edifice of the astral light. Immediately, she settled into her familiar astral cloak – the golden lioness. It felt good to be back amongst the warmth of her own kind.

Oh, how she'd missed the freedom of the astral light, where she could fly the universe at the speed of thought and take wing through the millions of years in an instant. Through her *ka*, she looked down on herself, lying on the bench. Would this be the last time she'd ever do so? She banished the thought. For now, she had to be meticulously correct. Her enemies were doubt, fear and hesitation.

She willed her *ka* towards Du'at, the realm of the dead within the Field of Rushes, and quickly located the pair of columns at its entrance, the colossal Anubis Gates. She expected to find the jackal-headed Anubis operating its gates, but they appeared unguarded. Her voyage to the underworld couldn't be easier – she'd enter Du'at, find the Hall of Truth, and rescue Horque's *ka*.

As she approached, a curtain of force shimmered between the gates. On its silky, misty surface appeared a thousand faces – young and old, happy and sad, and all strangely familiar people she'd met in her lifetime, human and Solarii – until one only remained. No. It couldn't be. It was her own face. She was so startled she nearly ruptured the precious umbilical connection to her physical body. Was it a mirror? No, it was a replica. It was more than that. It was her double.

The guard to Du'at was Issa herself. The face stared back at her, inspecting her, a most unnerving experience. To be investigated by oneself. She felt naked to the core. This was the inner point of no return.

"What do you want?" The double even spoke in her own voice.

"Entry to Du'at," she replied.

"This is the realm of the dead. You're still alive – go back to where you belong."

The face of her double stared back, eyes unflinching, scrutinising her inner being. There was nowhere to hide from oneself.

"No, I can't do that. Let me in. My son must live again."

"Many come to plead for their loved ones. Don't think you're the first," the face snarled. "Enter here at your peril, because you'll never leave."

"What does that mean? I'm more powerful than a mere guard dog," she scoffed. "Let me pass."

To her relief and surprise, the astral curtain disappeared. Her way was clear. However, the warning of her double was right about one thing. The astral light inside Du'at was bleak, dark and corrosive to her *ka*. She wouldn't survive long there. She moved quickly to the Hall of Truth, where Osiris sat on his throne, governing the scales of Ma'at.

Horque's *ka* was about to be placed on the scales. Once it was weighed, he would be lost, with no way to retrieve him.

"Stop!" she yelled. No one took any notice. Not even Thoth the scribe, nor the monster Ammut who was ready to eat Horque's *ka* should he fail the weighing.

"Stop or you'll never have any more souls to weigh!"

That got his attention. Slowly, contemptuously, the Lord Osiris turned his gaze upon her.

"What is the meaning of this rude interruption?" he said.

"I beg your leave, sire," she said hastily, "but if you don't let me take my son back to the land of the living, everyone will die."

"What difference will that make? Everyone is going to perish in the flood anyway."

"You might have a lot of souls coming here to be weighed, but to endure, to be of continual service to the gods, I have to take my son back with me to marry Akasha. They are the couple chosen by the Watchers. If Akasha marries Nimrod, their progeny will not survive the astral conditions after the flood. It has to be Horque. Between them, they will produce a new race, one that will last far beyond the duration of the present human race. We, the Solarii, will then be able to return home. The decision lies with you."

Osiris grunted. He didn't seem convinced.

"Sire," her Sekmet lioness growled, "you can save the human race, and that will give you a continual supply of souls entering these hallowed chambers. Otherwise, what good is there in being a God of the Underworld if there are no souls entering the Hall of Truth?"

All was quiet in the hall. Even Ammut stopped licking his lips. Thoth held his feather above the papyrus.

"I have decided. You can have him back," Osiris decreed. "In truth, his *ka* belongs to me. So I'll keep a small part as a guarantee. It will remind you of your debt. He'll return here sooner or later anyway."

"What part will you keep?" she wanted to know.

"That is between me and Horque."

The next moment she was free, Horque's *ka* by her side. As she flew past the Anubis Gate, she felt something tug at her *ka*, from which she pulled free. So elated was she at having achieved the impossible, she dismissed it from her mind.

Back in the chamber, she had to fulfil the last part of the Gods' Spell – to rekindle the nexus between Horque's *ka* and his physical body. She willed her *ka* to hover directly over his cadaver, her astral wings rustling gently. Waves of astral force surged into the chamber, pulsing rhythmically to the words of the resurrection utterance:

Wake up, you sleeper.
Rouse up, you Watcher.
Raise yourself like Osiris the King.

Out of the astral, a pale blue flame flickered above Horque's head. It was the eternal flame that did not burn. It was a slither of the Source. Exactly what she needed to transform the chamber into a God Crucible within which life and death were interchangeable. She fanned the blue flame and enshrouded the cadaver in its resurrective rays.

She willed her wings to beat, but they refused to move. She tried again. Nothing. Locked rigid. No! If she panicked, her umbilical connection would rupture; her *ka* would wither and die. Not a ruffle of the feathers on her wings. She was helpless, suspended in a netherworld.

Clouds of astral force shifted into two black dots, surrounded by blue circles, which then defined into two eyes. They wore that faraway, eternal look of the Sphinx. Then she realised. These were the Eyes of the Endless Ones, come to watch and guard against intruders like her. Yet they were the resurrective entity she had summoned, and they had come. She was alone with them, deep in an underground chamber only the dead knew existed. The time to trust had come.

Her son was the true twice-born. If he were not to marry Akasha, that would be the end of the Solarii. There would be no way back to the four mansions of the sun, to their doubles. No way out of this earthly prison. And no future for the humans either. Still she waited for the eyes. Still they watched. The power in the chamber was colossal. The walls of the chamber were frothing and melting with seething astral power. She couldn't hold herself together any longer. She lost her nerve for a moment. The umbilical to her physical body trembled and weakened, and she started to fall, back towards the Anubis Gates.

This time it wasn't her face that she saw. It was the jackal, Anubis himself, jaws snapping at her heels. He snarled and launched himself at her, ripping out a part of her *ka*. Suddenly, she was falling, falling. Then a movement. A ruffle. One wing, then the other. They moved. In a flash, she lifted herself out of the slough, back towards the light.

She'd passed the test. Delight, relief, joy, all at once. Beating the wings of her *ka*, she drew back into the chamber and fanned the pale blue flame, engulfing the chamber in its cool glow. She wrapped her wings underneath Horque's body, creating a magic sheath, a womb of life in which the flame could do its divine work.

Mother and son remained locked together for what seemed like an eternity, unified as one, womb and foetus, as before, as always. Time stood still. Everything stood still. She was in the midst of the Field of Rushes, the eternal Milky Way. Galaxies circled slowly in harmony. The feeling of awesome space filled her *ka*. She floated, feeling nothing, being nothing, joined to everything, for the millions of years.

Then – blackness.

CHAPTER 31

The Tenth Day

Waking up, Akasha looked through the window to see a light drizzle dampening the rays of the rising sun. She sighed. Today she had a sad duty to perform. For an enticing moment, she contemplated pulling the blanket over her head and going back to sleep. It would be wonderful to escape there, to a place where no one and nothing could disturb her peace. She couldn't do that, and she chided herself for being naive and disrespectful. There was no escape. Her spiritual tally wasn't going to switch off just because she wanted it to and didn't feel like making an effort at that moment. Whatever she did, however she felt, the tally was always on. In the end, that was just and fair, and she wouldn't have it any other way.

Her bones ached for her Samlios homeland. Every day it grew worse. The homesickness was abject. She delved into her basket and pulled out the sod of earth she'd retrieved from beneath the oak of Samlios. It enriched her being. She'd need all the strength she could muster because this was the day of Horque's funeral, the tenth day, and the day on which she'd cast a metaphorical pearl into the vessel of what might have been.

Dawn was still breaking. Sounds travelled as quick as the dead and new ideas were as prevalent as drops of dew. She glanced out of her window, which opened onto a courtyard at the back of Khephren's residence. Someone was banging on the back door and shouting.

"Uriah, are you there?"

What was her father up to at this time of the morning? The voice called again, this time a loud, insistent whisper.

"Uriah. Let me in."

It was Tarsus. What did he want with her father? As she left her room, and walked into the corridor, someone hurrying by crashed into her, sending her sprawling on the stone floor, her hands splayed out in front of her. Behind her was a loud thud as something heavy fell to the ground. Still in a daze, the next thing she heard was her father's voice.

"Akasha, I'm so sorry. Are you all right?" Uriah helped her sit upright. Grimacing, she rubbed her palms to take away the pain of the fall.

"Yes, I think so," she mumbled, groggy from the collision.

"I didn't see you there," he blurted out. "You came out of your chambers so quickly. I wasn't expecting you…at this early time of the day."

Her father's soft green eyes were plaintive and concerned.

"Someone was banging at the back door," she murmured as Shamira emerged from a neighbouring room.

"That's where I was going," Uriah admitted.

"What's all the commotion about? Akasha, are you all right?" Shamira asked, kneeling down to tend to her. The banging on the outer gate was now so loud they could barely hear each other speak.

"Father, you'd better let him in before he breaks it down," she suggested.

Uriah threw her with a sheepish grin and set off to the back door.

Shamira was examining a wooden box that lay on its side.

"What's this?" she asked.

"I think my father dropped it. Open it and find out."

It was full of carpenters' tools and utensils: one for shaping, another for shaving and a third for cutting, and many others Akasha did not recognise. Uriah returned with Tarsus, who was wearing a heavy pair of gloves and holding a similar wooden box.

"I see you found my tools," Uriah remarked.

"What are you building?" she asked, holding up a hammer. "And where are you and Tarsus going, so early in the morning?"

"Tarsus is a carpenter, I'm a sailor. Together we're building an ark." Uriah puffed out his chest.

"An ark, that's wonderful!" Akasha sprang to her feet. "Why didn't you tell us?"

Uriah looked guilty, so Shamira answered for him. "We didn't want to trouble you with it. Your mind was rightfully on Horque and his funeral."

"You knew all along?" She glared at Shamira, who held up her palms as a sign of acceptance. "As usual, I'm the last to know."

"We're going there now. Come with us." Tarsus was nothing if not enthusiastic.

"I would love to come, but…" She hesitated and puffed out her cheeks. "Horque's funeral is later today. Can we go there and get back in good time?" She glanced at Shamira, more in hope than fear. She craved her guidance.

"The funeral is at dusk," the pythoness confirmed.

163

"Then we have plenty of time. The site is in a disused dry dock by the river. It's not far from here." Uriah was evidently keen for her to come.

"We can manage to do both," Shamira concluded. "What about the escorts?"

"They're at the front gate, and as far as I am concerned, that's where they can stay," Akasha observed wryly.

They slipped out of the back door. Uriah went on ahead to alert the workers to Akasha's impending arrival. The ground was moist underfoot, as the overnight drizzle had stopped and given way to sparse white cloud against an evergreen sky.

"It's all because of Protector Horque, bless his soul," Tarsus said, doffing his skullcap. "He gave us permission to start building."

"I didn't know that." Her heart swelled with pride. So Horque had helped her own kind.

"There's a lot you don't know about the Solarii," Tarsus added.

"Tell me more," she said, her curiosity piqued.

"Take Lady Issa, for example," Tarsus said. "I've served the Horque household for many years but recently there've been some strange goings-on. They began six days ago, the day you both visited her. Later that night, I heard strange noises in the house. I went to investigate and found no one, yet she was in the house somewhere, I know it. In the end, I went back to sleep. After that, she disappeared for four whole days. Fryme couldn't rouse her from her chamber. Then out she comes looking pallid and gaunt, as if something's sucked the life force out of her marrow. Issa claimed that she'd suffered an uncontrollable spasm of the body. But as long as I've served her, she's never had a fit. So I don't know what happened to her. But I do know that the truth will out, sooner or later."

"You sound like a Solarii," she observed dryly.

"Ach," he sighed. "I've lived amongst them for too long. You can't help but adopt their ways of thinking."

As they made their way through copses and meadows, every now and again Akasha stopped and looked back, thinking she heard a twig snap, or the alarm cry of a bird. There was no one behind them, so she dismissed it, putting it down to anxiety.

When they finally reached the river, the fresh smells of the waterway and the banter of the men passing close by on their barges were a refreshing antidote to her grief. The sounds of hammers and building noises filled the air. The dry dock was nearby and so was Uriah, who came to greet them.

"Come, ladies, follow me," he said, ushering them along the steep riverbank. He led them to the edge of the dry dock. In it sat the keel of an enormous boat, with a long series of curved ribs jutting out from a thick central spine. Scores of men swarmed over it.

"What a piece of work," Akasha said with admiration.

As she followed her father down the slanting path to the base, the dock exploded into cheers of welcome. She returned their applause with a hearty smile and a vigorous wave. At the base, the bare bones of the ark reared high, a confusion of planks and boards of wood. Above her, men perched precariously on top of each of the struts of the great upward-curving ribs of the keel, forming an arch under which Uriah beckoned her to walk.

She breathed in every nuance of the scene before her. The men on the struts waved their skullcaps in the air, cheered and shouted her name. Behind her, the river ran cool and long. She grinned the whole way as her father led her to the beginning of the arch.

With moisture in his warm green eyes, he whispered to her, "This you must walk alone." He kissed her lightly on the forehead.

Alone, she joined the strength of the men and their collective endeavour. It was a moment of mutual respect. Her heart floated like a feather. As she walked under the first wooden rib, the men balancing on top released handfuls of petals that fluttered down on her. She was walking through a cloud of petals. Settling on the ground, they formed a magical coloured carpet, rich in fragrance. The bounty of petals bounced off her with a lightness as light as being itself.

The men cheered with abandon when, unable to contain her joy any longer, she skipped and danced under the arch of ribs. She peered up at the men's faces, strangers before today, now companions in life. All she could see was their misty eyes and broad smiles. She waved her hands high above her head. The men's cries and shouts echoed around the dry dock, amplified by its sheer walls.

Reaching the end of the starboard side, she paused and clasped her hands together, her grateful thoughts winging their way skywards. Surrounded by a kaleidoscope of petals, she walked down the second arch of joy, the ark's port side, with as much freedom and ecstasy as the first. Waiting for her at the river end of the dock were Uriah, Tarsus and Shamira, their smiles as wide as the river and as deep as the ocean.

"It's the traditional welcome for a nymph, a bride-to-be," her father explained.

Scores of men were filing down the paths on the sides of the riverbanks into the dock, while those on the ship's ribs clambered down to the ground, nimble as monkeys. As the men gathered around her, they hummed a tune, a joyous air that rose and fell, gently on the rise, subtle like a bumblebee. The tune swelled, full and rich.

It was a serenade, remembered from her early learning days, when there was harmony amongst men before the arrival of the renegade Helios. With this tune, a boy serenaded his first love. Alas, in the sad days of one-to-one replacements and the Emerald Cavern, no one sung it as a proper serenade. Despite that, each generation taught it to the next in the unflagging hope that one day those utopian days would return.

The men formed a crescent in front of her, their backs to the river. As they swayed back and forth, like a field of ripened corn moved by a summer breeze, they hummed the tune so quietly that it mingled with the gentle sound of the waves lapping on the riverbank and the soft rustling of the wind kissing the leaves in the trees. Their rough faces beamed with pride and their eyes blazed with joy.

This was a serenade by the raw passion of a group of Semite labourers, strangers all, carpenters, shipwrights and smiths. The wonder of the experience melted her to the quick. In the end, it was not just for her that they hummed and swayed, because the song was a serenade from all men, to all women. The courting played out and the tears wiped away, she stepped forwards.

"I am truly humbled by your welcome. Thank you, one and all. I wish you good fortune with the building of this huge ark."

"Now, we have something to ask of you," Tarsus said.

"Anything in my power to give, and it's yours," she replied.

"To finish the ark quickly, we need more willing men, but some are reluctant to join us. They say as Horque is no longer with us, his agreement to the work is invalid. They refuse to volunteer until the pharaoh himself endorses it. We beg you to help us to gain an audience with him."

"I will try," she said.

"Thank you. Also, our endeavour needs a name, a special name, a name that fits its grand purpose, to carry us through the eye of the apocalypse and enable us to sail into the calm, clear waters of the next epoch. Akasha, I humbly request your permission to call this sea craft the *Fair Maiden*."

She looked up and beamed. "A most fitting name. I agree with all my heart."

"Without further ado," Tarsus cried, "I name this ship the *Fair Maiden*."

The crowd broke into applause. Skullcaps cascaded into the air and cheers of joy again echoed around the walls of the dry dock. Men shook each other by the hand and slapped each other on the back. Akasha embraced Shamira and her father.

At that crescendo moment, the raucous sound of a trumpet bellowed out over the ark, curtailing the celebrations. Akasha peered up at the source of the clamour. Standing around the rim of the 'U' surrounding the dock was a line of Solarii guards. The silver metal of the ankhs in their holsters gave off a dull glint in the fading mid-afternoon sunlight.

"No one move," a stern voice called from the hilltop. It was Irex. "All of you are under arrest," he yelled. "My guards will escort you to the Temple of Ma'at where the vizier will examine you for the gross offence you have caused."

CHAPTER 32

The Temple of Ma'at

Limbs aching from the fast walk, Akasha followed Irex and his guards into the Temple of Ma'at. The two rows of pillars running along both sides of the temple quite dwarfed her. Busy officials and administrators carried papyrus scrolls under their arms, wielding reed pens and wearing black headdresses.

As the Semites entered the court, the attendants and officers turned as one towards them. Irex barked orders to his guards and one of them grabbed Uriah by the wrist and dragged him over the alternating black and white tiles like an animal to the slaughter.

"Let go of my father!" Akasha demanded, and hit the guard on the arm, but he fended her off and went on hauling Uriah across the chamber. The gallery of onlookers, banked along either side of the towering columns, quickly filled the court with their opprobrium. Akasha was having none of their idle threats.

Lasec stepped forwards and yelled. "Order! There will be order in court!"

At the far end, two Solarii were sitting on raised daises. They wore stately robes and glowing pectorals. One of them repeatedly thumped a gavel on the desk in front of him. The reports thundered through the vast colonnade, and eventually his noisy efforts succeeded in bringing about an uneasy quiet. She heard Lasec address him as the vizier. So was the Solarii sitting above him the pharaoh?

The vizier commanded, "Confine the rebels in the area for the accused."

Rebels? Since when have we been rebels?

The guards pushed and shoved the Semites down the aisle between the massed ranks of the public gallery. As they were harried along, the gallery stood up and threw insults.

"Ha, look at the little people!" they taunted.

One Solarii thumped his clenched fist into an open palm. So much for the special dispensation accorded to the pharaoh's family. In passing, she noticed that many of the Solarii had that same rash she'd seen on the faces of Marim and Javian, and some had blotches on their arms and legs.

The guards herded the Semites into the closed dock from where she could clearly see the two Solarii on the dais. Etched on the wall behind them was a large white ostrich feather, which Tarsus told her was the symbol of the goddess Ma'at. The Solarii sitting behind the vizier had his arms crossed over his chest and he clutched strange-looking objects in each hand.

"What he's holding?" she asked.

"A crook and flail, the two pharaonic symbols of state," Tarsus replied.

"That's Nimrod? The Solarii I'm to marry?" She was flabbergasted.

"He is, yes, but at least you kept your agreement," Tarsus said.

"How so?" she asked, screwing up her face.

"We asked for an audience with the pharaoh and you delivered, just not quite how we expected," he observed with a wry smile.

Her head swam with a maelstrom of impressions: of menacing Solarii guards, haughty court officials, an imposing temple, and last but not least, the sheer injustice of her and the Semites' situation, arrested for the construction of virtually their sole means of avoiding the imminent apocalypse. On top of that, the court process was confusing. Samlios had no prisons and no formulaic legal process. Those who transgressed beyond agreed boundaries suffered correction or exile.

The vizier was talking to Irex, who stood beneath his dais, peering up at him.

"I am pleased, Irex," Zoser was saying. "You've done well to bring the Semites here so promptly."

"Thank you. Can I ask what should I do with the girl?"

"The girl?" Zoser frowned.

"Yes, the nymph, the Lady Akasha," Irex said, pointing her out in the dock. She felt all the eyes in the court turn to her. She puffed out her chest. Yes, he's talking about me.

"She's here? I thought she was at Khephren's residence. You were her escort. What's she doing here? You've arrested her?" Zoser's face turned a deep shade of ruby as he realised what Irex had done.

"I arrested everyone. According to your orders. Have I offended?" Irex was clearly distraught.

Zoser threw up his hand in a gesture of quiet despair.

"No, but a member of the pharaoh's family can't be tried against their will."

Presumably seeking guidance, Zoser glanced behind him at the pharaoh, but none was forthcoming. Arms folded, Nimrod sat statuesque. The Solarii were good at that. There was a slight delay, and then Zoser seemed to have made up his own mind.

"Guardian of Justice, free the nymph Akasha."

Lasec approached the dock and spoke to her with barely concealed disgust.

"My Lady Akasha, by order of the vizier himself, you are free to leave this court."

An official opened the gate of the dock and gestured for her to leave.

Uriah regarded Akasha with a long face and motioned for her to go.

"Go, save yourself while you can," Tarsus urged.

What should she do? Stay and face an uncertain future with the Semites and risk rupturing the fragile accord between human and Solarii, or show her loyalty to her newfound tribe?

"The court wishes to proceed with the charges against the Semites. Leave the dock. Now." Lasec was typically abrupt.

A pregnant hush descended. She took a deep breath and slowly, deliberately closed the gate.

"I will remain here until the Semites are granted free leave to work on the ark," she said, planting her hands behind her back and thrusting her chin out. Come what may, she was going to honour the brilliant lance of loyalty those Semite men had shown her.

"You *want* to be tried?" Lasec stammered.

"What's she saying?" Zoser asked.

"Excellency, she refuses to leave the dock," Lasec answered.

"Refuses?" Zoser murmured with an air of disbelief.

"What is the court's decision? Should the nymph Akasha be freed from the dock?" Lasec cried, as his rasping voice echoed across the open spaces of the temple. A tense, moody silence smothered the court. Zoser consulted the pharaoh, then turned back and addressed the packed courtroom.

"Not even the mighty pharaoh wields the power to force a person against their will. The law of Ma'at is sacred and the pharaoh is as subject to it as he is to day and night. If she chooses to remain in the dock, there she shall remain, accused like the other wretches. So be it. Let it be done."

She had stood her ground, made a powerful statement of intent, and now she reaped the fruit of her actions. Both Tarsus and Uriah returned her gaze with steady and unflinching pride. Guided by principle rather than personal whim, she'd refused the easy path. With her integrity intact, she kept the hounds of doubt at bay.

Lasec read the charges, whatever they were.

"The Semites are accused of constructing a wooden boat without the pharaoh's permission and stealing all the tools and materials. They've also conspired to leave the pharaoh's service without his permission."

The murmurs of the gallery filled the court until Lasec asked Irex to begin the case against the Semites. Irex touched his heart three times with his closed right fist, the traditional Solarii signature for speaking the truth.

"This morning," he said, "the vizier instructed me to investigate the Semites' illegal activities at the dry dock, where I found them in flagrant contravention of the pharaoh's trust, constructing a boat using stolen tools and pilfered construction equipment."

"This evidence is compelling and appears incontrovertible," Lasec said. "Now, who speaks for the Semites?"

"I do," Tarsus said, his chin jutting out like a rocky outcrop.

"Then proceed and be quick about it," Lasec said. "We've other, more important matters to attend to today."

"Don't let him intimidate you," Akasha said to Tarsus so all could hear. "Take all the time you need."

Tarsus nodded. "On his return from the Mind Search," he said, "Protector Horque met us at a gathering in the market square and allayed our fears of the coming floodwaters. We'd build an ark. In return, we'd stay in Egypt and give service to Pharaoh until the flood started. This agreement would stand for as long as he lived. Alas, he has gone and we mourn his premature death. Yet we're detained on these spurious charges and prevented from paying our respects at his last rites."

"And that is all you have to say?" Lasec said, in that sneering, disparaging way of his.

Tarsus' face was pale and anxious as he continued. "Without the opportunity and materials to build the ark, we have no means to survive the flood. The Semites have accumulated years of loyal service to the pharaoh and his people, so all we ask is that he honour Horque's agreement. Will he or won't he?" Despite his reasonable request, there were worried faces in the dock, Semites biting their lips and wringing their hands.

The vizier said, "I shall confer." While he exchanged whispers with the pharaoh, three Solarii entering the court caught Akasha's eye. Two were women wearing white mourning clothes and face veils, and the third was a man with a pronounced limp who wore a black robe and a hood similar to Cheiron's, that concealed his face. With that attire, she assumed he was a priest.

Lasec called for quiet. "According to Ma'at," he said, "the pharaoh is under no obligation to honour the word of a deceased member of his Ennead Council."

That was bleak. Irex spoke up again.

"Let the truth be spoken here. Many Semites have recently tried to flee from the safety of Egypt and the pharaoh's welfare."

"Aha!" Lasec said, exulting in the Semites' despondency. "Is that so?"

"I swear on the feather of Ma'at," Irex confirmed.

"Then the Semites are hypocrites," Lasec declared loudly, "rendering them unfit to continue in service to the pharaoh, confirming the guilt of all the offenders on all charges. I defer to the vizier for sentencing."

There was a pause. This was all very hasty, and the arbitrary nature of the verdict was confusing. The Semites' heads dropped noticeably. Akasha wasn't having that. They were an honourable people, trying to appease the pharaoh and stay alive at the same time. Proud and defiant, she rose to the defence of her companions.

"Mighty Pharaoh," she began, "I am Akasha, the Nymph of Samlios, and the one true fair maiden. Your Goddess Ma'at loves fairness and justice, so I ask, is it fair and just to force these Semites to dedicate their service to you, only to let them perish in the waters and for their bodies to rot on the seabed? No, it's not. I plead for you to be sympathetic to their petition, they who have acted in good faith, following the word of the greatest Solarii I have so far had the honour to meet. Protector Horque."

"We defer to the pharaoh for a decision," the vizier declared.

Tarsus explained the etiquette. If the pharaoh lifted the crook, the accused was innocent, but if he tapped the flail, he or she was guilty.

As Nimrod weighed the decision, the sun was setting, a great green orb just above the horizon, sending slanting rays and long shadows across the temple court. The pharaoh lifted his left hand and touched the flail against his right shoulder.

No! It wasn't possible. The Semites were guilty. Horque's agreement was void.

The gallery erupted. Everyone stood up, shouting and waving their scrolls above their heads, yelling at the top of their voices. Amongst the din, Akasha was listening to the quiet, insistent voice of her conscience.

"If that is the court's ruling, hear my verdict," she stated, adamant to the last. At first, no one paid her any attention so she waited, fists clenched by her side, until everyone quietened enough to listen.

"I refuse to be the pharaoh's nymph. He can find another," she said. One by one, her words dropped onto the floor of the temple and lay there like coiled serpents. Then she unleashed her cold anger.

"Instead, I will honour the life and mourn the death of Protector Horque. I will attend his funeral." By then, the silence in the temple was as loud as the ferocity in her voice. "After that, I will head for Babylon, where I have friends awaiting me. I have none here. This place is full of hyenas."

Her limbs were trembling.

"Leave...funeral...Horque?" Zoser stammered.

Everyone in the gallery seemed to be gesticulating, and running up and down like hares on a moonlit night.

"Insult to the court!" one cried.

"Arrogant upstart," yelled another.

She didn't know what should happen next. An impasse blocked any possibility of agreement.

Into the hiatus stepped a tall, elegant woman, the one she'd seen entering moments before. The gallery seemed entranced by her sudden arrival as she walked with dignity to the centre of the court.

"I bring important news," she cried, removing her veil and releasing her ebony hair to fall over her shoulders. Her face and skin were as radiant as a young girl's.

It was Lady Issa.

Issa raised her arms. "Prepare yourselves for what I am about to tell you," she said. "Don't mock me, because I speak no lies. In this temple of truth, I give you the truth. In this temple of justice, I give you justice. I keep my promises, for I bring the promise of the future. When all is lost and dark, in despair, there is always the searing light of hope. Great Pharaoh, as promised, I bring you the true twice-born."

The audience muttered amongst themselves, bewildered by her words. No matter, she had their undivided attention.

"I reveal this man of hope to you," she said, gesturing to the man in the black priest's robe, his face still hidden by his hood. All eyes were on the Solarii as he walked towards her, a profound limp in his left leg, tapping his wooden staff on the tiled floor. As he stood by her, she cried out.

"Pharaoh, see and believe! Osiris and Anubis have granted the greatest boon."

She lifted the man's hood to reveal...

"Horque."

In the dock, she noticed poor Akasha faint into Shamira's arms.

Pharaoh murmured his name in shock. A dead man walked. Everyone – the high priest, the scribes, even the Semites – prostrated themselves.

"Pharaoh, I *am* Horque. I fell asleep, but now I'm awake." His voice was hoarse and weak.

Horque spoke. A dead man spoke. Issa's heart burst with joy to witness her son stir the hornet's nest. Now Nimrod had to deliver on her demands.

"But... How?" Nimrod stammered.

Horque gestured to her. In that moment everyone knew that she, Issa, Sekmet priestess, had conjured the Gods' Spell. She'd done it. She'd negotiated with Osiris and Anubis. She was the magi. The people should prostrate themselves before her, not Horque, but that was of little matter.

"Pharaoh, Issa has performed a miracle, she's delivered on her promise," the high priest stuttered as people peeled themselves off the floor, disbelief unfolding on ashen faces. The Semites were ecstatic. Horque was alive, and so was their agreement. So be it. Let it be done.

172

"Tell us, Great Pharaoh, is Horque really the true twice-born?" Cheiron demanded.

It was a canny question. Issa had no doubt in her mind as to the answer he'd give. The pharaoh needed to relinquish his claim and confirm Horque as the twice-born and this was the exactly the time and place to do it – in full view of the massed Solarii ranks. Should the pharaoh deny his claim, and it later turned out that Nimrod was not the true twice-born, it would jeopardise the return of the Solarii and the future of the human race. The gallery was so quiet it was as if everyone had stopped breathing.

She wondered what was going through his fevered mind. Would he raise the crook of hope or brandish the flail of denial? He had to follow the line of truth. Why procrastinate? There he was, all powerful, all seeing, yet he squirmed on his seat, facing public humiliation. How she savoured this moment.

As the decision hung in the balance, a small bird flew into the temple. It dived and weaved down the middle aisle, crying out in alarm. Behind it was a black hawk, wings wide, eyes blazing, claws set hard and sharp. It swerved to follow the sparrow high up into the hypostyle columns. The hawk screeched, a feather's distance behind it. They were a strange duet, the hawk's deft movements reflecting those of the sparrow. The hawk swooped on its prey in triumph and hung in the air, right above where the pharaoh sat. A drop of dark red blood oozed from the dead sparrow and dropped onto the pharaoh's crook.

This was the gods' sign. The last shadow of doubt was gone.

Issa grinned in deep satisfaction, her sacred work fulfilled. She uttered a prayer of thanks.

A sliver of the sun's disc hovered above the horizon, casting long shadows across the stunned courtroom. As it dipped below the horizon, the pharaoh thrust the bloody crook above his head.

The crowd burst out in rapturous applause, crying, "Horque. Horque. Horque."

PART 6

Union

CHAPTER 33

Reunion

Akasha screwed up her nose and pushed Shamira's hand away.

"Stop," she said.

"I was only trying to bring you round," Shamira replied, putting the smelling salts away. "How are you feeling?"

"Better. I feel better. Where am I?"

"Khephren's residence."

"Oh, back here again." Akasha lifted herself onto her elbows and gazed at a host of white-winged moths hovering around a glow lamp. Out of the window, the small, dark shadow of a bat swooped by.

"How long have I been out?" Her temples pounded like drums.

"Since you fainted in the Temple of Ma'at. Tarsus and Uriah brought you back," Shamira said.

"Now I remember. *It* came in with Lady Issa. The Horque I met in Samlios wasn't lame. That creature was, and it had a face as pale as death. That's how I knew it was an imposter. Then I blacked out…"

"You weren't the only one," Shamira replied. "Even those God-fearing Semites dropped to their knees. After that, the court was awash with perfume and swooning ladies."

"No, no, no. That was not Horque. The Semites were desperate for *it* to be that limping monster, so I'm not surprised they convinced themselves it was. I saw him in bits, body parts strewn over the wasteland near the Gates of Gades. He had to be *harvested*, remember?" She buried her face in her hands at the memory. "By all that's sacred, Shamira, the dead don't stand up and walk! It does not happen, not in our world, or even in that of the Solarii. *It's* an abomination."

"Don't make such a hasty decision." Shamira was pleading with her. "The

177

Solarii originate from a place of monumental astral power. I do not know all of what they are capable. They have solar furnaces and flying chairs and healing ankhs and irsutions and ashlars, and there's bound to be more we don't know about, nor can even imagine."

"That may be," Akasha replied. "But we're talking about someone *coming back to life*. How is that possible? Oh, it is so confusing. Are you telling me it's him?"

Shamira glanced at her; a knowing smile flickered on her lips. "Everyone else in the temple thought so. It wasn't a grey ghost they prostrated themselves before."

"Yes, but what do *you* think?" This was as profound as it got.

"It doesn't matter what I think, because the pharaoh endorsed him as your groom in front of the whole court."

"Did he?" Could it be him?

"Yes, he did."

"This morning I was going to attend his last rites and now I'm going to marry him. No, it's too incredible – there must be some other explanation."

"There isn't. The Solarii I saw in that temple looked and sounded like Horque."

"Then *it's* his double," she said. That must be it. "Every Solarii has a twin they left behind on their home planet."

"And?"

"The solar double has come to Earth, passed through the veil, and – what did they call it? – now it is a creature of the Casting of Shadows. Yes, like the original Solarii. They were once angels occupying the astral light and now they're physical, incarnate. After Horque died, his double came here and walks in his place."

Shamira sighed. "I don't know if that's true."

"I'm not going to grasp at false hope." Akasha's chest heaved with emotion. "I can't put myself through it all – not again."

Shamira placed a consoling arm around her shoulder. "Are you fit enough to walk?" she asked.

"Yes, why?"

Shamira took her by the hand. "Let's go and see him. He's at Issa's."

"Now? In the middle of the night?"

"Yes. We need to settle this once and for all."

"All right," Akasha reluctantly agreed.

"Don't you want to put on your cobra necklace?" Shamira asked, pointing at Demos' gift on her bedside table.

"No," she replied. "We have to go."

She didn't recognise any of the three escorts that accompanied them, but she noticed with pride that they wore the black hawk insignia of the Horque household. The three Solarii rasped and coughed, their breath chilled by the cool night air. Moths, attracted by the glow lamps the Solarii carried, danced around their heads in the bright moonlit night. Passing through the deserted streets, a Solarii man who wheezed hard into his kerchief surprised her. Deep red blotches disfigured his face. From inside the houses, she heard more coughing and retching. A malaise was sweeping through the city, breaching every threshold.

The closer she got to the Horque residence, the more nervous she grew. What was she going to find there? Some awful double, an imposter, or some ghostly apparition. Curiously, this time the hawk engraving on the stone lintel appeared benign and protective.

The gates creaked open and Tarsus welcomed them. He sunk to his knees in benediction in front of the glow lamp. Its light cast an eerie shadow on his jutting chin and sunken eyes.

Clasping his palms together and peering star-ward, he said, "Praise the Source, for today we've all witnessed a walking miracle."

As he led them into the main house, its gloomy corridors seemed alive with anticipation. Every muscle in Akasha's body was shaking, every nerve jangling as hope and doubt fought for supremacy in her mind.

"Uriah sent a message," Tarsus said with an air of excitement. "Scores of men have volunteered to work on the *Fair Maiden*. Protector Horque has saved us from the killing waters. Now we have a future."

She was too nervous to reply. Shamira wasn't. "That's good news," she said. "I'm very pleased. And what's happening to the Solarii? Their skin is discoloured, are they ill?"

"It's a terrible affliction," Tarsus said. "I hear it's a malfunction of the pyramids."

"If that's the case, it won't be long before it affects us as well," Shamira said, as Tarsus turned into the entrance to the water court.

Akasha's thoughts were as jumbled as leaves in the wind. Her skullcap sat crooked on her head. A lump rose in her throat. She swallowed hard but it was stuck there, stubborn to the end, like the double knot in the pit of her stomach.

As if in a dream, she heard Tarsus announce them.

"The Lady Akasha and the pythoness."

She waited at the entrance to the water court, her legs refusing to move. The daunting prospect of meeting Horque, a dead man supposedly alive again, was too much for her. The splatter of the water fountain thundered in her ears. Her head throbbed. She had the oddest sensation of walking on the bottom of the seabed. Her eyes were playing tricks on her and she was surrounded by vague shadowy outlines. A tall Solarii woman stood over her.

"Come." The woman led her to where a man sat on a high-backed chair, and Akasha took a seat next to him. She listened to the night, and the sound of crickets. The circadian rhythms of life carried on unabated. Next to her was a Solarii man, his breathing laboured and his face pallid and gaunt.

"Akasha." His voice sounded far away.

It was an apparition. It had to be. Her tongue was tied in so many places.

"Don't be afraid," the voice said.

She wanted it to be him, but it was a ghost.

"I *have* returned." The voice was muted, almost afraid.

It's impossible. The thought screamed in her head.

"It is I."

No, it can't be. She took a furtive glance, afraid to look him in the eye in case it was he, and equally in case it wasn't.

"Who are you?"

"I am Horque." The voice was firm, definite. Now that *did* sound like Horque.

He glanced at her. She looked away, staring instead at the water in the pool. His reflection leapt out at her from the water. *It* had body and substance. He was no apparition. The jawline was strong and the shoulders square, like the real Horque.

"Akasha, don't reject me," he pleaded as she looked away from his reflection. "I've made this long journey just for you."

Summoning all her courage, she turned to this thing.

"Are you a double?"

"No, I'm the same, it's me. I've come back." The voice was familiar.

"I don't...I can't believe you," she said, her chin trembling. "It's not you. You're his double, aren't you?" She was terrified of what the answer may bring.

"Believe me, Horque lives again. I am he, the same Solarii. I'm no solar double. My mother made a bargain with Osiris and Anubis. She brought me back from Du'at, the realm of the dead. I am alive again. They allowed me to leave so I could be with you."

"No." She felt smothered, stifled. "Horque is dead. You *must* be his double. You walk in his sandals – with a limp. Don't lie to me. Not now, not like this." Every fibre in her being was shaking.

"I tell no untruths," he said as if uttering some sigil. "I wanted to tell you that I found your necklace in Samlios."

"I know. Your mother told me, she gave it back to me," she said, remembering she'd refused to put it back on after the Temple of Ma'at.

He reached across and his hand brushed soft against her skin. It felt warm to the touch. As he withdrew it, she lifted hers and they touched. He left his hand there and she clutched it, at first with hesitation, then with growing certainty as it dawned on her that he was real. He was alive. A pulse of his immense warmth enveloped her body which she recognised as Horque's, as her Horque's. A vital relief spun through her body like a spring unwinding.

He turned his massive frame towards her, tall and powerful. He curled both his hands around hers. Cocooned in his web of might, she tilted her head on his hands, which still grasped hers. With closed eyes, she breathed in the delicious vapours of the moment.

She didn't know how long they stayed like that, with her head resting on his hands, the fountain splashing, the crickets clacking, the night owls hooting, the moths dancing. This was the joining of these two people, two beings, and two races. She had to learn to accept the will of the Source. At first, she'd denied Horque's resurrection, but he'd proved her wrong. She felt enormously blessed and graced. As long as she lived, she'd recall this moment with profound affection. In it, she was his and he was hers. It was the ecstasy. They were bound and unbound, separate and together.

She didn't know when she fell asleep. When she awoke, she began to feel as he did. A trickle at first, then a torrent, as his feelings transferred to her. Her limbs felt heavy. Her bones ached. She felt worn out to the core. Nausea covered her like a rash. It was like a vertiginous pain, a ubiquitous seasickness. She pulled her hand away from his. His eyes blinked and he yawned.

He let out a low whimper and groaned. "The return from Du'at – I'm beyond exhaustion. With you here now, my strength returns, the black hawk re-forms." He leant forwards to pick up his staff and limped around the water pool. The tapping of the staff on the stone floor sounded like thunder claps. How much labour must every step take from him?

"You must rest," she told him.

"I will." His voice faded into nothing.

"Will your leg heal for the union?"

Horque slumped down in the chair. "No, I'm afraid it won't."

"Then, when?" As she spoke, she knew the answer. "It's not going to heal, is it? It's never going to heal."

He murmured, "Osiris demanded that he keep a part of me, to retain until I return for good."

First he was dead, then against all the rules of life, he was alive – but lame. Soon, they were to be married. It was her dream. It was coming true, not as she'd expected, but when was life how she wanted it to be?

He cleared his throat. "Other than the limp and the profound tiredness, my body is in pristine condition."

"I give thanks for small mercies," she replied. "I'd rather have you with a hobble than not at all."

"We two will join together in marriage to make one. Between us, we carry the hopes and destinies of our two races. Let this be a communion for us both."

He poured water from the flagon into the glass and took a sip. Then he passed it to her and she drank from it too. The water tasted sweet. It was over. She accepted it was he, with a feeling of profound joy.

CHAPTER 34

The Beginning of the Last Days

Horque stifled a yawn as he heaved himself off his chair. In the twelve days since he'd held Akasha's hand in his, he'd not seen her again, and their union ceremony was fast approaching. In that time, matters of state had pressed hard on his fractured mind and tired body. In response to the unfolding crisis, the last six days of active duty had been full of unremitting toil.

"Come to the Temple of Hathor," was the message he'd received at dawn. Khephren only summoned him on matters of state importance.

His mother was still suffering from dreadful fits. To seek a cure, she'd visited Khephren in the Temple of Healing only the day before.

"You must go, my son," she insisted.

"I'm hard-pressed dealing with the pyramids – again. Tell me what you saw there."

"No, believe me, you need to see for yourself," she said, in that calm, reassuring way of hers.

As he left, she pressed something into his hand.

"What's this?" he asked.

"A headscarf – doused in rose water. You'll need it."

On the way, Marim tripped over some rubbish left in the street.

"That should not be there," Horque fumed. What had happened to Solarii standards of cleanliness? Where was their renowned civic pride?

This wasn't the first time his deputy had shown signs of fatigue. Marim appeared ill: his face was covered with dark pimples, while ruddy blotches marred his cheeks. The whites of his eyes were shot with red lines.

The way to the temple took them within sight of the three pyramids whose angled, polished surfaces emitted a tepid sheen. These last six days he'd spent trying to restore them to their normal incandescence, but without any success. This was why Marim was showing signs of the wasting disease. He wasn't alone. It was affecting all Solarii.

Casting his mind back to his first visit to the Temple of Hathor, Horque recalled how the healing priest had performed the circumcision ceremony on him, while whispering high moral platitudes that about instilling courage, fortitude and discipline in young Solarii men. As a nine-year-old, he hadn't understood the mores, but the extreme pain had been its own teacher.

He lifted his aching leg and tapped his staff on the ground. Strange how his view of the staff had changed since he'd whittled it from a bough of ash. At his appointment with destiny at the Temple of Ma'at, the staff had been a grace, a small counterbalance to the precious gift of life. Twelve days later, it was a gross encumbrance that gnawed at his soul. Osiris had played a trick on him by forcing him to walk with three legs well before his old age.

At the corner to the Temple of Hathor, he turned up his nose. Something smelt rancid. It was the smell of diseased flesh. Outside the two gleaming pillars that marked the temple entrance was a line of a hundred or more people waiting to get in. Heads bowed, some propped themselves up on roughly hewn crutches, unable to plant any weight on raw soles. Many had bloodstained cloths bound in haphazard fashion around their feet. Others wore rudimentary bandages around their heads, legs, arms and hands. As he passed by, a few mustered a glance, showing dull, vapid eyes and skin rashes as blood red as sard.

His headdress askew, a scrawny guard was slumped against an entrance pillar. Sheathed by his side, the guard had an ankh in the weapon position. He wore a scarf over the lower part of his face. Only his tired eyes, staring dreamily into the air, were visible.

"Protector," he said, the word bolting from his mouth.

"You're a Solarii," Horque stormed. "Stand upright. Pull in your shoulders. Adjust your headdress."

The guard straightened up and pulled a smart and brisk salute.

"Where's Khephren?"

The guard pointed at a white door at the far end of the temple.

Inside the temple, the smell of putrefaction hit him like a punch to the midriff. He fought to control the impulse to retch, and lifted his scarf to cover his mouth and nose. The rose water smelt sweet. Thank you, Mother.

Four rows of veined white marble columns stood like soldiers, obedient and ordered, symbolising the vaunting genius of Solarii medicine. Anything could be healed, from cuts and bruises to lesions and colds. Surgeons operated without physical anaesthesia, while nurses used ankhs to heal the sick. For more than three days, these marvellous abilities had been under threat.

184

Line after line of Solarii lay flat on the ground, while others were propped against the marble columns. Temple servants dressed in white headdresses emblazoned with the twin golden horns of the cow of Hathor bent over the sick. A nurse walked down the middle of the temple, emerging into and out of the long shadows cast by the hypostyle columns, the sun's rays alternately glinting on her ankh's shiny surface in a primeval dance of light and dark.

As Horque limped down the crowded aisle, a plaintive murmur rose from the sick. The scourge was terrible: some had skin peeling off, like rolls of a frieze falling off a damp wall. Soon Horque was recognised, and the word spread that the resurrected protector walked amongst them.

"Help us, heal us from the wasting disease," one man whimpered.

"Make it go away," another pleaded.

An old Solarii lying on a blanket grabbed Horque's withered ankle. Horque bent over him. A rash had closed the old man's right eye and the skin on his neck was rippled like a chicken's. He peered at Horque through dim, watery eyes.

"Bring things back to how they were," he croaked.

The words pierced Horque's heart. How could this old man articulate the very thing he himself craved? But Horque couldn't delude himself: they could never return to how they were. Instead, they were falling into the abyss.

Gently, he released the man's grip on his ankle and shuffled away.

Marim challenged him.

"What's happening to you, Protector? You allowed him to *touch* you."

It was true. The old man had dared to touch a member of the Ennead Council, a breach of the law of Ma'at punishable by death.

"He's dying," Horque replied. "That's why." On his way back from Du'at, he'd acquired a kindness, because he barely recognised the compassion in his own words.

Outside Khephren's chambers a woman lay on the floor, her face as staid as salt. A temple servant lifted an ankh into the healing position and the woman let out a soft whimper as her body hungrily absorbed the healing rays. That reminded him of the other reason for his visit. Before entering Khephren's chambers, he turned to Marim.

"The guard and temple servants have ankhs. Collect them and bring them to me."

Khephren was hunched over a desk, his eyes sunk deep in their sockets. He oozed fatigue.

"I wanted you to see how the people are suffering," he said.

"I have, it's terrible," Horque replied, heaving himself into a chair. He had this awful feeling in his guts that he'd been brought back to life to solve one crisis and now he was fighting another. How was that fair?

"It's more severe than after the last hybrids' attack," Khephren said, and then broke into a wretched coughing fit. When it subsided, he took a sip from a glass of water.

"And you're suffering from it too?"

Khephren nodded and pointed to the door. "Every one of them out there has a rash that burns their skin like fire and which is only soothed by the ankhs' healing rays. Over the past few days, the power of the ankhs has slowed to a miserable dribble during the night, because they rely on the pyramids for their charge. I want to heal the night-burn. I want it to stop."

"The seals are the problem," Horque replied. "The surfaces of the pyramids are so thin the dressed stone protrudes from beneath them. I've tried everything to thicken them, and nothing's worked. Without a proper seal, the pyramids don't store sun-fire ambience in the day, so there's none to release at night. For now, they're not much better than gigantic lumps of stone."

"I'm not interested in explanations," Khephren said, with a dismissive wave of his hand. "All I'm interested in is when they'll be working again."

"Tomorrow, I hope," Horque said wearily.

"Well, that's something." Khephren grunted. "And it's not just us. There's the Semites to think of as well. With no sun-fire ambience at night, they're suffering the growth of the hybrid seed. Benjamin's growing hair. Nails will be next. And he's not the only one."

"I know," Horque said. "Tell me, how is Akasha?"

"You may well ask," Khephren said, grimacing. "When she came back from her reunion with you, she was walking on air. Since then, I've been here. Talking of Akasha, what about the union ceremony?"

"It's in three days." How were they ever going to make it on time? The foreign dignitaries had already started arriving for the ceremony.

"Three?"

"Yes, and—" His reply was interrupted by sounds of a scuffle, and raised voices from outside the chamber. The door swung open and Marim walked in, carrying five ankhs slung over his forearm.

"I have them all," he said.

"Good," Horque said. "Lay them down here next to me."

"What's this? What's going on?" Khephren's voice was shrill. "What's he doing? Where's he taking those ankhs? He can't take them away!"

"This was what I was going to tell you," Horque said calmly. "I need every ankh we have to make one last attempt to thicken the seals."

"No," Khephren insisted, holding his hands on his head. "It's the only palliative we've got. You can't do this. At least leave me one."

"I wish I could, but I can't," Horque murmured. "It's for the greater good.

186

The seal on the pyramids must be repaired. If it works, everything will be fine and you can have them all back tomorrow."

"Take them and there'll be trouble," Khephren warned. "My patients are in such pain, they could turn violent."

"Khephren, this is our situation." Horque stood up, leaning forwards with both hands on the desk. "We've hardly established our cities and monuments in Egypt. We started with one pyramid, now we have three – all because of the deteriorating astral light. Soon we'll need fields of pyramids to generate enough sun-fire ambience to survive here. Other than that, everything's remained the same in our society for many years – the pharaoh, the Ennead Council and the pantheon. Then people hear a deluge is coming and they panic. Now the pyramids' failure is turning their world upside down. The oldest taboo, anthropophilia, is about to be broken. The Semites are building an ark and threatening to leave our service. Eventually, they'll do that anyway. Our own people are anxious about their survival. The very fabric of our civilisation is breaking down. It's not surprising they care less for the proprieties of Ma'at than they do for saving their own skins. These, my friend, are the beginnings of the last days."

"What does that mean? What can be done?"

"About the deluge? After the wedding, the Ennead will set in motion our own survival plans. About the pyramids? I'm going to try to strengthen the seals. Pray to Amen that I succeed – tonight." He picked up his staff.

Khephren planted both hands on his haunches.

"What about you, Horque?"

"What about me?"

"You've just travelled the Winding Waterway and come back to all this. Was it all worth it?"

"Life is not a choice, it's a prolonged duty." He covered his face with the rose water scarf. His leg hurt as he limped out of the chambers. From deep inside the dark realms of Du'at, he could have sworn he could hear the hollow rattle of Osiris' laughter.

CHAPTER 35

The Ark

As Akasha approached along the riverside path, a cloud of smoke billowed into the still morning air from the site of the ark. The shouts and calls of the men mingled with the grating sound of saws and the clash of hammers.

A flat barge had docked at the entrance, held tight by ropes against the bollards. Tarsus directed a gang of a hundred or so mud-besmirched men who were hauling one of the trunks off the barge. They shuffled it into place, then dropped it next to the others in the pile on the quay. The gang celebrated their efforts with slaps on the back, and greeted Akasha by waving their skullcaps above their heads. Her joy at their greeting was complete, until she noticed a light down of hair on their normally bald scalps. The hybrid seed was an ever-present and sinister companion.

Uriah showed her round the ark, which was cocooned with wooden scaffolding. Every cubit of the planking teemed with industry: men climbing up and down the adjoining ladders, standing on the baseplates, handing each other tools and planks of wood, carrying buckets of water and banging tools. The site buzzed with the frenetic activity of carpenters, shipwrights, smiths, water-carriers, and the scores of runners to ease their heavy burden.

"She's huge. How many decks?" she asked.

"Seven, each with nine subdivisions," Uriah explained. "We have to find room for all the Earth's little creatures."

"Why have you built the ark here, in this basin?" Shamira asked. "The keel's resting on ground that's just above the water level of the river, so how will she launch from here?"

"We won't launch her at all," Uriah said, giving her a knowing smile and earning one of Shamira's sterner frowns.

"Think about it," Akasha's father said, gesturing at the surrounding fields. "We could have built the ark in the middle of a meadow, it would have made no difference to the launch. We're only building it here next to the river jetty to unload the barges. The truth is, the rising floodwaters will launch the ark."

"Of course, now I see," Shamira said, bequeathing his explanation with a sly grin.

Akasha soon discovered the source of the plume of smoke. In the recesses of the dry dock, well away from the ark itself, a fierce fire blazed. It filled the air with the pungent smell of woodsmoke.

"Over there," Uriah pointed to a corner of the site opposite the fire, "are the barrels of pitch to make the bulkheads watertight. There's a plentiful store of logs to keep the fire ablaze all night – that way we can fire the torches."

Next to the barrels of pitch were several pitchers of water. An army of water-carriers milled around, ladling water into pelts that they carried up the ladders and along the planking to the thirsty labourers.

"I'm impressed," she said to Tarsus. "The men's spirit is indomitable."

"All because of you," Tarsus replied in those gruff tones of his.

"Me? You're the ones holding the hammers and chisels." She was coy.

"You fulfilled your promise and they'll never forget your courage and loyalty."

"Nor will I," she replied, a lump in her throat.

"You defied the pharaoh in the Temple of Ma'at," Tarsus reminded her. "It brought me to my knees. You have the heart of a lioness."

"I would never abandon you to those Solarii bullies."

"Don't let them hear you say that," Shamira rebuked her. "You're about to marry one – their chief, no less."

A small boat docked at the quay and a clutch of passengers emerged from it. One of them had a familiar face.

"Philo!" Akasha cried. "I'm so glad you came!"

"As am I," the Babylonian replied, his eyes sparkling with happiness.

"How is King Appolis? And his great tower?"

"It's finished and nearly reaches up to the sky waters," Philo said proudly.

"Have Callisto and Tros come with you?" she asked, looking around for them.

"No, sadly not," he replied, shaking his head. "They've stayed put, as have many other invited guests. These are dangerous times to be away from your family."

"What about you? Why did you come?"

"Sweet child, your wedding is a unique moment in the rich pageant of human history. I wouldn't miss it for the world."

"Well said, Philo," Shamira replied.

Akasha smiled, but she wasn't happy. All this was happening on the eve of her wedding. Like most normal brides, she would have loved to have the luxury of worrying about her appearance and her wedding dress, her bridesmaids and her bouquet. Instead, she worried about surviving an apocalyptic deluge. She was beginning to curse her own prediction. On top of that, she wouldn't mind catching a glimpse of her errant groom.

"Has anyone seen Horque?" she asked. "Why doesn't he visit me?"

Irex, who was guarding them today, knew the reason. "He's been trying to reseal the pyramids. He's going to make one last attempt this evening."

"I pray he succeeds," she murmured.

"As do we all," Shamira said.

"That's why we all have this abysmal growth," Akasha added, raising her skullcap to reveal a down of brown hair.

"The children you bear Horque will be free of it," Shamira said.

A question hung in the air, like a sword suspended above her head. She plucked up the courage to ask it.

"How is that possible, if I'm tainted by the hybrid seed?"

"Remember the Watchers' edict," Shamira answered. "*The Surge is paramount.* That's their promise for your children. The Surge will flourish in them."

Akasha wished it were that simple. The silhouette of the ark shimmered against the gossamer surface of the body of the water. Fireflies danced between the water lily pads, leaving a thin trace of light in the gathering evening gloom. Nearby, she could hear the clatter of tools, the crackle of the fire and the shouts between the men. The river flowed by, full of permanent impermanence.

It was a time of extremes, of hopes and dreams and preying fears. Seeking comfort, she reached for her avatar, the blue emerald birthstone Callisto had given her. Now her union with Horque was approaching, she conceived an idea of what to do with it. She would fashion him a wedding gift he'd never forget.

CHAPTER 36

Amen, Scarab God of the Sun

The first stars flickered on the verdant tapestry of the evening sky as Horque arrived back where the Horus Wing craft were located. The pyramids cast a dim light, a pale reflection of their former glory.

Marim was handing out ankhs like precious jewels to the flyers. Horque turned his mind to the union, only three days hence. This attempt to repair the seal had to work. If it didn't, there would be no union. He tried to conjure the warmth of his love for Akasha, but all he evoked was a dull ache in his leg. If only he could close his eyes without seeing images of the monster Ammut snapping at his heels in the Hall of Truth.

Marim brought him out of his reverie.

"Protector, your instructions?"

"Flyers," he said, leaning on his staff. "Tonight we're going to make a final attempt to replenish the seals. To do so, we need to create a potent astral light, which we'll temporarily engender by the simultaneous firing of our ankhs at the pyramids' surfaces. In such a powerful presence, motes of limestone can condense, like the way lichen deposits out of the air onto a rooftop, only far quicker. The method is dangerous, which is why it's a last resort."

"What's the danger?" Marim wanted to know.

"Instead of strengthening, the seal may be further punctured, releasing the remainder of the stored sun-fire energy. Pray to Amen, scarab God of the Sun, that it doesn't come to that."

He repeated the special utterance to cause the mental nexus to his new Horus Wing craft which shuddered into life with a deep growl, like a beast of prey rudely awoken from slumber. Low on charge, it responded with indolence. Exhausted, he could barely hold it steady in flight. He had to summon every morsel of his resolve to will the craft towards the pyramids, which stood like shadowed monoliths in the early evening twilight. Their surfaces pitted and uneven, they appeared like a thousand bared, gaping mouths full of jagged teeth, waiting to feed on Solarii souls.

The craft stalled and keeled forwards. The moment of his death flashed before him, when the hybrid birds had smashed into his craft. "Not again." He lost the mental nexus to his craft, which tipped over, his straps keeping him from a second death. He repeated the utterance. The craft purred and trembled beneath him. The panic subsided. The craft had ignored his mental instructions. That should never have happened. Was it his limp, his fatigue, or because it was a new craft?

Below him, the dark glint of the river snaked its way to the sea. Further up, a long tongue of smoke rose from a fire near the river's edge. That must be the fire for the pitch at the Semites' ark. Did they really believe they could sail through the floodwaters in that lump of wood?

Hovering directly above the Pyramid of Records, he took aim at the apex. A fiery astral bolt spat from the end of his ankh, lanced through the air, and struck the pyramid with such ferocity that sparks of luminescence flashed and vibrated over its four triangular surfaces.

The other flyers released their ankhs. Simultaneous beams of light erupted into the dusk and hit the pyramid's surfaces like bolts of lightning. At first, the pyramid drank the colossal amounts of astral energy like a thirsty child until she could suckle no more. The combined astral firepower of all the flyers began to concentrate and thicken the pyramid's slanted surfaces.

Throbbing with light, the pyramid shone like a stellar giant stalking the gathering night sky. The glow intensified until a thin film of luminescence coated the seals. These luminous threads grew into a gigantic astral dome that radiated from each face, first illuminating and then enveloping the flyers. As the wall of astral energy engulfed him, Horque heard a high-pitched hum resonate in his ears...then it was gone.

Buffeted by the dome of astral force, his craft shuddered again and bolted forwards. The motion caused him to loosen his grip on his ankh. He stopped firing. The other flyers took that as the signal to do the same. The giant ball of brilliant astral radiance that had been there at one moment disappeared in the next. At that same time, the upper rim of the sun sunk below the horizon, enshrouding them in a dim twilight.

Returning to the landing place, Horque had no idea if his plan had worked. At least the astral bolts hadn't ruptured the seal. As he stepped from the craft, he detected a high timbre in his ears. That was an excellent sign, as was the moment he turned to see the Pyramid of Records aglow, a sheen of luminescence coating its angled surfaces. As he'd hoped, the ankhs' fire created an astral ambience, allowing the seal to re-condense inside it.

Dawn would become a sacred moment. With the return of the light, the pyramid could go back to its sacred function as a solar furnace. He sank down on his knees. Ignoring an arc of pain that shot through his withered leg, he murmured a quiet prayer of thanksgiving to Amen, the great golden bull scarab.

At last, he could turn his attention to Akasha.

CHAPTER 37

The Nuptial Chamber

Akasha paced the floor in her chambers. To say she was restless would be an understatement. Her mind was feverish with images of Horque's visit to the Temple of Hathor and his brave ingenuity the night before at the Pyramid of Records, all conjured by stories Khephren had told her. The pyramids were all working fully once again, and now the whole of Egypt was in a state of frenzied preparation for the union.

There was a rap at the door. It had to be him. She opened it and frowned.

"What's the matter?" Shamira asked, and obviously realised the answer to her own question. "No, I'm sorry I'm not Horque, but I do have important news."

"Of him?" Akasha raised her eyebrows, and her expectations.

"No," Shamira said patiently. "I've met with Cheiron to discuss the details of the ceremony. It will take place in front of the Great Sphinx. Afterwards, the bride and groom will retire to the Nuptial Chamber in the Temple of Isis to consummate the marriage."

"I'd like to visit this chamber beforehand," she said.

"Cheiron said that it was strictly forbidden," Shamira retorted.

"Nothing is forbidden to the wife-to-be of the twice-born son of Egypt," Akasha replied. She marched out of the door, Shamira scuttling along behind her. She could get used to being important.

Outside Khephren's front gate was the ogre Irex. She'd never forgive him for his brutal behaviour towards the Semite workers. Marim stood next to him. Surely, he would have news of Horque.

"Where's the protector? How is he?"

"Resting," was all she managed to extract from him.

The marbled veins of the colonnades of the Temple of Isis were a wondrous spectacle, but it was the smaller chapel next to it that caught her eye, because standing in defiance on top of it was a sculpture of a mischievous dwarf. His most distinguishing feature was not his bearded smile nor his elf-like pointed ears; no, because in his hands he wielded an enormous phallus, an instrument as thick as his thigh. The sculptor had caught him in the throes of a huge ejaculation and drawn his face in an expression of wild ecstasy.

She was not going to be embarrassed. "Who is *that?*" she exclaimed.

"That is Bes, and this is his temple." Marim introduced the rampant dwarf.

Akasha peered through the entrance. Because all the window openings were up high, dimming the ambient light, the chamber was evidently built for privacy. The chamber walls were covered in a frieze of dancing men and cavorting women. On the ceiling was a painting of a naked woman, arched over a man writhing on the floor beneath her, his erection as stiff as the temple's supporting columns.

She was confused. In Samlios, Shamira had told her that the greatest aphrodisiac was the difference between the two genders. "Let nature work her magic," she always said. It was obviously different for the Solarii. If they needed images, that was harmless enough, wasn't it? Either way, she'd spend the first night of her marriage in that chamber with the man she loved. She'd enter it a girl and leave a woman, and hopefully a mother-to-be.

The sounds of chanting and bell-ringing came from inside the chamber. Clouds of incense wafted out of the entrance, quickly followed by the Lady Issa.

"Akasha, you shouldn't have come here," she said, ushering Marim to block the chamber entrance.

"I wanted to see inside," Akasha confessed, standing on tiptoe to peek into the chamber.

"That cannot be allowed. Cheiron has not finished his work." Issa turned to Shamira. "He warned you. Yet still you brought her. Why do you flout our customs?"

"I tried to tell her and she wouldn't listen," Shamira said, evidently taken aback at the stinging reprimand.

"Why? What have I done? I was only curious to see the Nuptial Chamber." Akasha feigned innocence.

"It's a bad omen for the bride to enter it before the wedding night." Issa's tone was guarded and hesitant.

Cheiron emerged and exchanged furtive glances with Issa. "The astral preparations are complete," he said.

"If Akasha is to spend the night in there with her groom," Shamira said, refusing to be intimidated, "then she has every right to know how you've prepared it. So what astral preparations are these?"

Cheiron replied. "The erotic paintings and objects will enhance their pleasure and enjoyment of one another, as will the conditioning of the astral light we've placed in there."

"Is that all?" Shamira hissed. "I heard religious chanting and incantations, both of which are used to summon an astral presence. So I ask again, what astral preparations did you carry out?"

Shamira's insistent questioning served to wake Akasha up from her romantic reverie and she became aware of the conversation's alarming undertones.

"Shamira's right," she added. "You're both priests, skilled in the invocation of entities from the astral light. To my mind, you've summoned an astral atmosphere…to interfere with the conception of the child. My, that's what you've been doing, isn't it?" she blurted out, as the full extent of their dark practices dawned on her.

"Like I said, it's a bad omen," Issa repeated. "Now I insist that we all leave."

Akasha was not going to be anyone's puppet. "You've conditioned the astral light in there to produce specific characteristics in our child. I'm not going anywhere until you tell me what they are."

Cheiron turned to Issa and sighed. "They have a right to know," he said. "It's for twins. A boy and a girl, both tall, well-built, good-looking and with strong libidos."

She felt a knot in the base of her stomach. So it was twins. With prominent Solarii characteristics. How had she trusted them?

"Cheiron, you mentioned nothing of this in our meeting. This is deceitful and totally unacceptable." Shamira spat out the condemnation.

"On the contrary, this is a purely practical decision," Issa said. "The new species has to guarantee continuance. Therefore, it has to be a boy and a girl, and the Solarii characteristics will equip them with the best opportunity of succeeding in a dark, dangerous world. You should thank us, not condemn us."

"What?" Akasha said, clenching her jaw. "No, this is sacrilege. I don't want any loading of the astral light in the Nuptial Chamber. If I find some, I'll refuse to step over the threshold."

"In that case, you won't find any," Issa said, with a calm nod of her head.

"I hope so," Akasha replied. She was going to have her way. "Lady Issa, I'll marry your son. I love him and he returned from the abode of the dead to marry me – that's how much he adores me. I'll marry into the Solarii race but he will also marry into the human race. As his bride, I'll happily embrace all your customs, but only in so far as they accord with my own beliefs."

Issa's ice blue eyes danced between her and Shamira, and after a moment, she said, "We need to confer." She and Cheiron retreated into the chamber.

After a while, from inside the Nuptial Chamber, the light timbre of the bell rang out and Cheiron started chanting. Issa returned alone.

"We agree," Issa said, now full of sweet reconciliation. "As you can hear, Cheiron is releasing the astral loading. You will see for yourself on your wedding night."

"Yes, I will." She hoped her defiant frown hid the knowledge that she didn't possess the astral skills to detect whether the Solarii would be true to their word – and nor did Shamira. Issa was a slippery adversary. What choice did Akasha have but to trust her word?

CHAPTER 38

The Union Ceremony

A pair of dappled steeds whinnied as they drew Akasha's wedding chariot ever closer to her appointment with destiny. With dry palms and a strong grip, she held the reins, proud to represent her race and her gender. She was dressed in a splendid wedding attire of silken crimson robes.

In front of her was the trio of pyramids, their apexes probing the clear mid-morning sky, their smooth surfaces reflecting the sun like so many glaciers. They loomed above her, three giant monoliths frozen in stone. Alien and incongruous, their size was as huge as the race into which she was about to marry.

The chariot pulled up at the head of the causeway in the thin shadow of the gigantic King's Pyramid. Shamira folded the train of her wedding dress and as Akasha descended from the chariot, the crowd roared and tossed handfuls of dried rose petals over her.

The musicians played the opening strains of the old serenade, the one the Semites had hummed to her on the ark site. As the flute added the high notes to the rhythm of lute and lyre, the human wedding guests hummed and clapped their hands to the familiar tune; feet and fingers alike tapped to the steady beat of the drum until everyone broke into a spontaneous dance.

While the musicians quickened the beat, Uriah, Tarsus and Philo, helped by the other Semite stewards, ushered all the ambassadors and dignitaries to their places in the bridal procession. They were still whistling and humming the tune well after the musicians had brought the music to a crescendo.

Shamira stood at the head of the bridal procession, looking nervous and elated at the same time. Philo was coaxing the last few errant guests into line, a task magnified in difficulty by a group of acrobats performing extravagant cartwheels and juggling acts to euphoric applause. All the bridesmaids, little cherubim dressed in pale blue dresses, giggled, laughed and urged each to hold the train of her dress higher than the other. Akasha gently chided them, to curb their excitement.

It was nearly high sun when Shamira gave the signal to start. The human musicians struck up another tune: cymbals clapped, the lute plucked, the bells rang and the drum beat. Trilling to the beat, everyone skipped down the causeway. Soon she could see the awesome Sphinx, evoking a sense of wonder. Close up, the hybrid appeared more mysterious than ever.

From where she was, some distance away, she noticed a chariot drawn by two fiery black steeds pull up in front of the Sphinx. A distinguished Solarii with a staff stepped down from its ramp. That was her groom. Her chin quivered as she fought to keep her emotions in check.

Arm-in-arm, Horque escorted Issa and Neferem towards the Great Sphinx. The stone beast, unperturbed by the festivities, stared implacably out to the ends of the universe. He'd always wondered why it was a hybrid, with an animal rump and the head and face of a virgin, the two insulated by a sliver of amber. Amidst the trauma of his death and resurrection, he couldn't remember the reason for the separation, nor to what the face of the virgin alluded.

The Solarii musicians struck the first chords of their welcoming tune while the Solarii onlookers cheered loudly and waved their red and white pennants to celebrate his arrival. On the top tier of the podium, the servants cooled Pharaoh Nimrod by waving large white-feathered ostrich fans. On the middle tier sat the members of the prestigious Ennead Council, stern and full of aristocratic pomp. On the lowest tier, he could see the governors of the twenty Nomes of Lower Egypt and of the twenty-two Upper Egyptian Nomes, not forgetting their administrative officials and wives, with fans aflutter and jewellery aglow.

Along the causeway, Akasha inhaled the sweet fragrances of the rose petals crushed by those ahead of her. With the delight of the moment, the heady rhythms of the music, the acclaim of the onlookers, and the gathering potency of the astral light, she felt dizzy. She grabbed her mother's hand for support.

As the bridal procession neared the Sphinx, and the massed ranks of the Solarii, she was ushered to join Shamira at the front of the procession. Across the short distance to the Sphinx, she could hear the strains of a tune from the Solarii musicians, which clashed with the wedding tune played by the human musicians in the bridal party. Unable to hear their own tune, each band played louder still, until the din became a cacophony. Eventually, Philo calmed the human musicians down and it was quickly resolved.

To arrive at this point, she'd left her home in Samlios, sailed the Northern Sea and flown in a flying machine. She'd suffered the grief and joy of seeing her groom die and – miraculously – live again. Only a score of paces separated her from him, and from her destiny. A score, that was all.

At the decisive moment, she stopped and screwed up her nose. What was that smell? It was like rotten eggs. And she could see it through her whites. Rising out of the bowels of the Earth in the gap between the two assembled races was a finger of black astral smoke. It twisted upwards, like a strand from a smouldering fire on a windless day. Next to it, another black tentacle appeared, and another. The smell was malevolent. She wanted to retch, but held it down.

A black cloud of astral fog billowed out of the ground and began to spin, slowly at first, then faster. A gust of wind blew up: now the cloud was incarnate. The wind grew stronger, whipping up a mix of spent flower petals, leaves, twigs and sand that showered over everyone and shrouded the Solarii tiers from view.

A malevolence crept up Akasha's legs and enveloped her soul. Her muscles tightened. Her arms hung rigid at her side. Invisible astral chains rooted her to the spot.

Horque sat next to Neferem and Issa, watching this strange phenomenon unfold. What was this swirling dust cloud and noxious smell? After all these preparations for his special day, it was ruined by a malevolent mist. What exactly was happening?

Around him, the Solarii were paralysed like the humans.

"Issa?" he called out. "Neferem?"

They were like statues, devoid of the power of speech or movement.

This was wrong, drastically wrong.

With her eyelids stuck open, the swirling sand particles stung Akasha's eyes.

"Help me!" She tried to cry out, but her tongue was as stiff and immobile as the rest of her body, and her cry of alarm stuck in her throat. To add to the misery, the stench was sickening. Her skin crawled. The plans for the ceremony were in chaos, the joy of the occasion dissipated and the people terrified. On the greatest day of her life, she was helpless in the face of this unknown adversary. Right now, she was in the very last place she wanted to be.

Despite being unable to move, her senses were acute. Out of the corner of her eye, she could see a long, thin body crawling towards her. The trace of slime the creature left behind glistened in the morning sunlight. It was ghastly. It was a cobra: her astral signature. This one was real enough, with hooded head and slippery body. She ached to run away. Her stubborn limbs refused.

The cobra-thing slithered into the spinning astral cloud and emerged out the other side of it, heading towards her. No one moved to help her. Her wedding dress rustled in the warm breeze. Her eyes bulged with fear as the snake slid right up to her sandals. She was desperate to raise the alarm, but no one could hear her silent screams. The cobra reared up in front of her, its hood open wide. Its head wavered, its forked tongue flickered. Its empty, soulless eyes glared into hers, its mouth open to reveal two sharp fangs.

She was hypnotised as the cobra swayed back to strike. Then everything happened so fast. A huge shape stumbled through the black cloud. A stick, brandished high in the air, crashed down on the cobra, which buckled under the impact of the heavy blow. The avenging arm lifted the stick and brought it down again on the neck of the snake, which spewed out its innards onto the bare rock in front of her.

At the moment of its death, the dark cloud dispersed, rupturing the astral lock that held Akasha and everyone else in its claws. A propitious gust of wind blew away the foul smell and heralded back in the sweet scent of rose bloom. Frightened screams betrayed the sudden release of taut nerves; the bridesmaids cried tears of terror.

Quaking with fear, she buried her head in Horque's strong arms. She'd never felt so safe, and yet so vulnerable. His grip was firm, his skin warm and supple, her hand was clasped in his. All her anxiety and dread melted away.

"Look," Uriah called out. Dangling on the end of a branch was the tattered remains of the cobra. By the Source, the snake had two heads! It was a mutant, a hybrid. Uriah hurled the branch high into the air and it twisted and looped like a piece of rope, back into the ravine from whence it had crawled.

"Crawling through the black astral cloud changed the snake. It grew another head, I saw it with my own eyes," Horque admitted.

"Only one entity has the astral power to change appearances like that," Shamira said.

There was no way Akasha was going to hear that Helios angel's name spoken aloud, not now. To think it was painful enough, but at this poignant moment in the history of humanity, it was incongruous and wrong. He had no place in these joyous proceedings. He was the rebel.

"Can we carry on with the ceremony?" she asked. It was more a demand than a question. Horque nodded. He persuaded the two sets of musicians to play the wedding anthem in tandem. At first, their efforts were awkward and the music discordant. Soon enough they adapted and out of the many songs, there was one.

Akasha wiped away the dust and flower petals that had landed on her dress and skullcap. Horque tried to help, though his clumsy efforts were more of a hindrance. He'd saved her life, he'd saved their love, so she could hardly chide him. She fingered her cobra necklace. Though far away, Demos had come to her rescue. He said his cobra necklace would protect her and it had.

Hand in hand with her groom, they took the first tentative steps across the open gap, pausing when they reached the spot where the black tentacles had first appeared. In silence, they stood there, a dual act of defiance against the foe that had sought to wreck their precious union. Then she followed Horque onto the Solarii podium and he escorted her to her seat.

Cheiron welcomed them, and began the union ceremony.

PART 7

Protector

CHAPTER 39

The Protector

The sporadic singing of the birds faded as the sun hung on the brim of the horizon. Akasha leaned against a tree until the giddy feeling passed. Staff in hand, Horque limped towards her between rows of bushy pomegranate trees. She crooked her neck to look up to him, and smiled.

"I'm happy."

"I am too," he replied. "Ever since my return, I've felt a stranger in my own skin. Until now. Today I feel my strengths, my loves and my desires are close by again. I feel like I've welcomed back an old friend who's just returned from a long and arduous journey."

Even in the midst of Issa's sumptuous gardens, tension lingered in the air. As soon as they'd returned from the Nuptial Chamber, some seven days before, Horque had introduced his new bride to the gardens. He knew of the human tradition whereby mothers spent their confinement in healing gardens. Every day they would stroll amongst the rock gardens, lily pools and orchards. They sat under his favourite pomegranate tree and enjoyed its luscious aromas. She even felt protected from the threat of the nefarious black cloud, which seemed to have receded. At least, no one had spoken of it since the union ceremony.

That night, she sat with Horque, Issa and Neferem in the water court and dozed on the chair. She awoke abruptly, as if from a nightmare, only to open her eyes and find herself confronted by one of the four Horus statues, glowering in the corner of the court.

"What's the matter?" Horque asked.

"These prowling statues…"

"They're of Horus," he said hastily.

"Yes, with hawk heads and human bodies," she snapped at him. "They're hybrids."

"They're guardians," he barked back.

She had to make him understand her predicament. "I don't want to even see them, let alone be near them. I don't want my baby, our baby, exposed to these hybrid impressions in any shape or form."

"The four Horus are there to protect you…"

"I don't care." She was adamant. "For all I know, it may already be too late. The hawk impressions may have entered my womb. After all this trouble, it would be a travesty if our child were born with the head of a raptor. Get rid of them."

"I can't. In Du'at, I faced Osiris, dread Lord of the Underworld, who Issa persuaded to allow me to return *from the dead*." He spoke with surprising passion for a Solarii. "Without his intercession, I wouldn't be here talking with you. Horus is his son. Out of respect to him, the statues must stay."

She tried again to make him understand. "So one moment, they're attacking your pyramids and threatening your entire race, but the next, you're lauding them as gods and saviours."

"They're antagonistic to us, it's true, and much of that stems from our rivalry with the Helios," he replied. "Speaking of which, these statues are now more important than ever."

"Why? What's happened?"

"The black astral cloud at the wedding…" He left the sentence hanging.

"What? What was it?" She knew what was coming and it made her shudder.

"That was Semjaza, the chief Helios angel."

"As I had suspected." Talk about an uninvited and unwanted guest. Semjaza was the fallen angel who had impregnated Irit. "I thought he died long ago, so how did he end up at our wedding?"

"I did too, but apparently not. A long time ago, before I was born, Semjaza adopted physical form and led an assault of hybrids on the Records Pyramid. He was captured and – it was assumed – killed by a rockfall inside it. Now it appears he survived by crossing back through the veil into astral form. But the seal on the pyramid had prevented his escape. As soon as the seal eroded and fractured, he slid out between the cracks."

"Our child must be free from the hybrid seed for the Surge to prosper. With Semjaza roaming the mansions of the astral light and these statues glaring down at me, I don't feel safe here anymore."

"What are you saying?"

"I may have to go," she said, trying hard to stay calm.

"Go? Go where? You can't go anywhere in your condition."

The choice was limited. She had to go to a city with healing gardens. The ones nearby in Sidon and Tyre, Byblos and Carthage, were a tangle of bindweed and broken promises. Their citizens had fled for higher ground, leaving the gardens to rot. Why maintain them anyway, since none of them boasted any women with child? Amongst all humans, only she – Akasha – was pregnant. Only one city had maintained their famous Hanging Gardens.

"I could go to Babylon," she said. "Philo's there, with Callisto, Tros and Rocor." Yes, that was a distinct possibility, although if there were a way for her to remain here, it would be better for the whole family.

"You must stay in Egypt," Horque said. His voice held the passion she'd heard before. "I can keep you and the child safe here, where I can protect you. We can talk about the statues. When the floodwaters ravage the city of Jizah, I can take you in the Horus Wing craft up into the ridges of Mount Hermon in Canaan."

That was a compromise. She sat quietly listening to the chirping crickets and the gentle flow of the fountain. Placing her palm on the surface of the water, the ripples cooled her hand. With a moist finger, she traced a blue vein that protruded beneath her lily-white skin.

"Please stay," he said. His face gleamed in the soft hues thrown up by the glow lamps.

"I'd prefer to. I'll have to think about it." His sentiments of loyalty and support moved her. It was another of those moments where the two of them were together, joined, like the moment which had summoned the Watchers. Perhaps she should stay after all.

Then it all happened in what seemed like an instant. A ripple of water sped across the pool. Horque reached towards her, stark panic on his face. A loud rumbling erupted under her feet, deep beneath the ground. The water court echoed with the groaning of the earth.

In the next moment, everything started to shake. In front of her, the table shuddered with such violence it was as if an invisible hand had grabbed it by the legs. Her glass smashed onto the alabaster floor, spraying shards. The shaking intensified. Akasha's legs gave way beneath her. She thrust out a hand to grab on to Horque's. Stumbling, she grabbed at the empty air. The shuddering dislodged a curtain of dust from the walls and floors. Water splashed from the pool.

As the ground juddered, the four Horus statues in the corners of the court shook and trembled in a macabre dance. Falling as one, they crashed to the ground; their heads and limbs breaking off and rolling around the court like apples on the deck of a storm-wrecked ship. One of them thundered into Akasha, knocking her further off balance. As she fell, her palm hit the floor hard and her wrist buckled under her own weight.

A gust of wind extinguished the glow lamps, plunging the water court into darkness. As quickly as they'd begun, the earth tremors ceased. An eerie silence followed.

"Are you all right?" Horque cried, his voice full of concern. He crawled over to her in the gloom.

"Yes, I think so." Akasha coughed in the dust-laden air. She trembled as she sat on her haunches, and clutched her belly. Her forehead was drenched in sweat.

In the streets outside, there were cries of alarm. Dogs howled at the round moon. Tarsus appeared at the entrance, holding up a glow lamp, which he thrust into the dark spaces of the water court. The light splashed onto his furrowed brow and ashen face.

"What's happened?" Akasha asked in a shaken voice. A thin film of dust spread into the room like a ghost, settling on everything and everyone. Neferem coughed a thin, rasping cough and then put a kerchief to her mouth as she bent down and tended to her mother.

"It was a quake of the earth. The underworld's in upheaval." Horque mopped Akasha's brow and gently helped her to her feet. She felt light-headed and clutched her belly. Her hand was stinging where she'd fallen on it. A blue fluid seeped from the cuts and gashes in her palm.

Issa looked pale and gaunt, but her mind remained as sharp as a reed.

"Tarsus, bring us face scarves, a bowl of water and bandages."

When he returned, Issa gently washed Akasha's cuts. The water dribbled into the bowl, slowly turning it blue.

"Your blue blood waters are not like ours," Issa said. "Ours are ruby-red."

Akasha smarted from the touch of the damp cloth.

"There, it's done," Issa said, tying the bandage.

"Are we safe now?" Akasha moaned, a ringing in her ears from the rumbling and her body still vibrating in shock.

"That should be the end of it," Horque said.

What did he mean – the end of what? She didn't have to wait long to find out.

"It's my duty to protect you and I failed," he told her, in a surprising admission. Why this sudden contrition?

"No, you haven't. You tried to warn me," she reassured him. "You told us it was a quake of the earth. So what caused it?"

Horque stirred uncomfortably. "I can tell no lies," he said eventually. He stared at her and then turned away, ashamed. "It's dreadful news. It's the Records Pyramid."

"I should've known," she grumbled. "It's exploded, hasn't it?"

"Yes." Horque nodded. "The temporary seal has ruptured, releasing all that stored sun-fire energy, like a plug removed from a volcano. The sudden effusion made the ground tremble."

"I see," she said. The quake had made her decision for her. He knew it too. She didn't know whether to feel joy or sadness. He'd done everything in his power to keep her in Egypt, and now this.

"Now I think about it, how did you know it was about to happen?"

"It's my duty to know. Veins and currents in the astral light connect me to the pyramids. The nexus is subtle but unbreakable."

She had to make herself clear. "It's not safe for me to stay in Egypt any longer. I must leave as soon as possible. You must escort me to Babylon."

At that moment, Tarsus announced the arrival of a messenger.

"Bring him to me," Issa commanded.

Irex appeared, wearing a brittle, determined look on his face. Grains of dust and fine particles of sand covered his clothing and an open gash slanted across his chin. On his tunic, emblazoned over his heart, was the crossed crook and flail.

"Speak," Issa said.

Irex bowed low and spoke in a stentorian voice. "I bear a message from mighty Nimrod, pharaoh of all Egypt. He gives thanks to the pantheon that you are all safe. He summons the Ennead Council to convene at noon tomorrow to discuss the ground thunder and the imminent flood."

"We hear his summons. Horque and I will attend," Issa said and turned away, dismissing him.

"There is another matter, Lady Issa," Irex said, standing his ground. "The Lady Akasha is also invited."

Akasha frowned. What was she to do in an Ennead Council meeting? She wanted to leave for Babylon, right now.

Horque answered on her behalf. "She'll be honoured to attend."

Irex bowed and backed out of the court.

"These are days of foreboding," Issa said, her voice ominous with presence. "The pharaoh is right to call a meeting. We can use the occasion to request an Isis Pass."

"An Isis Pass?" Akasha queried, although she guessed what it was on recalling that Isis was the Goddess of Travellers.

"Those who leave the sacred boundaries of the Two Lands must have an Isis Pass," Issa said.

"But I am Akasha, wife of Protector Horque…"

"…which means you're subject to Solarii law," Issa replied.

She was learning the rules of this strange people. Yet it always seemed that as she drew closer to them, some obscure impediment would appear of out of nowhere, blocking the way forwards, inhibiting, suppressing. This Isis Pass was another one.

In her imagination, she pictured herself walking in the midst of the glory and majesty of Hanging Gardens. That is where she was going. Nothing would stop her, certainly not an Isis Pass.

CHAPTER 40

The Hypogeum

Akasha set off with Horque and Issa to the Temple of Isis, tasked with persuading the pharaoh to put her safety and well-being above all else. To honour her invitation to the Ennead Council meeting, she'd dressed in the fashion of Solarii women: a simple white cloth headdress, a long flowing gown tied loosely at the waist and, on her slender wrists, some fine silver bangles. Fryme suggested a hint of rose-tinted perfume and helped her apply lapis lazuli eyeliner and carnelian lip make-up. While Akasha thought her appearance was rather fetching, all the Solarii women along the way gaped at her. This upset her until Issa pointed out it was unusual for a human woman to dress in Solarii garb.

Throughout the city, the dreadful aftermath of the quake was everywhere: uprooted trees, fallen statues and empty pedestals, streets littered with rubble and stones. Some people wore bandages around their arms and foreheads, stained with that distinctive ruddy Solarii blood. These were inauspicious omens. It was as if the entire Solarii civilisation was unravelling like a giant ball of cotton. This mayhem only served to strengthen Akasha's conviction that her future lay beyond the boundary stele of Egypt.

A sculpture of Isis suckling an infant adorned the temple roof. So Isis was also the Solarii Protector of Childbirth. Where had she heard that name before? Yes, Shamira had once told her that the dominant star in the sky at Akasha's birth was the Dog Star, Sirius, or the Star of Isis, as the Solarii named it. Soon she'd find out if that was a good omen or not.

The atrium swarmed with temple servants, guards, courtiers and administrators, all animated by the close proximity of the pharaoh. A black-shirted Solarii guard accompanied them to the meeting in the hypogeum. The temple walls were so high and sheer and the corridors so narrow that Akasha felt like she was at the bottom of a deep crevasse. On they went, corridor after labyrinthine corridor, until they halted before another guard. Beyond him, four black-shirts hauled the pharaoh's throne, mounted on two long poles, through a gap in the corridor wall. As soon as they were gone, the guard ushered them through the same gap.

The gap in the wall bewildered her. There was no door as such, just a space. Part of the enormous wall had separated out and that created a gap. There were no hinges on the part still attached to the main wall. Nor were there any lintels, handles, nor any other physical sign that identified it as a door.

As they emerged into an anteroom, the 'wall' grated closed behind them with the screech of stone on stone, slamming shut. No one had pushed it. It moved on its own, as if an invisible giant had closed it. Looking back at the 'door', not one sliver of light emerged through it. The seal was perfect. The technology of these Solarii was a marvel to behold.

The guard led them down a narrow, sloping tunnel. The smooth limestone blocks were damp and cold. They emerged into the hypogeum, a vast rectangular crypt. As Akasha's eyes adjusted, the silky blackness seeped through the stone floor and walls. The mountain of stone above her felt oppressive. If it collapsed, there'd be no escape. It would crush her and her growing child. Her breathing became shallow. A shiver of fear ran across her shoulders. This wasn't a good start to the meeting. She noticed what was housed in the hypogeum: arranged in neat, ordered rows were scores of long black rectangular boxes: granite sarcophagi. The place was full of empty coffins.

In the distance, she heard the growl of a big cat. Yet there were no cats down here. The sounds must have originated in the astral light. Enabling her other astral senses, she detected the sound of paws pacing towards her. Amidst the swirling curtains of astral energy, a lithe black panther stalked the perimeter of the hypogeum. An astral guardian, the panther protected the contents of the hypogeum – the black sarcophagi, along with who, or what, they would contain.

Horque and Issa strode passed two fierce-looking black-shirts into the hypogeum. As Akasha tried to follow them, the guards brought down their sabres in front of her nose. She yelped with fear and took an involuntary step back.

"No passage. Only Solarii can pass," the guard explained.

Horque turned in a flash. "She's married to me. She carries a Solarii in her womb. She *is* Solarii."

If Horque wanted to think that, it was up to him. She was human, and so would her child be.

"Let her pass. Now!" Horque snapped, and the guards gingerly lowered their sabres.

The inside of the hypogeum smelt of sweet river lilies. A temple servant wafted the stems before the pharaoh, who sat enthroned in a small annex with ten Solarii in two rows of seats facing him. Akasha took her seat in the front row, alongside Horque.

Issa, the newly reinstated vizier, began proceedings.

"We welcome our visitor today and congratulate her on being with child."

Akasha felt the eyes of the Solarii upon her. It made her distinctly uncomfortable.

Issa continued. "Now Cheiron will tell us about our plans for the flood."

"Thank you, Vizier," Cheiron replied. "This hypogeum will be our sanctuary from the flood."

So *that* was the purpose of the empty sarcophagi. Now the perfect seal on the outer wall made sense too.

"During the deluge," Cheiron explained, "the Solarii retainers and officials will be housed in a separate hypogeum. When the sky waters fall, the royal family and aristocracy will congregate here and fall into a suspended slumber. We'll awake when the silver trumpet of the new epoch echoes in our ears. By then, the earth will have drunk her fill of the sky waters and we'll be ready to return home."

She knew the Solarii were planning to leave Earth, but this made it personal. Was Horque going with them? As usual, he showed no emotion. The thought struck her like a chill wind. One of those cold sarcophagi was reserved for her. She could not imagine herself lying supine in a granite coffin, even for a moment.

Cheiron went on, "The birth of Horque's child will fulfil one of the Watchers' conditions for our return home. A second condition is their dictum, *the return is signed by the blue bow*. Once this mysterious blue bow appears, that will be a sign for us to leave. Before that, you must all walk the Sear Line."

This Sear Line sounded serious. Then again, everything to do with the Solarii was serious.

"Our returning souls must be pure, so as not pollute our doubles," Cheiron continued. "If one of us falls to the Twin Perils, it will taint our soul. If a degenerate soul returns home, it would poison all the solar doubles. Only those souls pure and fit enough to return home will pass the Sear Line."

"When will we have to submit to this mysterious Sear Line?" Zoser asked.

"When the trumpet rings out its clarion call, you must all come to the pavilion and make yourselves ready for the test," Cheiron promised.

"I doubt Horque will pass," Zoser added spitefully.

"What do you mean?" Horque asked, eyes glaring fire.

"Ruffled your hawk feathers?"

Horque glowered at him and mouthed, "How dare you?"

"Enough!" Issa growled. "We have other matters to consider. The Lady Akasha has put forward a petition."

Before she even stood up, Akasha's head was spinning with Solarii politics.

When she got to her feet, she felt awkward and incongruous in the Solarii attire. The headdress was tight around her forehead and she felt uncomfortable.

"I – we," she stammered, "meaning Horque and I, have to go to Babylon where we humans have a special garden. It's our tradition that a woman with child spends her time surrounded by natural impressions. After the explosion of the pyramid, Egypt is no longer safe for me. I can't bring up a child in one of those granite coffins. So I request an Isis Pass for Horque and me."

"What are the views of the Ennead?" Issa asked the questions.

Cheiron responded first. "The child in her womb is Solarii. We can protect both of them. People must respect our traditions too. Akasha should not be allowed to leave our boundary stele."

"I agree." Zoser was equally gruff. "Of course tradition is important, and it's our tradition that the woman gestates in the land of her husband. If the hypogeum is good enough for us, it's good enough for the Lady Akasha. Therefore, no Isis Pass."

She didn't like this snarling Zoser.

When Horque stood up to speak, the small chamber went so quiet she could hear a spider walking across the cold stone floor.

"We must listen to Akasha's wishes." Horque spoke clearly. "She must be shielded from any danger. She's ill at ease surrounded by our gods, and she fears she'll give birth to a hybrid. That would be a catastrophe for us all. It's essential the child is free from the scourge of the hybrid seed. She feels safer elsewhere, so she must have the pass."

"The omens for Horque are not auspicious," Zoser pointed out. "On the last occasion the protector was granted an Isis Pass to go to the Whispering Tower, he was mauled by hybrids. We wouldn't want that to happen again now, would we?"

Well, that was openly hostile.

Issa intervened. "That was entirely uncalled for."

"Then tell us *your* verdict, Vizier," Zoser snapped back at her.

Issa cleared her throat. "The pharaoh makes the final decision, but I will say this. I risked my life to bring my son back from Du'at. I believe in this union and its fruits. It must succeed. The mother's wishes are paramount. Horque supports her too. On that basis, grant them both an Isis Pass."

At least Horque and Issa stood by her. Would the pharaoh concur? Nimrod glared at Horque. The old feud between their families reared its ugly head. Everyone knew they did not like each other.

After an interminable delay, the pharaoh lifted his left hand: the flail of denial. He straightened his arm and held it high in the air above his head. Horque frowned, and Nimrod smirked.

Akasha was angry. For the second time, the pharaoh had defied her will. She was not going to suffocate in this claustrophobic place. Her child would gestate in Babylon, but how could she go there now? Without an Isis Pass, they'd both be vaporised if they tried to leave Egypt and pass through the astral shield of Dudael. These Solarii and their rigid rules made her want to scream.

Next to her, Issa whispered in Horque's ear. "Goodbye, my son."

Why the poignant valediction? Where was she going?

Issa stood up and turned to the pharaoh with quiet but determined authority. "No," she said.

A tense silence descended on the chamber. Even the astral guardian stopped prowling. For a moment, Akasha thought Issa had defied the pharaoh, but that couldn't be. Even Akasha, a mere human amongst these vaunted Solarii, was painfully aware that no one rebutted the pharaoh. She must have misheard. The pharaoh sat frozen like one of his statues, his hand still holding up the flail, staring at Issa with a mix of rage and incredulity. The atmosphere was full of nerves drawn taut, and minds in recoil.

In a voice stern with retribution, Issa uttered the fateful words. "Pharaoh, this petition calls for the crook, not the flail."

The chamber bristled with fear and horror. Issa had openly flouted Pharaoh's decision. This was anathema. On pain of death was Pharaoh countermanded.

Akasha put one hand over the other to stop them shaking. She felt like she was going to explode with the ferocity of the moment. With a malevolent glint in his eye, Nimrod lowered the flail in order to unleash a lethal astral bolt. Before he could, Issa strode up to him and whispered in his ear. Whatever she said must have been all powerful, because the pharaoh's face went white as snow.

Nimrod's last pharaonic act was to hand the crook and the flail to Issa.

This was unprecedented. The pharaoh was no more. Long live the pharaoh.

Issa was terrified, but exultant. This was her moment. She'd whispered the pharaoh's god name in his ear. He had to yield to her. A nomen and a prenomen were the core to a person's identity; a god name was more potent, even more so because it was hidden. To know the pharaoh's god name gave her the ultimate power of life and death over him. He'd divulged it to her soon after she'd presented her resurrected son Horque in the Temple of Ma'at. It was only a question of time before she used it.

This act was one of revenge and justice: revenge for Nimrod's interference in her husband's premature demise all those years ago, and today justice for Horque and Akasha. Nimrod had erred when he'd lifted the flail and she had to correct that. It was imperative that Horque left Egypt – Cheiron's timely reminder about the Sear Line had forced her hand. The knot she'd tied could not now be untied. Now to issue her first command.

"Horque, Akasha. I, Pharaoh Issa, grant you both an Isis Pass. Go safely in the arms of Isis. Akasha, you carry her seed, her genes."

Horque led the Ennead Council and bowed before her. When Nimrod prostrated himself, her journey of redemption was complete.

CHAPTER 41

Pharaoh

Not long after rise-sun the following day, Horque entered the pharaoh's inner chamber. Careful not to mix maternal sentiments when addressing the pharaoh, he bowed low.

"You summoned me," he said, casting an admiring glance at his mother. Her regal demeanour told him that she was undoubtedly in command. Since the hypogeum meeting, Issa had assumed all of the pharaoh's extensive obligations, prerogatives and astral powers. There had been no pomp or ceremony to mark the occasion – far from it. There had been no need for such overt trappings. Because at the precise moment Nimrod had handed over the crook and flail to her, every Solarii citizen, the solar doubles, the pantheon, the local astral entities, all knew through the astral and clairvoyant pathways what had transpired. As a matter of course, they deferred to her. As did he.

"Protector, where exactly do you intend to take your wife?" Issa asked.

At first Horque was confused, because his mother rarely addressed him by his function in the Ennead Council. The deeper, fuller tone of her voice was alien to the woman he knew. Gone were her usual flattering mannerisms and familiar feminine gestures. Instead, he faced a formidable woman of power. Of course, she was the pharaoh. She wasn't his mother anymore and never would be again. That was what she'd meant in the hypogeum when she'd said goodbye. From that point on, she had to dedicate her life in every intimate detail to the government of the Two Lands.

Whoever wielded the mace of power was attended by an array of preternatural astral entities. Now that Issa had risen to that elevated position, everything she did and thought was a matter of life and death, scrutinised by those same unforgiving and impersonal entities. She had to be correct, because, should she misuse their powers in any way, they would turn and rend her.

He straightened his back. "I will escort Akasha to Babylon in the Horus Wing craft and stay with her there."

"No. You must put our interests first," she replied stiffly, "and you and your flyers must take all the Horus Wing craft."

"*All* of them?"

"Yes, you will need them, and all the ankh weapons."

"What will I do with them?" Horque asked.

"Take Akasha and leave her in the Hanging Gardens. Then fly to the Zagros Mountains. Find a position high enough to survive the rising floodwaters, for they will come soon enough. Make an encampment there and guard all the Horus Wing craft and the ankhs with your lives."

His mind was reeling. She had thought it all through, that far ahead.

"And then what?"

"You are to remain there until the flood."

"And then?"

"I know what will unfold, but at this juncture, it's better you don't. However, when the time comes, it will be obvious what you have to do. If you are ever undecided, I urge you to remember the Watchers' edict. *The Surge is paramount.*"

"I will," he said. It was a timely reminder. The Surge was their visa home.

"Now," she went on, "ensconced in the High Zagros, you're going to miss the Sear Line. I want you to be able, on your own account, to return to your double after the flood, so before you leave for Babylon, I will impart to you the secret knowledge of how to cross the Winding Waterway."

"Thank you."

"Good," she said flatly. Ever since she'd returned from Du'at, she'd suffered awful fits which had conspired to harden her looks, lending them a cold, calculating aspect. That new face looked out at him now.

"You must understand our situation," she said. "I want you to know what the grand plan of the pantheon actually is."

"Please tell me," he replied.

"Humans were implanted on Earth as a preordained and divine trial, a journey that is obviously unfinished, since the human has latent capabilities which were meant to be activated by the Surge. The Helios tried to deliver it, but failed, and instead introduced the hybrid seed into the human. You and Akasha have produced a child in whom the Surge can work its magic."

He followed her thus far.

"But the human seed is weak," she continued. "It's like a rotting fruit without a seed, and it won't survive the rigours of the coming deluge. To protect it from certain extinction, the human needs the charisma of discipline, endurance and determination. All of these are the vaunted attributes of the Solarii. That was the secret reason the Watchers countenanced a union between human and Solarii – to toughen and fortify the human seed. Your progeny, Protector Horque, will carry the genes of our Goddess Isis, which will survive the flood and prosper thereafter."

"The genes of Isis," Horque murmured to himself.

"Yes, and in this way," Pharaoh went on, "do we fulfil the terms of our exile with the Watchers, who will shower us with their eternal gratitude."

"How will they do that?" he asked.

"The Solarii will permanently infiltrate the Earth and its history. After the deluge, there will be seismic physical changes. Every shoreline will shift. The seminal change will be in the astral light, which will lose its vibrant intensity. Humans of the future will measure and perceive everything according to the dim astral light of their day, preventing them from ever discovering the truth about the incandescent astral light we endure on a daily basis. For them, peering back at where we are now and gazing through the watery veil of the deluge, it will be as if they look through a glass, darkly."

An excited smile flashed across her face. A moment later, it was gone.

"This new seed will be a strange and wonderful concoction," he ventured.

"It will, Protector Horque, but mark my words. We, the Solarii of Egypt, will live forever on Earth. After the flood, humans will apotheosise our monumental achievements and see them as the great icons of civilisation: the Sphinx, the pyramids, the temples, the statues, our writing, religion, science, medicine, art, the occult, and government – everything from the sacred to the profane. The Solarii will be the mother and father of all things. For as long as humans revere us, their praise and adoration will keep us nourished and vibrant in the invisible halls of history: the astral light."

Horque rubbed his forehead. His temples were pounding from the sheer power of the astral entities that had gathered in the chamber.

"That is enough. Go to your wife," Pharaoh said with a dismissive wave of her hand.

As Horque left her presence, he wondered if he would ever see her again. Backing out of the chamber, he glanced at her, sitting there, glowing with the sheen of astral power, full of dignity, composure and imperial bearing. He was as proud of her as he'd ever been. She'd been mother to him – twice. She'd wrought a miracle on him, brought him back from the dead. She had risked her life for him, indeed, for all Solarii, in order to pursue what was right and just.

Turning to go, he caught a glint in her eye. Why *had* she allowed – no, wanted – him to leave with Akasha? As she'd said, he was unlikely to return to Egypt. She could easily have delegated Marim to fly Akasha to Babylon. Did she have some other reason? Was she protecting him?

CHAPTER 42

Departure

Soon after rise-sun the next day, beneath a dreary aquamarine sky, Akasha made ready to take to the air with Horque by her side. She had mixed feelings about leaving the ancient land of Egypt. A moon and a half ago, she'd left Samlios as a young maiden and protégé of the pythoness. In that short time, she'd grown up quickly, married a twice-born Solarii, and fallen pregnant with a child of the future.

Not only was her life changing, her body was too, as it prepared to support a new life. Her breasts and hips filled out and even her face was more rounded. Feeling softer, fuller, more feminine, she loved every moment. Only the vomiting and nausea were debilitating. Her only worry was that everything was happening much more rapidly than a normal pregnancy. Shamira reminded her that the maidens like Irit, whom the Helios had impregnated, had given birth in only three moons. To Akasha, it appeared her gestation was happening according to the same cycle. That was fine, so long as her progeny was not going to be the same as Irit's. She couldn't bear the thought of carrying a hybrid inside her.

Out of all the people she was leaving behind, the parting from her mother was the most painful, for both of them. Thera had always been there for her, but Akasha had wilfully taken her for granted. While her mother would be safe on the ark, they both sensed this parting had a strong air of finality about it.

Thera had shared every high point and witnessed every low point of her life. Together they'd rejoiced at the inception of her cleansing flow; she'd never forget the huge pride in her mother's eyes. Then there was the poignant moment Thera had comforted her in the dark stairwell of the Whispering Tower after receiving news of Horque's demise. Not long after, that was followed by the wonderful celebration of the union beneath the Sphinx's eternal and enigmatic gaze. Now as they embraced, her mother's tears wet on her shoulder, Akasha pressed her mother's thin frame to hers. They were both shaking with joy and sadness.

"We must go," Shamira insisted, and they parted in tears. Akasha climbed into the Horus Wing next to Horque, the vibrations of the machine trilling up her spine as it shuddered into life.

Soon they were gliding over the pyramid field. Where the apex should have been in the centre of the Records Pyramid, there was nothing but a gaping hole. A thin plume of smoke snaked its way into the tranquil morning air. Was that to be an epitaph to a once-supreme civilisation?

Horque in the lead, the score or more flyers formed into an arrowhead and headed for the river. Akasha craned her neck to catch a last fleeting glimpse of the ark and spotted a trio of tall wooden struts protruding into the aquamarine sky. From high above, she could see the gated compound for the animals. There seemed to be herds of them, so many she wondered how they would all fit.

She wouldn't forget those ruddy Semites who had serenaded her with a love song and stolen her heart. She knew they were watching out for the craft's distinctive vapour trail, and they'd be waving goodbye to her with a glint in their eyes. She put her hand over the side of the craft and waved back, the cool air rushing through her fingers.

Soon, the *Fair Maiden* was a speck in the distance. Her mind buzzed with thoughts of the past, her mother, the future, the Semites and her unborn child.

She'd pleaded with Horque to bring her parents to Babylon, but he'd shrugged and insisted they use the remaining passenger places to store and transport the ankhs, though he never explained what they were for, nor how they could be more important than her parents. Shamira was her only human companion on the flight.

As they turned east, they passed unscathed through the great astral shield of Dudael. The Isis Pass had worked. Issa had saved the day, and what a surprise that had been. From then on, the flight hugged the coastline, on one side a glass-smooth ocean, and on the other huge tracts of emerald forests.

To avoid a menacing waterspout, they descended near to the ground, where a herd of elephantine hybrids fled in terror at their arrival. Seeing them sent a shiver through her, a reaction that shocked her. Why did the hybrids revolt her so? They'd attacked Horque, that was why. However, there was a moment in Samlios when Jarda mysteriously appeared on a hill during Irit's last rites. He was no callous brute – he was clearly capable of finer, higher sentiments. She didn't understand why they weren't all like that.

Horque pointed to a broad, smooth-sloped mountain with three peaks joined by ridges and valleys, barely visible through faint wisps of cloud. He called it the Mountain of the Chiefs. She knew of it under a different name, Mount Hermon.

That was the fearsome place where the Helios had first manifested on Earth, and from where the angel Semjaza had led Azazel and his Helios cohorts on their voyage of rapture and insemination. That he was free and roaming the astral light again frightened her, yet with the protector by her side, she felt safer.

As they approached the Land Between the Two Rivers, she detected subtle changes in the astral radiation of the land. It was lighter and had lost the binding constraints of Egypt. Peering ahead, she saw her new home: the two rivers meandering through the plain, the mysterious oval city of Babylon. In the distance, the snow-capped Zagros Mountains shimmered in the fading evening light.

As Horque started their descent, the city and the river looked so beautiful, with glow lamps twinkling like a thousand and one stars. Easily recognisable in the centre of the city was the formidable Tower of Babylon. Beyond that, nestling against steep riverbanks, were the Hanging Gardens. Relief, at last. She already felt at home.

PART 8

The Facing

CHAPTER 43

The Giant's Dome

The day after arriving, Horque had a difficult conversation to negotiate. He had to tell his new wife that he was unable to remain in Babylon. To soften the blow, he gave her a parting gift. Ever the pragmatist, it was something useful: a hawk-headed staff whittled from a bough of the pomegranate tree under which they used to sit in his Jizah gardens.

"It's a fine piece of work, thank you," she said admiringly.

"I'm glad you like it," he replied. At least he was trying to learn these human conventions.

"I'll keep it with the Djed pillar," she said, showing him the green onyx pillar he'd presented to her as a wedding gift. In return, she'd given him part of herself, part of her very essence – half of her blue emerald birthstone. Out of it, she'd carved an exquisite gazelle, so elegant, free and fleet of foot.

"I have some bad news," he said. "I have to leave."

"Why? Were to?" she said, with an air of distress.

He swallowed hard and pointed to the snow-capped ridge in the distance. "Over there, the Zagros Mountains."

"I thought we'd be together. Why there? What's wrong with here?"

This was hard for him. "Orders from the pharaoh."

"What about orders from your wife? It's ironic that Issa sacrificed so much to bring us together and now she's breaking us apart."

What could he say? She was right. This was all his mother's doing. They were both pawns in her elaborate game. He had to follow orders, especially when they came from the pharaoh. "The Horus Wing craft must be saved for after the flood. I have to find and secure a holding bay for them, high enough to avoid the floodwaters. Come with me?" he added despairingly.

"Into the Zagros Mountains? You know that's impossible," she said. "I came here to tarry in the gardens with my growing child, and that's what I'll do. What are you going to do with all the ankhs, and all the Horus Wing craft?"

He knew she'd ask him that question. He couldn't tell her the whole truth, so he told her some of it.

"After the flood, I hope we'll rejoin our doubles once we've fulfilled the Watchers' edict. The craft will help us meet their requirements, such as searching out this blue bow."

"Oh yes, the mysterious blue bow," she said with a frown.

"I'll come back and see you whenever I can," he said.

She said a sad goodbye to him. Her eyes were moist and she turned quickly away. This was not how he'd expected to say farewell to the women he'd returned from the dead to be with. Just what else did his mother have in store for him?

On leaving, he led the twenty or more Horus Wing craft above the oval city. He cast his eyes along the sheer limestone cliffs until he found the Jasmine Gap. Marim had discovered the local legend and told him of the gap's genesis. Intoxicated on a brew of eucalyptus leaves, a giant stumbled towards the mountains and smashed his foot down so hard on the line of cliffs that he gouged out a deep, wide trough. To lesser mortals, this became the Jasmine Gap, the sole means of access into and out of the Zagros Mountains from Babylon and many leagues around.

Drunk as a god, the giant slept with a flat-topped hillock as a crude pillow. Livid at her husband's antics, his wife promptly cast a spell and turned him into a huge pillar of salt. Her regret was instant and she tried to revive him. Moulding lumps of salt with her bare hands, she made a rough-hewn similitude of her dearly departed. With warm breath and hot tears, she tried breathing life into the salt man. The first attempt failed, and the second, and the next, until she'd made scores of salt domes, alas, all with the same outcome. As a memento, she made a posy of jasmine flowers that grew profusely in the area. Later, they lent their name to the landmark: the Jasmine Gap.

Since those days of legend and lore, Marim concluded, the rain had eroded the limbs from the salt likenesses, depositing the brownish-white crystals evenly over the hills and valleys of the Zagros and leaving behind scores of rock salt domes as strange epitaphs to an unhappy marriage. The last remnants of the giant were enshrined in the salt dome adjacent to the flat-topped hillock. For obvious reasons, the crudely shaped pillar of salt was known as the Giant's Dome.

Horque chose the same hillock for the Solarii encampment. The even surface and steep falls on each side rendered it easily defensible and afforded panoramic views of all the plunging valleys and local hilltops.

"This is the place," he said as they stood on the crest of the hill. "These caves will grant welcome protection from the elements to both us and the craft. And I want an astral shield of the highest potency inserted around the perimeter."

"So be it," Marim said.

"Every craft must be flown and tested regularly, and we must scour the land for water and food, and other supplies," he added. "While they're up there, look out for hybrids. Sooner or later, the floodwaters will drive them up here."

Two moons waxed and waned without incident until, with a crescent moon in the morning sky, Marim came to see Horque with predictable news.

"The south guard reports a large concentration of hybrids." Marim's voice was a mix of fear and excitement. "The bird creature Pazazu is amongst them."

From afar, there came a distant retort, then a guard cried out loud, "They're coming!"

"That is the south guard again," Marim reported.

"Check the astral shield for gaps," Horque ordered. "With Pazazu out there, we'll have to seal the top of the dome. I don't want him or any of those other winged hybrids sneaking into our camp."

"One flyer is testing his craft. An astral seal over the dome would prevent him returning to the camp," Marim pointed out.

There *would* be someone outside. "Who is it?"

"Lasec," Marim said. "We must bring him back safely. The men would take it as a bad omen should he be killed. He's a man of justice. If he falls, we'll all fall."

Horque despised the men's primordial sense of superstition, a sentiment he had shared until his return from Du'at. After that, he changed. Because now if he could find the organ in his men that entertained this superstition, he'd cut it out and throw it to the hyenas. Then they'd stop moaning about every omen.

"The men are all important," he said. Marim looked at him askance; this was not his usual rhetoric. "But we can't risk the entire encampment for one man of justice. Seal the dome until the hybrids have retreated."

Irex whispered something to Marim.

"Protector, the east, west and north guards report hybrids on the plateau," Marim said. "We're surrounded."

That surprised Horque, because, if true, it displayed an alarming degree of planning and co-ordination for a bunch of mutant brutes.

"I'll see this with my own eyes," he said.

There were scores of hybrids. Horque had never seen so many at one time. The hoard beat their chests, shook their fists and roared their delight as the eagle-headed monster Pazazu circled above them, screeching and squawking. What a motley collection, every one different to the next: many had human torsos, but crowned by the head of a wolf, a raging bull or a bear. Some had human heads with the torso and legs of a lion, a crocodile or a rampant elephant. Others had wings tipped with human fingers, legs that narrowed into a cloven hoof, or a neck that flowered into the grace of a swan. They shared one thing: a common and vitriolic hatred of the Solarii.

Pazazu landed in the midst of the huge ring of hybrids encircling their hill. Wielding a wooden club in an apelike grip, he opened his broad wings, tipped his beak back and let out a long, high shriek that shot into the mountain air like an arrow from a bow. That appeared to be a prearranged signal, because the line of hybrids locked arms and wings around the shoulder or waist of their neighbour. Then Pazazu brought down the club and took a stride forwards, a stride followed by the hybrid hoard. He lifted and lowered the club again, strode forwards, and again the hybrids followed his lead. To tighten the net around the Solarii, the hoard was acting in unison. This was more than alarming – this was dangerous.

"Arrange the men in a ring," Horque ordered, "just inside the edge of the shield."

In their new position, the men were within a stone's throw of the hybrids. Step by step, the hybrids advanced, until the Solarii could see their rage and smell their hatred. Soon they were a single step away.

"Hold your positions!" Horque yelled.

With the next step, the hybrids walked into the smothering incandescence of the astral shield, which threw them violently backwards. The scene was surreal: scores of hybrids arcing backwards into the air in some grotesque synchronised movement, landing on their backsides, their flesh scorched by the searing astral shield. Squeals of pain punctured the gloom. Bemused and burnt, they scrambled to their feet and limped away.

The smell of burning fur and smouldering feathers was like incense to the Solarii, who cheered their foes' retreat. The battle was far from over, because the ferocious impact of the shield had scorched a few feathers, but hadn't actually killed any of them. Pazazu rallied the scattered remnants of his followers as they fell back to Giant's Dome. Heads low, they nursed their wounds and their injured pride.

During the brief hiatus, Horque rallied his men and assessed the hybrids' disarray. He had expected them to retreat beyond the Giant's Dome, but instead they were shouting and cavorting in front of it. A cacophony of hoots and shrieks accompanied their increasingly bizarre behaviour.

"What *are* they doing?"

"They seem to be kissing the salt on the Giant's Dome and rubbing it into their bodies," Marim said, with a bemused expression.

Next, they bowed low and some even prostrated themselves before the dome.

"It's as if they're in the presence of a divinity," Marim suggested. He sounded like he didn't quite believe his own words.

"Ha! What do dumb brutes know of shrines and deities?" Horque scoffed.

Marim shrugged. "Nonetheless, the hybrids have surprised us before. And I've never seen them collaborate so well together."

"Wait," Horque said. "You're right. Lasec's still up there, and armed. Order him to discharge his ankh into the hybrids. Let them feel the force of Solarii fire."

That was the best idea he'd had all day.

When he received the order to stay out and not return to the encampment, Lasec was shocked but not surprised. Horque had sacrificed him again to the vicissitudes of life on Earth – his life deemed so worthless, his return to the encampment forbidden. He wouldn't forget this in a hurry.

Despite that, Lasec had connections of his own. He counted Nimrod amongst his family and everyone knew of the long-standing feud between him and the Horque dynasty. Lasec was a hard worker, and regularly risked his life in the Solarii cause, just as he would this day against the hybrids. And this was how they repaid him? With an exclusion order?

At least now he'd received the second order – to wreak total vengeance on the hybrids. In one fell swoop, he'd satiate his bloodlust and redeem himself before his peers. How convenient of the hybrids to congregate by the Giant's Dome. He banked the craft for the attack. The dumb brutes even looked up at his vapour trail as he snaked towards them. One powerful, well-directed astral bolt would take out the lot of them.

Swooping down, he clutched the ankh, holding it steady. Despite his low trajectory and with the sun behind him, the hybrids weren't that stupid. They suddenly scattered to the four corners. Faster, he urged the craft forwards. As he released the astral bolt, the craft lurched forwards over an invisible air current, jerking his arm upwards. The astral bolt skewed past the hybrids and smashed into the Giant's Dome behind them, ripping a gaping hole in it. A cloud of dust and salt billowed up from the ground, forcing him to act promptly to avoid it. He was sick to the pit of his stomach. He'd missed his one chance to restore his credibility.

His pain wasn't over yet. The Giant's Dome lurched over on its side. With a loud ripping sound, it tilted and crashed to the ground, splintering into an uncountable number of salt crystal shards. The falling Giant's Dome crushed a few hybrids. The rest lived to fight another day.

The toppled salt pillar lay in a heap, a rebellious giant brought low by superior Solarii weaponry. The fallen pillar had revealed a deep cavern beneath it. Previously sealed by the salt dome, it was now open to the elements. A noxious stench of sulphur rose from it. Instinctively, Lasec looked through his whites to see a dark cloud of astral smoke extruding from the cavern. What beast had he woken from its ancient slumber?

His pain continued. The sheer force of the impact of the bolt fractured the

Earth's surface, dislodging gigantic rocks and boulders that rolled down the steep hillside. Gathering debris on the way, the landslide obliterated trees and demolished everything in its path as it thundered down the mountainside towards the Jasmine Gap.

Shrouded in swirls of dust and salt spray, an avalanche of boulders and trees thumped into the narrow neck of the gap. One rock collided into another until eventually the landslide ran itself into the ground. As the dust cloud cleared, Lasec could see it had blocked the head of the Jasmine Gap. So be it: the humans would have to find another way to escape Babylon.

As he flew back to the encampment, he passed over the fallen giant, where the sharp-beaked hybrids' leader perched on the edge of the cavern precipice. Pazazu was sniffing the air, like a predator smelling the blood of a frightened rabbit. Behind him, the massed ranks of the hybrids whooped in glee.

What were they doing? Then he realised. Cavorting in the black astral vapours, they were metamorphosing before his very eyes. It was unbelievable. Accompanied by excruciating cries, Pazazu's eagle wings grew and expanded until they were stronger and larger. Every hybrid was changing, increasing in size, growing bigger muscles, longer claws, sharper incisors. Sloughs of unwanted flesh littered the ground, testament to this spontaneous feast of growth.

From his vantage point on the rise, Horque was transfixed. The unfolding spectacle was mortifying. Even he, a Solarii of a hundred years who'd died, travelled to the grim caverns of Du'at and returned to tell the tale, had to blink twice. The metamorphoses didn't stop with physical prowess. A Cyclops grew a second eye; a goat with a human's head grew wings and flew off into the pale green yonder; a fish-headed human grew antennae and transformed into an enormous bee.

He dreaded to think what kind of enhanced senses, guile and cunning the hybrids had now acquired. Over by the fallen salt dome, a revived Pazazu was busy regrouping his motley crew for another attack. When Horque set up the encampment, he'd expected to meet stiff resistance from the hybrids, but he hadn't anticipated facing a demonic band of enhanced monsters.

"Protector?" Marim said.

"Yes, what is it?" he snapped.

"These metamorphoses are like the one we saw in the union ceremony when the snake grew a second head. The men are brave and strong, but they can't fight an entity with such vast and tenebrous astral tentacles."

Marim was correct. This astral chrysalis was an adversary with fearful transformative powers. If it could alter flesh and bone, change limbs to wings and tooth to fang, it could easily move through their astral shield. They were powerless, and helpless. Were they next?

"Listen to me," he said. "The snake entity was Semjaza. This one is just as vile. Long ago, when the first Solarii on Earth vanquished the Helios, they imprisoned them beneath the valleys of the Earth, fixing them there with plugs of salt."

Marim's face dropped. "Are you saying that a second Helios angel has been freed?"

"I believe so. And this one is Azazel, Semjaza's first subordinate."

Semjaza and Azazel, the two of them together again was a terrifying thought.

"What has Lasec done?" Marim asked.

"He's let loose an apocalypse."

CHAPTER 44

The Jasmine Gap

Weary and dusty, Tros was mightily relieved to reach the Jasmine Gap. From there, he could climb the pass and reach the safety of the High Zagros. His feet hurt and his legs ached, which wasn't surprising after trudging across the plain from the city. Accompanying him were scores of citizens from the oval city who'd also been refused a place in the Tower of Babylon. The king had only allowed members of the royal family, aristocracy and the elders. Typical! Reluctantly, Tros had entrusted Philo with Akasha's guardianship and headed for higher ground. He'd even had to leave his daughter behind – the hardest parting of all.

On the way past the sheer line of cliffs, he'd wondered about the plumes of smoke that had blotted the sky waters three days earlier. Masco, the chief gardener in the Hanging Gardens, swore that they boded ill. Tros liked him, not least because when he even sniffed at a bud, it flowered and grew. Those fingers of his had magic in them. Rocor was the same.

Arriving at the Jasmine Gap, he led the citizens into the pass, where he was surprised to find Kare standing on a precipice. Shoulder to shoulder with the High Priest of Babylon stood a motley bunch of men, guarding the passage. They looked like bandits. My, priests and thugs, that was an unholy alliance.

"Welcome, welcome," Kare intoned, sounding like he was reciting one of his precious sermons.

"What are you doing here? You're the last person I expected. Have you come to bless our path into the mountains?" Tros asked. The rock face up to where he stood was sheer and the climb well nigh impossible.

"We've cleared a narrow path through the landslide, and we're here to make it safe for all to use," Kare explained.

Tros was wary, and peered up at the priest to take a closer look. Above and behind the precipice was an entrance to the pass. A recent landslide had blocked it. They had created a narrow defile, wide enough for one person to squeeze through. But to get to it they had climb up the sheer precipice and get past Kare and his guards.

"I can see that," he said. "Throw us a rope then."

"I wish I could," Kare replied with mock reluctance. Now Tros was more than suspicious. "To enter the pass, you must first settle up."

"Settle up? How?" Tros asked. "We're ragged here. We've walked for three days. My legs feel like tree trunks. The flood's coming. So throw us the rope, will you?"

Kare looked down on him like he was some order of vermin. This smelt of dung.

"You misunderstand," Kare said. "To earn your salvation, you need to pay your dues. Give us your precious stones, your jewellery, your gold artefacts, *then* we'll throw you a rope."

Tros was stunned. These weren't priests. They were mercenaries.

"You're a man of god. You can save us all. Are you really standing there and demanding – *dues?*"

Kare stared him down without replying. Yes, he was.

Tros puffed out his cheeks. "We've no need of our riches in the next epoch so we left them behind," he replied.

"Go back and get them," Kare said impudently.

"How? Babylon is three days there and three days back. What do we do if the flood comes in the meantime? You might be condemning us to death."

"Who knows when the flood will come? Will it be the next moon, or the one after that?" Kare cackled. This man was possessed by *evil.*

The crowd hurled insults and stones up at the priest. By his side, Kare's minions flexed their muscles, menace oozing from every pore. This was ugly. Amidst the flying insults and flaring tempers, the crowd tried to scale the rock face by making a human pyramid. As soon as one reached the top and grasped at the ledge, one of Kare's minions stamped his foot on the man's fingers and he toppled backwards. The pyramid crumpled into a gnarled heap.

"Get down." Kare snorted. "And don't come back without your gold."

Tros shook his head. The human race had sunk this low, and a priest too. Kare's ice-cold stare was devoid of even a glimmer of humanity.

"You're mad," Tros railed at him. "What are you going to do with gold and precious stones? Make a boat and paddle it into the new epoch?"

Kare turned around, his attention drawn by shouts and a scuffle behind him on the defile. The priests and their henchmen were fighting a bunch of hybrids, which must have sneaked unnoticed down through the narrow defile. Taken by surprise, they fought back, their daggers and sabres flashing in the sunlight. The air was filled with blood-curdling cries. Out of nowhere, a monstrous bird-creature dived into the melee, swooped down on Kare and knocked him over the precipice. The high priest somersaulted through the air and landed in a crumpled heap at Tros' feet. He was still alive and sat up, examining the blue blood oozing from a deep gash on his head. The crowd surrounded him. Their mocking cheers grew muted and changed to gasps of horror. As they watched, Kare's face was changing. He was growing pink, hairy ears, a long black snout, and staring beady eyes. He was transforming into a…

"A goat!" Tros screamed.

Rocor knelt to tend to Kare but Tros forcibly pulled him away.

"Don't go near him," Tros said. "Look at what's happening. The hybrids touched Kare and now he's turned into one of them. They're contagious, and the disease they carry is turning people into monsters, mutants and hybrids."

Rocor clutched his head between his hands. The crowd yelled in terror. This was loathsome.

"We've got to get as far away from here as possible," Tros cried and hurried away, the crowd lurching behind him.

Tros never thought he'd be relieved to return to Babylon. Some things were worse than death, and this was one of them.

CHAPTER 45

The Dying Embers

Horque was ensconced in his camp. All day long, scuffles and shouts had come from the direction of the Jasmine Gap. Then he'd seen Pazazu lead an assault. As dusk fell, he'd ordered the astral shield lowered so that Lasec could return.

During the evening, a huge bonfire illuminated the gap. All through the night, the dark air was hollowed out with screams and yells of anguish. The bonfire bothered him the most. If the hybrids had built it, it would have marked a first. Up to now, the hybrids had been petrified of naked flame. What were they doing down there? Continuing their cultish worship?

At the first stirrings of dawn, Horque scanned the skies over the Jasmine Gap for Pazazu, but the hybrid was nowhere to be seen. Lasec knew the layout of the land down there, so Horque decided to give him a chance to redeem himself.

Across shortening shadows, Horque led their Horus Wing craft over the Giant's Dome, where all was silent. The debris from the avalanche was scattered all the way down the mountainside. Hovering over the area, and as the sun's rays slanted into the gap, Horque could see clearly. The hybrids had left bodies strewn on the rocks below the precipice. They were scores of human cadavers. On the precipice itself, the bonfire had almost burnt itself out. Otherwise, the area appeared deserted and safe to land.

Horque took the craft nearer the precipice and hovered for a while. He landed near the fire, Lasec next to him. The air was eerily still, like it was hiding a secret.

"Proceed with caution," Horque whispered. Was it a trap?

Horque stubbed his staff into the dying embers of the fire, overturning several half-burnt logs. The nauseating smell of burning flesh smacked his nostrils.

"Are these animal bones?" Lasec said with a frown.

They couldn't be. The smell was obnoxious. "What's that?" Horque said, prodding something shiny in the fire. "It's a necklace."

Lasec scrunched up his face. "What's that doing there?"

"These aren't animal bones." Horque felt like retching. "These are partially gnawed human remains."

There were human arms, legs and thighs. Humans had been torn apart, limb from limb, roasted and partially eaten.

Lasec stared blankly at the embers.

"This is disgusting," Horque said. "Damn them. Damn Azazel. Damn the Helios." Just when the Solarii had everything in place to deal with the hybrids, the Helios were free to wreak havoc with their well-laid plans to return home.

"This is Azazel's doing," Lasec murmured.

"No! This is your doing," Horque said. "Dolt! You aimed your ankh at the dome rather than the hybrids."

"I was following *your* orders," Lasec sneered.

"I didn't order you to free Azazel for him to mutate the hybrids into flesh-eating monsters!"

"No! As I aimed the ankh, the volatile air disturbed my aim."

"A lame excuse from a lame man."

"And you're the one saying that!" Lasec replied, with real venom.

"Never ever say that to me again," Horque snapped. He fought down the urge to have done with the wastrel and kick Lasec off the precipice. There'd be no point. "The damage is done," he railed. "And you've succeeded in removing the hybrids' fear of flame. We've nothing to fight them with, thanks to you."

"They're a virulent pest," Lasec murmured, "and always have been. If it had been up to me, I've have taken them all out at the beginning instead of playing safe, and trying to keep the humans happy. That's why we're in this situation, not because of anything I did or didn't do."

Perhaps Lasec was right. Either way, they were here now, and here they had to stay.

"You will fulfil my orders," Horque said slowly. "Now return to base."

CHAPTER 46

The Hanging Gardens

Akasha jerked her eyes open. It was dark. A cock crowed, birds chirped – but the sounds were muted. Amidst the shadows, on a pedestal by her bedside, was the onyx Djed pillar, Horque's wedding gift. It gave her strength, as if Horque was there in person. She was convinced it protected her from the dark presence of Semjaza.

As her belly had grown larger and Horque had not come to see her, she resigned herself to losing him. He'd go home to be with his kind. She missed him. The ache of emptiness was palpable. The baby kicked hard. Oof! He – or was it a she? – would never see and know their father. That was a sorrow. She picked up her pomegranate staff and held it close to her chest, as if she was holding a baby, cherishing it. It reminded her of him.

The day wore a strange unease, which was unusual in the gardens. She placed her few valued possessions in her shoulder bag: the Djed pillar, her half of the blue emerald avatar, Demos' cobra necklace, the sod of Samlios earth and the acorn from the oak of Samlios. She stepped gingerly into the terraces and probed the air with the staff. The air was cool, the grass dewy. Mother Nature was preparing for winter. The day oppressed her – it was in the birds' cries and now she heard it in gusts of wind that whispered to her of things to come. Grey clouds loomed in the eastern skies.

On the lowest terrace, she picked up her herb basket to tend the garden that she'd created soon after arriving. She'd gathered sprigs from every terrace and brought them together into one garden alongside a row of weeping willows. With the soft wind rustling through their leaves, they often sounded like the tender strains of the lyre, picking out a yearning melody of sadness and hope.

During the night, the river had risen like a writhing beast and sloughed its skin. The herb garden had sunk beneath a churning eddy. The river's swirling torrent dragged the lower branches of the willows. Leaves and roots floated on the murky tide. She'd put so much effort and love and care into her herb garden, and she felt pangs of sadness at its loss.

The soft rain pattered against her face and sprinkled into the swollen river. A dull thud nearby announced something falling out of the sky. It was a small bird with brown and white markings. One wing lay open, the other broken and twisted. The tiny feathers on its chest were still.

If only she could pass on the stirrings of this new life in her womb to the bird and bring it back to life. She felt so helpless. The sheer bulk of her belly prevented her from even bending over and picking it up. Instead, she caressed its mangled body with the tip of her staff. This was all wrong. Birds flew in the air; they weren't disgorged by it. The poor thing had no wounds or predatory marks, so what had killed it? A hawk? Now that would be ironic.

A wave of melancholy washed over her. The river had broken its banks and flooded her herb garden. A bird had plummeted out of the sky. To hide it, she sprinkled garden cuttings over its lifeless body. Beneath glowering skies, she stood alone in the slow, persistent rain, alone and vulnerable. Her time in the gardens had been serene but now her body tensed in preparation for something worse, much worse.

It was as if the dead bird had fallen through a tear in the mystical fabric of the world, a tear through which some vengeful deity was about to burst.

CHAPTER 47

The Zagros Gate

As Akasha wiped her muddy hands, Shamira and Callisto joined her. Droplets of rain trickled down her face as she pointed to the small burial mound of debris and cuttings.

"A bird dropped out of the sky like a stone."

"I know, that's why we're here," Shamira replied. "It's not only the birds. The city's dying too. Everything's breaking up. People are fleeing. The flood is coming. We need to get you to a safe, dry place."

"Where's that?"

"The Natal Chamber, a chamber beneath the Tower of Babylon."

As they tramped by the river, bobbing up and down in it like broken, useless twigs were scores of birds, great and small, innocent casualties all. Their unnatural deaths tugged at Akasha's soul, which ached to leave behind everything alive and beautiful in the gardens: the trees, the flowers, the shrubs, the grasses, not forgetting the birds, the animals, and even the red, white and black ants, the bees and the hornets. She'd forged a profound link to these marvellous expressions of the planet's maternal soul and the sublime feeling that enjoined it. In truth, she wasn't leaving the gardens; they were coming with her. Her child kicked her heartily in her belly, winding her. She smiled: the gardens had served their purpose. She knew this was the day. She patted her shoulder bag, full of valuables, and her baby, the most valuable thing of all.

On the other side of the gate, a man stood with his back to her.

"Tros," she cried, her face as expectant as the full moon.

The man turned to face her.

"Philo?" she asked. "Where's Tros?"

"He's left Babylon," Callisto said, a pained expression on her face.

"Left? He can't have. He promised to protect me."

"He went six days ago," Callisto revealed. "Soon after we all saw that huge plume of dust and smoke arise from the Jasmine Gap. Since then, Philo has stood guard in his stead."

"I wish he'd said goodbye," Akasha said ruefully. This was sad news. Tros, her rock, her stalwart. This flood was terrible – splitting families, dividing peoples, wreaking a terrible vengeance on all life. Why did *she* have to live through it? Couldn't it have happened some other time?

"He didn't want to upset you. Please understand, he did what he thought was best for you and the baby. It was a wrench for me too," Callisto said.

"Why isn't there room for Tros with us, in the Natal Chamber, or even in the tower?" she asked. "Well?"

"There's none in either place, I'm afraid," Shamira said. "I'm sorry."

What could she do? Another friend, gone. She hoped he would survive. She huddled her shoulders as a cold gust of wind blew right through her.

"Listen. The city's in upheaval," Philo said. "The route to the tower is via the Zagros Gate. Trouble is, the road for the Jasmine Gap starts from there so everyone is heading that way. I must warn you, this isn't Samlios, the Whispering Tower or Jizah. This is Babylon, where desperate times bring out the fury in people. So stay close to me."

"I will," she said, alerted by the tremor of fear in Philo's voice.

They traipsed through churning mud in the midst of a stream of people. They passed houses empty of people and life, their open doors creaking in the wind. Everyone had left in a hurry. At first, they made good progress and breached the edge of a broad square that gave onto two large wooden gates.

"This is the Zagros Gate," Philo said.

The square was crammed with people, arms waving, shouting excitedly. No one was moving due to a blockage at the gates, even though they were wide open. Philo got her to squeeze against a wall next to a wooden barrel, which he gamely climbed on top of to get a vantage point.

"What's the cause of the delay?" Shamira asked.

"A group of people are trying to get *in* through the gates," Philo declared.

"That doesn't make sense," Callisto said.

"I know, it's madness!" Philo had to shout to make himself heard above the rabble. "They're blocking all those wanting to leave."

Philo, Shamira and Callisto stood around the barrel, trying to shield Akasha from the burgeoning crowd. She felt crushed into this tiny space. The rain was pelting down and the feet of the crowd were churning up the ground. Dark clouds loomed in the distance and tornadoes skirted the horizon like a swarm of angry hornets.

"Isn't there another way?" Shamira asked.

"It's much longer, and I doubt Akasha can walk that far in her condition," Philo answered. "We're stuck here until the square clears."

"How long will that be?" Akasha's voice croaked with emotion.

Philo didn't reply. The longer they delayed, the more danger she and her baby were exposed to.

Pazazu squawked overhead as Tros ducked to avoid him, biting his tongue down on a curse. The whole way back from the Jasmine Gap, the grotesque bird had plagued their every step. With the Zagros Gates in view, Tros allowed himself a weary sigh of relief. Finally, he'd escape the clutches of the monster bird and his hoard of flesh-eating hybrids.

He, Masco and Rocor were bringing up the rear of several hundred people, all of whom, on discovering the horrors that awaited them at the Zagros Gate, had reluctantly returned to the city.

"Watch out!" Tros yelled at Masco, who darted forwards, flaming torch in hand, and shoved it into the face of a hybrid who was trying to attack him. Despite their best efforts, they'd failed to prevent the hybrids from dragging several men into the jaws of death.

"I can't keep this up much longer," Masco yelled, fending off another hybrid. "They've no fear of the flame and they're thirsty for our blood."

"We're nearly there," Tros shouted as he backed through the gates. Once he'd worn a rose of sympathy for the hybrids. Now that had pricked him. These hybrids were nothing less than murderous predators.

He and Rocor eased through the gates. Masco was backing towards them. Struggling to keep the hybrids at bay, his wicker torch was a mere smoking stub. A bird-creature swooped out of the air and knocked Masco to the ground. The poor man tried to get up, holding out a desperate hand. Rocor moved to help him, but Tros hauled him back.

"You can't. You'll be eaten alive," he snapped.

Pazazu had pinned Masco to the ground with claw-like hands while other hybrids ripped at his flesh. His cries for mercy filled the air. As more hybrids feasted on Masco's body, Rocor slammed the gates shut and brought the barrier down. From outside came the gnarling sounds of horrific death.

"What are you doing?" Rocor cried plaintively.

"I'm doing what needs to be done, even though I hate doing it," Tros replied.

"He needs us. We have to go outside, rescue him." Rocor was choking.

"I know. I'd like to do nothing else, but it's too late. If you go out there now, you'll expose us all. Bite your tongue. Accept it. Masco's gone."

Dim echoes and a raft of memories were all that remained of the man who was once the head gardener of the Hanging Gardens of Babylon. Tros felt cold, weary and alone. He'd lost a friend and companion. Now he faced an apocalypse.

"Tros!" Despite the cacophony in the square, he heard someone yelling his name. It was Callisto.

He embraced her.

"I'm so glad you're safe," she sobbed into his ear.

"My daughter," he whispered, holding her tight, never wanting to let her go again. He noticed she still wore the yellow topaz necklace. He remembered the day she was born and the day of its creation. Those were special, bygone days.

The square was in pandemonium. The squawking Pazazu flew back and forth over the heads of the crowd, depositing guano and panic with every dive. People were running for shelter, slipping in the mud and falling over each other. Outside, the hybrids were smashing pieces out of the gates.

Akasha and Shamira clasped his hands affectionately. For the first time in three days, Tros smiled, pleased to see old friends. Suddenly, the bird hybrid swooped over his head. He lost his footing and landed face first in the pool of churning mud.

Seeing Tros fall made Akasha take a step back. The monstrous bird swept down and landed on Callisto, digging huge claws into her shoulders. Callisto screamed for her life. The bird hauled her off the ground, leaving her legs kicking at thin air.

"Callisto!" Akasha yelled, reaching up as her friend was plucked off the face of the Earth.

This was chaos. This was a maelstrom.

Everyone around her seemed to freeze, peering upwards as the rain tumbled and the lighting flashed. Moments later, a large sack fell out of the sky, as if it had given birth to a thing. It splattered her with mud and spray. It wriggled in the muck.

Akasha stepped back in disgust. The thing was gawky and gangly. It righted itself, smeared with saliva, blood and mud. Its leonine snout sniffed the air. Baring its fangs, it let out a roar that could have woken the dead. The creature snarled at her, claws drawn. She was transfixed. It was a nightmare. Creatures with lion heads didn't just drop out of the sky. Birds didn't drop out of the sky. Yet in Babylon, they did.

Suddenly, a fierce blow from behind felled the lion-creature. It crumpled at her feet. Tros stood behind it, wielding a club with streams of blood and rainwater dripping off the end of it.

"Tros? You killed it."

His shoulders heaved with emotion and raindrops dribbled down his face. Or were they tears as well?

"Why are you crying?"

"Don't worry about me. Let's get you to safety," he said in a croaky voice. He was emotional because of their reunion – yes, that was it. He'd saved her from attack. Though why was the lion-creature wearing clothes...and shoes? And a yellow topaz necklace? Just like...Callisto's.

Oh no. That wasn't possible, was it? Oh, Callisto. Oh, Tros.

CHAPTER 48

The Sear Line

Cheiron dreaded its arrival, but it was here. Whatever runes he read, they all pointed to the same thing. The deluge was imminent. In some ways, it was incidental, although he'd never admit it because everyone could read the omens for themselves. The astral light was fragmenting; weird entities protruded through the veil. Even those blind to the portents couldn't miss the severe and inclement weather.

The sun reached its zenith. It was time for the Sear Line. The trumpets bellowed their clarion call from the top of the Temple of Isis, summoning the dignitaries. Avoiding the dead birds along the way, Cheiron strode into the pavilion, where the Solarii aristocracy had obediently gathered. It was a temporary construction, but everything these days wore the tawdry cloak of impermanence. The pavilion opened onto an avenue of sphinxes that in turn gave way to the architraves of the Temple of Isis. It seemed a long while ago that Horque and Akasha had strolled arm-in-arm through its honey-coloured columns into the nearby Temple of Bes, where they'd lain together in the Nuptial Chamber. Today, though, his concern was the hypogeum.

The dignitaries waited impatiently, anxious about the test they were about to undertake. Like the flood, it was unpredictable, potentially fatal and one that they all wanted to pass. If they did, they'd have a place in the hypogeum, and sanctuary from the killing waters. If they didn't, well, that was an entirely different matter. Their faces betrayed the usual insolence of office, but behind their eyes were nagging doubts.

How he relished their discomfort. For once, he was in control. He'd donned the black silk scapula that befitted his station. It was a black task. Only clear, fulsome light could penetrate back to the Source.

Stepping off her carriage, the new pharaoh barely acknowledged him.

"All is ready, Pharaoh," Cheiron said, bowing low. Still she unnerved him. Why was she so elegant and alluring?

"This day has been long in the making for our people," she murmured.

"It has," he replied, keeping his composure somehow, "but it is upon us. We must protect our solar doubles."

"Indeed." Issa nodded.

Zoser was less callow. "We're all here," he said. "Now will you tell us what this test is all about?"

"The Sear Line," Cheiron explained, "will hold a mirror to your soul and examine whether it still resonates with the blistering fires of your birthplace. Should there be any impurity, deviation or fracture from that original solar integrity, the Sear Line will *turn and rend you*." He particularly savoured the last phrase.

By the time the sun cast its smallest shadow, nearly threescore restless souls sat in the pavilion. A light rain pattered on its thin roof. Cheiron glanced at them: Nimrod was self-assured but uneasy; Khephren was dignified and twitchy; Zoser, bullish and almost blithe. The entirety of the Solarii ruling hegemony was present, except one.

"In front of you is an avenue of Sphinxes," he said. "You have all walked along it many times before, but today I have spoken the sacred utterance and brought it to life. Look through your whites and you'll see it pulsates with the intense astral fires of home."

In the astral, shafts of searing lines criss-crossed the avenue from side to side, from sphinx to opposing sphinx.

"One at a time, you will walk the avenue and it will test the fitness of your souls to return home," Cheiron said, fingering his black scapula.

The avenue consisted of two lines of supine sphinxes, paws out front, looping tails curled back and up against their hindquarters, each with stern faces on dressed maidens' heads with leonine bodies. There were twelve on each side.

"Saqqara, the first high priest, constructed this avenue. He foresaw that one day we'd be ready to return," he added. "The rock crystal eyes of the sphinxes align in an imaginary line drawn down the middle of the avenue. This is the Sear Line, along which you must walk. Reach the end of it and you are a true Solarii. You will have earned your place in the hypogeum. Ready? Then come forward when Irex calls your name."

"Let Nimrod present himself!" Irex cried out.

Stern in the eye and oozing confidence, Nimrod strode down the centre of the avenue. Cheiron was reluctant to admit it, but he was impressed. The man bore no doubts in his heart and certainly none in his soul. Reaching the end of the

Sear Line, the former pharaoh punched the air in celebration.

As the afternoon wore on, the rains thickened. The winds gusted and the Solarii shivered. One by one the aristocracy walked the Sear Line and reached the far end, alive but emotionally drained. By late afternoon, only Cheiron and Pharaoh Issa remained in the cold, damp pavilion. Tarsus, Issa's servant, remained too, although he was not, of course, to take the test. The pharaoh went last at most ceremonies, so everyone expected Cheiron would be next, but Irex called a different name.

"Protector Horque."

"What's the meaning of this?" Issa snapped. "Why call Horque?"

Cheiron had been afraid of her when she was vizier, afraid of her when she was Steward of the Granary – afraid not of her secular power, but of the power of her extraordinary beauty. It was the nearest he'd ever got to the first of the Twin Perils – love of an earthly power or woman. That was Issa. Despite having the power of right on his side, his knees still quaked and he stammered.

"There are no exemptions. If he wants to return home, Horque must walk the Sear Line."

"I know that," Issa grumbled.

She was seething, and trying desperately to hide it. Horque could not walk the Sear Line, not because of his physical absence, but because he would fail on the first of the Twin Perils. Osiris and Anubis, cheated of his soul at death, had retained a fragment of his fiery Solarii soul, which, on returning to Egypt, had been filled by a fragment of the Earth's soul.

From then on, she knew her son would fail the Sear Line. She had risked her life's work to remove him beyond the boundary stele of Egypt. How grateful she'd been to elicit Nimrod's god name. Without it, she'd never have been able to challenge him for the throne, and Horque would never have been given the Isis Pass. Her son knew nothing of this; he'd be devastated if he found out.

Cheiron was waiting for an answer.

"In case it's escaped your notice, Horque isn't here," she sneered.

"When he returns, he can walk the Sear Line, like everyone else." For once, Cheiron wasn't budging. He would choose this crucial moment to exert his pathetic influence over her. She was not having that.

"High Priest," she said, staring him down, "after the deluge, the astral light will be so dim the Sear Line won't exist. The sphinxes will be lumps of stone staring blankly into thin air, monuments to a forgotten age. Horque is protecting his wife, the mother whose child will be the future of the human race and our passage home. Obviously, he's an exception."

"No exceptions," Cheiron murmured, consulting the sacred Sear Line papyrus. When he cast a look as cold as the east wind, the pharaoh let out a soft whimper. She wasn't going to change his mind. Not this time. No one was above the law, not a protector, not even a pharaoh.

"So be it," she said. "Now, let us into the hypogeum."

Cheiron nodded at Irex, who cleared his throat and called out, "Pharaoh Issa."

"Me?"

"No exceptions." He seemed to delight in his words.

"A pharaoh is hardly susceptible to the soul of the Earth," Issa insisted.

"Hardly, but I must abide by what is written," Cheiron replied, pointing at the sacred papyrus. "And your insignia is here."

She swallowed hard. "Then I shall go forward, like the others," she said, with evident reluctance.

"Like all the others," Cheiron repeated, with an air of vengeful glee.

Her heart beating like a drum, she hesitated at the start of the Sear Line. She knew what was coming. She banished all doubts from her mind. She thought of the astral fires of the sun, her home. Fixing this noble image in her mind, she stepped gingerly onto the Sear Line. It felt like she was stepping on hot coals. Flinching, she took another step forwards. Her leg felt moist…watery. How was that possible? Her breath shallow, her head swimming, she cried out, a long, piercing cry of pain. Her body was burning. Her waters were scalding. As she took another step, a trace of steam escaped from beneath her foot as her body boiled. The integrity of her soul was corrupt. When she crossed the Anubis Gates, Anubis boasted that he'd take a fragment of her life from her. That was it. Like mother, like son, the same earthly impurity that tainted his soul had tainted hers. His was the limp; hers the fits and body spasms. The sphinxes' eyes emitted a ferocious astral heat and her impure soul had let it in. She was cooking from the inside.

A series of vivid images flashed before her mind's eye: her son's resurrection, the drama of his unveiling, his naming as the true twice-born, his union, her accession, her son's marital bliss, and finally Akasha's pregnancy.

All these came and went, memories melted by the heat of the Sear Line.

In the next step, her body was liquid, her form fluid, held together only by an invisible astral force that replicated her feminine shape. It was nearly over. Her time was up. Suddenly it burst asunder and the vapour was pulverised into tiny water droplets, which sprayed into the air, so small they evaporated almost instantly.

Cheiron looked on, mouth open. Tarsus and Irex looked horrified. He'd never seen a pharaoh vaporised, only hybrids. Recollecting his thoughts, he realised, in the event of such a failure on the Sear Line, that he was obliged to read from the sacred papyrus.

"We will not and cannot introduce impurities into the realm of our solar doubles. Thus have the enemies of the Solarii been rooted out. Issa is unfit. Under the stricture of the law, her soul had been weighed in the balance and found wanting. Not even a pharaoh is above the law of Ma'at."

What did it matter to him that a woman of inestimable courage had been vaporised? Or that a fine pharaoh had been de-robed in an appalling execution?

No, what mattered to him was that he'd performed his duty to the final sacred glyph. He gathered the pleats of his robe in one hand, and with the sacred papyrus in the other, he strolled down the Sear Line. Arriving at the other end unscathed, he ushered those waiting there for him into the hypogeum.

In his mind's eye, Tarsus replayed the moment Issa's body burst into sequins of water. To him, she was invincible, a woman who towered above the men around her, like a fortress lapped by the waves. Her violent and horrific death was more than unexpected. He slumped against the pavilion and wiped away an imaginary tear.

He didn't understand why the Solarii were so inflexible and severe. He shook his head in mourning for his mistress, and for all Solarii. A sorry lot. Why did they execute their laws with absolute relish? Without compassion or any allowance for mistakes, the Solarii continually failed to grasp these most fundamental of human virtues. Perhaps they would never embrace the human penchant for empathy and mercy. So be it. They were not of this world. Their fiery souls sat uncomfortably inside their human bodies. They were only able to remain here by inducing an artificial sun-fire ambience. At the end of the flood, they would go home. Let them. Humans would reclaim what was rightfully theirs.

He set off towards the ark, the rain slanting into his face. He walked through empty streets piled with discarded household goods. There were exquisite pieces of gold and jewellery, no longer of any value. He was terrified of the future. If the ark didn't survive the flood, there'd be no animals, no people, only a few birds, and plenty of fish. The world would be one shorn of the ability to bear witness to its perennial beauty. The question remained – could they sail the ark, this cumbersome hulk of a vessel, through the eye of the needle into the next epoch?

There was one vital call to make. He entered the precinct in the Nome of the White Wall and arrived at Zoser's residence. Thumping on the back door, the noise resounded through the empty house. Eventually he heard the soft patter of footsteps. From behind the door came a woman's voice.

"Who is it?"

"Tarsus."

The door swung ajar and a human woman stood there, holding two young children by the hand.

"I thought you weren't coming," the woman said, fear shadowing her face.

"I was delayed, but I'm here now. Come, this way, quickly." He beckoned her to follow him.

"Keep the hoods over your heads," the woman scolded the children – a boy and a girl. Tarsus paused. Momentarily the innocence of the children enchanted him, something he'd not witnessed for many a year.

"There's no time to tarry," he said, and set off again into the deserted streets, trudging through the mud and puddles.

Packs of dogs and hyenas, with no one to prevent them marauding the deserted city, sniffed the waste and howled at the crescent moon. Some had turned vicious and snarled at the four of them. The two children hid amidst their mother's skirts. Goats and chickens ran wild across the market square, where sodden pennants fluttered in the wet breeze. Horses and mules grazed on the grass sprouting out of the unkempt footpaths. Dead birds littered the ground, pawed at by wild cats and other scavengers.

The wind was rising as Tarsus pulled his coat up to cover his neck and chest. The woman walked behind him, to shelter from the rain as much as she could. On occasions, they had to slow down because the children were tired. Through the swirling rain, he could make out three struts protruding high into the air, and he knew them to be the masts of the ark. As they clambered on board, Uriah awaited them at the top of the gangplank, pulling his cloak fast around his body.

"Is that them?" Uriah glanced at the woman and her children struggling to get up the gangplank.

Tarsus nodded. As dusk settled, the wind howled around the ark and the rain pummelled the wooden decks. The animals growled and wailed.

"I hope you know what you're doing," Uriah muttered, out of earshot of the woman.

"We agreed they could come on board," Tarsus replied. "Well, there they are: Petra the Kushite and her children."

CHAPTER 49

The Field of Rushes

Horque surveyed the Solarii encampment. The old epoch was dying, and with it the embers of the sun, whose faint rays failed to penetrate the gathering gloom. From his mountain position, he witnessed the unremitting panorama of the coming storm. Darkening clouds enshrouded the horizon. Tornadoes gathered like buzzards beyond the foothills. Great sheets of fire burnt the air from the sky waters to the ground.

As if that was not enough, the ending of the epoch had precipitated a breakdown in the astral light, rendering unreliable any astral communication with Akasha. He yearned to know how she was, and how the baby was, all to no avail. He assumed she'd be heading for the Natal Chamber, so at least she'd give birth in a safe, dry place.

Marim, where was Marim?

"Why haven't the flyers tested their craft today? Don't we need water or food? We're not angels anymore," Horque said.

"I know, Protector. There are wild perturbations in the astral light. It's too unstable to send them out and it's more difficult to maintain an effective astral shield. Fortunately, the hybrids haven't discovered this."

"Yet. Because they will. Have you seen how canny they now are?" Horque stormed. "They're changelings, they're diseased."

"Lasec said you saw them chasing the humans towards Babylon."

"Yes, that's true." How could he protect his wife when he was so far away? He thought about flying off to Babylon, but even that was now impossible. "Strengthen the shield and close every gap," he ordered, dragging his weary body into his makeshift chambers, where he slumped down on his chair.

Issa, Issa…his thoughts flew to his mother and the Sear Line. Cheiron hadn't forgotten him. A short while before, he'd received the high priest's summons through the clairvoyant veins of astral light. Of course, he hadn't responded. The pharaoh's orders were to remain here. He had to obey her. Besides, Issa had convinced him not to undergo the Sear Line. She was privy to secret knowledge that would propel him across the Winding Waterway and home. At least his future was guaranteed.

His heart missed a beat. Something was wrong. His mother's reassuring presence in the astral felt distant, even absent. He peered into the astral light and glimpsed the gates of Anubis at the entrance to Du'at. He heard the rustle of reeds and a faint voice, right on the edge of hearing.

"Goodbye, my son."

His mother had arrived in the Field of Rushes. The pharaoh was dead. She had gone. He was lost without her. He wanted to be close to her, to feel the comfort she always gave him, mother to son.

He had an idea. Find it. Search his belongings. Yes, there was the white ribbon – the one she'd tied on the gates that signified the ten days of mourning for *his* death. It was his turn to mourn for her as she'd mourned for him.

Attaching it to his craft, he whispered, "Goodbye, Issa."

Outside the cave, the roar of the winds was deafening and torrential rains beat down on bare rock. Lightning flashes illuminated the olive sky, a macabre dance of the forces of nature.

He licked dry lips and swallowed hard.

The apocalypse had begun.

CHAPTER 50

The Facing

Akasha's belly hurt. The spasms shot through her, then faded. With Shamira's help, she waddled along behind Philo. The tower stood implacably ahead. From an enormous circular base, it spiralled into the sky, getting narrower as it got higher like a giant spindle. The apex was barely visible amidst the swirling mists and low cloud. In the darkening gloom, the hundreds of people who had taken shelter in the tower had lit glow lamps, that cast eerie shadows as they moved about in front of the window openings.

Obsidian clouds scudded in from the east, the horizon seared by constant flashes of lighting. In the distance, a tornado whirled its mayhem. This one seemed more menacing than the others she'd seen. She bit down on her fear.

The wind growled and the rain spat in her face. She wiped the moisture away, like so many tears for a dying epoch. A moment later, she was soaked again. There was no shelter. All around, people were inebriated, swimming in the ecstasy and exasperation of the apocalypse. It had a dull, parlous sound, this end of days: a cacophony of breaking strings, snapping branches and creaking doors.

With frantic gestures, Philo pushed the people ahead of him out of the way.

"The way's blocked – again." His voice was as hard as flint.

They were surrounded by scores of refugees from the Jasmine Gap, as well as drifters, rabble-rousers and lost souls all heading for the last place of possible sanctuary for many leagues around – the Tower of Babylon. Oh, she was so tired. Her baby was feeling her frustrations, an unwilling participant in a static crowd, so near and yet so far from her destination. Tros stood beside her. She felt guilty over his actions.

"I'll never forget your sacrifice," she told him.

"Nor will I," he murmured disconsolately.

Bats flitted through the mists. Dogs bayed at an invisible moon. A cock crowed and then another answered. Birds squawked cries of alarm and cats screeched like demons. An owl cried out overhead. Hordes of frightened, violent people worshipped at the altar of the atrophied old epoch.

None of them had glow lamps. The tenebrous night was closing in on them, and with it the storm of the millennium. Hemmed in, her breath shallow, Akasha was suffocating. She wanted to scream. Rain hissed out of the sky. She was drowning in an ocean of fear. Across the way, a turbulent wind gusted around the turret, making an eerie whistling sound. Locked in a weird embrace with the agents of death, they were all waiting for the apocalypse to break over their heads.

"We need to get over *there*!" Philo shouted, pointing at the tower, now less than a stone's throw from where they stood, hemmed in by the crowd. For a moment, there was a pause, a hiatus in the chaos. The crowd seemed to sense it too, and quietened. Then a moment later, it was gone, as if it never existed. And people were jostling, shouting and fighting with each other all over again.

It happened again. There was a note, a voice. Singing. No, it couldn't be. In this morass? The crowd surged behind Akasha, and she stumbled. That brought on another spasm. The child was awake, moving around inside her. Tros and Shamira grabbed an elbow each and hauled her upright.

Cloaked in the maelstrom, there was the singing again. Sweet sounds drifted in the air, blown this way and that by the gusting wind and slanting rain. People backed away, and Akasha stepped into a clear, open space. The singing originated from near the corner of the tower. The noise and hubbub subsided. A small gap appeared, and through the parting crowd walked a man holding a bright lantern out in front of him. It was Rocor.

His chest rose and fell as he sang. As if in response to a prearranged signal, the crowd parted to let him through. A wonderful paean rose up out of the maelstrom. Shamira and Tros joined the singing. Slowly, the crowd joined in with the singers and the joy of their voices extinguished the fear in their eyes. Amidst the rain, the drunks, the despair and the hopelessness, people raised their voices in the words of the hymn, incense to the Source. Those in the tower hung out of the windows and sang into the rain.

This unexpected transformation banished Akasha's pangs of doubt. In the midst of a spiritual vacuum, one man had restored her faith in humanity. Faced with an ugly apocalypse, she was dimly aware of witnessing something divine. She was not alone. That night in Babylon, all were equal in the eyes of men; they were always equal in eyes of the Source.

A belligerent gust of wind snuffed out the light in Rocor's lantern. This seemed to be an omen because he stopped singing and turned to leave. For a dreadful moment, Akasha thought he was stepping out alone into the tempest to meet his maker, as calmly as if he was going to tend his beloved gardens. Rocor's transformative singing had clearly moved Appolis the king, who insisted they found a place for him in the already overcrowded tower.

Such a small act of compassion had a large repercussion. Because, with her contractions increasing, Akasha's way to the Natal Chamber was clear, thanks to Rocor. Philo and Shamira helped her to the entrance to the chamber, round the back of the tower.

Philo cupped his hands and shouted, "Tros, there's room for you now – you can have Callisto's place!" Then he seemed to realise how grossly insensitive his remark was, because he immediately said, "Tros, I'm sorry, I didn't mean it like that."

"I didn't take it like that," Tros replied, magnanimous as ever. "Besides, I would be honoured to take my daughter's place."

"Good," Shamira said with evident relief. "That's agreed. Now, let's see this Natal Chamber."

Philo lifted a trapdoor. Down a score of steps, at the base of the stairwell, another door awaited them. Akasha was more than relieved to reach this point. Behind that door lay salvation and safety.

Philo pushed it open. Inside, the air smelt dank, thick like resin. He scuttled around the perimeter lighting the lamps on the walls, filling the chamber with a welcome glow.

Shamira assessed the chamber. It had a domed ceiling, and like the tower, it was oval-shaped. Occupying about one third of the available floor space were sleeping materials, birthing equipment, a plentiful supply of water, and various paraphernalia for their survival including glow lamps and candles. The chamber would easily have been large enough to accommodate Tros, if the other two thirds of the room weren't crammed with racks of shelving and scrolls.

"What on Earth are these doing here?" she demanded.

Akasha was already squatting on the birthing stool, grunting in between gasps for breath.

"It was the will of Kare, the high priest," Philo stammered, his fists clenched in frustration. "He persuaded the king to let him to store the temple's archives down here. What could I do but comply? At first, there were only a few. Then Kare ordered another lot, and then another, and that's how it's come to this." He waved his arm at the shelves.

"Kare – again," Tros said. "That man is a blight on the face of humanity."

"Philo, tell me," Shamira hissed. "What's written on the scrolls?"

"I don't know," Philo said. "The high priest told the king they contained everything we ever held sacred in Babylon."

"Let's find out what's so sacred." Shamira pulled out a scroll. "Here, read this."

Philo puffed out his cheeks.

"This one...yes...contains a list of all the water wells in the Zagros district of Babylon." Opening one scroll after another, he reported their contents. "These are details of property transactions... This is a list of quantities of herbs... This one's from someone complaining about the poor grade of copper ore he's been sent." He tossed them on the floor.

"This isn't sacred knowledge," Shamira said with a dismissive wave of her hand. "And even if it was, it'll never be as precious as a human being. Clear this chamber. Quickly!"

She erected some privacy screens for Akasha, while Philo and Tros emptied the chamber of cylinders and were soon removing the last shelving. Suddenly the chamber echoed with the sound of querulous voices from the top of the steps. Reluctantly, Shamira left Akasha alone and went to investigate.

"It's your fault," she heard Tros blurt out.

"It's not, it was broken..." Philo replied, hands on his head in desperation.

"What's the matter now?" she asked.

"The seal around the trapdoor is damaged," Tros said, pointing to a frayed edging around the wooden shutter.

This was ominous. For them to stay dry and safe, the seal on the trapdoor had to be watertight. Everything else had gone wrong, so perhaps this wasn't such a surprise.

"Can it be repaired?" she asked, more in hope than expectation.

"Yes and no," Philo said, with typical Babylonian ambivalence.

She glared at him until he explained.

"The trapdoor was designed so that when it was shut from beneath, the upper seal closed itself automatically."

"One of the shelves fell and broke the edge of the seal," Tros said, his face gnarled with trauma. "I killed my own daughter to save the human race from the blight of the hybrid seed. I won't let her death be in vain."

"What can be done?" Shamira asked.

"The seal can be made good, but..." Philo said, his voice trembling, "only if someone stays up here to close the trapdoor."

"I'll stay up here, tell me what to do," she said, without a moment's hesitation. What was her life worth against the continuance of the human race? Everyone was expendable, except Akasha.

"No!" Tros said. "Akasha needs you more than she needs me. I'll do it." The look in his eye was intense. He meant every word.

"All right," she said softly. Courage called for acquiescence.

In a flash, Pazazu appeared above them, a winged viper dancing in the air. A hoard of hybrids lurched around the corner, wielding torches and clubs, dripping venom. As Philo glanced at them and hesitated, Tros pushed him down the steps and slammed the trapdoor shut. Shamira and Philo tumbled to the bottom of the stairs. When Philo made to go back up to help Tros, the pythoness shook her head.

"He's made his decision," she said, and mouthed a prayer of thanksgiving to a brave man. Akasha called from the Natal Chamber.

"What is it?" Shamira answered, rushing to her side.

"My waters have broken."

PART 9

Apocalypse

Her waters burst asunder,
The rains began a-thunder,
The old epoch, God ends,
A new epoch, God sends.

EXTRACT FROM THE EPIC OF THE TWIN RIVERS

CHAPTER 51

Dewdrop to Dewdrop

Up above, Philo heard a loud thunder crack, then the inner door slammed shut. With heavy step, he entered the birthing area, sad at the waste of decent human life. But he was cheered by the sight of mother and newborn.

"Is it a...?" he stammered.

"It's a girl," Akasha replied with a beaming smile.

"That's wonderful. How is the mother?" he asked.

"Exhausted, but elated."

"And the child?"

"As healthy as can be," Akasha replied.

"She looks like her mother."

Shamira had her back to them. Now she turned, cradling a second child.

"Twins!" Philo exulted.

"And this one's a boy," Shamira said, her eyes gleaming like the blue of a tropical lagoon.

"Which came first?" he asked.

"The girl, of course," she replied, with a mischievous grin on her face.

"And...are they...both human?"

"Well," Shamira said, "we can see their tiny fingers, all different lengths. And no marks of the hybrid seed on either of them."

"What a relief."

Delirious with joy, Akasha lay her exhausted body down on the bed. Cradling the newborn to her breast, she felt alternate waves of relief and joy. The tiny babe squirmed and struggled, then let out a plaintive cry. Shamira hummed the birthing song, moving and swaying her body to its rhythm. Akasha joined in its soothing melody.

Milk to milk,
Water to water,
Dewdrop to dewdrop
A new daughter…

The light of thanksgiving filled the chamber, keeping at bay the creeping tentacles of the storm raging above them.

"What about my beautiful son?"

Milk to milk,
Joy to joy,
Dewdrop to dewdrop
A new boy…

They sang with such relish that the fairies, gnomes and astral entities of the Earth gathered around them to listen and sparkle.

"Don't you think the boy looks like his father?" Philo asked. "It's a shame he can't be here."

"He can be, at least in spirit," Akasha said, touching the onyx Djed carving by her bedside. "This pillar connects us both." Horque knew where they were, she was certain.

"The children need naming. He must be a part of that," Akasha said, wrapping the boy in swaddling clothes. For what seemed an age, they watched the babies sleep until Philo went to examine the seals.

"Now you have your wish – not once, but twice," Shamira said.

Akasha smiled. "I always knew I was going to be a mother. I was never going to sit in that Emerald Cavern, you knew that."

Shamira nodded. "It was my duty to try to persuade you."

"Even after that," she added, "the flame of motherhood burnt bright within me. I knew I'd bear children, though I never imagined the father would be a Solarii."

"I had an inkling when you were born," Shamira confessed with a wry smile. "That was when Sirius was most prominent in the skies."

"Yes, I remember you telling me… The Solarii call it the Star of Isis."

"There was a connection between you and the Solarii right from the beginning, and it carried through into your apprenticeship," Shamira added.

"I was wondering about that. What's happened to my apprenticeship?"

The pythoness' face seemed to be set like granite, and her eyes turned a deeper blue.

"It's finished," she said.

"Has it?" That was unexpected. "When?"

"Don't you know the moment it happened?" Now Shamira was teasing her. "It was in Egypt."

"What was?" So much had happened in Egypt.

"The moment you attained the development of a basilisk."

Oh yes, now she knew. A wave of realisation swept over her.

"In the dock at the Temple of Ma'at. The moment I defied the pharaoh's will."

"Exactly," the pythoness replied, a thin smile gracing her lips. "That was it. Even then, you knew what you'd achieved, at least instinctively."

"How was that?" Akasha screwed up her face. Shamira knew her better than she knew herself. How was that possible?

"You fainted in the temple, remember? When you awoke, I asked if you wanted to put Demos' cobra necklace back on."

"I refused, didn't I?" That sparked her curiosity.

"You didn't need it anymore. You knew the basilisk would provide the protection previously afforded by the necklace."

"What does that mean?" Akasha sought confirmation.

"That you're the custodian of the Basilisk That Slays. Know that it is as real as it is lethal."

Akasha had not known it consciously until this moment. Now it felt as natural as if she'd met a long-lost friend. In truth, she'd joined a part of her birthright.

"You used its power to slay that hybrid near the Gates of Gades. I'll never forget the look of dread on its face as you squeezed the life out of it."

"I am the pythoness, and that's how the power manifested in me," Shamira explained with pride. "In you, it's different. Demos saw that too."

"You mean...the cobra?"

"Yes, the hooded one. The astral power of the Basilisk That Slays emanates from the middle of your forehead and rears up from the top of your head. The Solarii call it the ureaus. In me, the basilisk emanated from the eyes."

It was true. Akasha was the White Cobra, Shamira the Blue Pythoness. There was a mutual respect between the two women, once protégée and mentor, now equals.

"I see that the power to slay is never to be used indiscriminately."

"The Basilisk That Slays will protect what is right and guard what is sacred. You're a protector, like your husband. A word of caution: like all high astral powers, the entity can cure or inflict. Abuse it at your peril."

"I understand."

"Understand too that from now on, you are alone."

"Alone?" Akasha was alarmed.

"The basilisk may serve only one. I've stepped down. Now it's your turn. How do you feel?"

"How do *you* feel?" Akasha asked in return.

"I feel like I've stepped into a void," Shamira confessed. "When I became the basilisk, I had to sacrifice part of my own path of development. I'm glad my service is over. I'm tired and jaded, my body aches. At this moment, I feel curiously empty. It's as if an old and trusted friend has suddenly died, which in a way is what's happened. Now it's left me for you, there's space for the real Shamira to take up residence. Now that my service is done, I'll tarry and rekindle connections young and old."

There was a long pause, as the basilisk reflected on her newfound responsibilities. She was aware of its profound presence deep in her soul, a Leviathan with the power to give life, and the power to take it. Above all, she had always to remember that it wasn't her power. It remained with her because it chose to, and because she abided by its requirements.

The storm raged above them. The percussive sound of thunder shook the foundations of the chamber, dislodging dust from the rafters. Some of the storm's might and wrath drifted down through the stones and the timbers, and interrupted her meditation.

Shamira heard it too. Glancing up, she said, "We are going to live through that."

"If we can survive the great winds, we can survive the falling of the sky waters. Sooner or later the rains will cease, the waters will drain away, and we'll walk out free as birds into the sun-filled air."

CHAPTER 52

Riders of the Storm

It was bitterly cold that morning, as Li Ching huddled together with her people on the summit of a hill. All along, she'd been confident they'd climbed high enough to survive the killing waters. Now, as the apocalypse wound itself into a frenzy, she was seized by doubt.

In the east, a huge black cloud smudged the horizon, turning the bright morning rays back on themselves, transforming day into night. Before the flood, the Cathay soothsayers had scared people with their predictions of the dread Lord of the Storm and his hoard of ghost riders, entities to which she'd never given any credence. Until now. Looking through her whites, she saw them. They were real, and they were coming.

Fearsome in their aspect, the Riders of the Storm followed their lord, riding upon the crest of the billowing cloud to chasten the living. In one hand, they gripped the reins of their phantom steeds, and in the other, they raised torches of livid gold and red. Every living thing quaked before the thunder of their hooves.

From her vantage point, Li Ching watched in terror as the astral riders galloped above the broad plains and mountains of the Land of the Yellow River, leaving a path of devastation behind them. Whirling tornadoes spun waters into a fury and destroyed villages and towns, temples and shrines. Hurricane winds cut a ruthless swathe through forests and woodlands. Hatching chaos, the riders spurred their steeds to bring the next proud land in their path to its knees.

In the High Zagros, Horque had a macabre view of the approach of the Riders of the Storm as the tempest rolled over the Solarii encampment. The rain hit the ground so hard that spurts of dust and droplets of water jumped up to the full height of a man. Lightning splintered through the roof of the sky, illuminating the pathetic faces of his flyers, who huddled behind the cave walls. Looking up at the sky waters as they descended upon them, they clasped their freezing hands together in futile prayer to the pantheon. They cried for help, they lauded their doubles, all in vain. Above the clamour of the storm, nothing could be heard.

The winds gusted with such ferocity that they clung to the rocks to keep from being sucked into the maelstrom. The rain whipped their faces and hands like a score of tiny nails plunged into the surface of their skin, puncturing it, tearing it, whipping it.

Amidst this terror, Horque's thoughts winged their way to his beloved. On the first night the sky waters had started to fall, he stood as near to the edge of the cave as he dared, watching in awe as the monumental forces of air, water and fire tore the earth apart. He turned to retreat into the inner part of the cave, when something rolled by his feet, blown into the cave by the storm winds. It was the burred surround of a horse chestnut casing. The casing was split, so that the top edge of a shiny brown nut protruded out of it. Prising it open, he found two nuts, nestling together.

It was a propitious omen. With his back to the storm, he stood there, hypnotised by the epiphany. Twins. Exactly as Issa had foretold after Akasha's visit to the Nuptial Chamber.

He had to find a way to visit his wife. Yet he couldn't feel her presence. Astrally, she was normally as close to him as if she was inside his own skin. The turbulence of the flood had disrupted the flux of the astral light, and all communications were erratic. He felt lost. As he grieved, all his experiences of her were plucked from him and cast into the empty darkness of Du'at. She was still alive, and he was desperate to stand by her side. He would have to wait until the worst of the flood passed over. He had to be strong, to endure, to survive, for her, and for his children.

Akasha's dreams were shot with stark images of ghost riders whipping up apocalyptic storms, and huge tsunamis that tore the earth asunder. When she finally awoke, she was more exhausted than when she fell asleep, yet her children needed feeding. As they suckled, she wondered about her Horque, hoping and praying he was still alive.

That the Natal Chamber remained dry was due in no small part due to Philo, whose examination of its seals was as severe as the storm that thundered above them. Should the seals rupture, there was nowhere for them to go to avoid death. She daren't think about it. The chamber was a cocoon: the claps of thunder and the battering of the rains were to her no more than muffled thuds. Thus far, her children were safe and she hugged them close to her, feeling their slender breath on her skin.

Rocor was ensconced in the Tower of Babylon watching the apocalypse unfold. He was squeezed together so tightly with those around him, he could barely move to relieve himself or take a sip of water. The panorama from the tower was awe-inspiring, until he watched the tempest demolish the terraces of his beloved Hanging Gardens. All that work, gone to waste.

As the riders passed overhead, they lit the sky with an arsenal of lightning bolts and fire in the heavens. Wielding such power in their torches, the riders could frighten a grown man out of his skin, as many were frozen in fear around him.

Rumour abounded amongst the populace, almost as fast as the waters swelled around the base of the tower. Even Appolis, they claimed, was fearful for his life – and he was their king. If he couldn't control the elements, no one could.

Rocor mouthed a silent prayer for Akasha and her children, who were hopefully safe beneath this whirling maelstrom.

As soon as Tarsus had returned from the Sear Test with Petra the Kushite, the crew had battened down the hatches. When the river broke her banks, the currents filled all the crevices beneath the ark. The waters swelled and lapped the keel and rose up the prow. As the Storm Riders passed by, claps of thunder deafened the crew. The scores of animals in the ark cowered and moaned in fear. The crew sought shelter from the killing rains that sent streams of water across the decks and over the sides. Tarsus and Uriah waited for the waters to surge around the *Fair Maiden* so she could launch on her maiden voyage into the burgeoning ocean.

In the High Pyrenes, Demos had climbed to the top of the Whispering Tower, glow lamp in hand. But the strong winds and rain prevented him from opening the door to the parapet, so he'd retreated to the relative safety of the stairwell, where he peered out of a slit opening onto the passion play of the elements.

He felt bitterly cold as the winds snaked up and down the stairwell. He fell to musing about how the Source could permit such a terrible onslaught. Surely, such wanton destruction was the recourse for fools, not a divine being of supreme intelligence.

Rain and cloud hung like a pall over the whole Earth; a darkness of the spirit obscured his light, because there was no mercy left in the humans' treasury. He was glad at least for his glow lamp, a flickering light that not even all the concentrated darkness of the storm could extinguish.

Big Qorus was still the proud Green Elder of the thriving city of Samlios, though it wasn't thriving much these days. In fact, it was deserted, with the exception of his ailing mother and a marauding pack of wild dogs. The astral light had become so polluted that swarms of a revolting new insect had emerged through the veil. They were the condensation of concentrated vermin – he called them 'flies' for short.

He'd stayed to care for Myriam, whose broken leg had prevented her joining the exodus from the isle after the Mind Search. He could have headed off beyond the Astral Dome in search of higher ground, but he was a loyal son. Besides, Samlios was his home and that was where he'd make his peace with her, flood or no flood. A full circle of birth and death – he enjoyed the symmetry.

Briefly, he'd made friends with Jarda and the lycans who, soon after the exodus, had crept through the west gate and over Out Hill, curious to see what had happened to the city. Later, with the flood coming, they'd followed their instinct and left. He hoped they'd survive in the distant mountains. They had treated him with respect.

Unlike the pirates who'd docked in Fishmouth Harbour. They'd ransacked the city, breaking it apart, smashing the carvings on the Avenue of Statues. For some unknown reason, they took especial delight in destroying Arka's bust of the Lady Li Ching. In the end, they'd reduced the city to a shadow of its former self. Like the flies, they fed off the carcass of a dying epoch. They were lower than the flies, since they knew better. Never mind. Judging by that dark, brooding hammer cloud on the horizon, he wouldn't be around for much longer anyway. He looked forward to standing before the Source and accounting for his life.

Savor the Andean never stopped encouraging people to climb the mountain peaks to survive the flood. His people already lived near to the sky waters, in the Land of the Clouds. Of late, their ranks had been swelled by hybrids that had followed an ever-lengthening trail of humans and animals heading there. As the rains plundered the land, he looked on in horror as many on the lower mountain passes were sucked into the vortex, or buried under treacherous landslides.

Birds sought what shelter they could find from the sheet rain and savage winds. They were blown about like flower petals, whipped up by the tempest, and dragged below the surface of the waves by grasping currents. While they still could, those of the feather flew, or rather swam through the rain, to perch on mountain peaks.

This was a time of culmination, so he made a point of thanking all who'd helped him in his life's journey. One way or another, hybrid seed or flood, it would end.

CHAPTER 53

The Natal Chamber

During the flood, Akasha cradled her babes in her arms for long periods, singing lullabies to them and staring with longing eyes into her twins' faces. Every one of their features – their high foreheads, sharp noses and thin lips – reminded her of Horque, who strode like a giant through the empty chambers of her heart. Although she yearned for him, her one hope was that he lived.

Since they had first met, she had walked by his side, holding his enormous hand in hers, for just two glorious, bittersweet moons, their period after the union in his residence in the Nome of the White Wall. After Babylon, he'd disappeared for a second time. Her life had barely started, yet here she was with two incredible twins and a serially errant husband. Like all newlyweds, she'd anticipated long years of contentment with her family, but even this had been snatched from her grasp by the vicissitudes of the flood.

She'd been desperate for Horque to be present at the birth, to smother her with his support, to cherish her and help her through the ardours of labour. She could easily imagine it: she would have shown off her twins, passed them to him like precious jewels. He'd have taken them in his strong, protective arms, where they would have squirmed like a pair of tiny, slippery serpents, then cried because they missed their mother's deep, musky odours.

The moment she would have prized the most was when a look of unfathomable pride swept across his broad and craggy features, like a sudden shower of rain that softened the hardness of arid ground. A doting father, he would have stared into his children's eyes, moving from one twin to the other. He would have seen how beautiful were her children, his children, their children; how quiet and handsome his son was, how he had his father's piercing blue eyes, and how the little girl had her mother's soft chestnut brown eyes and effervescent nature. At that moment, perhaps a rare tear of joy might have rolled down his cheek, and that smile of his would have spread right back to the stele of Egypt.

They would have amused themselves with endless debates about the babies' natures, seeking the clues to their characters and names. She'd have to be patient, and wait to hold these conversations with him until after he had fought his people's battles in the High Zagros. To console herself, she stared longingly at his onyx pillar, holding it until its strength seeped into her being like water dripping onto papyrus.

She felt the astral light diminishing in illumination as the rains fell and the storm hammered away at the earth, a demon freed from its shackles after a thousand years. More than anything else, she feared that vapid astral light. As each bright candle of the astral light was snuffed out by the flood, so the growth of the hybrid seed in her, in all humans, would strengthen. Sooner or later, the suppression would dissolve completely and the hybrid seed would sprout in them all. For how long would she be capable of caring for her babies?

Her main preoccupation was the marking of the passage of the day. Cocooned in an underground chamber with no windows, no natural light, the survivors needed a routine, something to govern their actions and replace the passage of the sun across the sky waters.

In the end, the solution was simple: the babies 'told' them. Their appetites were as regular as the rising and setting of the sun, the moon and the stars, which they could sense even if they couldn't see. The babes cried when they wanted feeding, at regular intervals during the day. To keep a daily tally, Akasha marked a line in the wall with a nugget of flint, just as she'd done during the great winds.

Their essential supplies were water and light, both of which needed careful monitoring. Philo had provisioned the chamber with several large barrels of clean, fresh water and ladles to match. There was plenty for Akasha, whose thirst was on occasion such that she was drinking for an army, rather than the just three of them. Her babies suckled her with an enthusiasm bordering on the delirious.

The babies did not need physical food, though she suspected they might inherit carnal appetites from their father.

Notch after notch she carved, until, on the twentieth day, she'd bonded with her babies and lavished them with love and kisses as only a mother could. They clasped her swollen breasts in their tiny paw-like hands and with eyes shut deep, drank their fill. With Shamira's help, she'd fuss over them until they slept the sleep of the innocents. To keep them warm, Shamira made them little hats, socks and mittens. The carers were so intent on the welfare of the babies that they hardly spared a thought for the destruction rent by the storm raging above them. Together they delighted in the early discovery of their characters. The girl was precocious, a quick learner, always wanting attention, crying and howling tantrums when precedence was given to her younger brother, who was as intense as he was curious.

Although their ark, their Natal Chamber, was not buffeted from the outside by undulating waves and tempestuous winds, their trials came from the inside, the cramped conditions and claustrophobic lack of space. They were accustomed to feeling the breath of the wind and the subtle rays of the sun on their skin, but in their ark there was not even a threshold to step over. But at least it preserved them from an almost certain death. Day by day, they were transported through the eye of the needle of the apocalypse. For that, they gave thanks and remembered those who'd given their lives so they could enjoy the safety of the chamber.

"I don't like the confinement here," Akasha declared. "If I had not been with child, I'd have preferred a place on the real ark, rather than while away the dark hours of the day and night accompanied by worms and earwigs."

"Are you sure?" Shamira asked wistfully.

"Oh, yes," she replied in all sincerity, "I have the credentials to be a toughened sailor of the highest calibre, and without doubt I'm a mistress of the ocean."

Shamira hid a snigger behind her hand.

"Don't laugh," Akasha complained. "May I remind you that Uriah is a skilled sailor, so it was undoubtedly in my seed? And have you forgotten that the ark is named after me? My blue blood is full of brine," she concluded, with a wink.

By this time, Shamira and Philo were in stitches.

"What about… What about…" Shamira said, gagging with laughter, "your escapade on the *Crucible*?"

"Oh, that," Akasha said with mock disdain. "That was a mistake. Those ropes…"

"Oh yes." Philo was laughing so much he could barely say the next words. "Those ropes were misbehaving, weren't they?"

There were more gales of laughter in the chamber than there were gales up above, at least for a while…until Akasha hushed them because they were waking the babies. But really, it was because she could not stop chuckling either.

CHAPTER 54

The Killing Rains

Rocor was humming a jaunty tune to himself when the wave crashed into the side of the tower, taking a chunk out of it, like a savage animal gnarling its prey. He kept on humming; he'd expected this for some time. It was difficult to ignore the rising waters, slowly swallowing the lower levels of the tower, as more and more people squeezed into less and less space. He wasn't sure why they were frightened of meeting the Source. They were screaming and yelling inconsolably.

Below him, the waves climbed the tower like a sentient being, a step at a time. Soon it would be his turn. Then a wave the size of a mountain arced over the tower like a gigantic fist and crashed down on it, dislodging the people in the lower floors, and throwing them to a watery grave.

This was the end and he was indifferent to it. Good old King Appolis had bequeathed him a place on the tower. His singing had earned him a few more days in which to give thanks for his extraordinary life, and the beauty and grace of the flowers and gardens he'd helped nurture. In the end, he could stand upright and say with pride that he had been a human being.

When another huge wave crashed into the tower, and its powerful under-currents sucked him out into the ocean swell, he was ready and prepared. For a moment, he bobbed up to the surface. He noticed that, by some miracle, the lower half of the tower poked up above the raging waters, no doubt a tombstone for the nameless dead and a welcome perch for passing birds.

As the voracious tide pulled him under, he was humming the lilting melody of the song of Samlios. Now that was a fine city.

The storm continued unabated and the winds blew with such ferocity Horque worried that his exposed location would be found wanting even though the flyers and the craft were sheltered by the caves. On a daily basis, he summoned his companions to remind them of their duties and keep their hearts and minds from fracturing.

"Embrace and welcome the flood. Once it peaks, we will complete our task here."

On occasion, he heard the pitiful cries of hybrids or humans, caught on high ground near the Giant's Dome, or what was left of it, then plucked by the baleful winds and tossed over the cliffs into the abyss, like leaves in the autumn gales.

Out on the exposed ridges with nothing to eat, the hybrids succumbed to a slow and painful death. From a distance, he heard muted cries, the horrible sounds of limbs devoured in a frenzy of cannibalism. Then the hybrids fought over the bloody fruits of their labour. Their silhouettes lit by flashes of lightning, they beat their chests to the sounds of thunderclaps, naively imagining themselves as Storm Lords.

In the recesses of his mind, Cheiron was aware that the rain was still pelting the ground, and that just above where he lay, water spouts with the girth of a city paraded across the once green and pleasant land of the pharaohs. The dreamer dreamt on, and imagined mammoth spouts of grit and earth and dirt lifted into the sky to form floating clouds of sand as big as seas. Blown by ferocious tempests, these great sky dunes were transported for leagues on end until, as the storm abated, they collapsed and spread their sand mountains across lands, like his land of Egypt, which had previously been bedewed with meadow and pasture, forest and dale.

Tarsus wondered whether many would survive the tempest, only to be killed by the flood. Out of the porthole of his cabin in the relative safety of the ark, he saw humans, animals and hybrids clinging in desperation to tree trunks and other floating debris. Sometimes the men on the ark were able to save them, oftentimes not. The ark was buffeted by towering waves, hail and rainstorms, and howling winds. Debris washed up on their bows, not least the rotting carcasses of those of the feather and the fur. Black clouds rolled overhead, lit beneath by sheet lightning.

Tarsus was no musician, but the Lord of the Storm conducted his own percussive orchestra: the constant booms of thunder presented a macabre requiem for those few survivors, whose physical strength and spiritual resolve wore thin, until it eventually snapped. Then they slipped silently from their tree trunks into unmarked graves at the bottom of the sea. After such a primeval battering, he thought it almost understandable that many willed their own deaths. Would any survive these killing waters?

The turbulence stretched its terrible hand into the ocean depths. Frothing waves disturbed the tranquillity of the even the deepest swimmers in the sea.

After a moon's cycle, a golden eagle roosted on the awning deck, its claws gripping the masthead, tight as a vice.

Demos sat huddled on the stairwell, palms absorbing what little heat was emitted by the glow lamp. For many days, he watched and waited, with Tamir as company. People pressed up the stairs to join him, chased by the swelling waters.

Day after day, night after night. Mostly, there was little difference between the two. Squinting through the slit opening, he saw swirling mist, drizzle fog and mounting tempest. Then one day, the clouds dispersed and – at least for a while – he could see through the watery veil. What he saw made him stumble. He edged towards the opening and peered down in wide-eyed terror.

There below him were…white-capped waves.

In the upper reaches of the Whispering Tower, he sat astonished, gazing out at what once had been an enchanting view of forests, fields and meadows, but which was now full of great eddies and whirling currents. He looked upon an all-encompassing slate-grey ocean.

He held his glow lamp at the slit for the world to see. The tower that whispered from the top of the world was now a beacon, a lighthouse at the world's end.

From the elevation of his cave, Horque watched the waters creep up the hills and valleys, ever deeper, ever nearer, shifting and depositing shells and stones along an ever-moving shore line. As the rains fell, the water levels crept up the slopes of the Jasmine Gap. After a moon's cycle, they had swallowed the fallen Giant's Dome. After another ten days, the waters lapped the slopes of the hill of his encampment. He was vigilant. The coming moment was not for pity, but for preparation. The final task would soon be upon him. *The Surge was paramount.* That was enough. Now he knew exactly what to do and how to do it.

"Forty notches now," Akasha said.

"So many," Shamira replied.

With their spirits at low ebb, Philo had an idea.

"I've just remembered," he said excitedly, delving into a chest. "Here, look at this!" He held up alternately a drum, a miniature harp, a rattle, and various other musical instruments.

"You'd forgotten you had these?" Shamira gently reprimanded him.

"It's the seals," he said. "They've kept me well occupied."

"As well they might," she said ruefully.

Akasha twanged the harp for all she was worth. The babies started crying, but this time they played on until the walls of the chamber resounded with music, singing and laughter. In between songs, Philo amused the children by blowing on a reed. Then they took turns to listen to a conch shell, summoning the susurrus sound of the sea into the depths of their chamber.

After Philo broke into his horsey laugh, Akasha put a finger to her lips and hushed him sharply.

"What is it?" Shamira asked.

"Listen," Akasha whispered.

Philo thrust an ear against a wall. "I can't hear a thing," he said.

"Exactly," she replied.

"It's over. Praise the Source, the flood has ended!" Philo beamed.

"And so it has begun," Akasha said prophetically. She was right about another new beginning; this one unlooked for and unwanted. They had survived. "My only prayer is," she said, "that the new epoch is an improvement on the old."

"The new epoch," Philo exclaimed, dancing on his tiptoes.

Reaching to pick up a rattle from the floor, something rubbed against Akasha's armpit. It was a small tuft of hair. A growth. If she had a growth, did the children? This was the moment of truth. They were so near to their destination, yet so far from it.

She looked all over their little bodies, and there was...nothing. Not a whisker. Thank the Source. Thank the Watchers.

Her stomach churned. What about her? Where would the growth end? How would she care for the children with webbed feet or eagle wings, or a cow's head? It was too horrific to contemplate. Her worst nightmare was to have got this far and then be rendered degenerate in faculty by the silent assassin, the hybrid seed. She whispered a prayer to the Source. The others thought it was a prayer of thanksgiving, but Akasha knew otherwise. She was praying she'd retain her wits for long enough to nurture her children to adulthood.

Though the rains had stopped, Tarsus knew they had to endure another uncertain wait as the waters drained away. On mountain peaks, the swollen waters deposited oyster shells, conch shells and the shells of other crustaceans; the sodden bones of creatures from the land, sea and air. As the sea level dropped, a mysterious and macabre trail of deposits was left around the hillsides. He imagined some huge synchronised movement, conducted by higher powers and orchestrated by the moon, the tides, the ocean swells and the currents that reached into places where the eye of man had never born witness.

After the flow came the ebb, the oceans drained into the deep, hidden recesses of the earth that had dried out during the epoch of the sky waters. Now the waters returned once again to the lowlands, the shallows, the marshes, the seabeds.

A drop became a trickle, the trickle a stream, and the stream a flood, all going the other way. The swirling waters ebbed into the underground caverns of the Earth, palaces of the deep never warmed by the rays of sun, nor glimpsed by the shadow of the moon.

That night, the night the rains stopped, Horque felt the unfolding of a brand new permission, a window of opportunity when the change in the universe was almost complete; when the world missed a heartbeat and paused. The riders drew breath, worn out by the colossal effort of the apocalypse. In this lacuna, this gap in the affairs of gods and men, a subtle hand stirred in the Natal Chamber.

He grasped this opportunity to dream-travel like a thirsty man drinks his first draught; a task which, during the maelstrom of the flood, he'd found impossible. He resolved to visit his family – if only in the astral.

Beremtha, his astral signature, came when summoned. So at least a semblance of stability had returned to the astral light. Repeating the sacred words of the heart utterance, he felt the black hawk flicker into form at the nape of his neck. The cool of its wing beat lulled him into that curious half-state between sleep and wakefulness. Spreading its broad wings, the raptor flew off into the astral light.

Within moments, he hovered over the area he assumed was Babylon. At first there seemed to be nothing left of it. A bland expanse of bleak waves and an ocean of debris stared back at him. No semblance of human emanation in the astral light. That was until he inadvertently flew through a hoard of lost wraiths, the astral entities of dead souls. If they were there, he must be close.

There – an astral emanation, and another. Life was down there. Bright balls, earthen reds, tan browns and forest greens. Ah, a flock of birds perched on a floating bough. No, this was the wrong shape. This was broad and rounded. Was he looking at the stub of the great Tower of Babylon?

He saw something else – yellow in astral hue, cylindrical in shape. It was his Djed pillar. Yes. There she was. She had left it out as an astral signpost for him, a lighthouse in these darkening days. Beneath the tower were five human emanations.

During the dead of night, he flew into the Natal Chamber. None of the astral emanations moved; they were asleep. He found Akasha and tried wake her. He flapped his hawk wings over her but all she did was flutter her eyelids. He hopped over to the children's cot. Oh, they were so tiny. Perching on the edge of the cot, he squawked loudly. No one heard him in the incarnate, nor would they ever. Nothing penetrated the invisible chasm of the veil. He knew that. But it was worth a try.

Sensing a presence, one of the children woke up, his astral emanation a bright azure blue. The boy. Horque pecked his cheek. All the boy would have felt was a light brush of air, a nuance. He did the same with his daughter, who slept the sleep of innocence. Like all girls, her emanation was a salmon pink.

Akasha hadn't named them. Why not? He'd heard the soft echoes of their names in the astral winds, so why hadn't she? Ah – out of respect, she was waiting for him. The link to his physical body weakened. Time to return. He pecked Akasha on both cheeks and opened his wings. Soon the hawk was nestling against the nape of his neck and feeling the chilling damp in the cave.

Shamira was already awake when Akasha broke her slumber.

"Today we name the children," Akasha said brightly. "Will you help?"

"Of course," Shamira replied with a wry grin. Nearly two decades before, she'd stood in the lee of the Crystal Cathedral in Samlios to name Akasha. So much had changed since then that she could hardly believe it.

Shamira held the girl-child up to the stars and announced:

Oh, Universe of Succour,
Accept this child unto the great Church of Life.
Offer to her the grace of resistance to the things she desires,
Keep her from the wayward path,
And grant her the full number of her days.
From thenceforth know this child by the name: Ora.

Akasha wore a deep, knowing smile as she repeated the prayer for Bahir.

Ora and Bahir. Children of the future.

CHAPTER 55

The Solarii Morning Prayer

Horque limped to the edge of precipice. This really was the dawn of a new day, a new epoch.

"So this is the new era!" he shouted, half expecting a response. There wasn't one. His voice barely carried. "Ha! With all this mist, she's evidently a lady and shy of revealing too much of herself."

"Yes, Protector," Lasec replied. At least the old order still had pliancy.

Forty days ago, he had looked out on a panorama of mountains and valleys. Now an ocean stretched out before him, until it was lost in swirling white mists. Sheets of fog hung like cobwebs of moisture, obliterating sun and sky. Something was different about the sky and the texture of the light, but he couldn't make out what it was.

A noxious stench smacked his nostrils. Floating around his feet were the festering carcasses of dead animals, hybrids and humans, as well as a heaving collection of tree trunks, rubbish and rotting fish. All the flotsam of a drowned world was strewn over the churning surface. These were the residue of the old epoch, of a race's broken dreams, the sole remaining detritus of a world sunk without trace. A few scraggy gulls squawked in triumph over the unexpected feast.

Kicking aside the bloated carcass of a hybrid, Horque thrust an exploratory toe into the ocean. It felt cold and unforgiving. He flung a stone into the killing waters, which absorbed the ripples as if it had never been thrown at all. Everything was empty and without resonance, as if some demon of the underworld had sucked the life out of every creature. The stench of death was oppressive. Yet this was all nature's work. By the pantheon, she was all powerful, and that merited a mighty respect and a healthy fear. Without compunction, she gave life and took it away. In the midst of weakness, there was strength. This was the moment to fulfil the Solarii dream. And what of the Solarii in that hypogeum? Had the subtle astral emanations of the new epoch awoken them? Had they crossed the Winding Waterway and rejoined their doubles?

Marim slid out of the cave, moving in the manner of a man who expected a wild animal to leap on him at any moment.

"Pull yourself together," Horque barked. "Yes there's a lot of water, but the rains stopped. If we were going to drown, if would have happened by now. It didn't, and we have survived."

"I don't fear death," Marim replied.

"What do you fear, then?"

"We're not men anymore." Marim glanced down at his manhood.

"What do you mean? Oh, *that*," he said, as realisation dawned. During the course of the flood, his manhood, normally rigid for long parts of the day and night, had grown increasingly flaccid. This morning, it was as soft and wrinkled as a baby's.

"Cheiron was right. The pellucid astral light was the cause of the 'Solarii condition'," he murmured. This was the very condition that had led to Berux falling foul of the Second Peril. Upon such small ironies great civilisations had turned.

"We can do nothing about that," he added, "although we can do something about our return."

Looking through his whites, he probed the astral light and found that its currents and streams weren't as diffuse as he'd feared. Pockets of vibrancy remained, and thankfully these were enough to fly the Horus Wing craft and fire the ankhs. Now was the time that Issa had foreseen all those moons ago. Now was the time to fly their final mission.

"What are your orders?" Marim's voice sounded more like his old self, stern and full of rebuke, even when asking a bald question.

A stiff breeze swirled hazy mists around the small band of flyers.

"Solarii, our moment of triumph has arrived."

No response. A score of them stared back at him, with furrowed brows and deep troughs under their eyes. Their uniforms were ragged and rain-soaked. If he sent them out on a task of this magnitude in this state of torpor, they'd fail miserably. They needed the warming breath of inspiration.

"Repeat after me," he said.

Raise yourself.
Make this the day the hybrid are banished from the face of the Earth and so
Rectify the faults of the Helios.

Since the beginning of their sojourn on Earth, the Solarii repeated this prayer every day to invest it with power and charisma in the astral light, from which the flyers now drew with its repetition. Next came the reminder of the fruits of their labour.

Fulfil thus the terms of our exile.
Heed then the call to cross the Winding Waterway in the sky
And return home to my double on the sun.

After decades of waiting, the agony of exile, the pain of imprisonment and the endurance of his people, the words rang sweet and true. He'd gained their full and undivided attention.

"What we're about to do requires courage and discipline," he went on. "Succeed and you will be saviours. Remember the flyers' code: *Nothing but order, efficiency and dedication.*"

The men stiffened their sinews. The repetition of the prayer had stirred the glowing embers in their souls.

"Out there," he beckoned at the ocean lapping at their feet, "the primordial flux envelops the world. When you stride forth across the dull waters, you'll see isolated outcrops protruding from the dark abyss. Like this one, these rocks were once the tips of the highest mountains, peaks that punctured the sky waters. Now the sky waters have become ground waters and the summits are no more, they are merely isles in a single huge ocean. These crags are the focus of our final mission."

A glint in their eyes, the flyers were visibly growing in resolve.

"We are few, and we have to fly over every remaining portion of dry land before the waters recede," he said. "Marim will inform you which portion is yours. Fly there, search every cubit of it and remove every last living hybrid, before they come for us."

The flyers raised a resounding cheer.

"Protector, on the crags and islets," Marim pointed out, "there may be humans and animals crowded alongside the hybrids."

"Do not give way to pity or compassion," he urged them. "If you find humans and hybrids together, remove them all. Follow my orders to the glyph and do not, *under any circumstances*, deviate from them."

The men glared back at him, stern in the eye. They had understood his orders.

"I myself will search the area around Babylon and the High Zagros," he said. "Once you've completed the search of your area, report to me telepathically and return here."

Marim took up the reins of the operation. "In a vapid astral light, your craft will operate on residual power. Use your ankh weapon sparingly. Make every firing count."

The flyers leapt onto their craft like hungry men invited to a sumptuous feast. Horque watched them fly off into the new epoch, their vapour trails quickly disappearing into the thickets of mist.

The great culling had begun.

CHAPTER 56

The Time of Necessity

The sky waters were a memory. The Riders of the Storm had dismounted, their steeds were stabled. The abiding tentacles of mist reached low into the seas and high into the sky, obscuring the rays of the new epoch sun.

Tarsus hauled on a rope hanging down from the crow's nest.

"Is it safe to go up there now?" Uriah asked, craning his neck.

"The winds have dropped and it's been dry for a day now," he replied.

"Do you think you'll be able to see anything?"

Tarsus shook his head. "We can't drift forever. We have to get our bearings."

"Bearings? On what? There's the odd islet out there. Everything else, from east to west and pole to pole, is one vast ocean. And when the waters drain away, all the familiar coastlines and river estuaries will have disappeared." Uriah was obviously upset about it.

"I'm going up there anyway," Tarsus said.

It was so foggy he couldn't see beyond the bow of the ship. The mist was like a blanket of cold water: it dripped off the end of his nose, ears, eyebrows and even his eyelids. His fingers and toes were frozen. The foot and handholds were loose. When one nearly fell out, he decided discretion was the better part of valour and like a sloth, he reversed back down the sodden mast.

"Too dangerous?" Uriah asked.

Tarsus nodded. "I'll wait for the mists to clear. Ring the fog bell."

"Why? We're hardly likely to run into another boat..."

"It doesn't matter," Tarsus insisted.

The ship's mate released the plunger and the dull thud of the bell resounded across the deck.

"Where do we go from here?" Uriah asked.

"What do you mean?"

"Well, where shall I start?" Uriah was winding up for another moan. "We can't see in front of our noses because of the freezing fog, the currents are unpredictable, the seas we're sailing on have never been navigated before, the crew are exhausted and desperate for fresh water and oh, we have a hold full of ravenous animals."

"True," Tarsus said. "But you've forgotten something."

"What's that?"

"We survived the apocalypse." He spoke with passion. "We've threaded ourselves through the eye of the needle, with guile and expert seamanship."

"And a lot of good fortune," Uriah added wryly.

"Although I must admit, there was the odd occasion when I thought our time was up."

"Only the odd occasion?" Uriah threw him a look of surprise, then realised he was joking. "I lost count of the how often we peered over the edge of the abyss."

"We had a few leaks," Tarsus said. Now that was an understatement. There must have been a score or more on the first day of sail alone. What a trauma that was.

"A few leaks." Uriah rolled his eyes. "Trying to fix the one in elephants' hold while avoiding being trampled was a memorable one."

"They're not exactly the most natural seafarers."

"Far from it." Uriah grinned. "Animals aren't shy about telling you that they're scared. What a cacophony!"

"I am glad it's over," Tarsus agreed. "Remember your promise at the Mind Search – to build a boat to survive the flood. Well, you've done it. I remember Akasha celebrated it with you."

A look of concern flitted across Uriah's face. "I hope she survived," he murmured.

"She should be safe beneath that big tower," Tarsus said. "By now she must have given birth and you're a grandfather."

A gust of wind blew off Uriah's skullcap and he scuttled across the sodden deck to retrieve it. Tarsus noticed a down of black hair on his head before he put it back on.

"You have it too, don't you?" Uriah observed.

"All the crew does."

"I hate to say it," Uriah said, but Tarsus knew he was going to say it anyway. "Despite sailing the *Fair Maiden* through the eye of the needle, our survival won't help us. We're all going to succumb to the hybrid seed. Those scheming Solarii will benefit the most. They'll leave as soon as they can, you mark my words."

Uriah sounded like Demos. "I disagree. I believe in them," Tarsus said. He always had, ever since he was young and Dashur, the great Solarii and first pharaoh, had healed his broken hand.

"How can you say that," Uriah asked, "after what happened to Issa?"

"I feel sorry for her," Tarsus said with a frown. "But I still trust them to deliver on their promise."

"The Solarii will do what they have to do," Uriah said. "All we can do is wait for the waters to subside. Then we can make landfall."

That, he looked forward to: the rest, they'd see soon enough.

Atop the Whispering Tower, Demos and Tamir peered into the gloom. Occasionally, a gust of wind would clear a path though the spiral banks of mist, yielding a fleeting glimpse of the new epoch, but mostly they couldn't see much farther than the parapet on which they stood.

"The mist is freezing," Tamir moaned. His son's hands were shaking: the immense shock of the floodwaters sat heavily on his young shoulders.

"You can leave if you want, but I'm staying to keep watch," Demos replied, hugging himself.

"Are we the only survivors?" Tamir murmured.

Demos wasn't sure if they were, but his son needed encouragement. "There are others out there," he said. "The whole of our village survived in the tower. As the waters rose, the flood brought up scores more from the surrounding plains, as well as a bunch of hybrids."

"I know. What I mean is, amongst the entire human race, are we the lone survivors?"

"Where the future's concerned, the most important thing is that Akasha and her children survived," Demos said, blowing into his hands. "The rest of us are at best incidental and at worst expendable. Akasha's a cobra – she'll renew herself. Do you want to know if there's anyone else out there? Then ring the bell."

Tamir pulled the plunger and released it. The giant bell reverberated with a single whispering note that pierced the gloom, reaching out across the watery abyss like a finger of hope. The vibrations rippled the surface of the ocean, disrupting its icy tranquillity, calling for a response. The ringing tone was slowly absorbed by the white-grey mists until after a while, only the vast stillness stared back at them.

His senses pitched to hear the slightest sound. Then a dull muffled tone skidded across the watery wastes.

"Did you hear that?" Demos asked, cupping his hands over his ears.

Tamir's face lit up. "It came from over there," he said excitedly, pointing in the direction of Avesta.

"Strata and his bird people survived," Tamir said, with an air of relief.

"So they did, so they did," Demos echoed.

"What do we do now?"

"We wait," he replied. "As the waters recede, we'll see what this next epoch is made of. Imagine: everything is new, pristine and untarnished. All the old charts and maps of the world are as useful as the scrawls of a child."

"Shame," Tamir murmured, almost to himself.

"You wanted to stay in the old epoch?" Demos asked, raising his eyebrows.

"It wasn't that bad," his son replied. "At least we weren't surrounded on all sides by ocean waves. How do we get off here? Perhaps the Solarii will fly here and rescue us. I saw their craft when they came here to collect Akasha."

"I doubt it," Demos said. "The Solarii are clever and ruthless. With the notable exception of Akasha's children, I doubt they'd be conspicuously interested in anyone but themselves."

"It's a new epoch. They could change. You said everything will be different, so why not them?" There was a glimmer of hope in Tamir's eye.

"They'll want to fulfil the Watchers' edict and comb the skies for the sign of their return."

"And what was that?" Tamir asked.

"The Watchers referred to it in their edict." Demos recited:

This is the time of necessity.
The Surge is paramount.
We proclaim the union between a twice-born Solarii
And a fair maiden daughter of man.
Let the return be signed by the blue bow.
Willing. Watchers. Waiting.

"Blue bow? What's that?" Tamir asked.

"I don't know." Demos shrugged. "Before that, the Solarii will seek to resolve the tragedy of the seed."

"What does that mean?"

"A good question. I believe the Watchers want to bring the human race to a point of rest. At that stasis, the hybrid seed will never reappear again. Then the Surge can appear."

A gust of wind cleared a gap in the hanging curtains of mists, and through them Demos saw an object, moving towards them through the air.

"By the Source, it's a bird," Tamir said, a look of wonder in his eye, as if he was seeing the great creature for the first time.

"It's an eagle, a golden eagle."

Gliding along invisible currents, the majestic creature flew with nonchalance. Master of the air, it screeched as it passed the tower.

"It could have flown for days in search of the sanctuary of a bough or a branch.

At least now it can be with its kind. Look, it's heading for Avesta." Tamir pointed towards the bird village.

"This is the first living thing we've seen since the rains stopped. It must be an omen," Demos said, stepping into the shoes of the soothsayer.

"Of what?"

"Of the nature of this new epoch." Demos had never been so sure of anything before. "Full of grace and agility, a golden eagle dominates a vast territory. It's powerful, imperial. These will be the ideals of tomorrow's empires."

"Shame we won't be here to see it for ourselves."

Demos was immersed in the wonder of the eagle's appearance and the prophecy that had burst so unexpectedly from his lips. Tamir rang the bell again. Its crystal clear tone rippled across the grey waters, and its echoes moved eerily amongst the fog banks.

Around the *Fair Maiden*, the mists had cleared sufficiently for Tarsus to heave himself up into the crow's nest. There wasn't much to see except fog and more fog, but every now and again, a gust blew away the tentacles of mist. Although chilled to the marrow, he was awed at what he was seeing – a newly formed ocean, as yet unnamed and unnavigated. He was conscious that he was the first human to do so on the first day of the new epoch. He felt privileged, and doubly fortunate to be alive.

There was a sound, muffled and ghostly. Was that a bell? No, it couldn't be, could it? It was hard to tell in the mists how far away it was, or from which direction it came. The breezes cleared the sheet of mist enough for him to see a dark speck of land on the horizon, before the mist drew in once more and he lost his line of sight. He'd try again later. He climbed down the mast to tell Uriah.

"I thought I heard something too," Uriah said. "Listen. There it is again!"

"Yes, I heard that. By the stars, there's someone out there! We're not alone!" His voice cracked with emotion.

"They can't be far away," Uriah said.

"What makes you so sure?"

"The golden eagle that had been perched on the cross mast for days took off a short while ago. It flew off into the mists."

"There must be land nearby. We're saved!" Tarsus cried, dropping onto his knees and mouthing a silent prayer. Uriah and the rest of the crew gathered around.

"Which way did it fly?"

"That way," Uriah said, pointing.

"That's the direction of the bell. Change course. Someone's out there."

The crew cheered and slapped each other on the back.

"Get back up there. If a fish so much as breaks the surface of the water, shout." Uriah said.

"I will," Tarsus cried, as he clambered back up the mast.

Demos saw a spot in the clearing mists approaching Avesta. Was that the golden eagle again? Then he saw another spot next to the first. Each of them lengthened into a thin vapour trail. They would be the Solarii flyers. They were coming in from the west, and Avesta was straight in front of them.

"There's an answer to your question," he said to his son, as he wiped the water from the end of his nose.

"I'm glad the Solarii survived," Tamir said. "With them, there's hope for us all."

Demos said nothing. Even in a brand new epoch, years of suspicion were hard to shift. What were the Solarii doing occupying the virgin skies anyway?

As the two craft approached, the bird people sent up a flare that arced above the village, sending shivers of colour and fire into the air that drifted back down upon the birds and avian-hybrids crowded on every sod of land. That rock had been their saviour, a laurel wreath upon an ocean of fury.

The Solarii craft banked above Avesta and entered a sharp dive. Suddenly, a bolt of force spat from one of them and slammed into the bird village. A tongue of flame leapt from the other flyer and pounded into the village with a thunderous crash and a blinding flash of light.

The roar of destruction was deafening. The blast threw lumps of stone and molten rock cascading into the air. Boulders as big as trees pitched into the surrounding waters, while plumes of water shot up into the sky. A silent scream raged over the empty ocean, shrouding Avesta in a cloud of white steam. Black smoke billowed up into the sky. Orange flames shot from the houses.

"What happened?" Tamir leant over the ramparts.

"Solarii treachery! I should've guessed why they've returned," Demos hissed, cursing his fatal lapse in judgement. How could he have been so stupid?

A cold wind gusted up to clear the smoke and mists to reveal...nothing. The lethal force of the blast had not only destroyed the village and murdered its inhabitants – all the humans, hybrids and animals that had taken sanctuary there – but also the buildings were devastated. The mountain peak on which the village stood was flattened. Avesta was now a scorched black table of rock. A fire raged with the fury of the underworld, sending a thick plume of smoke to mingle with the suffocating mists.

"Avesta. It's gone." Tamir pointed a quivering finger at the maelstrom.

Demos opened his mouth, but no sound came out. Ring the bell, raise the alarm, he wanted to say, but fear clamped his throat. Instead, he croaked and clutched the parapet until his knuckles turned white.

"*The time of necessity,*" Tamir said.

*

Marim banked his craft above the Whispering Tower. The last time he'd visited it was when he'd come bearing news of Horque's death. Times had changed, because now Horque had sent him to dispense death.

From his ankh, he unleashed a devastating astral bolt. A moment later, Lasec fired another bolt into the lower reaches of the tower. Flames leapt up the side, engulfing it in fire. The Whispering Tower disintegrated into a heap of molten stone, seared by phenomenal heat. It toppled over and collapsed onto the stone buildings below it, consuming the people, hybrids and animals in a fiery wave of death. As it folded in on itself, the stones of the tower ploughed into the molten fire at its base, sending shards and splinters vast distances into the surrounding seas.

The two vapour bolts brought death and destruction, but they were Marim's orders. He liked orders. He liked following orders. He knew where he was with orders.

What the flood hadn't done, they would finish. No hybrids. Anymore.

The *Fair Maiden* pitched over, the heavy waves rippling out from where the great rocks had plummeted into the seas. The twin astral bolts of fire transfixed Tarsus. His legs were trembling. This wasn't a manifestation of the divine.

It was the Solarii.

"Change course," he shouted. "Now!"

"Where to?" Uriah cried.

"Anywhere but here!" he yelled back.

They were next.

Marim saluted Lasec, his co-flyer. The swirling mists made it difficult to identify all the landmarks, but he was satisfied with his day's work. The Whispering Tower was their last target. He tried to telepath the message to Horque. But he couldn't reach him.

As he turned for home, he spotted the three large masts of the *Fair Maiden*. For a moment, he thought about destroying it, but he recalled his orders, which were to remove the hybrids from *dry* land. Shame they didn't include anything about boats.

The bows of the *Fair Maiden* broke through the mists. Up ahead, Tarsus could see two giant plumes of smoke and ash, one from each islet. The fires had burnt out, drenched by the moisture in the air. The smoke trail snaked into the sky and lingered long and heavy in the mists.

"Are you sure about this?" Uriah said.

"You know me," Tarsus scoffed. "Once, I was a Solarii apologist. If there were any way I was wrong, I'd admit it. But I know what I saw. Two vapour trails in the sky and they saw us, I'm sure of it."

"And they still flew off?" Uriah said with an air of incredulity.

"Yes. If they'd wanted us dead, we'd be vaporised."

"Why spare us?" Uriah cast a suspicious glance into the skies.

"They got their target already?" Tarsus guessed. How should he know?

"They were after hybrids. They must have thought we had none in our decks."

"We don't, but do you think it's that simple?"

"I do."

"Then it must be safe to land there," he said.

Uriah puffed his cheeks and sighed. "I doubt there are any survivors. This is tragic, to survive the rigours of the flood only to be butchered by the Solarii."

"I want to see for myself." Tarsus clambered into a rowing boat alongside the boatswain. Frightened by the explosions, the birds that had stayed on the *Fair Maiden* flew the roost and now circled the smoking crags, squawking and searching in vain for a safe perch.

He took the rowing boat around the lee of the islet. The closer he got to its scorched remains, the more acrid the smell of boiled flesh. He wanted to retch. The boatswain did. He beached the boat on the littoral of the isle. The other isle jutted out like a promontory in a windswept ocean. These two bits of molten rock were the burnt vestiges of Avesta and the Whispering Tower.

"They're better off than we are," the boatswain muttered under his breath.

The man had a point.

Tarsus took a tentative step onto dry land, his first in so many weeks of terror at the hand of the storm. The ferocity of the residual heat in the crag quickly dissolved his sense of achievement. Holding a damp cloth over his face, he hopped around on the shore to prevent his sandals from melting. The hot plume of acrid smoke billowed over him, forcing him back to the water's edge. He bent over double in a fit of coughing.

He'd suffered enough, and so had the boatswain. With a sense of relief and disappointment, they turned away from the scene of the atrocity to the relative sanctuary of the ark. He'd survived one apocalypse, yet courtesy of the Solarii, he'd witnessed a second.

With his head hung over the side, he vomited into the sea. By the time they returned to the *Fair Maiden*, Tarsus was determined to investigate the other plume of smoke a short distance away. If there was anything left alive there – a rat, an insect or a blade of grass – he wanted to know. This time, Uriah pulled on the oars.

Like the first isle, the rock fused into a grotesque conglomerate, a homogeneous mass of death, thrown together and sacrificed on the altar of the Solarii quest to return home. Amongst the debris washed up on the shore, an object jutted out of the water. It was an upturned bowl with glints of metal between the mud and gore.

"You know what that is, don't you?" Uriah said coldly.

Tarsus did, but he couldn't bring himself to admit it. He stared at it for a long time, the odour of molten flesh and burning rock assaulting his senses. "It's a bell, a large, upturned bell," he replied. "Or what's left of it."

That moment was an epiphany. The Solarii had done this, with the same ruthlessness with which they'd murdered one of their own – the Lady Issa. He was sick of their cruelty, sick of them all. In truth, he hated himself for swallowing their duplicity.

The ocean was endless. No land anywhere. He was fed up with it. The Semites were simple folk: stoneworkers, artisans and craftsmen, who thrived on the open meadow and the hedgerow, but natural sailors they weren't. He yearned for the firmness of the earth beneath his feet.

"What course are we setting?" Uriah asked.

Tarsus choked on the fumes, coughing and spluttering.

"I won't make our first landfall on either of these smoking islands of death. We sail on until we find a landfall that hasn't been tainted by the Solarii."

"That may be easier said than done," Uriah said ruefully.

"Then let's try and find the only place the Solarii won't have decimated."

"Babylon?"

"Yes." Tarsus nodded. "Babylon."

CHAPTER 57

The Guardian of Justice

Horque was chilled to the bone. The mists condensed on his headdress and eyebrows and dripped off the tip of his nose and ears. Banks of fog drifted across the face of the waters, as if guided by some divine wind, shrouding the skies and the sun from view and muffling every sound. More than ever, he felt like an alien, in an alien land.

His task was to find and remove all surviving hybrids in the High Zagros. The white ribbon was tied to his craft. The ten days of grieving for his mother had elapsed, yet he'd omitted to remove it. With a mournful smile, he put it in his pocket along with Akasha's wedding gift, the blue emerald gazelle. Ah, Akasha... For a fleeting moment the love he'd felt for her washed over him. Love, yes, that was it. That was what he couldn't remember about the Sphinx. The virgin represented the quality of love, absent in the lower animals, yet present in higher creatures. The insulation of a sliver of amber between the head and torso of the Sphinx best allowed the higher quality of love to operate.

Climbing into the craft, for a moment he forgot where he was, and he found himself waiting for Tarsus to tighten the straps. No, that was a different time, an earlier epoch. The old man of Samlios had served him and his family for all those years and he was grateful for his loyalty. Now Tarsus was probably another rotting corpse at the bottom of the pan-ocean.

The Horus Wing craft stuttered into life. Mentally, Horque directed the craft into the skies, seeking a safe route through the prevailing mists. His destination was a crag the size of a small meadow that jutted above the insidious waters. It was teeming with life of all shapes and sizes. The fist of the storm had battered them into submission, but they were still alive and defiant. Amongst the hybrids were goats, cows, sheep and wolves. Nearby another, smaller outcrop reached up forlornly into the mists, on which hundreds of birds had roosted and where ancient predatory rivalries had fallen into temporary abeyance.

With the crag in the distance, he hovered a few cubits above the water. As soon as they saw him, the hybrids flocked to the water's edge, snarling and waving their fists at him. That did not worry him. If Marim and the rest of the flyers had completed their tasks, then these pathetic few were the last hybrids on Earth, and the honour of removing them had fallen to him. He relished the task.

How to do it? Simple. Through the banks of mist, find the highest elevation and blast the crag. He mentally instructed his craft to gain height. The craft stubbornly refused to move. He growled. This would never have happened with his old Horus Wing. This replacement wasn't the same. Replacements never were. He willed the craft to elevate again, but with the same result – not a judder.

What else could the problem be? The craft was an intricate machine, directed by the subtle mental vibrations of its flyer. Should there be doubt, hesitancy or uncertainty in the flyer's instruction, the outcome could be a standoff like this.

Then it stuck him like a bolt of thunder. Despite his mother's reassurances to the contrary, he wasn't fully Solarii anymore. The craft didn't lie. She had. The strands of his mother's deceptive ruse unravelled before him.

It had started on the day of the Isis Pass. Issa had taken up the crook and the flail and ordered him to make camp in the High Zagros. Why did she really want him out of Egypt? It wasn't to escort Akasha to Babylon. Marim could have done that. So why? Because if he'd been in Jizah on the day of the Sear Line, he'd have walked into the same fate as her. By Osiris, she knew he'd fail the test. How had he not seen all this before? He clenched his fists until the blood drained from them; natron white on the armrests of his recalcitrant craft.

A plume of water shot into the air next to him. Pah! Hybrids, throwing stones. He ignored them. One thought ricocheted around the hollow caverns of his mind: his mother had sacrificed herself for him. She had the foresight. She knew he'd fail the Sear Line for one reason: he wasn't fully Solarii anymore.

No! A voice screamed inside his head.

Now it made sense. Why had she given him the knowledge of how to cross the Winding Waterway? It was a ruse to lure him into believing he could return home at will. Yet if he returned home in this half-Solarii state, he'd pollute the doubles and his kind would perish.

She knew he'd never do that.

He couldn't return: now the exile was exiled from his original land. With the guile and cunning of a jackal, she'd concealed her move until the last. By the God Horus, he thought he was a good player of the Intricacies of the Foxes and Hounds, yet from beginning to end, he had played pawn to her black queen.

He'd been born with a true Solarii soul, so why was it now tainted? The limp

– that was the origin of the impurity. Anubis and Osiris had retained a part of his soul, just as if they'd kept a part of his mother's. He was incomplete, with one toe in the Field of Rushes and the rest on Earth.

What could he do now? He was unable to return to his Solarii home, exiled on a planet where he didn't belong. Or was he? He was part human, so unlike other Solarii, he wouldn't be so susceptible to the dimming of the astral light. If he wanted one, he had a future on Earth. He was the father of twins who were also a blend of Solarii and human. They and Akasha were kin.

This dense web of consideration flashed before his mind in a moment. Then he heard the low drone of the returning Horus Wing craft. There were two of them. He couldn't let them find him impotent before the last remaining hybrids.

One more time, he urged the craft to elevate. It lurched forwards and came to an abrupt halt, the leather straps biting into his shoulders. He let out a long sigh of resignation. Finally, he understood. For all the intensity of his instruction to elevate and kill the hybrids, the compassionate human part of him weakened it. Actually, he wanted to spare them. The two forces collided inside him. His craft wasn't alone in detecting his contradiction.

He had to get the craft away from the crag, else the other flyers would read his mind. They'd know why the craft wasn't responding to his commands.

Too late.

In the next moment, a powerful blast hit him. Then another. The flyers in the two craft released their ankh weapons into the heart of the crag. The ferocity of the explosions threw up huge boulders that traced an arc of fire and ripped through the crag. Clouds of dust and debris billowed into the air and cascaded around him. To shield himself, he buried his head under his hands. A huge after-blast from the explosions rocked his craft and almost threw him out of the seat. The wind was acrid with the stench of the death.

A boulder of hot brimstone smashed his craft. Weighed down by the mass of molten rock, it plunged into the sea, while the reflection of the flames danced like a demon on the churned-up surface of the waves. It jettisoned Horque from the craft and he plummeted into the waters near the shore. Dazed and groggy, the bracing immersion revived him. He hated water. Unable to swim, he gasped for air. Flaming chunks of molten rock spewed out of the crag and threw up plumes of water all around him. He spat out another lungful of boiling water and thrashed his legs and arms in panic. His lame leg wouldn't move. With a mighty effort, he pulled himself from the murky water and rose to the surface, gulping for air. Lurching towards the burning crag, he grabbed onto a small rock in the shallows.

Lungs heaving, he pulled his aching body onto the last stub of land, where he lay like a beached whale. A searing pain flashed across his forehead and a trickle of blood oozed into one eye. He rolled over onto his back and reached inside his pocket for a cloth, and pulled out a piece of string and a small carving. As his vision cleared and the spasm of pain released its suffocating grip, he found he was clutching the white ribbon and a piece of blue stone – the gazelle carving.

A Horus Wing craft hovered in front of him above the shallows, eerily lit by the ambient flames. Emblazoned on its side were the scales of justice: it was Lasec.

Another craft arrived: Marim. "I've found one," his deputy sneered.

"Is he Solarii?" Lasec asked.

"No." Marim spat out the word.

"Then he's befallen the first of the Twin Perils. He's an abomination, a hybrid," Lasec said with the practised air of a judge.

Touching the gazelle figurine transported Horque's soul to the broad steppes of Afri, where he blithely imagined himself free and light. He smiled to himself and wiped the blood from his eye with the white ribbon.

"I remember every one of the instances of shame I've endured at your hands," Lasec snarled. "I am going to enjoy wreaking the most terrible revenge…"

"Our orders were to remove all hybrids," Marim added, "and we mustn't deviate from our orders – ever. The protector told us that himself."

Horque peered through the haze of pain and everything went quiet. It was as if the pantheon had thrown a pall over the whole world. Even the fires raging on the crag momentarily dimmed. Against the flames, cracked fragments of his life appeared, each one showing how Akasha had companioned his soul. She'd taught him about being human. In turn, her charismatic nature had nurtured the human part of him. Incredible though it seemed, the elegant gazelle had lived, walked, and prospered alongside the rampant Solarii lion.

Lasec sniggered. "The Eye of Horus will close forever." He fired a searing astral bolt.

Horque's body arced into the air and slumped back onto the wet rock with a thud. He grunted and rolled over on his side, twitching and writhing in his death throes. He opened his outstretched hand and from it fell the gazelle figurine to lie, forlorn, next to a white ribbon stained with crimson blood. As Beremtha left his body for the last time, he turned away from Lasec's cold-hearted gaze and breathed his last. The lion had devoured the gazelle.

With the fire raging on the crag, Lasec directed his Horus Wing craft to land on the temporary shore, the waters lapping against the base of his craft. He unstrapped himself and stumbled over to where Horque lay dead. Lit by the flames, he peered down at the corpse. The waters lapped against his feet. Floating on the water's edge with other detritus was a long wooden stick – Horque's staff. Lasec picked it up. A spume of red-hot flame leapt out towards him like a solar flare and he darted back to his craft to avoid it.

"Lasec, what are you doing? He's dead. Leave him be. We must go, now," Marim called to him, as he coughed into his kerchief.

"The end must be the end," Lasec growled. Cool as ice, he walked back towards the corpse, wielding the staff like a Rod of Erasure.

Tarsus and Uriah drifted through an enveloping curtain of fog. The wings of eventide closed around them and soon they were enshrouded in darkness.

During the night, the mists cleared to reveal a glorious sapphire night sky, where the stars of the universe shone like diamonds in quiet celebration of the new epoch. Tarsus wondered why the stars were so luminous; he'd never seen them so bright. Even Sirius, Star of Isis, was in her element. The gibbous moon rose over the dark rim of the horizon, where sea met sky. It was the milky colour of the sand of his favourite beach in old Samlios, which was odd, because the moon back in those days had always shone with a pale green hue.

Before dawn, Tarsus climbed up the mast to the crow's nest to witness the first dawn of the new epoch. The sky was clear. On the horizon, a pristine light appeared. The disc of the sun peeked over the rim of the universe.

He was dumbfounded. He pointed a shaking arm at the apparition.

It was bright yellow. Yellow?

It illuminated a sky of the palest blue. Blue?

It was majestic, awesome. Confused and fascinated, he watched the beams of the yellow sun play upon the blue-rimmed waters. Never had he seen sunlight like this. At any moment, he expected it to revert to the customary aquamarine. Below him on the deck, the crew knelt and prayed.

A squall of rain danced into view and drew moisture from the seas into the blue sky. The morning sun reflected off the myriad raindrops that coalesced with a natural colourful elegance into a clear dawn rainbow.

It was much more than that.

"Look!" he cried.

"What is it?" Uriah shouted from the deck.

"The rainbow set against the background of a blue sky. There's the new covenant, right there, that great arc in the sky – that's the blue bow of the Watchers' edict."

Lasec stood over Horque's mutilated corpse and smiled as he relished the thought of erasing the protector's astral record. All of his hard work would count for nothing. All that endeavour would have no continuance. All that life's quest, spent.

He knelt down and paused to look at Horque's face, covered in burns and cuts, discoloured by bruises, and soiled by mud and rain. He rammed the staff underneath Horque's neck and looked up at Marim's sudden shout.

"Lasec, come—"

At that moment, the fires raging on the crag exploded in a red-hot ball of flame and searing heat that threw him, burning, into the cold, grey seas.

In the icy depths of the hypogeum, Cheiron awoke. He floated above his physical body, in his astral form as a lynx. He was vaguely aware that the Watchers' edict was fulfilled. At the moment the rainbow manifested against an azure blue sky, a breach appeared in the womb of the planet's astral belts. It would remain open for a short while only, as the Earth changed from one epoch to another.

It was the great cycle, the cycle of cycles, which defined everything on Earth. He knew of it, all the Solarii lived in awe of it, because it was their crucial opportunity to renounce the place they called 'the planet of sighs'. The great winds had been part of that cycle; that was the beginning of the issue of the next epoch and the Earth made ready to receive it. After the winds came the flood. The human race prepared for it by helping remove the stain of the hybrid seed. The blue bow signified that attainment. The cycle was of cosmic proportion, in which the great unfinished work that was the human race rejoined its preordained path. Finally, they were ready to be instructed by the Surge.

While the sleek black panther stalked the unseen astral boundaries of the hypogeum, he and the other Solarii travelled astrally through the breach, there, finally and irrevocably, to return home to their doubles on the sun.

EPILOGUE

Mountain of the Chief

Mentally as sharp as a thorn, Akasha completed the circular walk around the neck of the mountain, which started and ended at the oak sapling. Tros had given her the acorn, which she'd planted there when they arrived on the mount some twenty years before. Every time she passed the tree, she felt the chill gust of the winds that had scythed through the oak of Samlios all those years ago. Yet here it was, a survivor of the old epoch, growing with youthful vigour and settling. Much like her son.

This was Mount Hermon: the place where the Helios had first descended to Earth. From here, Semjaza and Azazel had led their cohorts around the world, manifesting as hornets and stinging the maidens, siring the race of hybrids. Now it seemed like a terrible dream, but it wasn't, it was as real as her hand. That was why she had wanted so desperately to set up camp here, at the place of their arising, to defy them every moment of every day, because she knew that would be what it would take to keep them at bay.

"Bahir," she said. "Repeat the sacred utterance for us."

He spoke the words of power and she felt the astral shield strengthen.

"That's done," she said. "Semjaza and Azazel won't trouble us today." Her regular sacred dance of mental defiance to ward off the Helios had worked. But she was getting old. Fortunately, Bahir was a very able and occasionally willing apprentice.

"Mother, I've walked the mountain with you every day for the last three moons. Why can't you trust me to do it on my own?" he complained. He had inherited his arrogance from his father. How he revelled in being the son of an angel. Sometimes she wished she'd never told him about Horque.

"You'll be ready when you're ready, not before," she chastised him. "If the ritual isn't done properly every day, the Helios will rampage through the veil and tear us all to pieces. If you ever see a hornet…"

"The Helios! I doubt they actually exist anymore." He kept his voice low, but she heard him. She thought about reprimanding him, but decided against it. She was too tired.

"Of course they do," she murmured.

Her son wasn't the ideal apprentice. The flood had narrowed the choice. Other than Philo and Shamira, the only human survivors were those in the *Fair Maiden*; together they numbered no more than threescore. Akasha had settled on Bahir because there was no one else.

On their way back down the mountain path to the village, they walked by the small cemetery that contained only two cairns: Philo's and Petra's. Ashaka had a hollow ache whenever she thought of Philo, all those days shared in the womb of the Natal Chamber. Ashaka had known Petra only a short time before she passed. They joined the ranks of all the others taken by the killing waters, not least Tros and Callisto, father and daughter. So many memories, now seen through the watery veil of the flood.

The nearer they got, the stronger the smell of putrefaction became.

"Oh, what a stink." Bahir smirked. "Who would have thought that a man of Babylon and a Kushite girl could smell so bad?"

She threw him a look of stern disapproval. "Don't malign the dead. Philo and Petra survived the flood, but not the travails of the journey from Babylon. Show them some respect."

"You can smell them from leagues away," he said, pinching his nose for added effect.

"Cairns are part of our tradition," she corrected him with a sweet smile.

"Tradition!" he scoffed. "All those quaint practices were drowned in the flood. It's a new epoch. It's time for radical new ways. Bury them, I say."

"Don't be impertinent," she snapped. She wouldn't tolerate such talk from anyone, least of all her son. Conversations like these cast long shadows over her decision to leave the leadership of the survivors in his hands.

Suddenly, a pain stung her in the heart and she clasped her chest.

"Mother! What's the matter?" He raced to her side.

The world spun like a top. She slumped to her knees. Gasping for breath, she blacked out.

The next thing she knew, she awoke in her bed. Wracked with pain, her body felt as heavy as granite. She eased her astral body out, coiling into the familiar cobra until she floated above her physical body. What a relief to leave the aches behind. Below, she could 'see' the silhouettes of her friends and loved ones. Bahir was there, marshalling everyone as usual. Ora, her daughter, was there too, as were Tarsus, Shamira, Uriah and Thera.

"Oh, Mother, what's happened?" Ora asked, rubbing her hand tenderly.

"She collapsed on the mount," Bahir said, as calmly as if he was describing the sunset.

"Did you berate her about your apprenticeship?" Shamira asked him. The pythoness was one of the few who could stand up to Bahir.

"What do you mean?" Bahir replied, rolling his eyes.

"Everyone knows you want her to make you the basilisk, and you simply aren't ready," Shamira replied.

"On the contrary, Mother had just told me she was exhausted and looking forward to me taking over her duties," Bahir replied, a picture of feigned innocence.

That wasn't strictly true, but it was typical of her son. He was always stretching the truth to suit his own image.

The conversation stopped as Arran and Chalvia, Petra's children, entered the room. Akasha slipped back into her mortal coil.

"She's waking up," Thera said.

Akasha groaned, licking her dry lips.

"Drink," Thera said, gently lifting the back of her neck.

"No." She pushed the beaker away.

"But you must drink the water," Thera told her softly. "You told us so yourself after the flood. You said the waters that fell from the sky were sacred, and drinking them would halt the growth of the hybrid seed. If you don't drink..."

"I won't need it where I'm going," she said wearily.

Uriah crouched on the other side of the bed. "Don't talk like that," he said.

"Don't cry." She patted his hand. "It was always going to come to this. Let me speak to you all." With a huge effort, she propped herself up on the pillow.

"We're all here," Uriah replied.

Yes, they were, but Horque was missing, and sorely missed still. She had never found out what happened to him. She assumed he and the other Solarii had returned to the sun. Since the flood, no one had seen them, nor the hybrids for that matter.

The only things keeping her on Earth were the Helios and the Surge. The Helios were a palpable danger to the remnants of the human race. Bahir was as ready as he'd ever be.

"Bahir," she said. "You're to take leadership of the survivors. You're young and virile."

"I'm grateful," he said, although he didn't sound it. Then he added begrudgingly, "I'd better tell you now. I'm going to marry Chalvia."

Now that was wonderful news. That gave hope to the appearance of the Surge. She managed a wry smile.

"You have my blessing, both of you," she murmured.

Bahir took Chalvia by the hand. "Thank you."

"Ora, my sweet Ora," she pined. "One day I hope you will take Petra's son as your husband. That way, the Surge can bear fruit through the progeny of two families."

Ora blushed. Akasha could barely muster a smile in return, she was so tired.

"And I want you to have these gifts as early wedding presents," she said. "Chalvia, Demos' white bone cobra necklace is for you. Bahir, Horque's Djed pillar is for you."

Chalvia smiled and kissed her on the forehead. "Thank you," she said.

"You'll need it for protection," Akasha whispered, her voice failing.

"I'll put it on right now," Chalvia said, pride resonating in her voice.

"Mother, this is a wonderful gift," Bahir said. "My father was an angel. I am father of an angel, a twice-born. It is a symbol of his earthly regenerative power. I am chosen. I am ready."

"I hope so," Akasha said. "Chalvia, it's a shame your mother couldn't be here to witness this union."

"Yes, it is," Chalvia replied. "And our father too, Berux. You know, I've never told anyone but he was also born twice."

"How was that?" she asked. "Horque was my one and only true twice-born. How could Berux have been another?"

Chalvia related the story. "Mother told me that when Berux was born, his heart stopped and he died, but he was resuscitated."

She managed another smile. "Like Horque."

"The Watchers spoke of a twice-born Solarii," Shamira said. "They never said there was only one of them. That gives us great hope, and we pray the Surge can flourish in you and your children."

Akasha felt content. Her work was done. This was her time. She willed it so. As she let out a long sigh, she eased back into her astral body for the last time. Just before she closed her eyes, a pair of insects flew into the ray of sunlight and landed on Bahir's hand.

They were hornets.

ACKNOWLEDGEMENTS

A book is a coalescence of many strands and influences and this one is no exception. It has come about through the help and assistance of many people.

Thanks firstly to my lady, Irene, for her support, patience, and encouragement. My profound thanks go also to Nick, for his many promptings and suggestions, and for listening. More thanks go to the literary folk who have encouraged and guided me along the way: Ali, Kevan, and Jo to name but three, John Jarrold, and the Writers' Groups in Bath and Bristol. I would also like to thank my granddaughter Freja, whose reminder that 'you just have to imagine' was a constant source of inspiration.

My full appreciation goes to the monks of the Cistercian abbey in Orval, Belgium, and the Benedictines of Buckfast Abbey, Devon, where some of this book was written and edited in the peace and quiet of their respective grounds.

My profound thanks go to Raymond, without whose wondrous inspiration none of this book would have appeared. He taught me that the greatest debts are those that can never be fully repaid.

Finally, to my parents, who from an early age filled me with enthusiasm for travel, history, the arts, and above all, the written word.

Life. Will. Love.

Lightning Source UK Ltd.
Milton Keynes UK
UKOW01f0400150218

317900UK00003B/137/P